AS THE CROW FALLS

AS THE CROW FALLS

Greg, Carol, and Sherry Crow's statements as told to

Don Maddux

Copyright © 2015 by Don Maddux.

Library of Congress Control Number:		2015914430
ISBN:	Hardcover	978-1-5144-0435-5
	Softcover	978-1-5144-0436-2
	eBook	978-1-5144-0437-9

All rights reserved. No part of this book may be reproduced or transmitted in any form or by any means, electronic or mechanical, including photocopying, recording, or by any information storage and retrieval system, without permission in writing from the copyright owner.

This is a work of fiction. Names, characters, places and incidents either are the product of the author's imagination or are used fictitiously, and any resemblance to any actual persons, living or dead, events, or locales is entirely coincidental.

Any people depicted in stock imagery provided by Thinkstock are models, and such images are being used for illustrative purposes only. Certain stock imagery © Thinkstock.

Print information available on the last page.

Rev. date: 09/02/2015

To order additional copies of this book, contact:
Xlibris
1-888-795-4274
www.Xlibris.com
Orders@Xlibris.com
710763

For Darren Aue and Vince Cammisano,
my best friends at different points in my life.

I hope you guys have met up there and are having
a few drinks on me.

This one's for you.

BOOK 1

1

William "Willie the Rat" Cassivano rarely showers. Complete strangers often comment about his odor. He seldom shaves because he cannot grow a full beard, so, in turn, he always looks terrible.

Willie needs to carry out the assignment he and his crew have been selected for. Joseph Giovelli from Kansas City and his counterpart boss, John Scalto, from Cleveland, have been corresponding. They ordered the hit.

They needed to be given permission from Chicago's respective top families to perform the hit in the Chicago area. Since bosses from the north and south factions of Chicago's La Cosa Nostra are in a bright media spotlight, they need to keep a low profile because of minor legal trouble that can become major. The acting boss, consigliere Alfred Biandi, gave permission because he was convinced of the urgency.

Although secrecy, timing, and deceit are vital to a successful hit, this particular piece of work has been denied those three elements because of its nature. It is a delicate matter because an agent for the Federal Bureau of Investigations is the target. His home office is in Chicago. The man has been working undercover for more than seven years and has gained the confidence of many organized men in Kansas City and Cleveland. An FBI agent turncoat selling information to Joseph Giovelli tipped Joseph off that the guy is what he is: a nark. His real name is Dean Krabek.

The pickup for the hit needs to go down in Arlington Heights, a northern suburb of Chicago. The man, known as Scott Magdiano to the stand-up guys, lives in an apartment complex three blocks northwest from the intersection of Arlington Heights and Rand Roads. They notice he is on the apartment directory under his real name.

An attractive female law student and former exotic dancer from Kansas City is to seduce him at a Palantine nightclub, Chances, that he patronizes frequently.

For the last three evenings, she flirted loosely with him at the nightclub. Cognizant that time is running out, she slips a mild sedative in his drink. She teases him to the point that he wants to leave early and take her home. Convinced by her that he should not drive, she drives his red Chevrolet station wagon toward his apartment. Casually, she pulls the car into the parking lot of a White Hen convenience store to buy some beer and cigarettes.

As she cautiously drives into the parking lot, she notices the parking lot is full by her design. She nonchalantly turns to an alley on the east side of the shop and parks next to a blue Cadillac Fleetwood.

"Sweetie, come inside with me," she suggests with a kiss. He obeys and stumbles out of the car.

Quickly someone covers his eyes and mouth, while two other men grab him and throw him in the backseat of the Cadillac. They immediately frisk him and discover his snub revolver. Sam Digovanni from Kansas City jumps in the station wagon so he can follow; the driver of the Cadillac is a Chicagoan.

Leonardo "Leo Lips" Moraci from Cleveland and William "Willie the Rat" Cassivano are on the backseat waiting for Dean, a.k.a. Scott. He is forced to sit between these two legends. Shelly (her stage name) walks into the White Hen and purchases a soda, and then she and another man drive back to the nightclub to retrieve her car.

Dean/Scott, fearing this moment, knows one of the torture methods Willie is infamous for. He mentally prepares himself, hoping the procedure will not bother him. He cannot be more wrong.

Leo thoroughly searches the agent's wallet and finds a piece of paper with the name Dean Krabek. Leo smiles, considering this man has gone to this much routine trouble to obtain a driver's license, credit cards, and diverse identification in the name of Scott Magdiano and overlooked a simple return receipt from a department store in his real name. Leo compares the signature on the return receipt to the signature on the driver's license and smiles broadly because the penmanship is identical. Only the name is different.

As the Cadillac heads west on Highway 53 toward Schaumburg, none other than Leo Moraci finally breaks the eerie silence.

"Well, well, well, Mr. Krabek, we finally meet in person."

Dean/Scott cannot speak because of the garrote tied around his head. They take off the muzzle and replace it with a squalid rag that is saturated in hydrochloric acid.

"I don't know my way around here, so I don't have a clue where this warehouse is. Is that burning?" Willie the Rat asks, laughing. Willie smirks as he shoves his rubber-gloved acid-soaked index finger up Dean/Scott's nose.

"How much further, driver?" Leo asks, smiling.

"'Bout two miles."

They exit at Golf Road. In less than three minutes, they open the door to a three-car detached garage and park in the left bay. The garage is used to store swimming pool cleaning equipment, including hydrochloric acid.

Sam and the driver violently pull him from the car, strip him naked, then kick and knee him several times in the groin. The soldiers drag him to a chair, tie him to it, then turn on a garden hose full blast and spray it at Dean/Scott. They spray the water directly at his face to ease the burning sensation. The men then put a dry gag in Dean/Scott's mouth to muffle the screams.

Leo and Willie converse quietly in the corner. Torture is not usually necessary. This time they have no choice because there is no other way to retrieve information this critical. Joseph Giovelli and John Scalto do not know what Dean/Scott has already told the FBI, so it is imperative to be thorough. Willie has a reputation as a violent interrogator.

Prior to bringing Dean/Scott here, Willie prepared the materials he would need. He had the men build a sturdy plywood box of four walls at least four feet high and wide enough to fit around Dean/Scott.

The caged man is sitting with all limbs and his head immobilized on the chair that is anchored to sheet metal that is fastened to the floor. This whole contraption sits above a heavy sheet of plastic. The soldiers made sure to spread his legs before they were immobilized. Willie has the men grease down all four of the interior walls of the box before they gently place it around Dean/Scott. Willie walks to the cell and sprays Dean/Scott and his chair with a sticky substance that smells like maple syrup. The stuff is almost like glue. Willie takes two steps up on a stepladder and throws two large rats purchased earlier at a pet store on the lap of Dean/Scott. Willie reaches down and pulls off the gag towel.

"All right, I think you can see how pissed off I am." Willie grins. "Tell me now what you've told the other feds."

"Nothing! I swear I haven't even . . ."

"Not the answer I was looking for." Willie tosses in two more rats. The two he threw this time land on the metal floor and attempt to ascend the greasy wall. Willie smiles.

"Fuck you, you fat slob!" the prisoner yells.

Willie's phony smile is gone immediately. He hits his prisoner on the top of the head with his knife handle. Two more rats.

He knows they are going to kill him, so he has no intention of cooperating.

"I'll keep this up until I believe you. To show you that you can believe me, here are four more friends," Willie assures, grinning.

Willie dumps the rats on the prisoner's lap. Because his head is immobilized, he cannot see the size of the tails. They might only be mice. Like a good captive soldier, he stays silent. Willie throws in twelve more rats. One of the larger rats gnaws on the prisoner's right ankle. One rat chews at his toes. Four rats climb the sticky substance on his legs. The other rodents sense what their friends are doing and slowly join in. When they aren't gnawing at him or licking him, they fight.

"Tell me now, Dean, what have you told the other feds?" Willie waves the stiletto knife in front of the prisoner's eyes.

"I only told them about the casino money Joe is using. Please, I'm beggin' you."

"Good start, but I think it's only a fuckin' start!" Willie screams.

Willie opens the sharp stiletto knife and brings it down to the prisoner's right leg. He slowly makes a twelve-inch anterior cut on the top of his thigh toward his knee. It is not a deep cut at all. The cut is just deep enough to be extremely painful. Willie does not want the man to die of blood loss. There is too much information to obtain. Willie brings the knife up and clutches it in front of the prisoner's eyes. The scream is deafening as the rats bathe in and drink the blood gushing from the prisoner's leg.

"Can you be any more of a pain in the ass or are you gonna tell me? We have all night and a whole lot more of your little fuzzy friends." To show he is serious, Willie opens ten more boxes containing two rats each and throws them in the makeshift cell.

He thinks he remembers being told as a boy, "Mice and rats are more afraid of you than you are of them." Bullshit! Maybe one or two would be, but not this many. The captive has nothing more to tell Willie, so he knows he needs to make up something.

"I told them about the casinos and the Teamsters and other union funds Joe is using. I swear that's all I even know."

Willie brings the knife down to the other leg and makes an almost identical incision. Once again, the screams are thunderous. A few of the larger rats let out their own shrieks.

Leo and the other two men walk out the door. Although they cannot see in the box, none of them have ever witnessed such a barbaric and savage performance. Leonardo "Leo Lips" Moraci walks more than a hundred feet into the adjacent vacant lot and kneels to catch his breath.

"I'll give you another chance. Tell me now, what have you told them about the Scalto family in Cleveland?"

"Nothing, Willie. I swear. I told them there may be a plot against Mayor Kucinich and that Leo and Eugene are probably gonna kill Danny Gray, but I don't know anything for sure."

Willie knows Leo is out of the garage now. He does not care about Cleveland, Ohio. He just enjoys seeing this man suffer.

Willie has one more rat, and he hates not to use this one. This is an approximately seven-pound rat, nearly the size of a cat, that Willie has in a clear cage. Although rats and mice from pet stores are disease-free, Willie tells the inmate this one may have rabies. Willie needs to make sure he scares any last little bit of information from this man as possible, since he is, after all, an FBI agent. Willie holds the caged hideous gargantuan rat in front of the prisoner's eyes to hear him let out an inhuman wail.

"Please, no, god, please, no! Joseph's phones might be bugged, I don't know for sure." This is far too much. He is completely honest now.

Willie opens the cage and carefully drops the beast on the prisoner's bloody legs. He watches with an awe-inspired gaze as some of the rodents try to climb out of the slippery chamber as soon as they become aware of the emperor.

What a glorious thing to witness as they bite and shriek at the prisoner. There are forty rodents and one monster rat snuggling with him, and there may as well be a thousand. The stickiness of every part of his body above his blood-covered crotch and legs. Rats climbing on his sticky arms. Five rats have made their way to his head or shoulders. Two rodents begin gnawing at his neck. The huge rat gnaws at his blood-covered testicles. Having a smaller rat climbing on his sticky face and trying to crawl in his mouth is too much. He cannot scream because of that fear.

Willie smiles as he points an automatic pistol with a silencer down at Dean and shoots him between the eyes. The rats scurry. For good measure, Willie fires his trademark four more unnecessary shots.

Because the others are too weak to stay in the garage while this merriment took course, Willie has the hurtful and unpleasant task of extermination. Willie places the matching piece of wood on top of the stopgap cubicle. He uses duct tape to close all the seams. He drills a small hole in the top, puts on a gas mask, sprays the inside with noxious poison gas from an exterminator's tank, tapes up the hole, and walks out the door.

The two men standing by the garage, smoking, do not speak unless spoken to. Willie gives the soldiers instructions. He gives the man from Chicago $10,000 and reminds him the other $10,000 will be paid to him via the local consigliere. Willie's soldier, Sam Digovanni, is only given

$1,000 and understood previously that he would receive the remainder back at home.

After Willie the Rat and Leo Lips drive back to Arlington Heights, the two other men finally speak.

"I'm sorry. I don't even wanna know your real name. That guy is one sick, twisted motherfucker. Let's take this guy to the incinerator over at the dump. I know them, and they won't say nothin' when we show up. They're with us."

"Agreed. I wanna get this over with and never come here again. I'm sorry, dude. I never expected anything like this," Sam says.

The two silent accomplices follow the orders they were given. The plastic is all laid out under the box, so all they will need to do is wrap it up, then wrap it again and throw it in the station wagon, then dispose of the station wagon and other evidence. Then the man from here in Chicago can take Sam back to his car at the hotel, and the two will never speak during the ride or ever see one another again.

Dean Krabek is still officially a missing person.

2

August 16, 1972

11:52 a.m.

Gregory Crow had a real bad hangover. He tried desperately to think of the name of the girl sleeping next to him and where the hell he was. Today should have been different for Greg. For any other person in his position, it would be. Today was the morning after Greg's thirtieth birthday party. He realized what happened last night as he slowly came to. After all, that is what he celebrated last night—the thirtieth birthday party. Matchbooks, cocktail napkins, and balloons commemorated the occasion. Eighty or so friends, strippers, music, drugs and booze. Oh, so much booze. Greg loved booze, pot, cigarettes, cocaine, the occasional acid or mushroom trip, and women. And women most definitely loved Greg.

Who the hell is this one? Carol? Cindy? Cara? Maybe Sandy or Sarah. No, a name with a C. She's passed out. Look for something with her name on it. Whoa, that hurts, slow down, don't get up or move so fast. Slip on my underwear. Walk out of the bedroom slowly. Look for some mail or something with her name on it. A fuckin' hotel room! A suite, though. Where am I? Look out the window, at least fifteen floors up. On the Plaza, not that far from home. Oh, yeah, the party was in the banquet room downstairs. I'm here at the Ritz. Go back in the bedroom quietly. Look at her again, turn her head over, and get a quick look. I know I know her. What the hell is her name, though? If all else fails, just call her Honey and climb on top of her. Well, wait a minute, here's her purse unbuckled with the wallet on top. Embroidered. It's Carol. I remember now. Vince Giovelli's cousin. Oh shit! No, Vince was at the party last night. He was cool about it. Or was he? What the hell else did I do? Did I make an ass of myself again? Well, I couldn't have done too bad if I'm here with her. What a body! She's under the covers, but I can still tell. Gorgeous black hair too. She even paid for the suite. Here's the receipt

9

right here. She didn't need to do that, but, oh, that's right, it was my birthday, yeah, I remember now, I never paid for anything last night.

Greg stood up again and fell flat on his face.

I am really, really drunk.

"What're you doing?" Carol had been playing possum for a few minutes.

"I'm just trying to get my thoughts together."

"Do you think you could be a little quieter thinking?" she asked, laughing. "Why were you looking in my purse?"

"I'm sorry. When I first woke up, I had no clue where I was."

"And looking in my purse was gonna let you know where you were?"

"I thought we were in an apartment or house. I went looking for mail. Then I realized we were in a hotel." He was a pretty good liar. He did not have the heart to tell her he did not know who she was at first.

"Didn't you recognize me, though?" she asked with a hint of disappointment.

"Of course, I did, Carol, but I didn't know where we were, so I thought the driver's license would tell me. Until I realized we were in a hotel room on the Plaza," he rambled.

"What time is it?" she asked, yawning.

I wormed my way out of another one.

"I don't know. Well, wait a minute. My watch should be in here." With all his drunken, drug-induced episodes, he always managed to keep his wristwatch in his suit lapel pocket. "Ten minutes after twelve," he mumbled.

"It's after checkout time," she responded with another smile and a wink.

"Well, you know I don't have to be anywhere today. My brother was there last night. Saw how drunk I must have been. He probably knew what to expect," he muttered.

"You didn't act that bad until everyone started leaving. But after that you were stumbling around, giggling at everything. It was kinda cute actually. You were breathing on different things, then making them stick to your forehead, it was hilarious." She laughed.

"What do you mean 'things,' like what?" he asked, embarrassed.

"Just different things. You know, lighters, silverware, fountain pens, everything."

"Yeah, I can kinda remember that. Please tell me that's the worst of what I did?" he asked as a rhetorical question. He did not want a sincere answer.

"Pretty much, you were kinda slurring your speech. Then you came out of the bathroom with the straw and blade stuck to your forehead. We all started laughing hysterically. We started to shut things down after that. I got us a room, Vince helped you up here, and here we are," she said, stroking his hair.

"Vince helped me up here. That I do not remember at all," he said, trying to enunciate each word and failing miserably.

"Don't worry, he's cool about it," she said, as if she could read his mind.

"And your dad, oh shit!"

"I'm a big girl. And, besides, he likes you, your brother, your dad, all of you guys."

"Oh, I just mean I haven't been that wasted in a long time," he partially lied. He was inebriated nearly every night. Her father scared him a little bit also. His nickname was Willie the Rat.

"He'll be fine about it. I guess he knows I've had my eye on you for a while," she said, trying to reassure him. She grabbed him and kissed him. Another sexy smile. She surprised him with her aggressiveness.

"Let me call the office and talk to Gery. You wanna get something to eat?"

"Sure, just let me get cleaned up and find my clothes."

She pulled back the blanket to reveal the top half of her stunning body. She smiled at him yet again before removing the covers the rest of the way. She already had her panties on. She stood up to pick something up off the floor, then bent over seductively, knowing full well what she did to men.

"Oh shit! What the hell!" he shouted. "It looks like someone was stabbed in here!"

"I told you last night when we came in here from the living room that I was, you know, starting. It certainly didn't bother you then."

"You did!" he yelled, still loud but not shouting.

The bed was smeared with only a few minuscule drops of dry blood, but he could not handle the sight of even a tiny bit in his condition this morning.

He started gagging, stumbled into the bathroom, and vomited. Heaved and vomited again. Luckily for him, the lid on the toilet had already been lifted up. He would not have made it otherwise.

She stayed in the bedroom, putting on her clothes. Embarrassed and humiliated. He continued to lean over the toilet, trying to remember anything about her, or last night, for that matter.

Get hold of yourself, man. It's just natural, you stupid jerk. Go back in and tell her you just have a bad hangover. Tell her you can kinda remember her saying that. Well, wait a second. I do remember her saying that. Hmm? It didn't bother me then? Why am I making such a big deal about this? I must have been with women before during that time of the month. Hmm? I must have come in here to clean myself up after or during. Go back in and treat her like a queen.

"I'm sorry, Carol, I'm just hung way over," he said.

She was fully dressed. He wondered how long he had been in the bathroom.

"That's OK," she said with a tear in her eyes.

"I just kinda have a weak stomach for things like, ya know, things like that. This morning, I mean."

"Obviously," she said sarcastically.

A tear formed in her eyes because she had finally been with Gregory Crow, her dream guy since she was a little girl. Now he threw up because she had a monthly problem that all women have. What an immature jerk.

He stood six feet one, about 190 pounds, blond hair, baby-blue eyes, and a muscular structure that had everyone convinced he exercised religiously, when in truth his body required little maintenance. Push-ups on his fists now and then and some leg stretches at times, that would do. He did have a rather prominent chin that most women found appealing. Then, of course, there was the money.

He knelt before her and held her hand, brought it to his mouth, and gently kissed it.

"Let me make this up to you. I'm sorry." He kissed her other hand. "Let's go to lunch anywhere you want, and tonight we'll go to dinner anywhere you want."

"All right. Tell me why you made such a big deal out of this?" she asked without making eye contact.

"I'm just weak when it comes to, ya know,"—he could not find the right words—"it just kinda caught me off guard. And this is a world record for the worst hangover ever."

"Let's stop talking about this," she said, blushing. "Call your brother and we'll go."

Greg put on his pants and telephoned his brother.

"Crow Brothers Real Estate Company."

"Michelle, this is Greg, let me talk to Gery." Greg was on hold for about two minutes and hung up the telephone. He called back.

"Crow Brothers Real Estate Company."

"Michelle, this is Greg again. Don't put me on hold this time. Let me talk to Gery."

"I'm sorry. I thought he was in his office when you called. How are you feeling today? You looked like you were having fun last night."

I forgot she was there last night.

"I feel fine. Is Gery there?"

"He's coming down the hall right now, hold on. Gerald, it's Greg."

"I'll take it in my office!" Gerald shouted. Less than one minute later, "Yes, Gregory, what is it? Some of us work for a living."

"I'm sorry. Ya know it was the party last night, and I . . ."

"Look, I know it was your birthday and everybody had a good time, but this shit has to stop. You don't care what you're doing to yourself, that's fine. But you embarrassed the hell out of Sherry and me. Do yourself a favor and don't come near here for a few days. And when you do, please, *please* don't come in here reeking of booze. It evidently doesn't matter to you, but you're a gigantic laughing stock around here today, and I'm sick and tired of explaining your behavior. Granted everyone knew it was your birthday party, so there's a certain amount of understanding. But you have to learn be more professional."

"Why? It was just friends and stuff."

"No, that's wrong again. There were other developers there, potential tenants, other clients, employees, everybody. Not to mention my wife, who loves you, but was very embarrassed. You're the main reason we decided to leave so early. You better hope Dad doesn't find out about last night!" Gerald yelled.

Greg had no concern about his father learning of last night. Greg considered his brother to be much more anal retentive than their father. He did not want to argue right now, so he played into Gerald's hand.

"Are you gonna tell him?" Greg asked with a smile toward Carol.

"Of course not, but you have to assume he's probably going to find out."

"I'm a big boy. I'm sorry, but . . ."

"I don't want to hear how sorry you are. You're a big boy now, but you understand the unwritten rules. I'm sick of your half-drunk apologies. Just do me a favor, don't come in here for a few days. Let's see. It's Wednesday the sixteenth. Wait till Monday to come back in. Believe me, we're much better off if you let this blow over, so at least Monday. I have a lot of damage control to perform now because of you."

"Do you want me to come to your house or something?"

"You don't need to, but if you want to, be sure to call first so we're not caught off guard again. Sherry was embarrassed last night. The boys haven't seen you in a couple of weeks, and I know they want to."

"I'll call first."

"Good, but make sure you're sober. And for god's sake, grow up. You're thirty now, quit acting like a goddamn teenager. Good-bye." Gerald hung up the telephone without waiting to hear another phony drunken apology from his younger brother.

13

"What was that about? It didn't sound very friendly," Carol said with a smile.

"Just my brother being his typical pissed-off self, saying how embarrassed he and Sherry, his wife, were. Just his usual complaints," Greg said with a shrug.

"They weren't even there that long. It was almost like everyone waited for them to leave so we could start having fun. Finish getting dressed so we can leave."

"Is my car here?"

"I don't know, but I don't think so. Vince brought you here last night."

"Oh, yeah, I remember now. We left it at my house so I wouldn't drive home after the party."

"Good idea. You were in no condition."

He abruptly thought his chemical habits were not as secretive as he believed. *I'm so confused.* It was not a good idea to attempt to sort out this particular memory lapse.

Carol reminded Greg that his buddy Vince took precautions for him last night. Greg had known Vince Giovelli since the two were children. Vince never thought twice about covering for Greg anymore. Greg and Vince always looked out for one another.

"OK, let's go. Can you take me home to get my car first?"

She was bewildered at this quick change in his movement, suddenly appearing in perfect shape and not the least bit affected by a hangover.

"Why don't we just eat at one of the restaurants downstairs, then go home—I mean your home, you know?"

He looked at her as he methodically tied his tie without a mirror and smiled. Without speaking, he knew what she must have been thinking. He had seen this gaze before, but somehow this look was different. He could not be sure. But he thought maybe, just maybe, he might be looking at her the same way.

What's happening to me? Look at her. She's beautiful. Gorgeous black hair, incredible body, eyes that almost talk. But what is different about her than any of the others? Hmm? My best friend's cousin. There's something. Look at her, man. Those eyes. Wow.

"OK, let's go. You ready?"

"Sure, but before we go, would you mind zipping up? It's pretty suggestive," she said with another wink and a smile that was beyond sexy.

They walked out the door of the hotel suite arm in arm and walked to the elevator. They reached out at the same time to push the button for the lobby. The insignificance of that act brought a meager grin to both their faces.

14

At that moment in the plush elevator, he realized how spectacular her eyes were. They were not green, they were not brown, but they had a unique color he could not recall having ever been named. He couldn't recall ever seeing a color so beautiful. Whatever the color, her eyes were blindingly bright.

Greg and Carol went to lunch in one of the restaurants affiliated with the hotel and talked for hours over food and drinks. At one point, they pulled out cigarettes at precisely the same time. The brands were exactly alike. Neither of them had noticed this at the party last night. At the moment, it brought a slight chuckle.

She had one alcoholic beverage during lunch. Although she was not a prude, she could not help but count the fact that he consumed two Bloody Marys and seven beers during the three-hour lunch. The more he drank, the more impressed she became. Not because of the undeniable fact that he exhibited no signs of intoxication, but because she thought the same as any person would—*"Here's a guy who just turned thirty. Has a brother and business partner who probably doesn't even want him around. Drinks like a fish, great looking, and, to top it all off, has money to burn. Yet fails to see how lucky he is."*

They talked about nearly everything regarding business during this impromptu day off. The floral shop she started when she was eighteen. The deli she opened last year. The potential of expanding both businesses. Other small talk about her childhood, her ambitions, her goals, her dreams. Some things he was striving for. He became entranced with her the more they talked. He could tell that she would not be comfortable talking about her family. However, with his delicate sense of humor, she talked about them a little.

When it came time to pay the tab, the waitress informed them that another patron had covered it. They inquired as to who and were humorously apprised that it was a secret. He tipped the waitress handsomely.

As they were leaving, the hostess whispered to him that an important patron wanted to see him in private. He followed the hostess to a secluded banquet room, and, to Greg's surprise, his father, Gerome, stood there with a smile on his face.

"I guess you picked up the tab," Greg said, embarrassed.

"Of course. Just call it a birthday present. Look, Gregy, I'm not gonna bullshit you because I know she's waiting out there. I heard about last night and I'm pretty disappointed."

"I'm sorry. I guess I got a little carried away."

"You don't need to apologize to me. You need to apologize to your sister-in-law."

"What did I do to her anyway?" Greg asked, confused.

"You kept coming on to her while the two of you were dancing." Gerome laughed.

"Oh shit!"

"Don't worry, Gery doesn't know. She called me this morning and told me about it. She asked me to speak to you. She, of course, didn't say anything to this effect, but I think she was ashamed because if Gery hadn't been there, she would have been interested." Gerome smiled as Greg blushed. "Look, do what you want to do, but behavior like last night has got to stop, in public anyway."

"I'm sorry." Greg hung his head low. Worst of all, it was honest this time.

"Like I said, don't apologize to me. Apologize to Sherry. Now, she's Willie Cassivano's daughter, right?" Gerome asked.

"Yeah, sorry again." Greg smiled.

"Why? She's a cutie. And don't worry. Willie likes you. She's an adult, but if there's any problem about last night, I'll talk with him or Joe. Don't worry about that at all. Just be nice to her. You should get back out there with her. I'll talk to you later."

"How did you know we were still here?"

"I knew the party was here. I know you. I figured, birthday party, hotel, Gregy. It was pretty easy to figure out. Besides, I already had a dinner planned here tonight for the Optimist Club, so I just came in here early to make sure things are set up right. I spoke with Joe Giovelli this morning, and Charles told him he thought Carol spent the night with you. Look, you better go."

"You wanna walk out with me and say hi to Carol?"

Gerome nodded yes, so they walked out to the front of the restaurant. The entire conversation did not take five minutes, but it seemed as though it lasted hours to Greg.

"Carol, do you know my father, Gerome?"

"Of course, but it's nice to see you again," Carol responded, not knowing for sure why Gerome was there.

Gerome could always sense mental disarray in others. "I have a dinner here tonight with the Optimist Club and just happened to see you. So you don't need to think I followed you kids. You look great. I think the last time I saw you, you were this tall." Gerome put his hand up to his chest. "Look, I need to run. Tell your mom and dad I give them my best." Gerome shook Carol's hand, patted Greg's shoulder, then walked briskly to the banquet room.

As Greg and Carol walked toward her car, he held her hand while

16

making a poor attempt to take his eyes off her beautiful face. As they approached her car, they stopped and kissed.

She unlocked his door, walked around to the driver's door, opened it, waited for the violent heat to blast out of the car, sat down, turned her head as if expecting this, and immediately kissed him again. She always felt tingly when thinking of him. Now she was living her dream, and she feared she would wake up at any moment.

"Do you know where my house is?" he asked.

"Actually, yes. You keep forgetting Vince is my cousin. He and Sally live just down the street from you." He smiled, and, without any prompting, she said, "I know what you're thinking, and, yes, you're right, all us dagos are related." She giggled. "No, seriously, we do have a large family around here."

"Well, I was thinking you must have been stalking me lately, but that's on my mind too." They laughed and abruptly pulled onto Greg's driveway. As they stopped in front on the circular driveway, they kissed again, almost on cue.

It was a small home, but the exterior, including the landscaping, was elegant. The house had a crimson terra-cotta and brick facade with a vestibule, two bedrooms, and two bathrooms; it was a ranch-style home on a stone foundation. The home had been remodeled into two large bedrooms from five small ones.

The backyard was a sight to behold. It had a swimming pool and hot tub when he purchased the residence. He installed a well-lit fountain and many rose bushes to make a truly dramatic backyard.

It seemed a shame that a twelve-foot-high privacy fence needed to be installed to protect such an exquisite courtyard. She knew that because of the pool, law required a fence. However, twelve feet high wood with no space between boards for little eyes to peer in. Come on!

"Let me shower and shave, then you can decide where we're going tonight."

"I need to go home and shower too."

"OK, but you know you can shower here," he said, raising his eyebrows suggestively. He firmly moved his hands up her back.

She nearly passed out. "I still need to change clothes."

"How far away do you live?"

"You mean you haven't been stalking me too? About, I don't know, twenty, thirty, miles north of the river."

"It'll take you forever. That's probably fifty miles each way, and it'll be rush hour on top of that. I don't think I can live that long without seeing you."

They hugged passionately, swaying back and forth as if dancing to an uncommonly slow song. She took a deep breath and closed her eyes.

"Let's make it easy. We'll go shopping on the Plaza, and I'll buy you a whole new wardrobe. We can take a shower together and go shopping," he whispered.

Suddenly, reality came back to her. "Greg, we can't take a shower together after your reaction to my, you know, female problem."

"I forgot, but we don't have to take the shower together. Like I said this morning, it just caught me off guard, not to mention I had a bad hangover."

Not exactly Casanova-speak. However, she could acknowledge the fact that he tried to be mature in respect to the subject.

"You know, you're right about rush hour and all. I'll just do a quick cleanup here, go to the pharmacy, get what I'll need, and come back. Get ready, then we'll go out."

She gave him a list of certain unisex cosmetics to consider if she would need to purchase anything additional. She wore very little makeup, and what she did put on she always had in her purse.

While she went to the drugstore, she used a pay phone to telephone her roommate to inform her of her whereabouts. Carol's roommate was a girl named Patty, who was also her business partner. Patty informed Carol everything was fine and, "Please have a good time, finally."

Carol was an outgoing and domineering business-savvy woman. In personal matters, she could be considered shy and timid, so her behavior toward Greg in the past day alarmed yet excited her.

Carol was not a goody-goody. She also loved to party and go a little crazy. But she knew she was not in Greg's league chemically. She liked booze and pot at certain times as well as the infrequent lines of cocaine, but hallucinogenic drugs were out. She tried acid one time and had a bad trip.

Carol was certainly not promiscuous in the slightest. She had been abstinent for over a year until last night. She could not help feeling a little ashamed concerning her encounter with Greg. However, like Greg, she also believed there to be something beyond physical gratification, although the physical element went way beyond her restricted knowledge.

Carol counted three times Greg emptied himself inside of her last night, which equaled the three explosions of her own. She knew in her heart this was not destined to be another of his cheap, dirty, sex-only shows. After all, she had seen and understood the look in his eyes.

She purchased a few things from a boutique and pharmacy and opened her trunk. It startled her initially because once, when she was a girl of sixteen, she had a nightmare of an encounter when opening a car trunk. This time it had only been her dry cleaning, but anything unexpected in an automobile trunk caused her to flinch. The clothes must have been in there for three or four days. With the shoes she wore from last night, she was assured of putting together a nice outfit if need be. She would do anything to appease him. However, she desired to stay at his house and talk and listen and?

She flinched because one autumn day during her sixteenth year, she heard the automobile drive up that she had permission to drive. She had her own set of keys, so she went out to take the car. She opened the trunk of her father's car, and a dead man, bound, obviously badly beaten, and gagged, was the sight that greeted her.

What is almost comical about that is her father could not have been home for more than five minutes—probably to get shovels and knives to bury the poor bastard, or keys to an associate's funeral home to cremate him.

When she drove up to Greg's house, she was ecstatic to see him wearing a yellow tank top, white shorts, and white tennis shoes. He was talking to a neighbor in the front yard and had his customary bottle of beer in one hand.

He had obviously showered and shaved, and it made her feel filthy. It was not quite seven o'clock, so she was not sure if he wanted to go out or not. He reluctantly told her during the three-hour lunch today that his brother did not want him around the office for a few days, so she assumed he wanted to party all night as he so customarily did.

"Carol, this is my next-door neighbor, Mel. Mel, this is my friend Carol." The usual greetings and handshakes were exchanged. "Did you get everything you needed?" He kissed her on the lips. "I'll talk to you later, Mel. I need to go inside."

"See you later," Mel said with a grin and a shake of his head that said, "I know what you're going in there for."

As they walked in the front door, he grabbed her and kissed her.

"I missed you," he said, smiling.

She smiled back at him. "I missed you too. That doesn't look like an outfit you plan on wearing to a building ribbon cutting."

"I know. I had a change of heart in the shower. Would you mind terribly if we stayed here tonight? We can sit and talk,"—kiss and a hug— "maybe go for a swim,"—hug and kiss on the neck—"explore," he said.

She melted. "Can I take a shower now too so I don't feel like such a dirtbag?"

"Sure. Just let me show you where everything is." As they walked down the hall, he said, "You know, I've lived here over four years. Mel has lived there for about two years, and I still don't know his last name. Now I'm embarrassed to ask."

"Have you ever known it, or did you just forget it?" she asked casually.

A little perturbed at this kind of question, he abruptly stopped in his tracks, turned to her, and snarled. "What are you implying?"

"Nothing. I just wondered," she said, looking at him.

He knew when he became angry, his eyes would move in rapid fashion, so he looked away.

"You don't need to get defensive. Everyone forgets names. Just look up his address in the cross directory at your office." She smiled that unintentional seductive smile and shook her head.

He smiled back at her, not knowing full well if those magnificent eyes could see right through him.

Don't act that way, you stupid shithead. She wasn't accusing you of being a drunk. She just asked a question that you led her to ask. Just kiss her again, this time a long wet one. Moving my tongue down to her chest. God, what beautiful skin. She's as close to perfect as I've ever seen.

"OK, here's the shower. All the stuff you'll probably need is in the cabinets underneath the sink. And let me get you a towel." He opened a closet door, and she could see everything perfectly organized. "While you're in the shower, I'll whip up something for dinner. Yes, I still remember I promised you dinner wherever you wanna go, but tonight I just feel like lounging around."

"You cook?"

"Find out when you're out of the shower."

He closed the door to his own bedroom, all for her privacy. What a gentleman. This dream man could not possibly be better. Wrong.

She undressed to jump in the shower and looked at the surroundings. She felt like a snoop, but she was astonished to see everything in the bedroom in perfect order. She had been around men before, coming from such a large family. She could not recall one of them ever making a bed.

Her shower routine was quick and thorough. She shaved her long legs standing up and did not nick herself once. She dressed in the yellow blouse with no bra and tight white shorts she purchased at the boutique, slipped on her white tennis shoes, and put on just a little lipstick. She wonders what his reaction will be when he notices her outfit is identical to his.

She spent little time looking in the mirror. She knew she was a knockout in outfits like this.

She took a quick peek in the other closets, the dresser, and the chest. Everything was folded, placed on hangers, or hanging in wardrobe bags. Unbelievable.

She came out of the bedroom, leaving everything as perfect as she found it, glanced at her watch, and realized she had been in there for over thirty minutes.

He had yet another surprise for her. He wore an apron and methodically prepared dinner for two. Soft music coming from the living room, barely audible, was the background. The table in the dining room was set for two. The centerpiece was a hand-painted bottle of Perrier Jouet icing down in a crystal ice bucket. A freshly picked rose was lying across her plate, and petals from another rose covered her seat. The sun was already setting, and the small windowless dining room was illuminated by at least twenty candles. Perfect!

She could not smile anymore. Tears formed in her hypnotic eyes. This was heaven.

"I hope you like this. It isn't much, but if it sucks, then we'll have to go to McDonalds." He snickered.

When he bent down to kiss her, it was obvious to her that he had drunk several beers while she showered. However, she remained speechless and mesmerized by the atmosphere she now found herself surrounded by.

He poured the champagne and raised his glass in front of her to propose a toast.

"To us. I hope this is only a beginning."

They clinked glasses and began and finished eating the salad without a single word being spoken. They were lost in each other's eyes.

After the salad, they shared a long tender kiss, with him kneeling before her. The timer from the oven finally broke the tension. Both did not want this kiss to end. The telephone rang. He answered and informed the caller that he was busy and had company. A girl, no doubt. Being ever so conscious and caring toward her, he unplugged the telephone. He returned with the main course.

After dinner, he opened a bottle of port wine. They blew out the candles in the dining room and went to sit outside on the patio close to the romantically illuminated fountain.

She could not articulate. She could only gaze at him with more affection than she ever dreamed of. He could not take his eyes off her either. The affectionate light from behind her ravenous hair said more than he or anyone else could possibly verbalize. The emotional and physical attraction between them was intensely electric. They communicated effectively through the gleam in their eyes. They stared at each other and smiled brightly. The best part of it was the time. It was just after ten o'clock. They had all night.

"I have to admit this: I'm beyond impressed," she said breathlessly.

"Thank you again. If you're free tomorrow night, we'll go to the restaurant of your choice."

They sat silently for what seemed like an eternity, searching for the right words to begin this conversation. She casually crossed her legs. He reached out, picked up her left leg, placed it in his lap, delicately removed her shoe, and began massaging her foot. He then asked for her other foot and began massaging those beautiful feet as only he could do.

He gracefully stood up and just as quickly kneeled in front of her, managing to keep her legs locked around him. The powerful grip of his chest, abs, and arms around her thighs forced her to exhale the breath she had unconsciously been holding in and bite her bottom lip. For the fourth time in less than one day, she had an orgasm at his mercy. For the first time in her life, she had an orgasm while clothed.

"Love me now," she said, winded.

He lifted her as though she were in outer space, carried her inside, then gently set her on the bed, all in what seemed to her as one fluid motion.

He knew this was it. He wanted to say those three little words that he never said to a woman before. Not even his mother. Those three little words would need to wait.

After the third inning, she looked at the clock by the side of his bed to see it was nearly one o'clock in the morning. Her head rested on his left shoulder, while he caressed, almost tickled her arms, and began running his fingers through her sable hair.

The kiss this time was a soft, deliberate celebration of what now appeared to be the beginning of the relationship that seemed inevitable. The silence was finally broken. She whispered, "You are wonderful."

Wanting so desperately to say those three words to her, but having enough self-restraint not to, he used the only other three words that best described his feelings for her and replied, "you are perfect." Another soft kiss. "We need a cigarette," he said, lifting her head up to kiss her eyelids again.

"Agreed."

They looked at one another, blushing as she slowly picked her panties and shorts off the floor and walked to the bathroom. He picked up his own shorts and walked to the other bathroom.

He looked in the mirror at his slightly messed-up hair and rehearsed those three words. He left the bathroom to tend to the dirty dishes. He continued rehearsing those three little words as he walked.

He opened the refrigerator and quickly popped a bottle of beer. He chugged nearly half of it as he opened the dishwasher. He turned on the faucet and began washing the dishes by hand to put them in the dishwasher. Another beer. The silverware, the plates. Another beer. The pots, pans, and other items for the bottom shelf. The water glasses on the top shelf. The sponge from under the sink to clean up what little mess that could be seen on the counters. Another beer. He looked in the dining room to see if there was anything that needed to be cleaned. He methodically folded the tablecloth and went down the hall to put it in the laundry room while finishing his fourth beer in less than ten minutes.

Unfamiliar with his house, in the partial darkness, she made a little noise walking down the hall. He finished his beer and quietly placed the last empty bottle in the trash. He got two bottles of beer and opened one for her.

"Thank you." She wore her blouse unbuttoned but had obviously cleaned up a bit.

"Anything for you after that performance." He effortlessly lifted her off the floor and kissed her. It was obvious to him that she had brushed her teeth, so he thought fast. "I had cottonmouth so bad, I already chugged one beer while you were in the back."

"Man, you cleaned up in here fast," she said.

"Yeah, I'm fast sometimes, sorry." He smiled at her. "Look, I know you'll probably think I'm a real weirdo for saying this, but we've gotta go outside to smoke. I don't let anyone smoke in the house, including me."

"You've gotta be kidding. This is so wild. I don't allow it in mine either. It seems like everyone in my family smoked when I grew up, and I just hated the way it made my clothes smell." She smiled as she licked foam off the top of the bottle. He could not believe how sexy this looked.

"Would you like to smoke something else besides?" he asked. She nodded her head yes. He opened a drawer and pulled out a plastic bag of marijuana, some rolling papers, and a small tray and rolled a perfect joint faster than anyone she had seen in her life. He grabbed a couple of beers and headed for the backyard. "It's nice tonight," he said as he sat down and lit the joint.

The day had been miserably hot and humid as many summer days in the Midwest are. Just as everything else had been going, tonight was exceptionally cool. Tonight was perfect.

She needed to ask the question that had been with her since the spectacular cuisine he prepared earlier.

"So I can't wait to ask this anymore: How in the world did you learn to cook like that?" She smiled curiously.

"Well, I guess you know my mom died when I was really little. I never knew her actually. I mean, she died before I was a year old,"—he took a swallow of beer—"so my dad always had maids, gourmet cooks, around for us, everything."

"Look, we don't have to talk about this if you don't want to." She reached out to touch his leg. They passed the joint back and forth.

"No, no, I don't mind at all if you really wanna hear it."

"Absolutely I do." She moved closer to him.

"Well, my dad had no idea what to do with us, being the workhorse he is, so he hired all kinds of ladies to teach us things he thought our mom would teach us. Gery is a good cook too, when he wants to be, which is a rare occasion, but, anyway, I really developed a passion for it, so when I was old enough, I started taking cooking classes, experimenting with meals at night, and learned by trial and error."

"Why doesn't your brother ever cook if he's so good at it?"

"I think he works so much, he never has time for it. Plus, he's never enjoyed it as much as I do. I guess I'm saying too much too soon, but I kinda have a feeling that what I say to you will stay between us." He looked at her to receive a confirmation of this feeling and was enthralled to see she did not look at him like other women did. She was genuinely interested. "He never lifts a finger around the house, and what a house, jeez. About two miles from here over on the Kansas side. He has a beautiful wife. I know you've met her, but wait till you get to know her. Real nice girl. Two adorable boys, I'm pretty sure they like me more than him." He chuckled. He finished one beer and opened the other. "So, in addition to cooking, I just love going out to eat and party."

They finished the joint. He took one last hit before it slightly burned his fingers, and he smashed it out in the ashtray.

"I guess I'm being a little nosy, but is that why you keep everything so clean? I'm just amazed at how spotless everything in your home is. I, as you know, have a large family, and I've never seen my dad, cousins, brothers, uncles, any of them, do anything associated with what they refer to as 'women's work.'"

"There were all those maids doing all the cleaning, and after a while, I just started doing the work ahead of time so they wouldn't touch my stuff. I kinda have a privacy fixation." He finished the beer. "I'm going in for another beer, do you want one?"

"No, thanks. I'm fine."

Before he opened the refrigerator, he looked at the patio to see if she was looking toward the house. She was not. He grabbed three bottles and chugged one as he walked down the hall to the spare bathroom. He continued rehearsing those words as he chugged another beer. He returned after a few minutes.

24

"OK, where were we?" He opened one bottle while setting two others on the table.

"Well, I'm a florist, and I'm just blown away by your flowers. Who takes care of them?"

"You're looking at him. My dad always had someone to take care of the yard, shrubs, and everything, so I watched them and started taking care of the flowers myself. Read a few books. Although Dad could never talk about Mom without crying, he always smiled about that. Dad always said I inherited my green thumb from my mother." He smiled.

"Do you mind if I ask how your mother died?"

"Not at all. Apparently, she was gardening and slipped on something and hit her head on a shovel or rake. Penicillin was already available but still pretty new. She didn't know the wound was infected and died in her sleep a couple of days later. Dad told me she thought she was pregnant again and had a little morning sickness," he said.

"Tell me more about your brother. I know he and Charles are best friends, but I've never talked to Charles about him."

"Well, Gery is never home. He works like a dog. So, in turn, he's just an acquaintance of his wife and kids. I know he makes a lot more money than me, but he never—I mean never—has time to enjoy any of it. I know he's gonna regret it someday. I just get a base salary and some commissions. Even though Gery and I took control of the company earlier this year, Gery has been primed for it for years. He started with the company, like, uh, twelve years ago. I've only been there about six years. It took me a little bit, or should I say a lot longer than most to finish college. That's another story." He chuckled.

"What do you do there then?" she asked, wondering how he had all this money and so much free time.

"I'm just a front man and work better with people than Gery could ever dream of. Gery is more of a numbers guy, so he handles all the finances. When we meet potential tenants or builders, either one of the other officers of the company or I do most of the talking until the numbers start flying about. Then I'm completely honest with the people and tell them I should leave the room because that's Gery's forte." He smiled and laughed. "If you ever get the chance to listen to my brother talk, you'll crack up." He started imitating his brother. "He tries to speak very proper while he will try not to ever use any contractions." He laughed. "It's hilarious listening to him, especially in person."

"I know he and Charles are partners on some things."

"He and Charles are partners in property all over the country. Vince is an investor on some property with them. I'm just partners on twelve properties with them, and those are here locally. They buy the properties outside of the companies, then they pay Crow Brothers to manage them." He finished the beer and opened the other.

"Didn't your father start the company?"

"My grandfather started as a residential developer back in the '20s. He died a couple of years ago. Then my father turned it into a respectful commercial development company. With all the shit I could say about my brother and his nose-in-the-air attitude, he's making this company into a monster, and fast. He's so fuckin' smart. I have to admire him when it comes to business. He's so much better than my dad ever was. My dad is the first person to say that. Gery is the main reason Dad decided to let the company go and retire early. He truly thought he was holding Gery back. I know I should take business more seriously, but at least I have fun. Gery never does." She pondered this for a minute, then began to see his point. "Enough about me, tell me about you now."

He wanted to ask her how her father became known as Willie the Rat. He heard rumors about the guy and thought some of it had to be true.

"Well, there isn't much to tell after our lunch today. The things people read in the papers about my family—namely, my daddy—aren't true." She wanted to get that subject out of the way so his obvious interest about it would end. "I never went to college because I knew I had the opportunity to open the floral shop. So far, that has kept all the bills paid, and then some. Then the deli, I really wanna expand both businesses, especially the deli. I know they'd do even better in certain locations."

"Hold that thought. Would you like another beer?"

"Sure."

After a more than few minutes, he appeared with one beer for her and three for himself. She realized she was stoned and tired. She knew this needed to be her last beer. She tried to compute the drinks for him today, the lunch, the champagne, the wine and all that beer, plus a joint. Wow.

"OK. I'm sorry about that. You were talking about your deli and florist," he said as he took another large swig.

"Like I said, I never went to college because of that opportunity, but sometimes I regret not going. I never even thought I was making a mistake. I just always assumed I'd be fine without that piece of paper."

"Not many people have the opportunity you had, though. Besides, you're still so young—you have plenty of time for college. College was a real bitch for me," opening another beer. "Tell me more about your family."

"Well, there's two boys, me, and probably a million aunts, uncles, and cousins." She giggled.

"Tell me about your brothers? I'll bet I know them."

"Well, you've probably met my younger brother, Peter. He goes to Park College. So he's still close enough to live with Mom and Daddy. He wants to be a veterinarian, so I don't know where he'll go next, if he does at all," she said.

"Peter is the painter, right?" he asked.

"Yeah. He's a wonderful artist. He started drawing before he could write. Now he paints the most beautiful paintings you'll ever see. He's so talented. I wish he'd concentrate on painting instead of being a vet. But he just loves all kinds of animals. He paints these really weird paintings of animals, especially snakes. Real evil, demonic, fantasy, abstract portraits of animals. He loves snakes. He has a pet python. Mom and Daddy think he's nuts when he lets the snake crawl all over him. He wants his own apartment so he can have more snakes. Not girls, like most guys his age. Snakes," she said with a smirk.

"I've seen some of his mainstream paintings at art shows. I recognized the name. I'm amazed at some of his work, especially his real peaceful work. I've never seen his abstract paintings of snakes, though," he said, finishing a beer.

"He paints them as a joke. He never puts any of his abstract paintings up for sale. He actually makes money at the art shows where he enters his mainstream work. I think people would just love his abstracts. He says they're for nobody but him."

"What about your other brother?"

"My older brother, Paul, was killed in Vietnam about three years ago."

"You know, I know all kinds of guys that had to go there. I got an induction notice after I was expelled from my first of three schools. I failed the physical because I broke my right wrist when I was a teenager. I can't bend it back to do push-ups, but I do them on my fists almost every day. Actually, I already convinced myself I needed to go. The whole patriotic thing, I guess. Believe it or not, I was disappointed when I failed the physical. That was back when this bullshit war was supposed to be a peacekeeping mission. What a joke. Who would've known it would turn out this way? I hope everyone can see it now as a huge mistake. You probably do. I guess it's wrong to think of my wrist as a blessing, but it really was. I'm sure you've heard some horror stories about this stupid fuckin' war, and they scare me to death. Were you and your brother close?"

"Oh god, yes. He was the oldest, so he really watched out for us and cared for both of us a lot. Look, I've gotta stop talking about this. I start thinking about him, and I almost cry every time. So, please, no more Vietnam talk. It does nothing but make me sad or piss me off royally.

Let's talk about something else." She took a big swallow of beer and put her fingers to her lips in a "shh" motion.

"I'm sorry. I absolutely would've gone back then if it weren't for the physical," he pleaded.

"That's not your fault at all. You couldn't help it. Please, no more Vietnam talk. Please. I actually thought maybe I understood it when he went, but now I don't understand it at all. I just hate that fucking war. I can't believe we're still there, after all the lives lost. Excuse my language."

"I understand. I hate it too. And never ever worry about using any kind of language in front of me."

They sat together in silence for more than a minute. With their heads dropped down, it was almost as if they were in silent prayer, thinking about friends and loved ones they lost and others still on duty over there. They held hands and realized how tight the grip was.

Other pot she smoked was usually good. This stuff was spine-numbingly wicked. She suddenly thought, *I need to go in and pee. I hope I didn't think that out loud.* She looked at him. He did not pay attention to that statement, so she knew she did not think it out loud.

"I need to use the little girls' room. Do you need another beer or two, or three?"

"Sure. Come here first and look at me close so I don't forget what you look like when you're gone."

She bent over him, placing one hand on the table for balance. Smiling brightly, with her blouse still unbuttoned, she moved closer and closer to his face as he reached out with both hands. He put his hands under her blouse around her waist and kissed her lips, then kissed his way down her chest.

She walked into the house and then sprinted to the bathroom. After she peed, she looked in the mirror to see how obliterated her eyes looked. She immediately went for her purse to get some eyedrops. She went to the kitchen to get a few beers. On the way, she looked out the window to see what he was doing. He just sat there, chugging a beer.

"Here you go." She moved her lounge chair as close to the side of his as possible. As he began to speak, she could hear him slurring his words.

"Ya know, I'm thirty years old now. Maybe I should clean up my act and start actin' like it."

"What do you mean? You just finished telling me how your brother works so hard and never has time to enjoy anything," she said. They held hands again.

"I'm not talkin' 'bout anythin' that drastic. Never would wanna be like Gery. Just a little more. Ya know, not doin' anythin' for days. I should just start actin' more responsible. I'm not stupid. I know how lucky I've been. Nobody has the world mapped for 'em like I have," he mumbled.

"Look, honey, I'm real tired now. I hate to end this, but I need to go to sleep," she said, struggling to keep her eyes open. "Will you come and tuck me in?"

She jus' called me honey. I think I pretty tired too.

"I feelin' it too. Let's go inside."

He chugged one beer and brought the other inside the house as they held hands. He could not walk a straight line, and his speech was terrible. She had to hold him upright as they walked to the bedroom door. Once inside, they went straight to the bathroom sink to brush their teeth when he hit the bed, tripped, and fell on the carpet, spilling the beer. He struggled to stand up and made it to the bathroom to get a towel to sop up the wet mess. After he stumbled around in front of the sink brushing his teeth, they went to bed together quietly, skin to skin.

"I need to know, are you gonna remember any of this tomorrow?" she asked him.

His own eyes were a little less than half open. "Absolutely not, you'll have to refresh my memory in the mornin', and the mornin' afer dat, and every night too. G'night, you're my dream."

One more little kiss. It took her at least a few minutes to let sleep come into her.

As she drifted off to slumber, she whispered to him, "I think I'm falling for you."

He must have heard her say it because he briefly opened his eyes and whispered back to her, "I know I fallin' fer you. G'night." Silence. Even their breathing was in exact rhythm.

3

Gerald and Sherry Crow woke to their alarm at precisely five o'clock. The conversation was nonexistent, as it was every morning. Sherry went downstairs to prepare breakfast as her morning ritual dictated.

Gerald sprung from the bed with a fully erect penis. He masturbated in the bathroom and then showered. He shaved. He dressed. He walked downstairs to the kitchen and, without saying a word, poured himself a cup of coffee. He sat down at the breakfast table to open the financial section of the daily newspaper. Sherry brought him a grapefruit. She had French toast and bacon frying. She scrambled eggs. She also drank a cup of coffee and retrieved a section of the newspaper he finished. She turned the toast and bacon, stirred the eggs, and went upstairs to wake the children.

The boys came downstairs in their pajamas to sit at the table. Sherry served breakfast to both children and her husband.

"How are you today, boys?" Gerald asked them without looking from behind the newspaper.

"OK," Mark said.

Michael could barely keep his eyes open and did not respond.

"I don't believe I heard you, Michael." Michael gave his father the OK sign.

Everyone finished the breakfast. Gerald gave Mark and Michael a pat on the head and then kissed Sherry on the cheek before leaving for the office in his Mercedes.

Sherry helped the boys dress for school. She planned on taking them to educational day care today. She and her husband agreed that as soon as the boys were able, they would attend some sort of educational program year round.

She did not work. It is almost forbidden for a woman in her social position to possess an occupation or career. She needed to keep up appearances. Shopping and lunches are a foregone conclusion. Tennis

30

clubs and parent teacher association meetings are a prerequisite for parents who intend to portray the preeminent social compassion. As with every morning, she considered her marriage to be standard.

Gerald was a father to her children. A model husband that provided an extravagant lifestyle, a seven-thousand-square-foot home, luxury automobiles, fabulous exotic vacations, the finest jewelry available. The material list went on and on.

She grew up expecting to live a lifestyle similar to this. She did not expect her husband to be this wealthy this young, though. She did not expect him to be a workaholic that she would eventually only vaguely know. Although he provided this storybook life, Sherry had the sneaking suspicion her husband may be a closet homosexual. The only things she based this upon were his powerful effeminate physical traits and the undeniable fact that he showed no interest in her sexually.

His movements were either forcefully contrived or naturally effeminate, she could not decide which. His speech was precise in such a manner that people he spoke with immediately noticed the pitch change in his voice when he was not discussing business. Often it sounded as though he were the only adult living and everyone else was a slow, witless child to whom everything needed to be explained very elementarily and very slowly.

She always considered hiring private detectives to follow him. Gerald was too well known around Kansas City to act on those desires, if they were real. However, Sherry always suspected the worst when Gerald was out of town, especially when he went out of town alone. Travel alone was scarce for Gerald, but any travel time alone was too frequent for Sherry's peace of mind. When Gerald went to the larger cities alone, her concerns magnified.

AIDS was not a concern at the time. As far as our society knew, it probably did not exist yet. No, she was concerned of the mental problems society believed homosexuals had at the time. More than anything, she worried what effect it might have on the children if her suspicions about her husband were true.

After dropping the boys at summer school and running the daily errands, she met with her friend Louise for lunch. Sherry had spoken of the lack of amusement in the bedroom many times. Without mentioning her real concern, Sherry was able to tell Louise of the lack of passion in her marriage. Louise told Sherry that she and her husband did not "do it" anymore either. Louise talked to her sister and mother about it, and they informed her it is normal for a husband and wife to slow down after a few years. When Louise relayed this information to Sherry, she informed her that she and her husband only did it maybe five times per month. That was on a good month if she was lucky. When Sherry reluctantly informed Louise at the early lunch today that she and Gerald had not done it in nearly one year, Louise was shocked.

"I'm no psychiatrist, but that's definitely not normal. Are you sure he's OK medically?"

"For a fact, please don't tell this to anyone, all right?" Sherry requested.

"Of course not."

"Louise, I can hear him in the bathroom at times taking care of it himself,"—Sherry lowered the volume of her speech to a whisper—"you know, beating off."

"Oh my god!" Louise gasped. They started laughing.

"And almost every morning I see he still wakes up with a hard-on. Believe me, there are times I just want to attack him when I get so horny," Sherry whispered.

"Have the two of you talked about it?" Louise asked.

"If we had, do you think I would be telling you this out of sheer desperation?" Sherry exhaled.

"I guess not. Jesus, you poor rich girl."

"Ha-ha. Look who's talking!" Sherry displayed great frustration. "Louise, I'm gonna bust if I don't get laid soon."

"Has it always been this way?" Louise asked with a smile.

"Absolutely not. When we first got married, we could never get enough of each other. I mean, I don't know what other couples are like because I was still a virgin when I married Gery. But it was like we did it all the time. When we had Mark, we slowed down considerably. Then Michael came along seven years ago. He just turned seven about a week ago. After he was born, we slowed down to a snail's pace, then gradually less and less. For the last year, maybe only eleven months, it's been nonexistent."

"You had never been with a man before Gery. Wow," Louise said, genuinely shocked.

"That's not that hard to believe when you consider we've been married since I was nineteen. My freshman year we fell in love and got married about a year later." Sherry took a deep breath. "I'll tell you the worst part. I already told Gery's father, but keep it quiet." Sherry moved closer and whispered, "At Greg's birthday party the other night, Greg kept making passes toward me, and if Gery hadn't been there, I probably— no, I definitely would have gone for it. Greg is just a more fun version of his older brother. I know you've met Greg, but he and Gery are totally different, even if they do look alike."

"I don't think they look that much alike,"—Louise closed her eyes to visualize it—"A little, I guess. Greg has a reputation, though, as a heavy,

heavy-duty party guy and a bit of a drunk as of late. Does he even know that?"

"I think so. I really believe he doesn't care, though. I've never met anyone who has such a good time all the time. One thing I have to say about him is he never takes anything seriously and still does OK financially. If Greg didn't fall into Crow Brothers by birth, I don't know what he would do for a living. He's so much fun to be around." Sherry sighed.

"And Gery isn't?" Louise asked with a smile.

"In a different way. Gery is a terrific father. You've seen him with the boys. He just works so much that they almost consider him a stranger."

"Get back to the sex, the good stuff." Louise rubbed her hands together.

"There's nothing to tell, that's the problem."

"You think he has another woman?"

"I thought about that, but there's no way. Seriously, how would he have the energy to, you know, beat off all the time?" They started laughing again. "I swear, sometimes I hear him doing it three or four times a day on the weekends. Greg's sex drive is almost public common knowledge, so I guess Gery has a high sex drive also. Gery just chooses not to involve anyone else." They laughed again at the thought of it.

"I've caught my Jeff in the act at least seven times, maybe eight, during our entire relationship. And we've been together for, let's see, fifteen, almost sixteen years. Married for eleven. To tell you the truth, watching him do it kind of turned me on. That often, though, I don't think I could handle that," Louise said, shaking her head.

"Maybe only once in the morning during the week, but not every morning. God only knows how many trips he makes to the bathroom in his office during the week." They laughed hysterically now. People at the other tables thought they must have been telling jokes to one another. "I know guys do that more than us, especially when they're younger, but Gery, being married and at his age. it doesn't make sense."

"Just confront him about it. Be honest with him. Tell him he needs to expend all that energy on you," Louise said, as if it should be so easy.

"I've thought about that a bunch, but, you know, how can I approach him on this? 'Gerald, I want to be the one you make love to, not your hands.' Jesus! This may sound conceited to say, but I know I'm good looking. But I guess I'm not as good looking as his hands." They started to laugh so hard about the idea that the manager of the restaurant walked to the table and asked them to quiet down a bit.

"Sherry, please don't be offended by this. This isn't going to feel good when I ask this, OK?" Sherry nodded her head yes. Louise reached out to touch Sherry's hand and squeezed it. "Sherry, have you ever thought that Gery might be gay? You have to admit he's very feminine."

"No, that's ridiculous. No. No way."

Because of his femininity, Sherry knew people probably thought her husband was homosexual. However, Louise, being such a close friend and verbalizing it so easily, should have stunned Sherry. Instead, it eased her mind. She suddenly began wondering if the people who were around Gerald as much as Louise thought that. What about the people who just see him occasionally? Sherry instinctively knew she needed to hire a private detective the next time Gerald went out of town.

However, what if it was true? What would she do? Confront him and let him know she did not trust him? Ask for a divorce from this storybook marriage? Keep it silent to satisfy her mentally and keep the lifestyle? Definitely, she would need to do the latter.

"Louise, I need to run. None of this goes beyond this table. Do you understand? You've given me something I really need to think about." Sherry collected her purse and other items.

"How will you find out?" Louise asked.

"I don't know. I just need to be by myself for a while so I can think," Sherry said, looking at the floor.

"OK. Meet here again Monday?"

"Sure," Sherry said and walked out.

Sherry and Louise divided the tab, and, as usual, Louise needed to add a little extra for the tip. She did not mind. Louise had been a waitress in college, and Sherry had never worked a day in her life. How could Sherry know the tips she left for servers were inadequate? Louise always planned on mentioning this to Sherry, but the confused look on Sherry's face this morning warranted the tipping problem be mentioned at a more appropriate time.

Poor, poor little rich girl, her husband may be queer.

4

Gregory Crow, under orders from his older brother, was not to enter Crow Brothers Real Estate for at least a few days. Good. Greg never liked setting his alarm anyway. It was two minutes past noon.

Greg awoke in the state he woke to almost every afternoon. Greg was coming to and close to pole-vaulting out of bed. As he struggled to open his eyes, he realized someone was tickling his feet and sucking his toes, kissing her way up his leg. He did not have a hangover by his standards and immediately remembered the girl from last night.

"Carol, wait a minute, I need to use the restroom real bad."

After a couple of minutes, he reappeared wearing a robe. He brushed his teeth and gargled. Finally, he kissed her.

"I'm hungry as hell. Do you wanna eat something?"

"Well, I did until you decided not to be the main course," she said with a nasty smile. "OK, sure."

They went to the kitchen, and, to their surprise, the fire between them burned brighter than last night. As he fixed eggs and sausage for the brunch, she went outside to clean up what little mess remained from last night. She was not aware his orange juice contained nearly half a glass of vodka, almost four ounces. He poured himself another strong screwdriver and chugged it before she came back inside.

"I already called the florist and deli, so I don't need to go in today. They said things look pretty slow at the florist, but I've gotta go in to the deli tomorrow." She smiled.

He glanced at the telephone and realized she had plugged it in.

"How long have you been awake?" he asked, confused.

"Since about seven." She laughed. "No, seriously, about fifteen minutes before I woke you up!" They smiled then kissed.

She tasted the alcohol on his breath but easily came to the conclusion that it had lingered from all he had to drink last night.

35

"So if you don't need to go in today, what do you wanna do?"

Without saying a word, she kneeled in front of him, looked up at him with those eyes, opened his robe, massaged him a few times, then raised her head up so she could go way down.

That's OK with me if this is what she wants to do all day.

The telephone rang. He had no intention of answering it. It stopped ringing after ten rings. One minute later, the telephone rang again. It stopped after only five rings.

Stupid phone! Ring again, and I'll shove you in the oven.

"Oh god, Carol you're perfect." The phone started ringing again. She looked up. He let out a sigh of frustration.

"You'd better answer it, Greg." She got to her feet.

"Shit! How did the phone know I was enjoying you?" He picked up the phone and smiled at her. "Hello?"

"Gregory, it's your brother. Is she still there?"

Greg could almost see his brother grinning over the telephone.

"Yes, Gery, this is a real bad time." Greg rolled his eyes toward Carol.

"I talked to Vincey a little while ago. He said her car has been there all night."

"So what do you need, Gery? Make it fast."

"Gregory, I apologize for ruining your day, but you're going to need to meet me at my house in fifteen minutes," Gerald said.

Greg could hear his brother chuckling. "Can't. No way. I haven't even showered yet."

"I don't care, it's only me. We need to speak privately immediately. Do you understand?" The tone in his voice lent itself to a demand from Gerald, not a question.

"Yes, sir, buttface!" Greg shouted into the phone.

"You can bring her if you want. She can talk with Sherry, while you and I meet. Charley and Vincey will be there a little later, but I need to meet with you privately first and very soon. If you're not at my home in twenty minutes, I'm coming to your house." Gerald hung up the telephone abruptly.

"Carol, I'm sorry, but I've gotta meet my brother at his house right away. Charles and Vince are gonna be there later, so you're welcome to come, but I have to be there now. I'm sorry."

"I can't go looking like this,"—she smiled—"with hair that says I've been well screwed."

"It's just gonna be me and my brother and your cousins. You have time to take a shower. I should take a slow shower just to piss him off, but it sounded pretty urgent, so I won't. I'm gonna take a quick dip, towel off,

36

and go over there in shorts and a tank top. That should be enough to piss him off. Will you need directions if I give you the address?"

"Greg, I really don't wanna go."

"Come on, we'll be there for a few minutes, and then we'll have the rest of the day," he begged with a smile.

"No, that'll give me enough time to go home, clean up, and pick a restaurant for you to take me to tonight." She giggled.

"Oops. I forgot. I still owe that to you. OK."

"Do you want me to call you when I head back? I think I need your phone number. Here, I'll write mine down too." She wrote her telephone numbers on a notepad beside the phone.

"Well, considering it's my brother who loves to make an easy meeting difficult, long, and boring, phone numbers might not be enough. Let me give you another key."

As he retreated to the bedroom where he kept spare keys, he realized he had never supplied another woman with a key to his sanctuary. He was usually very cautious about his domain. In another trivial, silent, monumental event, he realized this was right. This was good. This was it.

"You don't have to do that, Carol," he said. She scrubbed the dishes to prepare them for the dishwasher.

"I want to. You need to get it together and go," she said, pointing at her watch.

"Here you go. I'm gonna jump in and out of the pool real quick and go." She held on to the key as if it were a precious jewel. "I need to hurry. I just wanna tell you something." He turned her around to face him. He gently took her face in his hands. "You're the first and hopefully only girl who will ever have this key." He kissed her and knew this was it.

37

5

Greg drove his Volkswagen Thing onto the steep circular driveway at his brother's estate. He also had a Porsche, but he decided to drive the Thing to his brother's home and park this piece of shit right out in plain view so all the neighbors could see it. Greg believed he owed some aggravation to Gerald in retaliation for interrupting him and Carol earlier.

Gerald and Sherry resided in Mission Hills, Kansas, a small township of mansions and exquisite estates. Although it was a fabulous estate, it was small in comparison to others. They were not financially able to reside in one of the upper echelon estates. Yet.

Greg pushed the doorbell and rolled his eyes as his brother came on the intercom to ask who was there.

"It is I, Sir Needle Dick. Open the door right fuckin' now!" Greg shouted.

"Just a moment."

Who does he think he's trying to impress? He probably thinks Carol is with me. I'll give him thirty seconds.

Sherry opened the door laughing. "Hi, Greg, he's in the den. That was hilarious. You're alone, I see. Do you want something to drink?"

In a lame British accent, Greg replied, "No need, luv, just hit me over the head with a bottle of his finest sixteen-year-old scotch." Back to his real voice. "Actually, I'll have a beer if you don't mind, only because I know it'll bother him." Greg followed Sherry into the kitchen. "Look, I'm real sorry about the other night. I didn't know I did that until someone told me."

"It's OK, water under the bridge." Sherry then whispered, "Greg, I was flattered." She smiled.

Greg did not like the way Sherry looked at him. She reached in the refrigerator and pulled out a beer for both of them. She blew a kiss to him from between her legs as she reached in. She wore tight pink shorts that covered very little and made sure Greg had a perfect view when she bent

38

down. If only she were not married to his brother, she would be stripped and on all fours already. She opened the imported beer and filled two frosted glasses. As she brought his beer to him, she flicked foam from her own glass to the tip of her rather prominent nose, then showed exactly what she wanted by licking it off and holding the white foam on her still protruding tongue.

"Sherry, cut it out, my brother is here." Greg laughed.

"Greg, I need to talk to you soon. Please call me," Sherry begged.

"Sherry, you're my sister-in-law."

"Gregory, you slow-brained idiot, did you get lost again? Come into the study *today* please," Gerald said over the intercom.

Greg smiled. "When he says 'study,' he means the den, doesn't he?" Greg immediately raced from the kitchen out of fear he would be trampled by his sister-in-law. He did not bother knocking on the door. He walked in sweating, hiding his chuckles over what had just happened with Sherry.

Gerald and Gregory had many of the same features, but Greg seemed to have received the sharper part of the chisel. He plopped down loudly in an English Chippendale chair, knowing how obsessed Gerald was with his antique chairs. Greg hoped to break one of these chairs "accidentally" sometime.

"This better be important, Gery. You grounded me, remember, so start talking. You've already managed to fuck up a pretty good day again. So make your point quick."

Gerald would not make eye contact. He wrote on a legal pad while he spoke from behind his mahogany desk. Greg set his beer glass on the desk next to a coaster, then plopped his feet on the antique desk.

"Please take your worthless feet off my valuable desk. As usual, your beer is not on a coaster. Please move it to a coaster before I throw it in your face."

"Just messing with you. What's up?" Greg did as instructed and smiled.

"As you may or may not know, we may be in a bit of trouble. My educated guess is you do not know because you never will understand the way the real world works."

"Stop talking to me like I'm a kid, Gery. Cut the bullshit and make your fuckin' point."

"Do you remember Weitzer Construction Company, out of Minnesota?" Gerald asked.

"We worked with them almost four years ago when Dad was still running things."

"Correct. However, the agreement with Dad did not have any insurance provisions for miscalculations that may be made on the buffer zone, only on the strip shopping center in Inver Grove Heights and the apartment complex in Maplewood. So when we chose to go ahead with the apartment complex as a buffer zone in Inver Grove against the existing residential development, the complex was not zoned properly. I looked it over and did not think it was necessary to apply for a variance. The residents of the existing developments directly adjacent to our buffer zone sued the county zoning commission. The county sued Weitzer Construction Company. Weitzer sued us. I—so, in effect, 'we' did not hire a surveyor for the apartments, only the shopping center."

"Then it's your problem, not mine," Greg said.

"You're an equal partner, though. You're responsible for it, whether you like it or not."

"Go on then, douche bag."

"I tried to cut corners on the buffer because I knew it was not the real purpose of the project. Dad had no knowledge of it. I was responsible for it all. Sorry. Hopefully we can establish a grandfather clause to the county, but the way the state of Minnesota is, who knows? I would love just to sell those properties and never do business in Minnesota again. Too many regulations and the taxes are outrageous. I don't know any of the county commissioners there, so a cash payoff is out of the question. Anyway, Weitzer Construction sued us. Word got out that we are in trouble in the Minneapolis-St. Paul area, and word spread to Rochester . . ."

"Hold it, Gery, OK?" Greg cut Gerald off midsentence. "I'm sorry. You've lost me already."

"Thank you. Now that I know where you stand, I'm giving you a list of banks, who to talk with, and how much to ask for, secured or unsecured." Like a teacher speaking down to a kindergartener, Gerald said, "Do you understand the difference between secured loans and unsecured?"

"Fuck you, Gery." Greg's gesture reciprocated his words.

"Basically, we are just in a cash shortfall right now. So just do as I have written on the list and we'll be fine in about two or three months," Gerald said.

Greg looked over the list his brother handed him. His eyes bugged out.

"Shit! Gery, this is over $9 million in loans. I don't have that kinda collateral."

"Yes, you do, Gregory. You're one of the two principals of Crow Brothers. Anything that is owned by the company has your name on the deed. Dad made sure of that, against my better judgment, of course. The property I purchased separate from the company has nothing to do with you, thankfully." Greg rolled his eyes and pretended to yawn. "Look, I pledge to you in two, possibly three months, this will be well under control. Your obligation to us is to procure and submit the applications to all those banks starting Monday morning and conclude before two o'clock on Tuesday, all on the Kansas side. The ones I'm going to are the big banks on the Missouri side. You have no choice but this, or you're bankrupt. I, on the other hand, would just take a financial hit." Gerald smiled.

"You have me getting loans from nine different banks. You wanna kite these checks across the state line for months, I'm guessing. This is check kiting. It's illegal as hell, and I'm not gonna do it," Greg said as he threw the list back on the desk.

"Then we will see how long you survive without Crow Brothers. I promise—do everything just as I have told you and nobody will get caught. And in the one-in-a-billion chance we do get caught, just have the feds give you an IQ test so they can see that you . . ."

"Fuck you again, Gery."

"Look, you do nothing to help the company. You sit on your drunken ass, making hundreds of thousands a year. By my calculations, it was over eight hundred grand last year and you do absolutely nothing for it. You spend it on booze, probably drugs, and God only knows what else."

"It's none of your business, but I save most of it, dickhead! I don't go around buying things I don't need to impress people I don't even like."

"Touché. I'm sorry I said that. I will admit, you're a great salesman. You're a much better salesman than I am. That's your strong point. I found a flaw in my strong point. I got a little power hungry and made a few mistakes. I'm truly sorry." Greg rolled his eyes again. "This will get us out of the bind. I'll never make these kinds of mistakes again. So, please, Monday morning get to those banks, follow the script, and, please, I'm begging you, please go sober." Gerald pointed at Greg.

Greg knew he was beaten after Gerald reminded him he could not and would not survive without Crow Brothers.

"All right, you win. Tell me now what Vince and Charles are coming for."

"Since a portion of this is your money, you have the right to know. Charley told me about a few casinos in Las Vegas that we can purchase dirt cheap. Nothing compared to what they are actually worth. You and I are going to be the front men even though Charley and Vincey are putting up 50 percent of the money. They trust us. They don't believe they'll be able to pass the Nevada Gaming Commission background check required by law because of their notorious family history. Even though they have never committed crimes, I think you know who I'm talking about. If all goes according to plan, we can legally place them on the ownership deeds about six months after we take ownership."

41

"What happens if we can't add their names?" Greg asked, confused as usual.

"That is precisely what we are going to discuss today. I imagine we put them on as 'straw men' in that case. You and I will be approved, no doubt. Crow Brothers already owns three properties in Nevada, the apartments, and the strip shopping center. Dad bought them outside the company, so he's the only one that makes anything on them, but our names are on the deeds now. If, for some reason, we cannot put them on, we'll need to pay them under the table as 'straw men.' If we can add their names, we simply pay them back with interest."

"How many casinos are we talking about? And since some of this is my money, naturally I would like to know the names of what you're buying?" Greg demanded.

"Three small ones for now. I honestly don't know which ones. I'm going to discuss it with Charley and Vincey, but it sounds as if they are pointing toward several more in the next few years."

"Whatever. Look, you can handle the numbers on it. The less I know about it, the better off I probably am. Something about this doesn't sound right. And, as I've told you for years, he hates the name Vincey."

"I've always referred to him as Vincey," Gerald said, bewildered.

"And he's always hated it. Answer this: what do you need me to borrow this kind of money for—if this casino thing goes to hell?" Greg asked.

Gerald smiled at the fact that his brother actually asked an intelligent question.

"Gregory, I hope you understand the delicacy of this proposition, so, as usual, please do not discuss it with anyone."

"Call me Greg, Mr. Twat."

"Fine, Greg Mr. Twat. We are still a little short on cash to make some of the balloon payments coming due."

"Stop right there. I don't wanna know anything else. This check-kiting thing has me worried. The less I know, the better. You're smarter than I am when it comes to business. I have no trouble admitting that, but you leave something to be desired when it comes to human relations. Regardless, I'm not going to Nevada with you at your request. If Vince or Charles needs me to go for them, then maybe I'll consider it. This all sounds like something you can go to prison and get butt-fucked over. You would probably enjoy that, though, so it wouldn't really be punishment."

"Shut up!" Gerald screamed. He usually paid no attention to his brother's rambling.

Greg stifled a smile and laughter because he knew he'd hit a sensitive spot.

Sherry happened to be walking past the closed door of the den when Greg issued the statement on prison. Part of her was shocked, and part of her wanted to burst out laughing. Sherry knew nothing of the discussion between her husband and brother-in-law. She just assumed Greg was being his usual self to Gerald.

Greg gathered the papers his brother had prepared for him and was ready to walk out the door, singing his version of "If I Only Had a Brain" from *The Wizard of Oz*. The parody version Greg sang was titled "If You Only Had a Dick." Gerald sang his own rendition, "If You Only Had a Brain." It was a tradition for them to sing this or another critical song to one another, and both were smiling as usual.

Suddenly, like a baseball bat to the stomach, a vile, malevolent vision appeared in Greg's mind of himself drowning in the trunk of a sinking car. He turned around, terrified.

"Is one of the Giovelli relatives you were talking about Willie Cassivano?" All color instantly faded from Greg. He thought he would drop dead from a coronary.

"I honestly have no idea. Vincey told me Carol's car was outside your house this morning, and everyone knows you spent the night with her at the Ritz after your birthday party." Gerald thought about it for a second, and then he realized what his brother must have been thinking. He looked up to see the pale, ghostlike statue his brother had just become. Lightning quick, Gerald raced across the room to keep his brother from hitting his head on the floor as Greg passed out cold.

"Oh my god! Oh my god! Sherry, come here! Sherry, in here now!"

Sherry never heard her husband shout this loud, so she knew something was horribly wrong. She burst through the door and did not expect to see her brother-in-law gravely pale. She saw Greg lying there with his eyes closed and his head in his brother's hands. The bottom of her husband's hands appeared to be the only padding that prevented Greg from banging his head on the parquet floor.

In college, Sherry majored in nursing and was legally a registered nurse. Without a thought, she knew exactly what to do.

She ran faster than she ever had to the kitchen, where she always stored a medical bag and first aid kit. When she ran back into the den, she saw her husband shaking. He did not have the stomach for this. Name-calling and verbal torment since they were kids was part of the fun they had with one another. However, they were still brothers who cared and loved one another unconditionally.

"Gery, get those pillows from the couch." Sherry had her stethoscope on and listened to her patient's heartbeat. Greg was always a picture of health. Sherry calmly gave medical orders to her husband. He obeyed. Gerald feared his brother had just suffered a stroke or heart attack. He was confident Sherry knew what she was doing. "He's dehydrated. Go pour a glass of orange juice and a glass of water." Gerald did exactly as instructed. "Greg, can you hear me?"

"Of course."

"I'm not going to say anything to Gery, but you reeked of alcohol when you came in, so drinking a beer in front of him was a good move on my part." Sherry smiled. Just as quickly as the color had faded from Greg, it reappeared.

Gerald entered the den again, oblivious to current the situation. He set the orange juice and water by Greg. Sherry directed her husband back to the kitchen and told him to get a straw.

"You owe me now, mister. I'm not going to say one word to him about the fact it was alcohol that made you pass out. Plus, the meeting sounded intense. Also, it's ninety-four degrees outside and you just entered a house that Gery keeps as cold as a refrigerator. I'll tell him you're more than likely coming down with a flu bug."

"He knows I never get sick."

"Shut up and open your mouth." Sherry grabbed a thermometer from her medical bag, licked it, ran it around her lips, then showed Greg how far she could stick the thermometer and her fingers down her throat before she abruptly stuck it under his tongue. Coincidentally, Gerald walked in the room that very second.

"He OK?" Gerald asked, shaking.

"He'll be all right, sweetie, but right now he's burning up, so I'm taking his temperature to see how bad it is. If it's higher than 102, we'll need to take him to Dr. Stein right away." Greg felt fine. He could not believe the bullshit Sherry fed her husband. "Honey, go upstairs to the linen closet and get a hand towel, wet it down with cool water, and bring it down." Again, Gerald did as instructed. As Sherry heard Gerald go up the staircase, she again tended to herself. "You really are dehydrated, Greg. Sip some of the orange juice. All jokes aside, you need to drink more water and juice if you plan on drinking everything else." Sherry put his hand up her shirt.

The very idea that her husband was just a few feet away thrilled her. It scared Greg to death, but it got him excited, as she could see. She saw it twitch and stuck her hand down the front of his shorts aggressively to grab all she could. While she played, she heard her husband descending the stairs and rolled her eyes.

"Here's the towel. Goddamn, Gregory, you almost scared me to death."

"Honey, let's get him to the sofa in the family room so he can be close to the bathroom. You're running a bit of a temperature, but not that bad. I do need to keep an eye on it, though." His temperature was normal. Gerald stood behind her as she told lie after lie. "Do you think you can stand up now, Greg?" Sherry asked with false concern, which seemed real.

"Yeah. I'm sorry, Gery. All of a sudden, I just started getting cold and blacked out. Ya know, I'm still cold." Greg figured he may as well play her little game.

"Well, look what you're wearing, Gregory. Sherry, should I get a blanket or something?"

"Good call. There should be an afghan on the couch, but go upstairs to the linen closet again and get one of the big quilts."

Sherry forced Greg down on the couch and rubbed her face on his crotch.

"Sherry, this is way too much. Stop it or he's gonna kill both of us," Greg begged with a smile.

"Don't worry. When he comes down from upstairs, say you need to leave."

"You're fuckin' nuts, Sherry."

Two minutes later, Gerald walked into the family room with the quilt and pillow. Sherry stood up and pulled Gerald into the other room and spoke quietly.

"You know, Gery, you should take him home so he doesn't leave any flu germs behind for the boys to pick up."

"I can't leave right now. Charley and Vincey will be here soon. Honey, you better check my pulse now. That's as close to what Gregory calls freaking out as I've ever come in my life. I really thought he was dying just now."

Sherry put her arms around Gerald. "Honey, your heart is beating too fast. Sit down so I can take your pulse." She went back to the family room and winked at Greg as she picked up her stethoscope and blood pressure kit. She listened to her husband's heart, knowing full well he was fine, but she wanted to play this out to the hilt. She took his blood pressure and pulse. Then she cleared him medically. "You had a bit of a scare, that's all. You're fine." She reluctantly kissed her husband.

"Is Gregory really OK?" Gerald asked.

"He'll be fine. He just has a little flu bug. He has a temperature, but nothing to be alarmed about."

"Sherry, he can't hear me, but if you would have seen what I saw. As soon as he began thinking of William Cassivano, then it occurred to me that Gregory has spent the last two nights with his daughter. Gregory turned white as a ghost, passed out, and I freaked out at almost the same time. That was strange."

Sherry listened with genuine concern but immediately changed the subject. "Gery, what time is your meeting with them?"

"Two thirty. They're always on time."

"It's already two. I'll just take Greg home, make sure he has everything he needs, if you'll pick the boys up at day care later. Or you know what, I'll just leave a message with the workers at the school to send them home with the Carmichaels, and I'll pick them up later. Get it together so you at least would look OK for your meeting." Sherry collected her medical instruments and placed them in the medical bag to take with her to Greg's home.

"You name when and where you want to go on vacation next, and it's all yours," Gerald said with a smile.

"OK. I'm going to take him home now. You know what? I wouldn't talk about this to anyone. It might sound a little crazy," Sherry winced.

"Thank you. You're right again."

Sherry went back to the family room and loudly informed Greg she was taking him home.

"Sherry, I feel fine now. I can drive." Greg smiled.

"I haven't released you yet. OK, but at least I'm following you, then going to the store," Sherry said.

Greg knew he could not refuse, so he reluctantly gave her the thumbs-up.

Sherry followed too close and appeared dangerously eager to be alone with Greg in his bachelor pad. He really was in good health after drinking a few nonalcoholic liquids. He desperately tried to think his way out of this soon-to-be encounter alone with his rabid sister-in-law.

As he unlocked the front door, they heard the telephone ringing. He hoped to stop this relentless pursuit. He hoped the telephone call was from someone needing to see him right away. No such luck. It was Carol saying she had swung by the deli to check on things and, as habit dictated, she started working. She told Greg she could not be there until at least six o'clock. He thought fast and asked if he should come by the deli and they could go out from there. No good. She informed him she would stink to high heaven when she finished work. She would go home, clean up, and, if he wanted, she could bring a change of clothes for morning. He ran out of ideas so he told her, "That's a winner."

Greg hung up the telephone hesitantly. Before turning to Sherry, he let her know Carol would be there at six o'clock. He looked at the oven clock and was sorry to see it was just now two thirty.

46

Shit.

"I don't want to waste another second!" She kneeled in front of him and ripped his shorts, violently tearing the top button completely off. She ripped his underwear and, in fact, wasted no time. For the second time in less than three hours, he received oral sex in his kitchen. The first woman was the most beautiful woman he had ever seen. This one was his only brother's wife. He knew this was not right at all, but he could not speak, and it did feel good.

He closed his eyes and attempted to imagine the woman giving him this extraordinary gift was the girl he had fallen for. It was of no hope. He knew it was his sister-in-law. He then wanted to put his brother out of his mind. How in the world would he be able to do that? His brother's wife was on her knees in his kitchen giving him a blowjob.

"Sherry, this is wrong," Greg said breathlessly.

"Hmm, mm," she mumbled.

"You're my brother's wife."

"I'm not your sister, so this is legal. This is just between us. No one will ever know, and, besides, you owe me." She looked up. "If it makes you feel better, it's a little bigger than Gery's—from what I can remember anyway."

That did not help. After a long while of this, she forced him to lie down. She carefully removed her own shorts and climbed on top of her husband's brother.

6

A black Lincoln Continental with bulletproof and tinted glass pulled slowly onto the driveway at Gerald and Sherry Crow's estate. Before the tanklike car pulled to a complete stop, the passenger door opened. Out stepped a man impeccably dressed for someone of his proportions. He was in his early thirties and carried a briefcase. He stood at least six feet five and weighed at least 280 pounds. This was not anybody's imagination. This guy was mostly muscle. The man was visually intimidating. Medium brown hair neatly trimmed, beady eyes that did not match his other broad facial features. Looks were deceiving. This was Vincenzo Giovelli.

A bashful and gentle man who hated the fact that people were scared of him because of his physical stature and primarily because of his name. He was proud of his heritage, but the notoriety was something he could definitely live without.

The driver's door opened, and Charles Giovelli presented an equally menacing presence as his younger brother. Charles was not as tall or heavy as his brother, but he was close.

His jet-black hair looked like a wretched dye job. Charles had a receding hairline, and his eyebrows nearly touched in the middle. He dressed meticulously in a black suit with black sunglasses. From a distance, he looked as demonic as any character in a horror film. Up close, he looked like a man in his mid to late thirties, trying desperately to hang on to any semblance of his fast-fading youthful looks.

Charles was a chain smoker who averaged three and a half packs per day. Sometimes as many as five packs of cigarettes would pass through his system daily. When he removed his sunglasses, his eyes were baggy as if he had not slept. His cheeks were sunken, and the skin on his neck was loose. Friends and family begged him to see a doctor. The prognosis: negative. He was just getting old very fast.

Charles was always paranoid over this or that. He always carried an automatic pistol concealed under his suit jacket. He left the gun behind in the automobile because this was only Gery.

"It doesn't look like Greg is here," Charles voiced the obvious.

"Carol's car was at his house this morning. That's two nights in a row. He might be out celebrating—that's a long relationship for him." They laughed as they walked to the front door. "I sometimes stop by in the morning just to wake him up, but when I saw her car there, I passed. I don't know if she would see the humor in it. She told me at the party the other night how hot she thinks he is, asking all kinds of stupid questions about him." Charles pushed the doorbell. Vince imitated a girl with his highest voice possible, "You know him, Vince. What does he like? How do I get him to notice me? Should I do this or that? Does he like this music or that music?" Back to his real voice, "It was exhausting listening to her ramble on and on and on about him."

Charles hit the doorbell again. "I guess when guys look like him and have that kind of money, it doesn't matter how bombed you are." Charles shook his head, laughing. "God, he made such an ass of himself that night."

"That's Greg, though. What you see is what you get. He's great. He never has said a bad word about anybody, to me at least. I really believe he likes everyone. He never thinks less of anyone else. He is without a doubt the most nonjudgmental person I'll probably ever meet," Vince said, smiling.

"Guys, I'm sorry. I'll be right down," Gerald said over the intercom.

"So do you think we need to do anything or just give Gery the financial statements?" Vince asked.

Charles noticed the light on the intercom was still on, which meant Gerald was still listening.

Charles whispered, "Be careful, he's listening." Normal volume for the benefit of the intercom, "No, just give them to him and we'll shut up. He'll look over them tonight and have his decision by tomorrow. He doesn't pussyfoot around on anything if it involves business. He's pretty smart," Charles said, whispering to Vince that the light meant Gerald continued to listen.

Vince decided to play along. "Yeah, I didn't really need to be here. I just wanted to see Greg. Maybe ask him about Carol. If she's there again tonight, then I'd bet on it—this is going to get serious, and I'll owe Sally a new car if it turns out that way."

Vince did not believe Greg could ever be serious about a woman. Sally, Vince's wife, predicted to Vince the night of the party that Carol was perfect for Greg. Sally, the hopeless romantic, said she believed a marriage was imminent. Vince laughed so hard, his eyes watered and he drove off the road for a second. He reminded his wife several times, "You don't know Greg the way I do." He promised to purchase a new Cadillac for her if the relationship lasted more than a month.

Gerald opened the door. "Sorry, guys, I was just upstairs."

"So I take it Greg isn't coming over?" Vince inquired, although he already knew.

"Actually, he came over earlier in his finest attire—shorts and a tank top," Gerald said.

"Vince said he saw Carol's car there again this morning. Did Greg say anything?" Charles asked.

"No, I don't talk to Greg about those things anymore. He became ill after he was here for a little while. Sherry took his temperature. He had a fever. He was pale and said he was dizzy. Then Sherry followed him home. Just a flu bug, she said. She knows what she's doing, though. You guys might remember she's a nurse."

"I'm sure I'll talk to him later," Vince said.

"He wouldn't need to be here for this. I gave him the basics already from what you have told me, Charley, and he gave me permission to use his funds. Let's go sit down and talk." Gerald led them to the den and pulled up his Chippendale chairs. Being the two huge specimens that the Giovelli brothers were, Gerald worried one of his antique chairs may break.

"So here are the profit and loss statements on the three casinos. You can read those later. What we couldn't discuss on the phone is the silent partner covenant." Charley pulled out a cigarette to light. Gerald despised cigarette smoke, but this was Charley, so he retrieved an ashtray. "We can invest as much as $15 million. If you guys can invest it and put up your own fifteen, we shouldn't have any problems. These three are small casinos with ramshackle hotels. No one knows they're for sale. Dad told us about it and suggested you and Greg as partners," Charley said.

"For almost twenty years now, as you probably know, Dad has been funneling millions of dollars in cash from certain casinos out in Vegas. I honestly don't know which ones," Vince said.

"If the casinos are in your name, you give the company we choose the contract for the renovation of them. We set it up through a construction company we have in Las Vegas that is actually our own company working under a 'Doing Business As' name. We give it a moronic and probably non-Italian name, like, oh, Uncle Joe's Repair and Renovation. Run a few big ads in newspapers for a few weeks, like 'Uncle Joe's Repair: No job too big or small.' You then give them the contract. The repairs aren't going to be that extensive anyway," Charley said.

"You have a disagreement over the money to pay Uncle Joe, so a mechanic's lien goes on the casinos. Not on you personally, though. Then as soon as they open remodeled and the cold hard cash rolls in, our people there start bringing the cash here bimonthly. You work it out with Uncle Joe's to settle for less money, Uncle Joe's removes the lien, and the four of us are sitting pretty. The head cashiers or skimmers fix the books, so it all goes down legal. Then they give the runners the cash and they bring it here," Vince said.

"Then before you add our name to the deeds, we agree on an equity swap on a property here, Arkansas, Colorado, wherever. We give you the equity on that. In return, you put our corporate name on the ownership warranty deed for the casinos if you need to. So you have some land in Bumfuck, Arkansas, and sell it to Giovelli Construction Company because we actually really still own it. You take a loss for your taxes, and we're done," Charley said.

"The equity swap sounds like an unnecessary step. We could just as easily give Uncle Joe's part ownership in exchange for removing the mechanic's lien," Gerald said.

"See, I told you, Charley," Vince chimed in. "We thought about that, and it can work if we agree to buy Uncle Joe's, all of his contracts, liens, tools, everything. That would be a more sensible approach. If we put too many steps in this, we're all going to lose track of it. We don't want to get any more people involved in this, but we could get someone we know to start up Uncle Joe's, or another company name, and get them to obtain the right licenses. Just not go into details over the purpose of it."

"When is this supposed to take place?" Gerald asked.

"We need to drive out there, but you can fly. It'll probably take two days to drive, but we could start out as early as next weekend. You can fly out one week from Monday, the twenty-eighth. Our people in the Nevada Gaming Commission office could have your ownership settled legally within a week or two after that. Our legal ownership would need to take place after the bogus renovations are done, but no sooner than six months and no later than a year. We might not want to be on the deeds, though. We might want to purchase others in a few years. We'll just play it by ear. We can work out the lettuce so you don't get hit with too many taxes." Charley finished his cigarette at the same time and immediately chained another one.

"I can do that. Greg doesn't want to go. Do you think it would be all right to take my wife?" Gerald asked. "She just loves Las Vegas, the shows and everything."

"Greg has to go, no choice," Charley protested.

"I'll talk with him. He has to be there to sign papers. He can even bring Carol. Jesus, if he's still with Carol by then," Vince said, and all three laughed.

"I'll look through the profit and loss statements and give you an answer by the weekend." Gerald organized the items for his briefcase to proclaim the business portion of the meeting over. "Guys, look, I know this might sound paranoid, and I really don't want Greg to know I asked this of you. Does Greg have anything to worry about regarding William Cassivano?"

"I haven't thought about that, but I'll check it out," Charley said comfortably.

"I never thought about that either, but that's probably a legitimate concern," Vince said.

"Of course, this needs to stay among us. Willie is a real asshole. He's not really our uncle—he's more like an embarrassment. He just happens to be our dad's wife's brother. I can't really call her my stepmom. I was already twenty-one when they were married. Sometime I'll tell you what I think of her too." Charley laughed. "You've seen her. She's just a few years older than me and looks younger than I do. I call her Sister Sandy because my wife is Sandy, so I tell her that keeps us from getting confused. Actually, Dad's brother Angelo was her first husband." Charley attempted to laugh but let out a rough smoker's cough instead. "I'm sure I speak for Vince too when I say I can't stand Willie, even if he's part of the family by marriage. He's lucky he isn't in prison or dead. He's such a lunatic."

"Willie is incorrigible. I hate when he tries to act like a caring uncle. All the old-fashioned kissing us on the cheeks and shit. Yuck, use a breath mint, you fuckin' rat," Vince said, holding his nose.

"He doesn't even realize how phony he comes across. Then two minutes later he's screaming at people, but never the two of us, throwing things around. Greg doesn't have anything to worry about. I'll talk with my dad as soon as I get back to the office, meet him later, and tell him the situation. He'll straighten Willie out right away before Willie ever has a chance to think about it. I do know Willie is out of town right now. Greg will have absolutely nothing to worry about. I'll tell him that," Charley said, trying to reassure Gerald.

"Guys, I don't want Greg to know I even spoke to you about it. He might be offended if he thinks I got involved in his personal life," Gerald pleaded.

"All right, but you can at least be assured that Greg will be fine. I don't want to get into the details, but Willie has no choice but to do exactly as my father says." Charley smiled. Gerald knew Joseph Giovelli was the boss. "Willie has no choice. Enough said. When we have more time, I can be a little more specific. Willie is a real dick."

52

Charley did not worry about anything said in the presence of Gerald. Charley knew and had sworn secrecy years earlier about the secret Gerald did not want anyone to know. Presumably, Charley never told his wife or brother. Gerald had a secret, and it was safe with the only person he had ever confessed to.

After more than an hour of discussing other business and personal talk, the meeting was obviously over.

"Well, I'll call one of you by Saturday morning. We can meet somewhere to work the rest of this out," Gerald said, standing up and stretching his arms.

As Charley and Vince walked to the front door, Sherry entered from the garage. She came out to the foyer and hugged the Giovelli brothers. They asked how Greg was feeling.

"He's fine, just dehydrated and maybe a little cold." She made the motion of drinking.

Gerald placed his arm around his wife to show how proud he was of her. She placed her arm around his waist. What a show. Nothing was wrong. Everything was just fine. Gerald said good-bye, excused himself, then went upstairs and locked the bathroom door.

Sherry informed Charley and Vince that Carol would be at Greg's later to spend the night. Vince told Sherry of the wager he made with his wife. Sherry forewarned Vince he'd better start shopping for a new Cadillac. Vince shook his head, smiling.

Sherry was fidgety and severely uncomfortable. She kept glancing at her watch. Vince glanced at his watch and determined she needed to pick the boys up. They all said good-bye. Vince and Charley walked out to the car and drove away.

Sherry walked up the stairs as Gerald came out of the master bath.

"Honey, go pick the boys up. I need to take a bath," Sherry said loudly, trying everything to avoid any eye contact with her husband.

"Can't you pick them up? I still need to go back to the office," Gerald whined.

"If Greg really has something, I need to clean up and change clothes so I don't give it to them."

"You're right again. I'll get them. Where are they?"

"The Carmichaels, remember?" Sherry said with unnecessary sarcasm.

Gerald never argued with his wife. That would require too much time speaking to his token.

"Tell me again where they live."

"I'll do better than that—I'll write it down. Then you write it in your address book, OK?" Sherry said loudly but not angrily. They tried to speak

53

through the sound of running water in the master bath. Sherry came out in her robe, wrote the address, and gave it to her husband.

"Sherry, if all goes according to plan, we're going to Las Vegas one week from Monday."

"Who is 'we'?"

"You and me. Charley and Sandy, Vincey and Sally, then Greg and whoever he wants to bring."

"That sounds crowded."

"It'll be fun. We need to tend to business there, but we might as well make a vacation out of it. We might be out there for two or three weeks."

"Go pick up the boys. I'll get dinner ready." She closed the door and got in the tub with a smile on her face.

7

Greg got out of the shower to see a confused look on his face as he shaved. Between strokes of the razor, he took one sip after another of straight gin. He brushed his teeth thoroughly and then gargled twice. He finished his gin, then immediately walked to the kitchen to get a beer. He stopped in his tracks and saw Carol's telephone numbers next to the refrigerator. He convinced himself that no one would ever know of what happened earlier. He dialed the telephone number for the deli and asked for Carol.

"Carol, this is Greg. When are you coming?"

"Well, right now if I think about it real hard." She tried not to laugh. "No, actually, more like seven. Then I need to be here by eight tomorrow morning. Why?"

"Oh, I'm just wondering. I'm gonna take a swim and crash for a bit. Being with my brother is exhausting. You have the key, so just come on in."

"I'm sorry, but we're still busy. I really need to go."

"I'll see you later." Long pause. "Carol, you're my dream. See you when you get here." They set the telephones down. Her spectacular eyes twinkled.

He put six beers on ice in a small cooler, grabbed a towel, and headed for the pool. He did not feel right. He went back inside and grabbed a bong, went outside, took three one-hitters, then quickly dove in the pool, hoping he could drown the disdain he harbored for himself right now. Sherry was not his sister, but incestuous relations would cease to leave his mind in a conscious mental state just then. Greg should not get ripped this early, but he hoped the pot could help him forget. Wrong.

This sucks. What will I do if she ever says anything? I shouldn't have let her inside. What the hell is wrong with me? I didn't owe her anything. I certainly could've told her no. I'm stronger than her. I could have forced her to leave. What could make her want me anyway? She has Gery. This is a sick, sick thing I did. I feel like I cheated on Carol. Shit, I feel like I cheated on Gery too. I need to take

55

a Valium. Another beer and a couple more bong hits, then crash for a bit. Carol has the key. She can wake me up. God, I'm sorry. Carol is the one for me. Why did I do this? What the hell is wrong with me?

Carol quietly walked into the bedroom. It smelled obvious to her that he had been drinking, and she reminded herself again it was none of her business. She put her arm around him gently as he gradually came to. He smiled and then closed his eyes again. She moved closer to him and planted a kiss on his nose.

"I guess that's my alarm telling me to wake up."

"No, not at all. I just couldn't resist." Her smile was absolutely beautiful. *Those eyes.*

"You look nice. Where do you wanna eat tonight?" Greg asked.

She wore tight bleached jeans, a purple blouse, and white tennis shoes.

"I don't care. Anywhere is fine, but it's gonna be impossible to top your dinner last night."

"Well, do you want steak, seafood, Chinese, Mexican, Italian, Ger . . . ?"

"Anything but Italian. I've seen enough marinara sauce today to last me a lifetime." She giggled.

"I forgot. Do you like German food?" He struggled to hold his eyes open.

"I don't think I've ever had it before."

"You're kidding?"

"No." She smiled.

"There's a great place over on Wornall called Berliner Bear. You'll think you're in Munich. The food is so good."

"Sounds fun. Let's go."

"That means I need to get out of bed and get ready."

He brushed his teeth and put on a pair of bleached jeans, a purple short-sleeved pullover shirt, and white tennis shoes. She looked down at her own outfit as they laughed.

"People are gonna start thinking you're my brother if we keep dressing alike."

"Oh,"—he slapped his face—"I must have put this on as a complete accident. No, they won't think that—I'm much taller than you."

As they went to the garage to take his Porsche, she was amazed again at how quickly he appeared to sober up. The Porsche was bright red and, as with all of his possessions, spotless.

At dinner, they ordered two Becks Dark. She was honest with him about her lack of knowledge of German cuisine and asked him to order for her.

During the meal, he was thrilled to learn she was a baseball fan. She was almost as astute at baseball trivia as him. They talked about the Royals, the old Kansas City A's, and the sports complex that was about to open.

She asked how the meeting with his brother and her cousins went. He informed her it was just boring business stuff. He was pissed off at his brother, so he chose to leave early before Vince and Charles arrived. He temporarily forgot his vision of her father and his incestuous encounter with his sister-in-law.

What the hell is wrong with me?

During the conversation about this and that, he learned her father was out of town on business. She thought he was in Chicago.

Business. Right.

They went back to his home, and she spent the night. She woke at six thirty in the morning so she could divide her time equally between the deli and the floral shop to give her partner the day off. Greg spent the day swimming, getting stoned, and drinking.

Vince and Greg met alone briefly to discuss the casinos that weekend. Greg and Carol spent the majority of the weekend alone together, eating, drinking, smoking, joking, laughing, skinny-dipping, touching, kissing, and loving.

On Sunday evening, Greg stopped drinking at seven o'clock because of the bank meetings the next morning. He smoked pot instead.

8

Brian has just come from a friend's bat - mitzvah. His friend is almost one year younger and is now supposedly a man. Brian is not Jewish. He is upset that he is not also considered a man. Only two things could make a soon-to-be-fourteen-year-old boy a real man, and a ceremony is not one of them.

The first thing that makes you a man: women will always be there. Brian has already experienced that twice. As far as Brian is concerned, there is only one other thing that will truly help him become a man. Because of the situation in the park down the street from his house, he can become a real man now.

Brian knows he is already an incredible human specimen. Football, basketball, and other sports do not appeal to him; although, with his incredible size at such a young age, he could be a star athlete. He likes drums and piano.

A bunch of older teenagers are drinking, smoking, and partying. They are leaving together in groups of four and five. One guy lingers behind, sitting on a park bench. Brian knows him because he lives just a few doors away. The guy is obviously walking home later after he puts on a major buzz. Brian walks down and sits next to the guy. This is his chance to be a man.

"How ya doin', Brian?"

"Pretty good. I just came from a friend's bat - mitzvah."

"Sounds fun. I've been to a few before. I guess that makes them men." The guy laughed. Brian is nervous but is able to let out a faint laugh. "Have you ever gotten high, Brian?" Brian shakes his head no. "I got high for the first time when I was your age." The guy pulled out a pipe and filled it with pot. He gave Brian a lighter. "Fire it up!"

"Why don't you? I'll try it, but I may cough and spill it if I try to light it," Brian said.

The older kid begins to light the pipe when Brian's massive fist hits him so hard in mouth that it knocks him off the bench. Another fist hits him in the left eye and dazes him. Yet another gloved fist hits him in the right eye.

"What are ya doin' to me?" The kid tries to shout through broken teeth, yet his voice is filled with surprised anguish and terror. He barely screams a whisper.

"Guess!" This time Brian's adult, almost inhuman strength lets out a flurry of punches.

The fatal punch must have been the blow to the kid's nose. Nevertheless, to make sure the kid is dead, Brian strangles him with his gloved hands.

Brian sat down with a friend, and less than three minutes later, the friend was dead. Brian can feel the life drain out of the kid, and Brian feels more alive now than ever before.

Brian has absolutely no interest in anything that would alter his mind, so he jams the dope-filled pipe in his friend's eye socket, squishing his eyeball.

Calmly, Brian walks home and plans on disposing the gloves tomorrow. He looks at his hands and can see no scratches or bruises. He looks in the mirror and smiles.

"That," Brian said to the mirror, "is what makes a boy into a man. I am a man now."

Seventeen-year-old Frank Blascati was buried three days later. A closed casket was needed because of his facial trauma.

Thirteen-year-old Brian Nivaro was a pallbearer. Rivers of tears streamed down his face.

9

On Monday morning, Greg arose from bed well rested, clearheaded, and sober. After his brief workout and shower, he ate breakfast while looking over the documents supplied by his brother on Thursday. He examined the script he had been required to memorize to discover that only three of the nine loans needed collateral.

Because his home was owned by the corporation for tax purposes and did not have a mortgage attached to it, it was one of the properties that would be used as collateral. He knew his brother did have a mortgage on his home, so he presumed Gerald would place a second mortgage on his residence.

Greg deduced from reading the list that one signature and two secured loans were not necessary. He did not live a life of extravagance compared to Gerald, so, in turn, a considerable amount of his money was safely in the bank. He telephoned his brother.

"Crow Brothers Real Estate Company."

"Michelle, I need to talk to Gery."

Less than fifteen seconds. "Gregory, when are you going to the banks? This is urgent."

"Good morning to you too, ass wipe. There are three that I don't need to go to. I have that much in cash."

"Yeah, right," Gerald said sarcastically. "Which three can you possibly be talking about?"

"Traders, Southeastern, and Southgate," Greg replied.

"Wait a second. That's over, let me see,— Gerald used an adding machine—"1.4 million. How can you have that much cash?"

"Because I don't spend like you, dick hole. I put it in the bank."

"Are you serious? I figured that's just your booze budget alone."

"Fuck you. Well, I'm gonna go and probably wrap this up today."

"Gregory, be serious for just a second. If you really have that much in cash, then wipe out two others too. On second thought, forget it. How much do you have total?"

"That's none of your business, but I will say enough to get by for a while if you manage to lose this."

"I won't lose it, Gregory. You don't need to tell me how much you have, but we might need it later. Since it's yours, we would work something out. As soon as you hit the first three, call me. If there's any trouble at the first three, which there shouldn't be, call me. Are you coming in today?"

"Yes, Gery. I talked to Vince this weekend. He explained everything in English. We're cool."

"Well then, how are you feeling?"

"It was nothing, Gery. Don't worry. I'll see you later."

This time Greg hung up on Gerald. After Gerald mentioned the illness Thursday, Greg remembered Sherry.

What the hell is wrong with me?

Greg drove out by ten o'clock and had two secured loan applications completed before noon. After making two swift unsecured applications and eating lunch at a fast-food restaurant, Greg went in the office at two o'clock.

Everybody was either too absorbed in their work to speak or had honestly forgotten the party scene last week. Greg did not care. He was treated with genuine respect at Crow Brothers.

Jacob Rosenstingel, the comptroller for Crow Brothers, immediately confronted him.

"Greg, I take it you talked to your brother about the loans?" Jacob asked.

"Yeah, Jacob, I did. I'm not crazy about it, but I guess I have no choice. I applied for four loans today."

"It'll work. Believe me," Jacob said with a smile.

"I've got some things to do," Greg said, walking down the hall.

Fuckin' Jew bastard.

He saw there were no messages for him on his secretary Tracy's desk. Greg laughed under his breath. Tracy, his private secretary, sat at her desk, filing her nails, and talked on the telephone. She did not hide the fact that it was a personal call. Next to Greg, Tracy occupied the most blow-off job in the world.

Tracy was a beautiful girl in her early thirties. She had bleached blond hair and braces. She never wore a dress because her figure looked better in tight pants.

Greg went into his immaculate office. He opened his daily planner to make it appear as if he actually had work. He began thinking of Carol and started to pick up the telephone when a knock at his door stopped him. Tracy entered and then closed the door behind her.

"Hi, Greg. Look, I'm sorry about the other night. I already had something planned."

"Good Lord, Tracy. I thought somebody died by the look on your face. Don't worry about that at all." Greg smiled.

"Well, I just heard it was so much fun, especially you." Tracy laughed. "Everyone told me I missed a great time."

"Tracy, I have something to tend to. Would you excuse me?"

"Greg, we need to talk."

"What is it?" Greg realized by the look in her eyes that this was serious.

"Look, I overheard something with Gery on Wednesday. I haven't talked to anyone. I wanted to talk with you. I went by your house, but somebody was there. I know it's none of my business, but you've always been so cool to me, I didn't wanna see you get hurt." Greg listened intently. "Are you in some sort of trouble?" Tracy inquired.

"Not that I know of. What did you hear?"

"OK. I just heard this by accident. I was leaving the girls' room and I was talking to Michelle. The phone in her office rang, so she asked me if I would answer it while she went. I picked it up and must have picked up the wrong line because I heard a phone ringing, like when you're making a call. I should have just hung up, but I stayed on the line and heard Gery yelling about you to someone. That he'd had it with you. This was the last straw. He wanted to buy you out and get you out of here."

"Who was he talking to?"

"Well, at first, I thought maybe it was your dad. But I know his voice. I mean, I worked for your dad for seven years."

"Are you sure it was Wednesday?" Greg asked in a paranoid voice.

"For sure. It was the day after your birthday party."

Good. Gery doesn't know about Sherry and me.

"Make this simple. Tell me what you did hear."

"Gery told someone named Nick that he was through with you."

"Nick Cibella?" Greg asked.

"Yeah, that sounds right. How did you know?"

"He's a friend of Gery's. I know him but not very well. Don't worry. Gery can't buy me out. I own just as much of Crow Brothers as he does. What was his problem with me?"

"I only know he called you a drunken embarrassment. That you didn't understand anything as far as business. That if you wouldn't do this, he would need help in getting you bought out. Blah, blah, blah."

"Did he say what it was that I had to do?"

62

"Absolutely not. I listened to the whole conversation and I still don't know what it was." Tracy held her hands up in a defensive position.

Greg thought it was probably something to do with purchasing the casinos or the fraudulent loans.

"Tracy, do me a big favor and don't mention this to anyone, ever." Greg reached into his pocket and pulled out a money clip with hundred-dollar bills in it. He counted out $1,000 and gave it to Tracy. "Do you understand?" While he silently counted out the cash, she looked at the quantity he held and guessed at minimum another $4,000.

"Greg, I wouldn't tell anyway. You don't need to do that," Tracy said, smiling through her braces.

"I want to. Besides, we don't pay you enough anyway. Just promise me you'll do something fun with it."

"Thank you, I will." As Tracy was leaving, she turned back. "You know, I won't say anything to her, but Michelle can't stand Gery. If you ever get the chance, you could talk to her. Believe me, you could trust her."

"I really don't think that will be necessary, but thanks for the idea."

"Who is Nick Cibella, and what would he have to do with Crow Brothers?" Tracy asked.

"He's just a real rich guy. One of our commercial agents, Vick Spelo, is his cousin. I really don't know where his money comes from, but, needless to say, he's not the kind of person I wanna associate with. If Gery could buy me out, and I assure you he can't, Nick would probably front him the money. Tracy, we've talked enough, there are some things I need to do." Tracy exited the room, and Greg instantly telephoned Vince.

"Giovelli Construction."

"Vince Giovelli please. Tell him it's Greg Crow." Greg knew the mention of his name warranted immediate attention from everyone.

Vince thought a call from Greg was personal. Rarely did Greg call for business purposes.

"Hey, Greg, what's goin' on?"

"Vince, I just found out Gery has been talking to Nick Cibella about buying . . ."

"Greg, I really can't talk right now," Vince said urgently. "When can you meet me at your house?"

"Well, let's make it in about an hour. Do me a favor and . . ."

"I'll see you then. We have a real mess with an architect on a hotel right now, and I have to go. I'll see you in an hour." Vince obviously lied. He did not want communication on the telephones. He had been warned the lines might be bugged.

Greg did not want to violate the confidence bestowed upon him from

Tracy. He could not mention the Nick Cibella information to his brother. Gerald incessantly kept his office door closed and occasionally locked. This time it was not locked, so Greg walked in without knocking. Gerald had his nose in a filing cabinet and was mildly shocked when someone exhibited enough nerve to enter his domain unannounced.

"That's discourteous behavior, Gregory. You should learn to knock or have Michelle tell me you are waiting."

"You're such a weasel, Gery. Sit down. I need to talk with you about something."

"Just a moment, I'm in the middle of something."

"Sit down right now, fuck face! I have a meeting with Vince in a bit. This will only take two minutes out of your precious day," Greg demanded.

"What do you need?" Gerald asked, refusing to make eye contact.

"I made four of the six applications today. I actually think I'll have the money by Wednesday or Thursday at the latest."

"Sounds fantastic. I presume, following your rendezvous with Vincey this weekend, you're joining us in Las Vegas?"

"Yeah, I guess I have no choice. Can Michelle handle the arrangements for the plane and hotel?"

"About that. Will you be traveling with Sherry and me? And who will accompany you so Michelle can give the name to the travel agent?" Gerald asked, smiling.

"Well, I haven't asked Carol yet. But tell Michelle to hold off until I find out. If Carol isn't going, I'll more than likely go alone."

"You've got to be kidding. Is this getting that serious?"

"I honestly have no idea. But it's getting serious, I think. I have nothing else to go on, but it feels like it is. We haven't even been together for a full week yet. She's just perfect for me. I really don't know."

"Well, good for you. But be careful. If you know who I'm referring to . . ."

"I will. Gery, be serious with me. If we're buying the casinos, what's the rest of the money for? And don't bullshit me." Greg pointed his finger, demanding the truth.

"Gregory, there are problems we could go into, but it might take an hour or two. The problems in Minnesota are working themselves out. I have a few attorneys there at this moment representing us. I might need to fly up there Thursday to complete the papers. If we can do everything, I'm going to list them for sale that day. There are some serious problems, including some earnest money that was accidentally commingled with another account in the property management department."

"You're losing me again, dick weed. Did that happen in Minnesota or what?"

"That happened here. I didn't understand it before I sat down with Jacob and had him explain them to me. They are too convoluted for you to comprehend in a few minutes, so, unless you can sit down with me tomorrow evening for a few hours,"—Gerald shrugged—"it's my failing totally. I proved to be too creative financially and stopped watching the register. I'm confident that after you talked with Vincey, you understand the cash from Las Vegas will be used to remedy these predicaments. Until the cash begins arriving, we have no choice other than this. I went to five Missouri banks today. We can pull this off. It just takes timing. Jacob explained to me how it would work after we receive the money. He said he would take care of the rest. So in the unlikely event something happened, he would know more than me. Consequently, he would be guiltier than me. He wouldn't be doing this if he wasn't 110 percent sure that he could make it work."

"Gery, that's enough. I should've never asked. I have no idea what the fuck you just said. You speak a different language. If Jacob is sure of this, then that's good enough for me. I told you the other day, check kiting is a serious crime, and the amount we're kiting is beyond anything I could ever imagine. If something fucks up, then I have a perfect explanation: I only did what my dickless older brother told me to do. I didn't know anything." Greg looked at his watch, then got up from the chair, wanting desperately to say something about Nick Cibella.

"What are you meeting Vincey for?" Gerald asked.

"It's Vince, boner breath. Nothing important." Then Greg thought he should mess with Gerald's mind. "We might buy an apartment complex down south."

Suddenly, the greedy ears of Gerald Crow were interested in anything dealing with money. He finally made continual eye contact.

"Wait, Gregory, don't walk out right now. What apartments are you interested in?" Gerald asked.

"You just have to know everything, you greedy dog-pecker gnat. I don't know yet," Greg said, smiling.

"Well, when you find out, can you let me know?" Gerald attempted a smile.

"Why, hmm? So you can do some more creative financing and be assured you get butt-fucked in jail? No, seriously. If it looks like something of interest to me, I might, I repeat, *might* let you know." Before Gerald could get one more word out, Greg walked out and slammed the door.

As Greg pulled onto his driveway approximately ten minutes early, he noticed that Vince was already there. He was not surprised and figured Vince had called it a day and would head home afterward. Then, suddenly, Charles pulled up, and Greg knew something was wrong.

"Charles, is this more serious than I thought? I was just gonna meet with Vince," Greg said, shocked.

"Greg, look, I'm sorry. But we really have to know about Nick Cibella and what he wants," Charles said, visibly uncomfortable.

"I don't know. That's why I called Vince." Greg shrugged his shoulders.

"Greg, I'm sorry. What did you need with Nick?" Vince asked, trying to keep everything calm.

"Nothing, guys. What the fuck is going on?" Greg put his hands up.

"Just tell us what you know," Vince said calmly.

"Just what I said . . . nothing. Apparently, Gery talked to Nick Cibella last week when I was out. Remember, I spent the night with Carol after my birthday. I wasn't there that day. My secretary told me today that she was on the phone and overheard Gery talking to someone named Nick about trying to buy me out. I figured it must be Nick Cibella. Nick's cousin Vick Spelo is a commercial agent with us. Jesus, Charles, do you need a beer?" Charles attempted to calm down but was still obviously nervous.

"Actually, yes. Sorry, Greg," Charles said.

"So when did this conversation between Gery and Nick take place?" Vince asked, substantially calmer and not sweating like Charles.

"Tracy, my secretary, said it was Wednesday. I know Vick Spelo wants to start his own development company. It might have something to do with that. Look, I'm getting a bad vibe here, so I'm sorry I asked. Let me say this, don't tell me anything more. I don't wanna know. As it says in the Bible, uh, dumb motherfuckers shall inherit the earth. So don't tell me anything," Greg said.

Vince laughed. Charles chugged his beer.

"Greg, just let me ask one question. What do you know about Nick Cibella?" Vince asked.

"All I know is what I told Tracy. I don't know him. I've met him and would prefer not to have anything to do with him. That's it, I swear."

The Giovelli brothers were content with that answer and changed the subject.

"So, after Sally and I were here, I noticed Carol's car was here again. What's going on with that?" Vince asked with a smile.

"Vince, I'm not gonna kiss and tell on this one, except to say I don't have a clue yet. I can say I don't wanna do anything to screw this up. She's perfect," Greg said, knowing full well it would get back to Carol.

"She's a pretty girl. I wish she weren't related." Charles verbalized the obvious.

"Yeah, I'm sure that's your only problem, Charley." Vince rolled his eyes and patted Charles on his receding hairline.

"It's not just the way she looks, you perverts. I swear, I've never met anyone that's so . . ." Greg could not find the right words to describe his feelings for Carol. "I don't know, perfect, in every way."

"You know, Vince and Sally made a bet that"—Vince tried to cover Charles's mouth—"you and her would not last——"

"Shut up, Charley," Vince shouted, smiling.

"A month was it? Or Vince will have to buy her a new car." Charles laughed.

Greg shook his head offensively. "Are you serious, Vince? Please, *please* don't let that get back to Carol," he begged.

"I just said it in jest. I didn't know Charley was going to tell the world. Why don't you take an ad out in the paper, loudmouth?"

"Both of you shut up. Please, I'm begging you, don't let that get back to Carol," Greg pleaded.

The three talked for more than an hour.

After Charles left, Greg and Vince snorted nearly three and a half grams of cocaine between them, with Vince snorting the majority. Greg knew when Vince did cocaine, his tongue would get loose. Greg asked what Vince knew about Nick Cibella.

"He's been around here for a long time. He has this opinion of my father that's not very favorable. Dad has always been too focused on legitimate business. Nick's from that old school and thinks my dad sold out." Vince shrugged his shoulders.

"Why would he be resentful that Joseph has been successful?" Greg asked, bewildered.

"Greg, someday I can tell you more. You know this shit always makes me talk too much. Why do you think Gery is talking to Nick?"

"Gery might be looking for financial help in buying me out of Crow. Or it might have something to do with Vick. I don't know."

"Gery can't buy you out, can he?" Vince asked, alarmed.

"No way," Greg said, shaking his head accordingly.

"Look, the way Nick is, if he ever got his bony fingers wrapped around even a fraction of Crow Brothers, he could make life a living hell for everyone close to it," Vince said as he and Greg divided the last line of cocaine. "I'll get a message to Gery to stay the hell away from him. If he can persuade Gery to sell part of his interest, then he'll wind up owning the whole company and running it in the ground. And he'll have you out of there quick. Or he'll have his violent cousin Vick Spelo running it. Nick Cibella is one mean son of a bitch. He can't stand the fact that Dad is the boss around here. Maybe we could make it easy for Vick to start his own company. Get Nick and Vick out of the picture fast. I'm talking way, way too much. Look at me. I'm shaking like a leaf. I need to go." As he walked out the door, Vince turned to Greg. "If Carol goes out to Vegas with you, she'll need to go on the plane under another name. I'm losing it, Greg. I need to calm down before I see Sally. She hates it when I do coke without her."

"You're talking a mile a minute. Let me get you something to help calm you down. You're gonna need to stay here for a minute to let this take effect," Greg said with a smile.

Vince required a few beers and a Valium before he could leave. He was grinding his teeth, moving his jaw back and forth, and moving all of his fingers as if he were a pianist. Every time he got jonesed with Greg on cocaine, he would wake up the next day with sore thumbs from moving them back and forth so fast. Greg could do cocaine all day and never show any of those signs.

When Vince left, Greg telephoned Carol at her deli. She was gone. He tried the florist. No answer. He tried her at home. The roommate said she had not seen her. Greg put on a swimsuit and took a dip.

He came inside after an hour, and, to his surprise, Carol was in the kitchen preparing dinner.

"Oh, it's you," he said, surprised.

"Were you expecting someone else?" she asked solemnly.

"No. I just mean I didn't hear or see you come in."

"Would you like me to leave?"

"Come on. What are you making?" he asked as he kissed the back of her neck.

"It's already made. I'm just warming some things from the deli. I guarantee you'll like it."

"Before I forget, I need to ask you. Will you go to Las Vegas with me next week? Gery, Vince, and Charles are going and bringing their wives. I need to go, but I don't wanna go without you. We have business there."

"All week? I don't know. I need to talk with my partner and see."

"OK. I just need to know soon so we can make reservations."

"I'll talk to her in the morning and call you tomorrow before our lunch hour hits." Long silence, and the look on her face said it all.

"What's wrong, Carol?"

"I don't know if it's even something I should be concerned about. I

68

talked to Sandy Giovelli today, the younger one. She told me Vince was gonna buy Sally a new car if we stay together for a month."

"That had absolutely nothing to do with me. I swear, Vince and Charles were over earlier, and Charles told me about it. It started as a joke between Vince and Sally and got blown out of proportion. Carol, please don't make a big deal out of this."

"Why would Vince say that?" she asked solemnly.

"Vince and I've known each other forever. He just said it as a joke. I've probably gotten a reputation for, ya know. Carol, it's nothing." *I'm gonna say it now.* "Carol, I don't know how to say this. I might be thinking it too soon, but here it is." He moved close to her and took her face in his hands. "I think I'm in love with you."

"I love you too. I've dreamed of hearing that from you forever."

"We haven't even been together for a full week." He smiled.

"Since I met you when I was a little girl."

Their clothes were torn off in seconds, and they did it on the kitchen floor. After they ate and talked for a few hours, they did it in the swimming pool. After the pool, they were trying to do it in the living room when a story on the ten o'clock evening news grabbed her attention . . . hard.

"What the hell? I know him. He worked with Daddy."

The reporter said,

"A man from Kansas City has been gunned down in his northeast-side home today. At approximately 4:00 p.m., his wife discovered him. There are no suspects. There are no signs of forced entry. Police and federal agents believed Salvatore Digovanni, or Sam, as he was known, to be a member of the Kansas City underworld. Relatives have been contacted. Police are not releasing any further information until a thorough investigation is complete."

She knew Sam Digovanni was out of town with her father last weekend. She quickly got sick to her stomach. She, of course, would never know for sure, but she knew: Daddy killed again.

"Are you OK, Carol?" Greg asked.

She immediately showed no concern. "Oh yeah. I only knew him in passing anyway. I've only met him maybe three or four times. I just recognized the name." She hated the fact that she needed to lie to him. She needed to change the subject. "So I think I'll be able to go next week."

"You already told me that."

At that response, she decided to go down on him. It was of no use. He'd obviously had enough for the night.

He pulled her face up to his and kissed her. "Carol, I think I'm done tonight. I'm sorry." He smiled.

"I love you. Let's go to bed."

"Carol, I don't think I can sleep right now, even though I need to get up early tomorrow."

"Then just hold me. Why can't you sleep?" she asked.

"Well, I'll tell you, but this can't get back to Sally. Vince and I did almost an eight ball earlier. I'm wired." He laughed.

"What's an eight ball?" she asked innocently.

He forgot for a second that not everyone spoke drug lingo. "We did coke together, and a bunch of it." She looked up at him with a smile and asked him if he had any more. "Yeah, but you don't wanna do it this late. You'll be awake all night."

"I'll pay you for it," she begged.

"Carol, I don't care about that. I just don't wanna see you going into work on little or no sleep."

"I can handle it. I've done it before and handled it fine."

"All right, but I'm not doing any more tonight."

They went into the kitchen, where he kept a container of rice next to the containers of salt, sugar, and flour on the countertop.

He poured out a small amount of rice, reached in, and pulled out a plastic bag nearly one-quarter full of cocaine. In addition to the loose cocaine in the baggie, there were thirty to forty individually wrapped magazine paper packets containing three and a half grams each. He went to a cabinet where he stored very organized a custom-made bevel-edged mirror and a gold razor. He went to his bedroom, and, just for fun, he tightly rolled a $1,000 bill around a fountain pen. When he returned, he went directly to the kitchen table where he reached a gold spoon in the bag four times and used the razor to cut up four huge lines. She did two of the gigantic lines in six snorts. She dipped her finger in a glass of plain tap water and snorted it to clear her nostrils. The cocaine was the same quality of everything associated with him, and the numbing effect was beyond anything she'd ever experienced.

"Greg, are you sure you can't do any?" she asked while picking up the remnants of powder with her index finger and running her finger around her full lips. He thought this was the sexiest sight ever.

"What the hell, it's only ten thirty." He snorted one line and handed the bill to her. Against his better judgment, he opened two beers.

They talked for a while and did two smaller lines each. They went outside to smoke. Of course, he brought two beers for himself and one for her. Obviously she was able to keep up with him on beer tonight, so he loaded down a cooler and brought it outside. She went inside to use the

70

bathroom and asked if she could do another line. Twenty minutes later, two lines for her, one for him.

That's it, no more tonight. I need to get up early. No more beer either. I've done a shitload of this today. I'll have one more beer and a couple of downers. I need sleep tonight. I'll let her do as much as she wants. She knows when to stop. One hard day at work will do her good.

"Carol, let's go back outside. If you want any more tonight, you're more than welcome. I'm gonna die if I don't have a cigarette."

"Let me do one more little line?" she asked, almost begging.

"It's all yours." He laughed and smiled.

He looked at the clock to see it was already two thirty. Where had the time gone? He had taken the downers at least an hour ago. One more would not hurt.

She chain-smoked, talked, and switched subjects every minute or so, then would go back to a subject she abandoned nearly ten minutes earlier. She did one more little line every time she went to the bathroom. Then she moved her fingers back and forth as Vince always did.

It must be an Italian thing.

"Carol, it's almost four now. I've gotta try and get some sleep."

"I'm sorry, Greg, there's no way I can sleep." She looked around constantly.

"I told you this would happen. What time do you need to be at work?" he asked, laughing.

"What time is it now? It doesn't matter. I open the florist today at nine. You haven't been to the deli, but it's not my day to work there. No later than nine thirty. Maybe I do work at the deli. We go back and forth every other day. The food is excellent. No, I don't work there today. I need another beer. Then we switch every other weekend. Do you want one? We're closed on Sundays at both the florist and deli. What time is it? I'm gonna get another beer."

"Carol, just don't do any more. Don't try to use it as a substitute for sleep. In a few hours, you're gonna come down hard and wanna sleep. However tired you are, you have to suck it up. Don't do any more."

"Suck it up, huh? I can do that." She got down on her knees again. With regretful yet gentle force, he pulled her up and kissed her.

"Carol, I really need to try and sleep for a few hours. I imagine you're gonna be awake for a few hours. So I'll leave it to you to use this energy however you want. I'm speaking from experience. Don't try and use coke to stay awake." He hugged her as she reached under his robe. He looked at her and knew it. "Carol, I know it for sure now. You're the only girl I've ever said it to. I love you."

"I have some pot in my purse. Maybe that'll mellow me out. Do you have any Valium or anything? I can't remember if I put in the orders today or not. I think I'll have another beer. I love you too. She might not get the right produce tomorrow or today if I didn't. I'm gonna get another beer. Do you want one?" She looked in every direction as she spoke.

He wanted to burst out laughing. "Carol, this is against my better judgment, but I'm gonna give you a relaxant. You can have as much beer as you want. But please don't do any more coke this morning. You're talking a mile a minute just like Vince always does. Tell you what. I'll sleep in the other bedroom tonight for a few hours. You can use your energy to clean up the kitchen if you want, but please no more."

He followed her into the kitchen as she opened another beer. He gave her a Valium. Then, without using, she cleaned up the table of all the paraphernalia. He said good night one last time. He set the alarm in the guest room for nine o'clock.

She chugged one beer after another by the pool as she smoked almost another full pack of cigarettes and two pipes filled with marijuana. She finally tried to sleep in the master bedroom at seven thirty.

When his alarm sounded at nine, he woke a bit groggy. He shut off the alarm and decided he could sleep for two more hours. Suddenly he realized he was in the guest bedroom. He then bobbed and stumbled his way to the master bedroom. He walked in and did not see her. The bed did not look to have been slept in, so he assumed she'd already gone to work. He walked back into the guest room and was about to go to sleep again when he noticed her car out front. He alertly came out of the sleeplike state he was in and searched the house. He looked in the master bath to find her leaning over the toilet with blood coming from her nose. She wiped her nose and mouth with a tissue.

"You were right. I did too much and didn't realize how much I was drinking. I'm just getting rid of the hangover." She could not look at him.

"Did you sleep at all?" He made a failing attempt to hide his smile.

"Very little."

"It's after nine."

"I need to get it together and go."

"Let me make you something." He returned with a glass of tomato juice and beer spiced with Tabasco. "Chug this and you'll be fine. When you get to work, start eating everything you can find. You have the key, so just come in when you can. I need to sleep a little more."

She cleaned up and would struggle her way through work. He went back to sleep for a couple of needed hours.

Waking struck him like a lightning bolt when he realized it was almost one o'clock in the afternoon. He knew he needed to go to the last two banks by two o'clock and panicked. He did a world-record cleanup and barely made the second bank by two. He came back home to sleep.

Carol called and said she needed to stay at home and sleep. She had spoken to her father and told him she was going to Las Vegas with Vince and Charles. Gerald and Gregory Crow were also going.

William Cassivano said he already knew about her and Greg. He gave his blessing and instructed her what name to use for the airline ticket. He would have the appropriate identification for her before she left.

Tonight was the first night Greg and Carol would not spend together in a week. They both needed the rest.

As he predicted, the banks telephoned and informed him he was authorized for approximately $7.6 million in loans. He signed the remaining documents, picked up the checks, and took them to his brother. He informed Gerald of his unwillingness to work the remainder of the week because of this. He told Gerald he would have the various banks cut cashier's checks totaling $1.4 million from his savings. He gave Michelle the name of the girl he would bring to Las Vegas next week. Her name was Carol Jones.

Carol received the identification from her less-than-well-groomed father. People who knew him well would never comment on his hygiene. Carol was his daughter. She could say anything to him. She told him, "Take a shower, shave, and, for god's sake, put on something other than filthy sweat pants." Willie obeyed.

10

Carol Jones, Gregory, Gerald, and Sherry Crow flew out to Las Vegas. Vincenzo, Charles, Sally, and Sandra Giovelli had started driving out two days earlier.

Everything in Las Vegas went according to plan. The twenty-seven people, Joseph Giovelli, along with La Cosa Nostra bosses in Chicago, Cleveland, Milwaukee, and St. Louis, had placed in the approval office of the Nevada Gaming Commission had Crow Brothers Real Estate Company sanctioned for the purchase of the Starlight, Freebird, and Cactus Inn hotels and casinos within five business days of the offer to purchase contract signatures. It was vehemently stated by the commission that any purchase also needed to include major renovations of the casinos and the attached hotels for them to be up to building codes. The current owners were retiring cash short, and Crow Brothers inherited the impending health department violations and structural problems. Following several bids, Uncle Joe's Repair was the local contractor decided upon.

While everyone else was seeing shows, gambling, and having a good old time, Greg and Carol spent the majority of the time alone in the room. They could not get enough of one another. They admitted it verbally now. This was it.

The only reason they did not get married in one of the all-night chapels in Las Vegas was the fact that Carol Cassivano had been using a counterfeit name.

Greg volunteered to pay Carol's portion of the rent in her apartment if she would move in with him when they arrived back in Kansas City.

"Greg, it's a duplex. Patty and I own both halves. We only live together because the rent from the top unit pays for ours. She has no monthly payment."

"Well then, she's not losing anything. Tell her I'll personally pay her utilities or, I don't know, something, until she has a roommate."

"Greg, she'll take advantage of your generosity, so let me talk to her first before we do anything rash." She smiled.

"OK, that's settled. Do I need to worry about any particular girl's father?"

She understood and did not attempt to hide that she had also considered her father's reputation and temper.

"Believe me, Greg, you have nothing to worry about. Nobody would ever touch you if I tell him to lay off of you. In his eyes, I'm the queen, and he does whatever I say."

He did not want to jeopardize this, but he needed to ask.

"Does that mean if you wanted me hurt, you could ask him?"

"Greg, someday I'll tell you what you're hinting at. You and I are gonna have arguments living together—that's only normal. Daddy is just coming up to this century, so he's gonna object to me living with a man that's not my husband. But I'll tell him to back off and leave us alone. I'll tell him the truth—that we almost got married here," she said.

Without a doubt, he knew marrying her in Las Vegas could have easily been the biggest drunken blunder of his life. Nevertheless, both knew marriage was imminent. Although they had only been together for a brief time, they were convinced the chemistry was magic.

"Before you move in, we need to establish some ground rules. You go first," he said.

"I really don't have any. I mean, it's your house and all. Just promise me you won't bring girls home without letting me know first."

He looked at her and realized she was serious.

"I might not be real smart, but I'm not stupid." He took a sip of beer as they sat naked in the bed. "Girls will probably call sometimes or even come by. You can't get mad at me about that. That'll slow down after a while. If you happen to answer the phone or door when one calls and I'm not there, just be polite. As you can probably see, I like things clean, so please be sensitive to that. I can't even go to sleep if I know there's one fork in the sink. And whatever you do, don't be like Gery and never, ever lecture me once about drinking or partying. It's part of me. Always has been and probably always will be. Other than that, I really can't foresee any problems." He kissed her stomach.

"I can do that. I actually think we'll have fun together. And I know you think I'm joking about letting me know about the girls, but I'm serious as a heart attack. Just let me know first and I get to be there to watch." She calmly took a sip of beer while he spit his out, laughing.

"Carol, come on, you'd go nuts." He chuckled.

"Greg, I'm totally serious. I don't care about your past sexual experiences and I don't care how many there've been. Don't even wanna know. Of course, I've heard things. For me, you're more than enough. I love you and would do anything for you."

"Carol, we need to stop talking about this. This is freakin' me out. You're the one I want, and that's it. If, for some reason, you think I'd wanna be with other women, then you don't believe me when I take your hand, look in those enthralling eyes, and say I love you. You're the only girl I want."

"I do understand. I just wanna make you happy and I'll do whatever it takes to prove it. Besides, it would turn me on. I'd even participate." She smiled that seductive yet nasty smile.

"Carol, let's drop this subject and not even bring it up again unless the situation ever arises."

They held one another tight. When the time was physically permissible, they made love again.

11

Greg and Carol returned to Kansas City after a fourteen-day business trip turned personal vacation in Las Vegas. Carol informed her roommate/partner, Patty, of her intention to move in with Greg. Everything was cool.

Carol met her father one afternoon in his mechanics garage. When she told her father her decision, the shit almost hit the fan. She was an adult now and was going to move in with Greg. Period.

"Daddy, I'm telling you now, if so much as a finger is laid on Greg by anyone, I'll never speak to you again. I'm in love with him and will probably eventually marry him. He hasn't said anything, but he's afraid of you. I can tell. I need your word right now that he has nothing to worry about."

"Carolyn, you have it. Joseph told me a couple of weeks ago that everything he owns he owes to Greg's father. Greg does have a reputation as a drunk, though, and if he ever loses control and hits you, I'll personally . . ."

"He'd never do that and he's not a drunk, so don't ever say that about him again. Ever! Not to me, not to anyone. He's exactly the opposite of you. Vince told me he has never seen Greg lay a finger on anyone, and they've known each other their whole lives. He's so incredibly gentle, kind, and considerate—everything you've never been."

"Carolyn, I don't understand why you think of me that way. I've never laid a hand on you or your brothers, except for spanking you when you were kids. And, believe me, all three of you deserved it every single time."

"Daddy, I know things that I probably shouldn't know, and some of them scare me. I'm never gonna say what I suspect to anyone, including you. But, so help me God, if Greg is ever hurt, you might as well kill me because I'll never speak to you again."

"I just don't wanna see you get hurt. Neither would your mother. She and I have talked about you and Greg and his reputation every night for the past couple of weeks. We only want what's best for you."

"Daddy, this is what's best for me. I never could've imagined I could feel this way about anyone. And he feels the same way. Even Greg's sister-in-law said she never has seen Greg so goo-goo over a woman before. And I'm sure there've been a lot of them."

"Carolyn, why do you think that is, hmm?" Willie answered himself. "Because he only thinks of himself is why. I know his type. I know his father and I've met Greg and his faggot brother." Willie sighed. "I don't know why you don't try to find a nice, honorable Italian boy. You don't need to land a rich spoiled brat to please me."

"I knew that was gonna come out." Carol rolled her eyes. "Why in the world are you so hung up on me finding an Italian?"

"Because I don't think outsiders can be trusted."

"Daddy, if only you could stand where I am and hear how ridiculous that sounds. He's none of what you just described. And Gery is married to a gorgeous woman. They have two adorable little boys together. I think calling him a faggot is way out of line. Even for a prejudiced racist like you. And what does Greg need to be trusted with anyway?"

"Carolyn, don't call me names. I'm still your father and you will respect me, little girl."

"I'm not a little girl anymore. In case you haven't noticed, I'm an adult now. I've only pointed that out to you a couple of million times. What, did you think I was still a virgin?" Carol asked sarcastically.

Willie quickly turned red as if he were about to explode. For the first time in her life, her father smacked her across the face hard enough to knock her to the ground. She immediately brushed herself off, stood up, and smiled at her father.

"That was brilliant, you pig. Maybe I should tell Greg that you hit me. This conversation is over. Greg would never ever do that to me or anyone else. You need some work on making your points. I'm enough of an adult to let this blow over, but I don't wanna speak to you for a long time. I'm moving in with Greg, that's it. If you call and I answer, expect to hear only a click. If Greg answers, he's so polite, he'd take a message. Also, Greg is the cleanest person I've ever met. He showers every day—sometimes two or three times a day, and your body odor would not be welcome there."

Willie's blood boiled at that.

"I'm sorry. I just don't wanna lose you."

For pure shock value, Carol reached into her purse, pulled out a loaded small automatic pistol, and held it right against her father's head. She clicked off the safety. The look on his face was priceless as he now had the unpleasant experience of being on the opposite end of a gun.

"I would never hurt you, Carolyn."

"You have a funny fucking way of showing it. Don't call me for a long while, do you understand?" She walked outside to her car, pointing the gun at her father the entire time. She pulled out of the gravel parking lot and punched the accelerator in such a way that rocks shot toward the rundown garage. Willie sat, attempting desperately to slow his heart rate.

William Cassivano, underboss of one of the nation's most powerful organizations, sat mentally beaten and broken by his own daughter. Worst of all, he'd hit his little princess in the face, hard. He sat alone in his garage for hours, crying.

12

Greg and Carol moved items from her place to his house. Considering the house was amply furnished, there was no need to move anything other than her personal property. A moving truck would not be necessary.

Greg noticed most of her later records were identical to his: Amboy Dukes, Beatles, Led Zeppelin, Black Sabbath, Jimi Hendrix, and Rolling Stones. All of these records were the same as his. Carol made the decision to leave those duplicate albums with her roommate, Patty, for now. Because he was a little older, he owned various albums from an earlier era: Elvis, Chuck Berry, Fats Domino, and Chubby Checker. They were making the third and final trip.

"This is wild, Carol. I have most of these. People think I'm too old for this music, but I really get into it. You have a Wicked Lester album too. I didn't think anyone else knew about them."

"You can't have that one, no way."

"Got it. I was with Vince in New York about six months ago on business for ten days or so. Vince and I had nothing to do one night, so we went to a show at this neighborhood bar. Lo and behold, Wicked Lester played, and I just fell in love with them. They were strange looking and kinda bizarre, but it was pretty cool. That lead singer and the bass player were awesome. I didn't think much of the rest of the band. I got this album at the show."

"I saw them at a place in New York too. A few girls and I drove up there just to experience big city life for a couple of weeks. We saw them and a bunch of other bands and a few shows on Broadway when we were there. I didn't think much of any of the bands, but Wicked Lester was great."

"Some woman at that show told me that the bass player is a history teacher. When you were a kid, could you imagine having a teacher that looked that wild?" He chuckled. She shook her head and smiled. "Not to mention his tongue. Could you believe the size of that bass player's tongue?" He tried to mimic the bass player with the long tongue.

"Greg, I can't tell a bass guitar from a regular guitar. I know the guy you're talking about, though. His tongue disgusted me, it's so long."

"Oh, you would just hate it if my tongue were that long," he said sarcastically.

"Well, if it were attached to you, I could deal with it." She blushed.

"Both of those guys had great voices, especially that guy with the regular guitar. His voice was absolutely incredible. I guess both of them are like co–lead singers. I can't believe people here don't know about them yet. They need to get rid of the rest of that band or they'll probably never make it out of New York."

"What are those guys' names?" she asked. "The bass player and the lead singer."

"Let me see. Gene Simmons, lead vocals and bass guitar. He's the guy with the tongue. And uh . . . Paul Stanley, lead vocals and rhythm guitar."

"Greg, let's finish this up and get to your house."

He planted a kiss on her and forced her to drop the remaining box.

"Carol, I don't ever wanna hear you say it that way again. It's not my house, it's our home."

She flashed a glistening smile and said, with a lump in her throat and tears in her twinkling eyes, "Let's go home."

13

The atmosphere Greg and Carol created living together was absolutely spellbinding. She added a subtle, yet needed female touch to the decor. They were both astounding cooks, but he enjoyed going out to party so much that they seldom ate at home. When they did dine in, more marvelous gourmet meals were served than could be ordered at any restaurant.

The lovemaking seemed to be more meaningful every day or night. She was an early riser and frequently a prompt businesswoman. He usually went to sleep a great deal later than she did, so, in turn, he would sporadically sleep in the spare bedroom. The booze and drugs were plentiful, but never a problem.

The only argument they ever had occurred when he became aware that she carried a gun in her purse. He worried she would get angry with him and shoot him in the balls. She assured him she would not carry it in their home ever again. She knew a girl who had been raped and murdered downtown. Several other women in the newspapers had been raped and murdered. The only occasion she carried it was when she was alone downtown and in the deli or florist to protect herself in case of a robbery. He despised guns, but in this case, he thought she might be right.

Greg gradually attempted to carry a greater responsibility toward the company. At first, it was to his brother's consternation. At times, Gerald appreciated the effort Greg made.

The cash from the casinos in Las Vegas started arriving immediately in abundance. Before Greg was supplied any amount, his brother funneled and laundered it for payment of the fraudulent loans. The fraudulent loans were under control and would be paid off considerably faster than Greg anticipated.

Greg had no idea what to do with that much cash. He did not believe he was smart enough to launder money. He had Vince install a waterproof/fireproof safe beneath the floor in his basement. The safe had been fiendishly

82

covered by a piece of plywood and a rug under his weight set. The cash Carol and her partner continuously skimmed from the deli and florist was a pittance compared to what arrived from Las Vegas.

Greg wanted Carol to have access to the safe, so he attempted to give her the combination. She held up her hands in a defensive position, as if to say if she had the combination, then he would believe she was only interested in his money. That was clearly not the case.

Greg rationalized it and knew any other girl he had been with not only would have wanted the combination but also would probably steal the money and disappear. Following her refusal to hear the combination, Greg decided to pop the question.

He heard somewhere that men were supposed to ask the girl's father for permission first. Not this time. Willie the Rat scared him. He would do the next best thing and speak to Joseph and Vince Giovelli. He telephoned Vince at work one day. Vince telephoned right back to tell Greg to meet at his father's estate that night at five thirty.

14

The Giovelli estate was a contemporary-style mansion. Joseph had designed the estate. The architecture was unique, complete with a sitting area and garden on the roof overlooking the Country Club Plaza. There was a side entrance five-car garage; three of the bays were tandem and filled with luxury automobiles. An additional tandem five-car detached garage was only partially filled. The interior had been professionally decorated and furnished with no expense spared. There was an Italian marble foyer with an indoor white marble fountain. The two-story exquisite atrium ceiling proved Joseph Giovelli to be way ahead of his time, architecturally. The chateau was situated in such a manner that in back of the circular staircase was a wall constructed completely of glass with a breathtaking view of the Country Club Plaza. The remainder of the mansion was almost as spectacular as the entryway. Each room on the first floor and basement of this twenty-one-thousand-square-foot palace was exquisite.

Sandra Giovelli decorated the bedrooms on the second floor. Joseph cringed when his wife announced she desired to choose the decor for the upstairs, but he allowed it. His only request was that the sections of the second floor that were visible from the first floor needed to have a smooth flow and remain with the continuity of the atrium.

It was a righteous notion to do it that way, considering the second floor was the epitome of vulgarity. Sandra had the impression that the more expensive furnishings were, the more attractive they would be. Every room upstairs contained a different theme. What those themes were supposed to be was anybody's guess. When Joe took people on a tour of his mansion, he never brought them upstairs because that was just the bedrooms and there was nothing special. An elevator stopped at the basement, both floors and the garden roof.

Joe lost his first wife after a bomb exploded in her deli nearly twenty-two years earlier. As tragic as her death was, the insurance money allowed

Joe to open Giovelli Construction Company. His rise as boss of Kansas City La Cosa Nostra came shortly after his wife was killed. The murders of the boss and underboss at the time did not hurt.

Vince knew Greg had never met his mother, and sometimes he wondered if that was a plus. Vince was old enough to remember his mother and wondered if that made it harder for him and his brother.

When Greg and Vince arrived and went inside, Sandra greeted them. There was no argument about whether Sandra Giovelli was a beautiful woman—she was. It was mid-November, and she insisted on wearing short skirts and high heels inside the house. She knew that it was what Joseph liked. Her first marriage was to Joseph's younger brother, Angelo. Angelo died nearly nineteen years earlier.

Her nasal voice almost forced people to laugh when they heard her speak. "Hi, boys, Joseph is in his office. Go right in. He's expecting you." Vince and Greg laughed on the way to the den. They knocked, and Joe yelled,

"Come on in, the door ain't locked!"

When Vince and Greg walked in, they saw Joe sitting at his desk, smoking a cigarette, and drinking a beer while watching television. He only wore a plain white T-shirt and dress pants. His body was in perfect shape, with muscular arms and virtually no fat anywhere. He looked his age or older in the face with his white hair and wrinkles. It was obvious, when someone looked at Joe and Vince together, that Vince did not inherit his height from his father.

"So what's up, boys?" Joe smiled.

"Well, Greg needs to ask you something about . . ."

"He can talk, Vincey. What do you need, Gregy?" Joe looked at Gregy with admiration and thought of Gregy as his own son.

"Well, I'm nervous right now, so bear with me." Greg cleared his throat.

"Why are you nervous, Gregy?" Joe asked, smiling. "You're like my own kid."

"No, not because of you, Mr. Giovelli. Just the subject."

"Let me stop you for a second. Please, I've told you to never call me mister. Just Joe."

"Joe, I'm sorry. Anyway, I wanna ask Carol to marry me, and I really don't know her father that well."

"Plus, he's scared of Willie," Vince interjected.

"Vincey, go in the other room, you aggravate me. Finishing other people's sentences. Go make yourself a fuckin' sandwich or something.

Make sure it's not real fattening, though. That muscle is turning to fat. Go on, Gregy, as soon as Vincey gets his fat ass out of here."

Vince walked out grinning because his father had been saying he would turn into fat since he was a teenager. Vince shut the door and looked down at his body to see that his muscle mass may be turning flabby.

"Are you really scared of Willie?" Joe asked, perplexed.

"Sort of. Since Carol moved in with me, he and Mrs. Cassivano have been over a few times, and I think he understands that I really love Carol and Carol loves me. So he's a little less abrasive toward me now."

"Well, Gregy, I'll tell you. Carol is his daughter, and he's overprotective of her. I know Willie is a bit of an asshole. And, by the way, her mother's name is Margaret."

"Oh, I know. It's just a force of habit with me," Greg said.

"Look, if you wanna marry Carol, I think it's great. She's probably gonna want a big wedding, so if Willie balks at the prices, I'll help out. Don't let Carol know that."

"I actually don't think she will want a big wedding. The cost of it's not an issue for me." Greg smiled.

"You don't think she will. Does that mean you haven't even asked her yet?"

"No, I thought I needed to ask her father first or, as it happens, you."

"What century are you living in, son? Before you ask one of us, you better hope she says yes or you're making a complete ass of yourself." Joe laughed.

"I'm pretty confident she'll say yes. We've hinted at it, and I know she will. We almost got married in Las Vegas last summer. We didn't because she flew out there under a false name."

"Is that all going all right for you? What're you doing with the cash?" Joe asked.

"Actually, I don't know what to do with it. I'm smart enough to know not to put it in the bank, so I'm just keeping it in a safe."

"That's real dangerous, Gregy. You should never have that much cash around. You need to start funneling it through the company. Or move it offshore."

"I really don't know how to do that." Greg had an annoying habit of not displaying any confidence in himself intellectually.

"Well, just talk to Gery about it. Or better yet, when the cash comes here, I'll tell you how much your share is and I'll take care of it for you. I'm taking care of it for Charley and Vincey. They still get some cash, but I take care of the majority of it for them at no charge. But it's your choice. If you're comfortable keeping it around, then it's yours. You could start

86

buying things for Carol and use it that way. You know, you're legitimately high profile enough that you could buy things like jewelry and trips. You're young, Gregy, you should enjoy it."

"So should I go ahead and ask Mr. Cassivano for permission about Carol or not?"

"Don't worry about him, Gregy. I'll take care of it. I'm glad to see that you're finally ready to grow up and settle down. Gerome and I always worried about you."

"Well, I never thought it could happen to me, but she's just perfect. When I tried to give her the combination for the safe, she said she didn't want it because I'd think she was only with me for money. I knew then how special she is."

"You mean you've never noticed what a nice ass she has?" Joe wanted Gregy to lighten up and laugh.

"At first, it was the way she looked, but I'm serious when I say I love her more than life."

"Gregy, I'm happy for both of you. You need to watch the booze and drugs. Don't give me any excuses. Clean up your act. Or, as your father always says, at least in public." Joe smiled.

"Thank you, Joe. Talking to you makes me comfortable."

"If you ever need anything—I mean anything at all—including trouble with Willie, you contact me directly. You don't need to go through Vincey ever again." As Greg walked out, Joe stopped him. "Gregy, I'm interested, what do you know about commercial developer Victor Spelo?"

"I just know he left us to start his own company."

"That's all?"

"Mr. . . . I mean, Joe, that's everybody's dream—to start their own company. He's harmless."

"Gregy, send in that son of mine. I need to talk to him about something. Stay here, though. I might need to talk to you again." Greg exited.

Vince entered immediately. "Yes, Dad?"

"Sit down, Vincey." He motioned to the chair in front of his desk. "Vincey, you need to watch your weight. You're turning fat and disgusting. But I'm sorry, the jokes were in poor taste."

"It's OK, Dad."

"Let me ask you something. Does Gregory ever say anything about his knowledge of us?"

"Dad, he knows more than he lets on, but, believe me, he can be trusted with anything."

"What about Gerald?" Joe asked.

"Brilliant guy, kind of prissy, but he's trustworthy. He knows what to keep secret. Charley and I have talked with him about Nick Cibella and told him to stay away. You might remember that we had your permission to talk with him about Nick. Believe me, Gery can be trusted," Vince assured.

"You know to keep his proposal to Carol quiet. I don't want her finding out before he asks her. You know Willie doesn't trust anyone that's not Italian. I don't know why, but that's the way he is." Joe shrugged his shoulders. "I wanna make Gerald and Gregory. It goes against the rules, but screw them. I owe everything to Gerome Crow. You're the consigliere. What do you think?"

"I think it's a great idea, for Greg at least. I do know him and I know he could never take out another person."

"You could never do that either," Joe said matter-of-factly. "I'd never ask you or him to." Joe closed his eyes to think. "Gerald is a little more cold-blooded. I might set something up for him to take out somebody to see if he will. Somebody around us is bound to screw up. We need proper guys like Gregory and Gerald."

"I might need some time to think about making Gery."

"Either both of them are made or neither."

"You're right. Give me some time to think about it—say, two days."

Joe motioned to Vince that was fine. "Bring Gregory in again. I wanna talk with him with you present." Vince retrieved Greg.

"Gregy, we need to talk business now," Joe growled.

Oh shit, they're gonna see I don't know much.

"Have you ever eaten at Italian Deli? Carol's place in the Quay?" Joe inquired.

"Oh, yeah, the food is amazing. She works so hard there, you wouldn't believe it. Even at home, she's always talking about ways to improve it," Greg said.

"I don't know if it would ease Willie's mind toward you or if he'd resent it, but suggest to Carol that she look for other locations and you'll invest in it."

"You know, she always talks about expanding, and that never even occurred to me."

"She might not have the time to find other locations. So you could ask a commercial agent in your office to help you, or you could find the locations yourself. That would give you something to funnel a little of the cash through. I could pay you as a real estate consultant for things, and we could funnel the majority of it that way," Joe said.

"That's a great idea, Mr. Giovelli—I'm sorry, I mean Joe," Greg said with a smile.

"Then if Willie ever says anything, I could point out that without your idea, Carol would be running the same deli forever because he doesn't have the brains to think the way you do. As far as anyone is concerned, this is your idea."

"Thank you. I'll start on it right away." Greg blushed and smiled ear to ear.

"Vincey, you understand that you never heard this from me. Gregy brought this brilliant idea up to you." Vince understood that Joe wanted to see for himself how Greg would handle this. "Gregy, no one thought this through but you. This is your brainchild." They all looked at one another for confirmation. "Gregy, have you ever seen the basement here since we installed the bowling lanes and shooting gallery?" Greg shook his head no. Vince knew what was coming. Joe needed to see how Greg would handle a gun.

They walked to the finished walkout basement. Joe showed with pride the Olympic-size swimming pool outside and the kidney-shaped indoor pool with a waterfall at one end. The rear of the mansion was spectacular. Every room had a door with a deck protected by green retractable awnings. Twelve decks in all. They walked back inside, and Joe turned on all the retracted lights to show a fully stocked commercial-style bar with seats for twenty people, a small commercial-style kitchen, a walk-in cooler, and a climate-controlled wine cellar, and a recreation room with a pool table, dart boards, several poker tables, pinball machines, and two regulation bowling lanes.

In the front of the basement, underneath the stairs, was a closed room with a shooting range. It had been professionally installed and was very state of the art. They entered, and Greg remained so impressed with the bar that he had difficulty concentrating on the gallery.

Joe turned on the lights, put on his soundproof ear mufflers, and clasped a target to a mechanical runner. He pushed a button and set the target approximately fifty feet away.

Vince and Greg put on ear mufflers and watched as Joe fired six shots from a .38 revolver. He brought the target back to see one bullet had hit the bull's-eye, and others were scattered about the target. Not bad for an old guy. Joe reloaded the gun and had Vince do the same thing. Joe brought the target back to see two bullets hit the bull's-eye, but the others were closer than Joe's shots. Vince reloaded the gun and asked Greg to try.

"Guys, I don't know what I'm doing. I've never fired a gun in my life."

"Gregy, it's simple. This is revolver action." Joe fired two shots. "This is single action." He pulled back the hammer and fired one shot. Joe reloaded the gun and warned Greg that the gun would recoil on him, but he needed to try to hold it steady. They moved the new target only twenty-five feet

89

away. Despite the fact that he was uneducated about firearms and visibly nervous handling a gun, Gregory Crow fired a shot. He did not come close to the paper target.

"I think I understand what you mean by recoil now. Let me try again." Bull's-eye. He fired again. Bull's-eye. They brought the target back. Joe and Vince laughed. They clamped on a new target and mechanically moved it back fifty feet. They reloaded the three previously fired bullets and handed it back to Greg. One shot. Bull's-eye. Bull's-eye. Bull's-eye. Bull's-eye. Bull's-eye. Joe and Vince looked at the target with their mouths open.

"Gregy, that's incredible. Are you sure you've never fired a gun before?" Joe reloaded the gun while he talked. Vince stood speechless.

"Maybe a BB or pellet gun at beer cans, but never a real gun," Greg said, obviously amazed at himself.

Joe motioned for Greg to attempt again. Joe moved the target back to approximately seventy-five feet. Six bull's-eyes later, Vince and Joe shook their heads. During the seventy-five-foot shoot, Joe noticed Gregy did not even use the gunsights properly. Joe watched this as if he were an egotistical father.

Joe clamped on another target and moved it back to the maximum of 115 feet. Vince showed Greg how to load the gun. Joe instructed Vince to watch Greg because of the gunsights. Five bull's-eyes and one borderline. Joe unlocked a cabinet where he stored other guns. He and Vince stood bewildered at Greg and his ability as a marksman. Different guns, different calibers, different distances. After one shot from any gun, Greg would make adjustments then he would needle the bull's-eye no matter what. Left hand, right hand, one bull's-eye after another. If not on the bull's-eye, then fatally close.

"Gregy, son, we need to bring you to a professional outdoor shooting range that can accommodate further distances."

Greg looked at his watch and announced he wanted to go home to Carol. Joe handed him a towel with a cleaning substance and pointed to a washroom. As Greg cleaned up, Joe and Vince stood flabbergasted over the marksmanship they just witnessed. Vince finally broke the silence with a whisper.

"Dad, have you ever seen anything like that?"

"No. I know he's telling the truth, though. Gerome hates guns. I gave Gerome a real nice .45 revolver with his name engraved on it a long time ago. I know he kept it, but Gerome hates guns." Joe shrugged.

"See if you can get Greg to shoot your bow and arrow. I know for a fact he did that in college," Vince said.

"Forget it, this is too much for him now. Forget it!"

"Guys, I need to go home. I'm gonna buy the engagement ring at Tivol's tomorrow. Then hopefully I can order the wedding ring from them. I'm sure they don't have anything like what I wanna see on her finger in stock."

"I know you have the best intentions, Gregy. But you'll also need to get her a smaller one." Joe laughed. "You don't want a classy-looking broad like her walking around with a $10,000 rock on her hand. She might as well wear a sign that says 'Please mug and rape me.'"

"You're right, I didn't think of it that way Mr.—I mean, Joe. Actually, I was thinking more expensive than that."

"Look, son. Don't go overboard with an engagement or wedding ring. You can buy her other jewelry and all after you kids get married." Joe pointed, shaking his finger jokingly. "I can tell you right now that you two are not gonna stay in that house after you're married. That's assuming she says yes." Joe and Vince laughed.

"Why couldn't we stay in that house?" Greg asked, honestly confused.

"Jesus, Gregy, did Gerome never explain women to you, or should I sit you on my lap and explain the birds and bees?" Joe and Vince laughed again. Greg did not understand the humor, so he faked a laugh. "Women don't wanna live in a house their husband lived in while he was single, especially with a husband who has a past like yours. Right, Vincey?"

"How the hell would I know? I didn't have a real past when Sally and I got married. I was only nineteen. Sally was only eighteen. Three kids later, I still haven't had a past." Vince shrugged and smiled.

"I never thought of that. Jesus, there's a bunch of stuff I'm gonna need."

"Welcome to the wonderful world of marriage, son," Joe said.

"Well, I'm sorry to inform you two, but this marriage really is gonna be wonderful. I mean, look at me." All three laughed hysterically at that.

Greg gave one last good-bye. Vince and Greg made some meaningless chitchat before Greg drove away. Vince immediately rushed down the stairs where his father gazed at the paper targets that Greg seemed to have reached out and poked precise holes through.

"Dad, what do you want me to do?" Vince asked, smiling.

"He's such a sweet kid, and his father is a god to me. So I don't know. He doesn't realize what an extraordinary gift he has. We need to somehow see if Gerald is as marvelous at this as Gregory. Tell you what, when Gregory announces his and Carol's engagement, we'll have a party here next week. You and Sally, Charley and his bitch wife Sandy, Gerald and Sherry, Gregory and Carolyn, Gerome and a date, me and Sandy, and I guess Willie and Margaret. We can—nah, forget that. I don't want Willie to see Gregory use a gun. Too many people anyway. Somebody would talk. Let me think. We could just have Gregory, Gerald, you, me, and Charley meet here for a payday on the casinos. Greg announces the engagement. Then we can celebrate and take a tour. Maybe even bowl a few games."

15

The following day, he bought an engagement ring. He wracked his brain trying to think of an unanticipated and unique way to propose to her. He was usually very creative. This made him nervous. He wanted to propose today, but on such short notice, he could only think of one way to ask her.

He made plans with a friend who owned her favorite Mexican restaurant to assist with the proposal. They went to dinner that evening and ordered margaritas and dinner. After the margaritas, he knew she would order a Corona to show she could keep up with him drinking. When the Coronas were brought to the table, the lime on top of her bottle had a plastic skewer with a piece of folded-up paper attached.

"That's disgusting. What do they think I'd put anything in my beer? It's probably the bartender's phone number. Yuck!"

"Just open it up and see."

She carefully took the piece of paper off the skewer and could feel an object wrapped inside. As though "the something inside" smelled bad, she slowly unfolded the paper to see the handwritten message saying, "I love you, Carol. Make me the happiest man in the world and marry me." The something inside was a seven-karat diamond ring taped to the paper. She screamed and cried as he slipped the loose-fitting ring on her delicate finger. All the patrons in the restaurant knew something was going on but were uncertain of what.

"Carol, I still need your answer." Still speechless, with tears streaming down her face, she nodded her head yes. "Carol, in a court of law, they don't acknowledge a head shake. I need to hear you."

Barely able to speak, she said, "Yes."

They stood at the side of the table and embraced passionately.

He began to cry, then shouted to the restaurant, "She said yes!"

Everyone clapped, hooted, and hollered as Greg and Carol kissed. He strutted around the room and started shaking or slapping hands. At one

93

table, Greg recognized the man as someone from a construction site. He looked at the woman to see that she also looked vaguely familiar. As Greg made his way around the room shaking hands, he realized the man made a failing attempt not to stare at him.

He gave the owner of the restaurant and bartender instructions to buy a drink for everybody in the restaurant, roughly seventy people. He gave the owner $400. He then went to the bartender and his waitress and gave them $200 each. All of the other fourteen servers and busboys were given one hundred dollars each. They put on their coats and walked out the door to a chorus of many cheers, when he noticed that the man and woman had disappeared.

On the way to his car, she dropped her purse. When he bent down to pick it up, the sound of the gunshot was unmistakable. He tackled her and rolled behind a parked car. Quick like a cat, he reached in her purse to grab her small automatic only to find she possessed a .38 revolver instead. As though it was instinct, he placed his arm over the car and fired three shots in the direction of the Dodge Duster. The shots rang and penetrated the metal of the trunk. The driver jumped back in the car and hit the accelerator. Greg hesitated, then used the sights and fired the fourth shot at the right rear tire. Bull's-eye.

Carol sat with her hands over her ears. Restaurants and shops filled with people as the streets emptied. People were not accustomed to hearing gunshots in that area of town. Even on a flat tire, the car was still able to drive onto a residential street. The police sirens sounded closer.

He looked at his shoulder. If he had been standing upright at the time, the bullet would have drilled his chest. It did graze the left shoulder of his coat but thankfully did not pierce his flesh. It only scratched him.

He put the gun back in her purse and asked her if she was OK. She trembled, but, otherwise, she was fine. He instructed her to walk back into the restaurant casually. He would talk to the police. She obeyed.

One of the police officers was a good friend of Greg's who moonlighted as a security guard at office complexes and small strip shopping centers.

"What happened, Greg?" Officer Kenneth Bondano asked.

"I don't know, Kenny. Someone tried to kill me. I knew they were in a car. I could hear the tires squealing. There were guns goin' off, so I just dove behind a car," Greg said, desperately trying to hide his shaking.

"You don't have a gun, do you?"

The officer with Kenny looked around for evidence.

"Of course not. You know me better than that."

"Did you see what kind of car it was?" Kenny asked, grinning.

"No."

"Then you probably didn't see which way it went." Kenny obviously asked for the other officers' benefit.

"Of course not." Greg shrugged his shoulders as Kenny deviously winked at him.

"We had a murder maybe three blocks from here a few days ago, a drive-by shooting. This sounds like the same thing. I don't know what this world is coming to, but it was probably random. Are you sure you're fine?"

"Oh, yeah, the bullets didn't hit me."

"Go on," Kenny whispered. "I'll talk to you later."

Several other police officers arrived and asked people if they witnessed anything. There were the usual stories of what happened—usual because none of the stories coordinated. Someone pointed at Greg to say he must have fired a gun. Kenny knew that could not have happened and informed the other officers. Case closed.

Carol walked out of the restaurant and blended in with the crowd. She made her way over to Greg as he wrapped up with Kenny. Carol and Kenny also knew one another, but at the time, Kenny gave a nod to Carol that said, "Leave now." Greg and Carol casually walked to his Porsche and drove away. They were barely out of the parking lot when the conversation began.

"Greg, I wet my pants when that was going on. I'll clean it off the seat later. What just happened?"

He instantly began thinking of his daydream last summer. "Don't worry about the seat."

"Greg, what just happened?"

"Someone tried to kill me." He figured it had to be someone associated with Carol's father.

"Or me." She looked at him. "I know you must be thinking it was someone in my father's crew. But I guarantee you it wasn't."

"Carol, we'll be home in a second. I can't drive and talk at the same time right now." She respected his wishes.

As soon as they pulled into the garage, he let out a nervous quivering breath and opened the car door. She went into their home and immediately went to shower. She changed her clothes and threw the urine-soaked pants in the washer. He sat quietly at the kitchen table, drinking straight scotch and smoking a cigarette inside for the first time ever. She went out to clean the seat of the car. After she finished cleaning, she sat down at the table with him.

He tried to piece together why a man from a construction site would want to assassinate him. Gradually, he realized it more than likely had nothing to do with his future father-in-law, Willie the Rat.

"Tell me why you had a large gun in your purse instead of the small one?"

"Patty has been carrying a small purse. She couldn't fit that one in her purse. We keep that .38 in the drawer at the florist. I took it when I left this afternoon because it gets dark so early."

He pondered this for a moment and easily came to the conclusion that she had no reason to lie.

"I'm actually glad you had it. I'm sure whoever the guy is would've killed us both if I hadn't fired back."

"Greg, you told me you've never handled a gun before." Her volume grew louder. "That car must have been two hundred feet away when you blew out that tire."

"I met with Vince and Joseph yesterday for business. Joseph has a shooting gallery in his basement. They had me try it."

"You've only handled a gun once and you're that good of a shot?"

"I'm not that good. It was just luck." He shrugged.

"Greg, it was a moving target, and moving fast!"

"Carol, do me a favor and never say one word of this to anyone . . . ever. I got the license plate and I'm going over to Vince's to give it to him."

"I'm not staying here alone," she begged.

"Well then, come over there with me and show Sally the ring. Please don't tell her about this."

Greg telephoned Vince and told him they had a surprise and were coming over. They drove Carol's Vega to Vince and Sally's house. In a minute, they pulled on the driveway. Greg instructed Carol to make a big deal of the ring so Sally would think the engagement is the reason for the visit. She did just that. Everyone hugged everyone else. Vince suggested they open a bottle of Dom Perignon to celebrate.

After the celebration, Greg pulled Vince to another room and told him what just happened. Vince assured Greg that the seemingly spontaneous manner was too sloppy and unprepared to be a professional hit.

"Can I still call you Uncle Gregy? Or do I change to just Gregy?" Amber Giovelli, the middle child at six years old, asked, whimpering. She had a crush on Gregy.

"You can still call me Uncle Gregy." Gregy picked her off the floor and whispered loudly enough for Vince, Sally, and Carol to hear. "I'm still your uncle, and you can talk to me about anything that you can't talk to Mommy or Daddy about." Gregy kissed Amber loudly on the lips and set her down.

"Honey, Greg and I'll be right back. We need to go to Dad's house and tell him this personally." Greg and Vince drove away in Sally's new Cadillac. When they were approximately halfway during the two-mile trip, Vince grinned while asking a serious question.

As the Crow Falls

"So Carol freaked out and peed her pants?" Vince could not help laughing.

"Shit, Vince, I don't believe I didn't lose it too. Have you ever had anyone try to kill you?"

"No, except Sally when she was pregnant."

"She shot at you?" Greg asked, puzzled.

"Not with a gun. She did throw things at me like dishes, bottles. One time, when she was changing Amber and was pregnant with Vincey Jr., she threw a big glob of baby shit at me. Hit me right in the mouth with it. You wouldn't believe how crazy they get when they're preg——"

"Shut the fuck up, Vince! This is serious shit here. I don't wanna hear about you getting hit with baby shit. Someone, for some reason, just tried to blow me away, and you have the fuckin' nerve to compare that to getting hit with baby shit. Jesus Christ!"

"Sorry. I'm just trying to calm you down."

"Excuse the fuck out of me, Vince, but you're pissing me off. I just got shot at, and you're comparing it to getting hit in the fuckin' mouth with baby shit."

"I said I was sorry. You do the talking to Dad."

They got out of the car, and Greg kept mumbling those two words. *Baby shit.*

When they met with Joe, Greg recounted the story of what had just happened. Joe immediately telephoned a police officer he owned and gave him the license plate number. The officer was at home when Joe called and promised he would have an answer within two hours. Joe then suggested to Greg that he and Carol should stay with him or Gerome until this blew over.

That's not gonna happen.

"Carol and I were just engaged."

"Well, I don't think we should worry Gerome right now. When are you gonna call him and let him know the good news?" Joe asked, smiling.

"Well, tonight probably. He goes to bed pretty early, so maybe tomorrow," Greg said, obviously nervous.

"Make it tomorrow. He's on a date tonight anyway. He might go to bed early tonight, but he won't be going to sleep if you know what I mean. Have you kids decided on a date for the wedding?"

"No, we just got engaged. We were heading home when all this happened."

"Vincey, get that elephant ass out of the chair and call the Ant and give him the address. Have him watch Gregy and Carol's house for a few days. Go in the other room to call him." As soon as Vincey walked out, Joe lit a cigarette. Gregy pulled one out, and Joe lit it for him. "Gregy, you need to give up smoking soon. When the two of you start having kids, she can't smoke when she's pregnant. It's only fair if you give it up too."

"You're right. Thank you. I will."

"Gregy, come downstairs with me."

Greg had the unmistakable feeling that Joe was bound to give him a gun. Joe turned on the lights and unlocked a gun cabinet. There had to be eighty handguns in this cabinet.

"I want you to keep this one with you at all times. It should fit right in a suit lapel or pants pocket. You're not supposed to have a concealed weapon here, but no one will ever find out if you're just carrying it from your car to somewhere you're walking into. Don't go into some bar and get drunk when you're carrying it. But a shop or office, that's fine. Then keep this one in your car. That's perfectly legal as long as it ain't concealed. When you get out of the car, just put the gun under the seat or in the glove box. Here are two boxes of ammunition for each one and a vest."

They were an automatic pistol of some sort and, of course, the .38 revolver that Greg was now a professional at firing.

"I'm kind of leery about it, but I know I need to. I'm just worried that with an automatic, I might accidentally shoot myself in the side," Greg worried aloud.

"Not with this one. If it makes you feel better, I'll give you a shoulder holster. All you do is put this safety on, and there's no way it can slip and fire." Joe stood at a table close to the entrance of the shooting range, dropping the gun and banging it on all sides to show it would not fire with the safety active. Joe showed Greg how to load the magazine and do general maintenance to the gun. Without intending it, though, Greg showed Joe how to shoot.

"I need to go. I've gotta get back to Carol. I'll bring these back to you whenever you want them."

"Don't worry about it. Call me directly if you ever wanna use the shooting range. Anthony Gilante and one of his men will be watching your house and the street in general for a few days. I know Carol always carries a gun in her purse, but please make sure she doesn't forget. She has a vest too. Make sure she wears it until I say she can take it off."

Greg went upstairs carrying four boxes of ammunition, a bulletproof vest, and two gift-type cases with a shoulder holster.

My life has certainly changed in the last couple of days. I don't know if I could actually kill somebody. Forget it, there's no way. I'll just carry them to make Carol feel more comfortable. And me.

When Greg and Vince drove back to the house, they loaded the guns and ammunition in Carol's car. The customary good-byes and congratulations were exchanged. Carol decided to call her mother while Greg was with Vince. She said her mother was ecstatic and would tell her father as soon as he got home.

"Carol, we're only gonna talk about this for a minute. Then we're gonna drink ourselves into oblivion, get stoned, and talk about the wedding." He opened a beer and was ready to go outside when a jolt of paranoia dictated that it would be permissible to go ahead and smoke in the house again. He went and closed all the bedroom doors and opened a kitchen window. He turned on a fan, and both lit cigarettes. "I gave the license plate to Vince and Joseph. Joseph said they'd take care of it."

"Greg, you said you've never fired gun before yesterday. Now I see you have a complete arsenal."

"Joseph gave me two guns and four boxes of ammunition and this bulky vest. He said you need to wear yours also. Joseph's order."

"These fit my .38. What's the other gun?" She had not stopped shaking.

"I think Vince said it was a nine-liter or something."

"Nine-millimeter."

"Isn't that what I just said?" he asked, frustrated.

"You said liter. It's millimeter. Liter is liquid. Do you know how to use an automatic already?"

"Joseph showed me how. I'll be all right with it."

"He gave you a holster for it too. That means you wanna carry it underneath your jacket?"

"I don't want to, no. I think I have to. But he said it should fit in a suit lapel pocket. It's Friday now, so I don't need to go anywhere this weekend. Have plenty of beer, plenty of smoke, plenty of food, plenty of guns. Everything a growing boy needs."

"I know you don't like guns, Greg. But as you said, if I didn't have one tonight . . ."

"Carol, no more pro-gun talk. I don't like them, but I guess I have no choice. Joseph is sending someone over with Vince in a while to check my cars for bombs just to be safe. But they said it was too sloppy to be a professional hit." He sighed. "I know I've seen the guy. I just don't know where. I'm pretty sure it was at a site."

"A site?"

"A construction site. Carol, no more tonight. It's over. We're both fine. No more." He took her hand. "Let's talk about something more pleasant." He smiled and kissed her softly. She stopped shaking.

"Let's talk about the wedding." She smiled brightly as she finally took off her coat. She collected his new guns and placed them in the utility closet. She left her .38 on the table. She got two beers for them, sat down, moved close to him so she could place her head on his lap, and hugged his legs. "Greg, I think it should be up to you when and where. We could get married in front of a judge as far as I'm concerned."

"Carol, you'd regret it. We can't do that. What about your mom? You're the only daughter she has. You can't deprive her of that."

"I read a book a few years ago, and this couple got married on New Year's Eve. That would be pretty cool." Carol smiled.

"I thought about that today. I'm afraid if we got married on New Year's Eve and didn't have the ceremony early enough, everyone we know would show up wasted. Imagine what would happen if we waited until right at midnight for the preacher to say, 'I now pronounce you man and wife. You may kiss the bride.' And everyone started screaming, dumping champagne on people's heads, not to mention the preacher's and ours. Knowing some friends, they'd start throwing bottles. Start mooning us. New Year's Eve is out."

"Priest." She corrected him.

"What?"

"Priest. If we don't get married by a judge and have a religious ceremony, we have to get married by a priest, not a preacher," she said.

"What's the difference?"

She tried not to laugh because she knew he was not educated theologically.

"I'm Catholic. Greg, we need to be married by a priest. My mom and daddy would go crazy if it weren't a Catholic wedding."

"Whatever. If your dad bitches about the price of it, then I'll take care of it."

"He's not gonna complain about that," she said.

"Meaning he would find something else to bitch about," he said sarcastically.

I shouldn't say shit like that. She's gonna get mad.

"Probably. We still need to think of a date. Do you wanna wait until Valentine's Day?" she asked, smiling.

"Why do we need to get married on a holiday? Thanksgiving is soon, we could get married during halftime of a football game." He laughed.

"Greg, be serious. At least I'm trying."

"I know, I know. I will. I'm just,"—he interrupted himself—"I got it. Let me see a calendar. Do you have one in your purse?" He studied the calendar. "Christmas Eve, no, forget that, it's on a Sunday this year. Saturday the twenty-third, that's it. The day before Christmas Eve."

"That would be fun. We could get married in the afternoon. Have a

Christmas-themed reception afterward. Then we could have a Christmas party that night, a real party. I know most women would want a big wedding, but I really don't. Just forty, fifty people. We could have it in a banquet room at a hotel on the Plaza, looking out over the Christmas lights. That would be romantic. Besides, all the Cathedrals will be full that weekend."

The doorbell rang and startled Greg. Carol was so shocked, she dropped her cigarette on the table but was able to catch it before it hit the floor. Greg looked out the window to see Vince, Joseph, and another man he had never seen. His heart pounded. Carol had her hand on the loaded gun.

"Shit, it's just Vince. I'm so paranoid," Greg said as Carol quickly put the gun in the utility closet. Greg welcomed them in. Carol stood to give Joseph a kiss. "Hi, guys. We just came up with a date for the wedding a few minutes ago," Greg said with a smile.

"Hello, Uncle Joe." Carol gave Joseph a big hug and kiss. "Oh my god. Anthony, it's you. I haven't seen you in ages. Where have you been?" Just as Carol said that, she remembered Anthony Gilante had been in prison.

"I've been away on vacation for 180 days."

His voice was raspy and his laugh very melodic. He was a handsome man in his thirties. He had light-brown hair, neatly trimmed. Brown eyes. His height-to-weight proportions were ideal for a man only five foot five with lifts. His nickname was appropriately the Ant. With the lifts in his shoes, he was still three to four inches shorter than Carol. He and Carol hugged and quietly conversed.

"What were you in for, Ant?"

"I decided this cop pulled me over because he was so tall and I'm not. Then I decided it was OK to spit in his face. I was so drunk that I forgot I had a trunk full of guns." Anthony laughed with his raspy breath.

"Where did you spend your time?" Carol asked.

"Duluth, Minnesota. It was a federal crime, since I'd transported firearms across the state line. It was stupid of me to drive drunk. I would've never been caught if it weren't for the fact I was driving like a fool. Then I acted like an idiot once he pulled me over."

"Well, nice to see you again. Do you know my boyfriend, Greg?" Carol began to make the introductions, when Joseph stepped in.

"Gregory Crow, this is Anthony Gilante. Ant, this is Gregory Crow." The two shook hands.

Vince decided to make the necessary corrections. "I think it's safe to say Greg is your fiancé now, Carol." Greg and Carol smiled.

"Ant, Vincey. Go check the cars," Joe said.

101

Anthony and Vince walked back out to Joseph's Mercedes to get three toolboxes. After unloading the heavy toolboxes, Vince walked back into the kitchen.

"Greg, Ant can check all the cars in just a few minutes. He's an expert," Vince said with assurance.

"Joe, Carol and I have already driven two of the three tonight. My Porsche and her Vega. The only car we haven't driven is the Thing," Greg said.

"Just to be safe, Gregy. So when and where is the wedding?" Joe asked with a smile.

"Well, we decided on a date not three minutes before you came in—the day before Christmas Eve. We haven't even discussed a place yet. Neither one of us want a real large wedding, just quality and beauty." Greg and Carol were hugging and squeezing.

"Just move it to Christmas Eve. That would be unique," Joe said.

"We thought about that, but Carol was hinting that we couldn't find a Catholic preacher guy."

Joe and Vince could not hold in their laughter at that. Carol could not stifle her own laugh.

"You know what? This is totally up to you, but I'd be honored if you'd have the wedding at my house. We could decorate the entrance and have the wedding in front of the fountain. The house lights dimmed so you could see the Christmas lights on the Plaza. We could have the reception on the roof. I'd get a heated tent that night. Then if you kids wanted, you could have a real party that night in the basement," Joe said.

"You've put quite a bit of thought into this, Joe." Greg knew this had to be a rehearsed concept.

"Sandy and I finally finished the house a little over a year ago. I don't consider the upstairs finished, but that's another story." Joe and Vince snickered. "I'd like to have a big gathering like that. I know it's selfish, but I'd really like to show it off. Plus the fact that the two of you mean a lot to me, and I want everything to be first class."

"That would be fun, Greg." Carol gazed excitedly. "We could get out of there early so everyone with kids could be home early. We could start the ceremony at five o'clock just when the sun is going down. Looking out over the Plaza lights," Carol said with her spectacular eyes twinkling.

"What do you say, Greg? Just give me an answer of approximately how many people before the wedding." Anthony entered the kitchen. "Say two weeks before the wedding. Anything, Ant?" Joe asked.

"Nothing. Everything was clean. As a mechanic, Carol, I can tell you the transmission and the U-joint on your Vega are both about to go. You really need to replace them this week. If I were you, I wouldn't even drive it again. I'd have it towed."

"I knew something was wrong with it." Carol sighed.

"You can drive either one of mine for a while. We'll buy you a new car after the wedding. It gets cold this time of year. My Thing is good in the snow." Everyone laughed because of what that implied. "I'm talking about the Volkswagen Thing, you perverts."

The Ant could not resist. "That would make a great billboard: My Thing Is Good in the Snow."

"Carol, you should make that part of your wedding vow. I will never be cold when I have his Thing," Vince said.

Beer started coming from Carol's nose as Joe continued.

"I could never get out of the deep end until I grabbed his Thing." Everybody laughed harder. "Well, if we sit here long enough, I'm sure we could think of a bunch of stuff that could be done with your Thing, Gregy. But we should go and leave Carol alone with Gregy and his Thingy." In the midst of the laughter, Joseph whispered, "Gregy, come in the other room. I need to speak with you." Vince and Anthony sat down at the table with Carol. Greg and Joseph walked into the living room. "I got the word from my guy in the police who that was. He brought the DMV photo to me. Here it is." Joe showed Greg the photograph. "He's a guy named Harold Trafficanly from Tampa. I guess he was in trouble with the outfit down there. They warned him to get out of the city. That was one or two years ago. He's with the pipe fitters' union here. Vincey knows him, barely. He's been working with some plumbing company up here, and Vincey recognized the picture of the guy from a plumbing subcontractor on a job. Vincey can't remember which company. They know him in Tampa as a loose cannon. Is that him?"

"No doubt. I wouldn't forget that mug as long as I live." Greg breathed heavily and sat down. "There was a woman with him too."

"That's his wife, Rebecca. Now here's the bad part." Joe sat down beside Greg on the couch. "I opened up the books, and he works in Nick Cibella's crew. He's a made guy, and if he tried to kill you unauthorized, he might be in trouble with Nick himself." Greg lost all color momentarily. "Are you fine, Gregy?"

"Why would he wanna kill me? I'm just a dumb-ass developer that wouldn't hurt a flea."

"Just like the guy in Tampa said, he's a loose cannon. I know you need to get back to Carol. We have his address and are gonna have somebody watch him for a few days. I've put in a word for Nick to meet with me

103

tomorrow. I'll take care of him with Nick, and I'll take care of it for you because I love you as a son. I just need to know if you're fine with that."

Greg hated the fact he was giving a death sentence to someone. But it was the prick that tried to murder him and made his precious Carol pee her pants.

"Absolutely. Do what you think is right. Only two conditions: I never wanna know about it unless it's on the news and I can't help but hear it, and, most importantly, I never want Carol to know any of this. She has been around stuff that she hates all her life. This fits right into all of that. I'm scared about this. She's a goddess, and I wanna take her away from this life she has and treat her like a queen the way she deserves."

"Has she ever said anything?" Joe asked.

"Of course not, Joe. But I've lived around here my whole life. I've heard things about her family. I read the papers. I'm not stupid. If it walks like a duck . . ."

"If you're concerned over her family—meaning us—then why have any more dealings with her?" Joe interrupted as he'd heard this cliché many times.

"First, I don't consider these 'dealings.' That's business talk to me. I can't explain it any better than I have. I love her. I'd lay down my life for hers. Is that plain enough for you?" Greg said angrily and then calmed himself. "Please don't tell that to her father," Greg said with a smile.

Joe chuckled and realized he was speaking like a gangster instead of a friend.

"Gregy, I can tell you right now, you never have anything to worry over. Your father gave me a great life in construction and many chances to take advantage of him. I never would with him and I'm not gonna with you, Gery, your kids, anyone. I might speak to you like a grandfather at times, but I admire and respect you. I know you're an honorable man, and you should consider yourself part of the family. From a man like me who never needs to ask anything of anyone, I'm asking you for permission to take care of your attempted murderer. Without your permission, I can only tell Nick of the incident and have him do as he chooses."

"Joseph, you can do whatever you want," Greg said sternly. "Don't bullshit me."

"Gregy, let me put it this way. I won't do it without your blessing. You're with me, I wanna be with you." Joe kissed Gregy on both cheeks and asked him again. "I'm with you, Gregy. Are you with me?"

What the fuck, this is scaring me. I can't go around feeling scared for Carol's life. Or my life, for that matter.

"Joe, I'm with you. Just promise me that Carol and I will be protected

104

and neither of us ever finds out about this unless it's on the news and we can't help hearing it."

"You have my word, Gregy son." Joe kissed Gregy on both cheeks again and walked out of the room, stopping first to wipe a tear from his eyes. Joe informed Carol that he would have a garage tow the Vega to her father's mechanic's garage tomorrow. Joe hugged Carol again and kissed her on the lips. "I'm proud of you, Carol. You have a hell of a guy here. I just told him he had a hell of a girl too. So you don't need to think we were talking about his Thing." Everyone just chuckled as Joe, Vince, and Anthony drove away.

Carol knew what her uncle and soon-to-be husband had to be talking about. She was the daughter of the underboss.

Vincey and Joe dropped Anthony at his car less than three blocks away. Anthony and one of his men would watch Greg and Carol's residence until Harold Trafficanly was safely out of the picture.

"Vincey, I want you to set this thing up with Gerald early next week. Gregory needs to be made! For us. What incredible timing. He must have shown some balls out there. For that to have scared the piss out of Carol the way it did and him to be in such control." Joe smiled.

"I'll do it, Dad." Vince yawned. "When are you meeting with Nick?"

"Tomorrow, at eight in the morning. I'm driving myself. There's no reason for Nick to suspect anything. If someone drove me, he'd think there is. I just wanna see if he handles this the honorable way. He's a nice guy. I know him well enough to know he wouldn't get angry in a public place. If he wants to be the boss, let him be the boss. I'll tell him that. None of us need this shit anymore. I'm really tired of this. I just wanna be sure Nick is there when we make Gerald and Gregory. I'm supposed to be semiretired now. I'd love to be able to retire from this shit totally. I could work in my woodshop anytime I wanted to. I'm making a real nice dining room hutch and china cabinet for this guy I met in the Optimist Club. He and his wife are gonna have their thirtieth or fortieth anniversary soon. I don't care, it just gives me an excuse to be a carpenter." Vincey and Joe pulled in the garage. "Tell Sally and the kids I'll see them Sunday afternoon."

"I'll see you this weekend, Dad."

"Vincey, come here." Joe hugged Vincey. "Vincey, please do something about the weight. I know I shouldn't give you so much trouble or talk to you so bad. I just have a lousy way of telling you it's not good for you. You need to lose it for Sally and the kids. You're getting old, and the muscle is turning to blubber. You're fat and disgusting now. It doesn't look good."

"I'll call you tomorrow." Vince looked in the rearview mirror and knew he needed to lose weight.

Vince smiled because his father had all the money in the world just so he could finally relax and work his ass off as a carpenter. With the quality craftsmanship Joseph displayed and the attention to every tiny detail, he could easily charge any amount he chose. Instead, he never charged a dime to anyone for wood carving.

16

Nicholas Cibella and Joseph Giovelli met at a cafe in the River Quay for breakfast. Nick and Joe were approximately the same age, same hair, same height and weight, yet looked nothing alike.

Out of the respect and admiration Nick had for Joe, he wore a suit, while Joe wore jeans and a sweater. Due to the nature of the meeting, it was resolved that it needed to be discussed in a private setting. The breakfast was used to break the ice. Both men agreed by telephone to meet alone, without bodyguards. After a short breakfast, Joe convinced Nick that the remainder of the discussion needed to occur in a more intimate setting. As the two were leaving, the cafe patrons stared. Two men of their prestige and reputation meeting together warranted a few stares. Joseph Giovelli and Nicholas Cibella were two of the most feared men in the Midwest, and rightfully so. They drove to Joe's woodshop and walked inside.

"Nick, one of your guys tried to take out a friend of mine last night. Needless to say, I need to know if you're gonna handle this the honorable way."

"What're you talking about?" Nick asked, genuinely confused.

"Harold Trafficanly shot at a friend of mine. Soon to be a Friend of Ours."

"Harold isn't in my crew. He never really was. I took him in when he came up from Tampa. He's a lunatic. He can't keep a job, nothing. My guys never even used him for anything outside of minor running. Nobody could stand being around him, so he eventually disappeared. At least, I thought he did," Nick said.

"Look, Nick. When I looked into it last night, they said he was in your crew."

"I promise you he isn't. We tried to use him for certain things when he first came up here. His father, Santo, told me personally to keep an eye on him but to treat him right. He's gone back to Tampa several times. The guy

107

is a loser. He belongs in a mental home. I haven't seen Harold in months. Believe me, the guy is a fuckin' nut. I'd never have anything to do with him." Nick held his hands up.

"Well, if this was not authorized by you, what're you gonna do?"

"Joseph, you're the boss of your family and crew. I can promise you we had nothing to do with this."

"Nick, we both know Kansas City isn't big enough for two bosses. I really wanna retire soon. I want our organizations to be one classy unit, and silent. The way La Cosa Nostra was meant to be. I'll call you next week. We might have a ceremony soon. I want you to be there to show that we're one. I'm gonna have a few of my men handle this."

"That's fine. I don't want you to think I'd have anything to do with that madman. I have the utmost respect for you."

"Nick, we need to work together as one, and you know it. Look around here, and what do you see? A woodshop. This is what I want. I'm a handyman and carpenter who has been fortunate. Neither of us is a boss. I was a boss once, and you know what? It was as the boss of Giovelli Construction. The world is changing, and if Kansas City La Cosa Nostra doesn't change with it, we're gonna be extinct soon. The old ways of doing things are coming to an end. If you still think you need to be the boss, then fine, you're the boss. Just do yourself a favor and be more discreet unless you can find something legitimate that warrants someone flashing that kind of money around," Joe said with a grin.

"Joseph, I have never and will never try to take your place. I don't understand why we're talking about this. We came to talk business. I then found out Harold Trafficanly took a shot at a friend of yours, and that's what the purpose of this meeting was supposed to be. Tell me what you want from me," Nick said.

"I want you to start associating with me. I don't want my sons to be any more a part of this than they already are. You were there when Charley became a Friend of Ours. Vincey became a Friend of Ours when you were away for a few years. Charley and Vincey are making so much money right now as president and vice president of Giovelli Construction that they don't need this. I want you to join me. I want us to be one."

"I agree, Joseph. I will say that I've never considered myself the boss of anything. Just the supervisor of some people who need some direction." Nick hesitated. "Who is it that you're making into a Friend of Ours?"

"I'll let you know as soon as I'm sure. Probably this week. I'm gonna have one of the people I wanna make into a Friend of Ours take care of Harold."

"I'll have someone take care of it if you want."

"No need. I need to see how the potential Friend of Ours handles it. We need to start appearing together in public, especially in front of Friends of Ours. Why don't you and your wife meet Sandy and me for dinner tonight? You pick the place and call me at home. We need to be seen together frequently so people know we're one."

17

November 13, 1972

Gerald and Gregory Crow were summoned to Joseph Giovelli's estate along with Charles and Vincenzo Giovelli for payouts on the Las Vegas casinos. In the driveway, Gerald approached Gregory.

"So what happened Friday? I just heard from someone fifteen minutes ago that you were the target in a drive-by shooting."

"Yep. I dove behind a car. That's about it. Who did you hear it from?"

"Kenneth told me he was one of the first officers on the scene. Anything else to know?"

"Nope."

"You're so eloquent with words, Gregory." Gerald rolled his eyes and laughed.

"It's Greg, you wimp."

"I'm so sorry, Greg U. Wimp."

After the bimonthly payout of the Las Vegas casino money, Greg announced his engagement to Charles and Gery. This was the first time Gerald heard of his brother's impending wedding. A brief celebration ensued.

While on the tour, all decided to show their stuff at the Giovelli shooting gallery. Everyone was impressed with the marksmanship of Gregory. Gerald went to his Mercedes to get the automatic he preferred. Gerald confessed that he was an experienced marksman and validated that statement by drilling the bull's-eye as equally natural as his brother. Gerald confessed that at times he carried a concealed weapon with him.

"I never thought I would need to. I began carrying one about a year ago. I read about someone getting mugged in the parking lot of one of the banks we use. I became a little paranoid, since I occasionally have a hefty

110

sum of cash on account of Vegas. So I carry it all the time now," Gerald said.

"I never knew you carried a gun, Gery," Charley said, chain-smoking.

"That's why it's concealed, so nobody knows. I know it's against the law, but so is robbing someone at gunpoint. It's just for my peace of mind," Gerald responded.

"Guys, I need to go. I have a lunch date with Carol. Then we're gonna look for a wedding ring. I don't wanna be late. She's taking the day off for this." Greg was obviously tiring of the gun talk.

"Gregy, have you decided where to have the wedding yet?" Joe said as Gregy headed up the stairs.

"Well, we decided to go ahead and have it here. What is the limit you could tolerate on the amount of people?" The two were far enough away from the remainder of the group that Greg was comfortable.

"I can accommodate any amount that you need." Joe smiled.

"Carol doesn't want a huge wedding, and neither do I. Just give me a couple of weeks to give you a roundabout number. How many people she wants to invite is the only thing I can't tell you right now. Ya know, just call her to discuss all the plans. Other than Dad, Gery, Sherry, and the boys, I'll probably only invite three other couples. Well, Vince is gonna be the best man, so I don't need to invite him. Make that two other couples."

"I see you're wearing the vest. Are you carrying your piece now, Gregy?"

Greg opened his winter coat and suit jacket to show he was indeed wearing the shoulder holster. He told Joe that one of the guns was safely in the car. Joe hugged and kissed Greg yet again.

This is getting fuckin' ridiculous.

Joe walked back to the shooting range. Joe and Charles informed Gerald of the need to meet privately. Vince announced his intention to leave, since Gerald was comfortable speaking openly only in the presence of Charley. The three sat at the bar.

Joseph proceeded to inform Gerald of Harold Trafficanly and his attempted murder of Gregory. Gerald was not as adept as his younger brother at hiding his feelings. The anger in his eyes at the mention of Harold Trafficanly was unmistakable. The possible relationship between Harold Trafficanly and Nicholas Cibella did not matter. This was not business at all. Greg was his brother. Gerald wanted this bastard dead. After several hours of verbal intimidation from Joseph, Gerald wanted to kill this motherfucker himself. He informed Joseph and Charley of his business trip to San Francisco on Wednesday evening. He would not be back in Kansas City until Saturday. An ironclad alibi.

The picture and address were given to Gerald. For supervision,

Anthony "the Ant" Gilante and Kenneth "Kenny the Cop" Bondano were summoned to the Giovelli estate. Kenny introduced Ant to Gerald.

On Friday morning, November 17, 1972, the bodies of Harold and Rebecca Trafficanly were found floating in the Missouri River. Rebecca Trafficanly had been shot twice in the back of the head. Harold had been shot a total of seventeen times. Although eight of the gunshots had been powerful enough to travel through his body, nine bullets remained lodged in his spine or head. Three different caliber bullets were found in his body. Harold Trafficanly was a known member of the Tampa, Florida, underworld.

18

November 19, 1972

The ceremony making Gerald and Gregory Crow into Friends of Ours did not go off without a hitch. The Crow brothers were a minority for the first time in their lives. William Cassivano was hesitant to have non-Italian members of La Cosa Nostra. That did not happen. It was unheard of. A violation of the most basic rules of this secret society. Willie calmed down after Joseph explained to him that the two Crow boys were essential to launder money. Crow Brothers Real Estate Company, along with Giovelli Construction, was a perfect setup. Willie began to understand the benefits of having his soon-to-be son-in-law as a made member.

Greg was not Italian. But Willie could see, with the help of his wife Margaret in the past few months, what Carol was attracted to. Sure he drinks too much, but he is so nice to everyone. He is so clean. He is so respectful of Carol. He plans on investing in her deli and florist. He wants them to be huge chains. He is rich and getting richer.

Convincing Nicholas Cibella was impossible. Nick was outraged. He was pissed off when he arrived for the ceremony that day to find out the men who were now going to be Friends of Ours were not Italian. Joe explained the benefits to Nick. Nick did not care. He did not want to stay at the ceremony, except everyone else thought it was a good idea. Nick needed to sit still and pretend to go along with it. During the ceremony, Nick began to visualize the benefit to himself by having Gerald and Gregory Crow as members. Still, Nick was old-fashioned enough that he did not believe non-Italian persons belonged. Something had to be done to provide Kansas City La Cosa Nostra with tradition. This may be the new world, but Nick Cibella would be damned if he were going to accept this.

Gerald was exhilarated to be a made member of La Cosa Nostra. Greg thought La Cosa Nostra was a ridiculous organization. He would not kill at all. He would have Vince relay that message at a pertinent date. Greg did comprehend and would maintain and respect the fact that La Cosa Nostra was a clandestine society.

It is suspected that Gerald and Gregory Crow are the only non-Italian people ever to become made members of the American La Cosa Nostra.

19

Sherry Crow hired a local private detective who belonged to a network of affiliate detectives in other cities. It was imperative to Sherry that this particular vacation be closely monitored.

When Sherry had her meeting with the detective at his office, he confirmed her suspicions. Sherry had to sign papers waiving responsibility from the local detective as well as the detectives from San Francisco. He translated the San Francisco detectives' report:

"Gerald arrived early Wednesday evening. He promptly checked into the hotel and then patronized a bar frequented by homosexuals. Two young Hispanic men accompanied Gerald back to his suite at the hotel." The detective snapped twenty-four pictures for proof. "Gerald attended a seminar on Thursday. Thursday evening, his whereabouts were unknown." They lost him. "Sometime during the night, Gerald reappeared. Friday, he attended a morning tax seminar. At noon, he went back to his hotel and checked out. He was picked up by limousine and taken to a private residence in Sausalito. A small cottage with direct access to the beach.

Gerald then spent the entire day with another man driving to the wine country, going into all the wineries. The couple finished the evening with dinner in a gourmet restaurant at Fisherman's Wharf. They drove back to the private residence, and the detectives snapped over three hundred surveillance photographs of Gerald and his male partner having sex on the back porch of the residence overlooking the beach."

Sherry did not cry, as this was finally a huge relief not to wonder. She could not look at all the photographs. Many of them were redundancies and may as well have been reprints. The detective assured her they were not. He was under legal obligation to destroy the photographs and negatives if she did not want possession of them. She wanted the negatives to be in her safe deposit box.

Her husband, the father of her sons, in pornographic pictures with another man. She needed a few days to think of how and when she could, or even if she should, approach her husband on this.

Sherry decided to confront Gerald the day after Thanksgiving. Mark and Michael traveled with their grandparents that day. Sherry's parents drove in from their farm in Grain Valley, Missouri, for Thanksgiving. Her parents took Mark and Michael back home with them for the long weekend.

Sherry was from an area that was not very open-minded. Consequently, the femininity Gerald displayed by nature was troublesome, to say the least. Years earlier, before Gerald and Sherry were wed, Sherry explained to her parents that Gerald was very well mannered and proper. That was the only reason he came across as feminine to people (meaning rednecks) like them.

She wanted to give Gerald the opportunity to tell a barefaced lie. Gerald sat on the sofa, reading the daily paper.

"Gery, we need to talk." Gerald mumbled something and continued to look at the paper while barely acknowledging his wife. She grabbed the newspaper and pulled it down to look him straight in the eyes. "Gery, we need to talk now." He set the newspaper aside as if this were a routine husband-and-wife conversation.

"What is it?"

"What did you do last week in San Francisco?"

"I went to a few business seminars and one tax seminar. Why?" Gerald continued to ignore Sherry.

"I'm going to ask you one time. Are you having an affair? We've only had sex once in the last year."

Gerald informed Sherry after the ceremony that he was a made man now and this had to have something to with that.

"I'm sorry. I didn't realize I was neglecting you. That's selfish on my part. No, I'm not having an affair."

"Gery, I know you are! Tell me what her name is?"

"Sherry, I assure you, I'm not having an affair," Gerald said, smiling. Sherry started crying. "Then tell me what *his* name is."

This was not a question. Sherry threw five pornographic pictures of Gerald with a man toward him. Gerald was numb. He was void of all expression. He could not speak as Sherry just stared at him with a look of dejection accompanied by a tear.

"Sherry, what do you want me to do?"

"This is why you haven't been interested in me sexually?"

Gerald put his head in his hands. He then tore up the photographs and placed them in the fireplace on burning logs. He turned up the gas to the maximum to make sure the photographs burned beyond recognition.

Sherry reached into a shopping bag and pulled out three more pornographic pictures and gave them to Gery.

"How many of these do you have?"

"A few hundred. Plus the negatives in my safety deposit box."

Gerald knew his life might as well be over. He knew she would want a divorce and would use these pictures to blackmail him forever.

He was a made man now, though. He could have one of his associates take her out. However, he could never do that to his sons. He remembered what it was like growing up without a mother. It was hell. Although his father supposedly raised him and his brother, Gerome was obsessed with business, and, in turn, he'd never been available for fatherly things—much the way Gerald was to his own boys.

"What do you want from me?" Gerald asked.

"An explanation would be nice."

Sherry was the woman Gerald had promised to love forever. How in the world could he explain his sexual preference to her?

"I don't know what to say, Sherry. I'll give you however much you want."

"I resent the fact that you think you can buy me off with money."

"If not money, then what do you want?" Gerald asked, genuinely confused.

"I just want an explanation. How long have you been gay?"

"I think since I was born." Gerald exhaled a breath that sounded as if he had been retaining it his entire life. "I don't know if I am entirely. I'm obviously not destined for an attempt at worming my way out of this, but I really do love you, Sherry."

"I love you too. I would never try to blackmail you. I love Mark and Michael. I love to see you with them. You're a wonderful father when you're there, which is rare. So maybe I am blackmailing you. I want you to start spending more time with them. Do what they want to do. Just the three of you. I can't be a father to them."

Without a doubt, he knew she was correct.

"I will. My dad was constantly too busy for Gregory and me. I've seen that in myself recently, and I don't like it."

"I don't want them to know this." Sherry pointed at the shopping bag containing the pornographic photographs.

"Of course not. I don't want anyone to know. I never wanted you to know. I have to say I'm relieved, though."

"Me too. Here's what I do want. I'll be your wife in public. We'll be parents together. No one ever needs to know any of this. I get to do what I want sexually as long as it doesn't affect appearances in public or in front

117

of the boys. You can also do whatever it is that you want sexually. Same boundaries. That'll be OK with you, won't it?" Again, this was not a question.

"Do I have a choice?" Gerald asked, slightly smiling.

"No! I'll even burn all the pictures. That is, unless you want to look at them for some reason. The negatives stay in my safety deposit box." Sherry slowly burned all the pornographic pictures of her husband with an unknown man.

Gerald and Sherry talked about endless subjects that day. For as long as Gerald could remember, he had not been this comfortable talking, for fear his secret would come out. It was like the old cliché: "A huge weight was lifted off his shoulders."

The two made popcorn and played Scrabble like they had not done in years. They started getting a bit tipsy and could no longer concentrate on the Scrabble board. After a while, they started blasting music and danced like two kids again. Gerald was mentally looser than Sherry had ever seen him. By eight o'clock, they were falling down drunk.

Someway, for some unexpected reason, they made love that evening on the sofa. Following a few Thanksgiving leftover sandwiches and veggies, they made love on the floor. For the first time in years, they fell asleep in one another's clutches.

The next morning, they awoke to hangovers they were inexperienced dealing with. Gerald mixed a gourmet breakfast cuisine as only a true connoisseur of cooking could do. After they gratified their craving for food, they made love in the bathtub.

They telephoned Greg and Carol and asked them to come over to celebrate the engagement. Everybody exchanged hugs with everybody else. Greg had never seen his brother so delighted. Greg thought Gery was overjoyed for him. He was. Nevertheless, everything under the sun was brighter to Gerald Crow today.

20

The wedding between Gregory Crow and Carolyn Cassivano was as unpretentious as possible in a mansion that reeked of magniloquence. There was only a superficial modification in the Christmas ornamentation. Greg and Carol requested that appearance. They desired the wedding to be as Christmas themed as possible.

It was intended to be a modest ceremony. The invitations were only delivered to forty people. The majority of the invitations were to close family or intimate friends and their children. There were beyond 150 people in attendance. It was a good idea to conduct the wedding ceremony on Christmas Eve. If not on a holiday, there would assuredly have been a greater number of unwanted guests. The elder Sandra Giovelli made the arrangements with caterers to accommodate for, at minimum, two hundred people.

It is invariably unique how, at a wedding or funeral, people who never dress their best can become visibly exceptional. The biggest shock of the day went to Willie Cassivano. Willie could not be recognized at first glance. He cleaned up well. Underneath all the grime and clean-shaven, a strikingly handsome man appeared.

Carol spent the evening before with Sherry Crow. Sally and the younger Sandy Giovelli came over to help Carol carry on the tradition of not seeing the groom the day of the wedding. Gerald, Vince, and Charles drank a final mini bachelor party at Greg's soon-to-be-no-longer bachelor pad.

Gerome needed to talk privately with his son before the ceremony, so he entered the den where Greg waited in nervous anticipation. Gerome had never been an excessively affectionate father. Nevertheless, today he and his son shared a tight embrace, the kind only a father and son can relate to. Gerome sobbed while he smiled.

"I love you, Gregy. I hope you know that."

"Of course I do, Dad. I love you too." Greg began to cry as well.

"I tried to do the best I could. I never could find another woman to take her place. I'm sorry," Gerome said with a broken voice.

"Dad, you have nothing to apologize for. You always did right."

"When I was there, maybe. I was never there for you."

"Dad, you always did what you thought was right. You never yelled at us. You never hit us. You could have abandoned us."

"Sometimes I feel like I did." Gerome erupted into tears.

"Dad, don't ever think that. Ever! Just think of all that you've given to Gery and me."

"I can't help but think that I should have given you more than just materials."

"Dad, we need to get ready. It's gonna start soon."

They reluctantly severed the embrace, and Gerome looked at his son.

"Look at you! You look so much like her. Your mother would be so proud. I wish she were here."

"I know. You know I'm not that religious, Dad, but I think she is proud. I think she is here." They hugged once more and went to the attached half bathroom to splash water on their faces.

"One thing I need to remind you of, Gregy. Remember Vincey's wedding?" Although Greg could not remember, he nodded his head yes. "All these Italians give cash at the reception afterward, so don't be offended."

"What do you mean *cash*? Like how much?"

"Hell if I know."

Vince entered the den to announce it was time. Greg and Vince took their spots adjacent to the fountain. The music began, and drop-dead gorgeous Carol and her father descended the stairs with several bridesmaids lifting the train of her sweeping wedding gown. The dimmed interior lights on the fountain, the dazzling Christmas lights on the opposite side of the glass, and the general ambiance of the scene made a truly dramatic wedding portrait. The vestibule in the Giovelli estate adequately accommodated enough people for this ceremony that it looked like the lobby of a hotel.

Although it was a Catholic ceremony, it had been significantly toned down for the obvious reason: Greg was not Catholic. He could never be positive what religious persuasion he was. All he knew was that he held belief in God.

During the formal ceremony, Greg learned that Carol was actually Carolyn.

The priest ended by saying, "I now pronounce you man and wife. You may kiss the bride." Greg and Carol did something that many people thought was sacrilegious. Other people thought it was hilarious. They gave one another a high five before the kiss.

I did it. I don't feel any different. Hmm? Well, maybe I am different now. God, look at her. She is it.

The reception quickly moved from the frigid roof to the basement recreation room. Greg and Carol sat in chairs next to one another as everybody passed by, giving them envelopes full of cash. Greg was a wee bit offended, but he understood this was a tradition.

When Willie and Margaret stopped by, Willie leaned in and whispered to his new son-in-law, "I don't give a shit who you are. If you ever cheat on or hit my daughter, I'll kill you. I won't have anyone do it. I'll do it myself."

Greg wanted to jump up and say something smart-ass. He knew it was not appropriate, so he whispered to Willie, "You have nothing to worry about, old man."

Gerome Crow and Joseph Giovelli stopped by. Together, they gave the newlyweds two small boxes that looked as if they contained jewelry. They opened the boxes, and inside were Hot Wheel models of brand-new Corvettes—his and hers Corvettes. Mr. and Mrs. Crow could pick the colors when they returned from the honeymoon. Greg and Carol were overwhelmed and were told what dealership to pick the Corvettes up at when they returned.

Greg and Carol wanted the honeymoon to begin as soon as possible. It was only a little after seven o'clock, so the plan to get out of there by eight was very practical.

After accepting congratulations from everyone and leading two dances, Greg and Carol announced they were leaving. Greg informed Joe that Willie had just threatened him.

"I'll take care of it, Gregy." Joe instantly grabbed Willie's arm, tugged him aside, and attempted to straighten him out.

"I mean it, Joe. I would say the same thing to any man marrying my daughter."

"You're not gonna touch Gregory Crow! You got it?"

"I'll never have a reason to as long as he doesn't hit my Carolyn."

"He won't do that. I'm telling you now, don't ever fuckin' touch him. Discussion and decision over."

Carol tossed the bouquet to the single girls. Greg slipped off Carol's garter and threw it to the single guys.

Joe had one last word for Gregy. "I just talked to Willie. Never worry, Gregy, you're with me."

Greg and Carol had a personal word with their own fathers before leaving.

A limousine took Greg and Carol to a hotel for the evening. They had packed previously and would leave for the honeymoon Christmas Day. The suite was no accident; it was the exact suite where they had first encountered one another's bodies in August.

She counted the money—$74,000 in cash. Two new Corvettes, numerous gifts, and priceless drawings from children, especially Sarah Giovelli. Her drawing showed great promise as an excellent artist. Greg and Carol could not refrain from showing it to everyone. Professional artist Peter Cassivano was impressed. Peter recommended private lessons to enhance Sarah's gift. Vince and Sally told everyone who asked that, at eight years old, Sarah's drawings were framed and in houses all over.

The whereabouts of Greg and Carol on the honeymoon were unknown by intent. Vince was the only person who knew how to reach them and only in the event of an emergency. Many people joked that they did not even leave town. They stayed in bed for the entire thirty-day honeymoon. They did go to Hawaii, but staying in bed was not that far-fetched.

At Greg's request, Carol had an appointment with a gynecologist promptly after she and Greg became engaged. She stopped taking birth control pills immediately.

Approximately the end of the second week in Hawaii, the dream honeymoon was marred by a calamitous telephone call from Gerald.

"Gregory, I know you guys aren't coming back until next week, but there's information that can't wait."

If he starts discussing business, I'm gonna scream.

"Gregory, you need to sit down for this." Greg's heart sank, yet he continued standing. "Vincey gave me your phone number. He's too upset to talk. A bomb went off in Joseph's woodshop three days ago. I didn't even know about it until I got back from Chicago last night." Gerald breathed deeply. "Gregory, he lost his right leg and part of his left foot. His right arm. I guess he's burned pretty bad. The doctors and the other staff won't let anyone except Charley or Vincey see him. I guess police are guarding his ICU pretty tight."

Greg attempted not to frighten Carol. She understood by the expression on his face that something was terribly wrong.

"Is he gonna, ya know?"

"Not yet. The doctors didn't expect him to make it through the first night. That was Monday. He can barely see. He was wearing some protective eye gear that saved some of his eyesight. A hard hat with some respirator to keep lacquer spray and fumes out of his lungs and hair saved his brain. He started talking a little yesterday. He can speak, but barely. The doctors don't understand that at all. He can write left-handed, so he has been able to communicate with Charley and Vincey. I guess the bomb was under some power tool or something. Look, I don't know all the circumstances yet—just the basics. I spoke with Charley last night. Apparently, Joseph doesn't remember anything. Some big piece of oak or something that he was working on saved his life."

I would rather be dead than live like that.

"Gery, we weren't scheduled to come back till the end of next week, but I'm sure we can make it sooner."

"No, don't do that. Charley and Vincey specifically asked me to call you and inform you not to come back early. So far, the media has been pretty respectful. No television stations or newspapers know anything yet. They just know that Joseph Giovelli was injured in a bomb blast. Here's why I called you, Gregory. I know you need to sit down for this."

Greg followed the recommendation of his brother and sat down. Carol started to get enraged over the fact that Greg was not communicating to her what had happened. The sunken expression on his face said it was something horrible.

Please don't let Gery say this is because of Carol and me.

"Charley and Vincey have some connections with the police. I don't have the specifics yet, but the reason you shouldn't come home till scheduled is that Carol's father is one of the suspects right now. Charley and Vincey thought you should know for that reason alone before William can persuade you to end the honeymoon early. I told them I would call you. Charley and Vincey said they only wanted you to hear this from me. Gregory, there is nothing you could do. There are too many people here now. Friends and family everywhere. If Carol is right there, just say yes."

"Yes."

"Do you want me to speak to her?" Gerald asked.

"No. I'll do it. Where can I call you later?"

"Call me at home about midnight, our time. There's, what, four or five hours difference? Don't tell her now that her father is a suspect. I'll call you when he dies, then it'll be all right to come back early." Gerald and Greg were equally shocked at that statement. "Shit, I can't believe I said that. Call me between twelve and one tonight. I don't think I'll be sleeping."

"I'll talk to you then." He placed the telephone down carefully as if it were the bomb itself. He blankly gazed at her as she skittishly paced the room, smoking.

"Tell me what's going on, Greg."

He lit a cigarette and took a deep drag. "Carol, someone bombed"—he had trouble looking at his new wife—"I mean, a bomb exploded in Joseph's woodshop a few days ago. He's hurt pretty bad. The doctors don't think he'll live very long. The doctors are surprised he's made it this long."

Tears immediately filled her suntanned face. One trembling hand covered her sensual mouth.

"Oh fuck! No! God, please no. We need to go back. My aunt Sandy is probably hysterical."

"Gery said we shouldn't come back right now. He asked me to call him tonight. There's nothing we can do right now." He continued to gaze away from her with an expressionless look on his face.

"Greg, we have no choice but to go back early, unless there's something you're not telling me." She stared at him intently as he continued looking away.

"I can't even imagine what Vince is going through. I feel like we should go too, but we shouldn't."

"Why not?" She threw her hands up.

"Too many people. Gery said he would call us if Joseph dies."

"I'm calling Daddy."

He could not keep her from using the telephone. He began crying and went to the restroom. He did not cry for Joseph, or even himself. He cried for his best buddy Vince.

Carol and her brother Peter had a secret telephone ring code with their mother and father. Allow the telephone to ring three times and hang up. Dial back, let it ring once, and hang up. Then dial again. It was a nuisance, especially when calling long distance. Nevertheless, the process was the rule. Peter answered.

"Carol, how's your honeymoon?"

"Peter, let me talk to Mom or Dad."

"I asked you a question, rich bitch. How's your honeymoon?"

"It's wonderful, Peter. And I don't appreciate the nickname. Put Daddy on now," Carol demanded.

"I'm sorry, Carol. I didn't mean that. It's been rough here the last couple of days. Hold on."

Carol and her brother had always been close. At the moment, he was royally jealous of her newfound wealth. She could hear her brother in the background shouting for her father to "pick up the damn phone."

"Hello, Carolyn."

"Daddy, what's going on? Greg's brother just called."

"What did he tell you?"

"I didn't talk to him. Greg did."

"What did he tell Greg?"

"That Uncle Joseph was in an explosion and that he's almost dead."

"That's about the size of it."

Following a lengthy awkward pause, she asked, "Daddy, should we come home now?"

"No. Absolutely not. It's a madhouse here. There ain't nothing for you to do here now anyway. If Joe takes a turn for the worse, then I'll make sure Gery or Vincey gets in touch with you, since they're the only people that know where you are. Of course, Vincey gave Gery the privilege of knowing your number," Willie said, intensely sarcastic.

"Daddy, I'll give you the number if you want it that bad."

"No. I shouldn't have said it like that. Everyone knows you're in Hawaii right now. I know it's tough, but just try to enjoy the honeymoon. What was Greg's reaction?"

"He just sat there stone-faced. He's in the bathroom now. I think he's crying."

"I know Joe is important to him. I know how very important he is to Joe." There remained an inkling of sarcasm in Willie's voice. "Carolyn, just try not to think about this."

"That's impossible, Daddy."

"Carolyn, there ain't nothing nobody can do. I'll have Gery contact you."

"What about Aunt Sandy?"

"I haven't seen her. I heard she's a fuckin' wreck. Could you expect anything other than that?"

"I guess not. Oh shit! I forgot. That's how Angelo died too."

Greg entered the room and could not avoid hearing that.

Carol and her father said good-bye, and he promised again to have Vince or Gerald call her as soon as anything happened. Greg sat on the floor, guzzling one beer, while two other beers sat prepared. He lit a joint, took a hit, and passed it to her.

"Who was Angelo?" Greg asked.

"Aunt Sandy's first husband. Uncle Joseph's brother. Daddy is Sandy's brother, so Angelo was Daddy's brother-in-law too. I know it's strange, but in addition to brothers-in-law, Angelo was also Daddy's third cousin by Uncle Angelo's first marriage and Mom's nephew by her uncle's marriage to Angelo's aunt by her first marriage."

Greg agonized to figure that one out, but to no avail.

Either this shit is really good or that makes no sense.

"How your family is able to keep relationships fuckin' straight without some sort of inbreeding taking place on occasion is nothing short of a fuckin' miracle. Cousins four times removed being married to their second wife's third cousins and shit. Jesus Christ!"

"I know. I'm glad I married outside the family," she said. They could not help but laugh.

"Where was Angelo?" he asked.

"In his toolshed. From what I've heard over the years, he and Daddy were making a bomb. Angelo was still working on it when Daddy went home. He went inside to eat dinner and wasn't paying attention. Then he and Aunt Sandy's kids, all three of them, two girls and one boy, were playing in the toolshed. When Angelo noticed, he ran to get the kids out of there. He tripped over something, and the bomb went off. The kids died on the spot. Angelo hung on for a few days. He told the cops what happened before he died. Aunt Sandy spent the next three years in and out of nuthouses. Daddy went to prison for a year."

"What was he charged with?"

"I really don't know. I was only three when it happened. I've heard over the years that he was charged with all kinds of things. He ended up pleading guilty to illegal possession of explosive material. Illegal possession of firearms. Then he pleaded guilty to some minor stuff too."

"Carol, I never thought I would need to tell you this, especially this soon. When everyone was bringing us the money at the wedding, your dad leaned down and told me he'd kill me if I ever hit you or cheated on you. I told Joseph about it right then. Joseph was the last person I spoke to other than my dad before you and I got in the limo. He told me he warned Willie and for me not to worry. I'm gonna ask you this point-blank. Do you think your dad did this because of us?"

Carol avoided speaking ill of her father her entire life. Presently, she found herself at a crossroads. She could

1. Recount everything she suspected her father of.
2. Continue to verbally defend him and tell a blatant lie to the man she loved.
3. Stay quiet.

She decided on a combination of one and three. The joint they passed back and forth was gone.

"Greg, I don't think he would've done this because of us. Sandy is his sister, so I don't believe he could do that to her. I don't know, but I don't think so." Carol hesitated. "I'm not gonna defend him to you ever again. He's my father, though, and I need to defend him to other people. I hope you understand that. Anything you ever wanna know, ask me. You ought to ask now, while I'm stoned."

"I'm just having real trouble thinking of anything other than Vince

126

right now." Greg could not talk about Willie the Rat at the moment. Nevertheless, he did have one rather trivial question. "Carol, why do people call your father Willie the Rat?"

Carol cast a perplexed look upon Greg. She expected a flurry of questions. This was an enigmatic question. This was the query she feared the most above all others, considering she did not believe the explanation.

"I'll tell you what he told me. When I asked him, he said that he used to loan his dog out to neighbors for a few days to get rid of the rats in their houses. Word got around, and everybody wanted to borrow his dog now and then to chase off the rats. A neighbor called him Willie the Rat, and the name stuck. Probably because of his hygiene. Or lack of it."

"Where did he live when he grew up with this rat-scaring dog?"

"KC. I'm just telling you what he told me."

"Carol, unless the people in his neighborhood were outrageous slobs or lived next to a sewer, Kansas City isn't a haven to big fuckin' rats. None of his neighbors had dogs? His was the only dog capable of chasing away or scaring rats? Come on, Carol."

"Greg, please don't do this. I told you, that's what I've been told. I'm the one who loves you. I'm not my father's keeper."

As day turned into dusk, Greg and Carol talked about their memories of Joseph Giovelli. They spoke of different functions they both attended. He was ashamed he did not remember seeing Carol at those parties, picnics, and other gatherings. However, she understood it was because she had evolved from a girl to a woman gradually over the last few years. She was a bit of a late bloomer.

21

In the intensive care unit of St. Luke's Hospital, a mangled, burned, seemingly partial outer covering of a body that was formerly Joseph Giovelli lay in the hospital bed, mentally and physically wandering in an out of an anesthesia-induced coma. He had written on an Etch-A-Sketch to Vincey that he needed to see a priest immediately.

In less than fifteen minutes, the father that Joseph preferred arrived to give him his last rites of passage. The priest spoke to Joseph. Joseph confessed his sins in scarcely legible writing on the Etch-A-Sketch. Joseph was forgiven. Charley and Vincey spoke to him now.

"Dad, it's me, Vincey." Joseph tried to speak at almost a whisper. His voice was inaudible, so he wrote the words "I love U."

"I love you, too, Dad," Vincey said.

Joseph then showed the words to Charley.

"I love you, too, Dad."

"I lived the bomb. I die by bomb."

Charley and Vincey cried and held hands. The brothers had their free hands on their father.

"I want U 2 decide who take over."

"Who would you like?" Charley asked.

"1 of U 4 now."

"It'll be Charley. He's older, it's only right," Vincey replied.

Joseph fell into anesthetized unconsciousness for thirty minutes, then woke up and began writing exactly where he stopped.

"Get out soon as can 4 kids."

"We've talked about it. We both want to," Vince said. Charley nodded his head yes.

After a long hesitation, Joseph wrote.

"U 2 always knew didn't U."

128

"Know what, Dad?" Charley asked as he and Vincey looked at one another.

"Mom."

The brothers started crying harder. They shook their heads up and down and whispered, "Yes."

"I sorry. I thought it wood help."

Joseph motioned his sons to move in closer so he could speak.

"I sorry, Chary. I love u. I sorry, Vcy. I love u. Tke cre of kids. U shuud get ot soon." With his last breath, Joseph said, "I go see Mom and Dad now. N Angy. U Mom 2." Joseph inhaled then exhaled slowly.

On January 9, 1973, Joseph Giovelli died.

Charles and Vincenzo Giovelli hugged one another, crying. They had funeral arrangements to make.

Joseph had composed on notarized documents his settlements in a living will years before. In several clauses in the will, Joseph preferred cremation if he were to ever perish in any sort of way that would render his body unacceptable for viewing. His death fit with the request.

22

At a quarter past midnight (central time), Greg telephoned his brother to find that Joseph passed away that afternoon. Greg and Carol were unfettered to return home. Greg chartered an airplane that evening.

They were in agony from major jet lag. After two nights in his no-longer bachelor pad, they attended the visitation for Joseph Giovelli.

A wood-based and copper-trimmed urn, crafted by Joseph himself years beforehand, was used for his cremains. The next morning was the funeral. A studio photograph taken less than one month earlier of Joseph and Sandra, Charles and Sandy, Vince and Sally, and all of the grandchildren was symbolically placed in front of the urn.

Gerome Crow spent his entire existence despising violence of any sort. Now he seriously wondered if he squandered feeling that way. Most troublesome to him were the thoughts of revenge he harbored. Gerome did know that someone murdered his best friend. As antiprejudice and antiracist as Gerome had always been, he could not help thinking that it must have been some greaseball that annihilated Joe.

When most La Cosa Nostra bosses passed away, it had been little less than a monumental event. Joseph Giovelli was not the typical boss. Infamous La Cosa Nostra members from around the United States were present to pay their respects. Unlike many bosses or members, Joseph had never spent one minute in jail. It had also been rumored among members that Joseph was a renegade that made two non-Italian persons into Friends of Ours.

Although there would be no organized procession after the service, the cavalcade of vehicles destined for the Giovelli estate was mind-boggling. To make this gloomy episode even more surreal, several marked and unmarked police cruisers lined the streets in unmistakable fashion. Local police and federal government helicopters swarmed the cloudy, snowy skies above.

Police lightly interrogated William Cassivano in his home. At the time,

130

he was not a suspect. He was at the visitation and funeral. Substantially more noticeable than all the infamous figures present was the absence of one individual: Nicholas Cibella. Nick was in Las Vegas at the time of the explosion and subsequent death. Presumably, Nick did not know.

During the reception, the elder Sandra Giovelli looked older than her age. She was obedient to the unmistakable care of a psychiatrist.

Following the reception, Gerald, Greg, Charles, and Vince parted with their wives briefly and discussed the location of where to meet tomorrow. This time, Greg suggested his own home.

Hugs all around. Greg and Vince spent a tearful ten minutes away from the remainder of the group reminiscing about Joseph. Greg was positively on some sort of tranquilizer. His speech was intensely lethargic and slurred. Nobody noticed except for Vince. Vince was difficult for Greg to offend. Carol witnessed Greg take it previously and did not wish to take one. In comparison to Greg, she had little experience with downers. She only knew that downers or depressants of any kind, including alcohol, affected her memory. She needed to remember this.

Greg asked her to drive. They slid into her new black Corvette and drove home at a leisurely pace. The first full day back at home, she had selected her black Corvette. Greg had not selected his new Corvette yet. It would be a constant remembrance of Joseph. When Carol reminded him it was a wedding present from his father as well, he promised her he would select the new automobile after the honeymoon.

From the interior of a home neighboring the Giovelli estate, surveillance photographs of the visitors were taken.

23

Before the meeting started, Gerald and Charles questioned Greg. They asked if he could function. Greg was obviously severely intoxicated. Was he drunk now, or did he just stink of booze from last night? Last night it was. Greg perceived that Vince was not concerned.

"I'm still on my honeymoon. What I do on my time in my house is guess whose business? That's right . . . mine. Now it's Carol's business too. When I told her the three of you were meeting me here to discuss *bussssinessss*, she went out in the cold to shop instead of staying in here where she should be. It's still our honeymoon. I didn't know the two of you were perfect," Greg said sarcastically. "I didn't know the two of you were gonna judge or analyze me. I think you guys should leave now if you're concerned with me."

Just to show Gerald and Charles that he did not care what they thought of him, Greg opened the refrigerator and retrieved three beers. He handed Vince one, chugged most of one, dumped the remaining swallow on Gerald's head, threw the empty bottle in the trash, and sat down at the table with one. He opened it and flicked the cap at his brother's face. Gerald and Charles got the message. Vince could not ward off the temptation and busted his gut laughing. Charles joined in as Gerald wiped beer foam from his face and used paper towels to mop his hair.

"I get the point, Gregory. Let's begin and end this quick so I can go home, shower, and change clothes so I don't reek of a brewery like you."

Following a momentary period of clearing the laughter, the meeting began.

During the conference, Gerald was assured that the skimming from the Las Vegas casinos would continue, with the payouts going directly to Charles. Although he did not express his feelings, Greg did not worry about the skimming either way. The money they were making lawfully in Las Vegas was more than enough.

By designation of Joseph, his son Charles would now be the boss. *Boss of a stupid club for Boy Scouts who like to murder.*

Charles and Vincenzo Giovelli easily realized that Nicholas Cibella was responsible for their father's death. Nick was disgusted with the fact that Joseph had made two men who were non-Italians. They were convinced that William Cassivano was not involved in this. The Giovelli brothers assured Greg that his new father-in-law was intelligent enough not to have his sister's second husband murdered in virtually the same method her first husband was killed. Willie would not put his sister through this again. Willie knew his sister could become suicidal. Joe was a friend and brother-in-law to Willie anyway. Emotionally, Willie could not have murdered Joe.

"Vince and I talked about it before the funeral and then a little bit again this morning. Sandy isn't going to be able to stay in that house. It's a constant reminder of Dad. She has spent the last four nights alone in a hotel. We have a shrink talking to her twice every day," Charles said.

"What's going to happen to the house?" Gerald asked. Everyone could see that Gerald visualized himself in the contemporary castle.

Have a little gall, you twerp. These guys just lost their father.

Greg flicked a little more beer foam at Gery.

"Guys, let's stop talking business for now. My guardian angel doesn't have enough self-restraint to keep me from pouring beer on Gery right now," Greg said.

In the distance, they could hear sirens from police, ambulances, and fire trucks. Greg walked outside and could not see smoke from a fire. They were accustomed to the sirens this time of year. Kansas City has never been known for quality drivers, particularly in the winter, so they assumed that another traffic accident had occurred on the snowy, icy roads.

Gerald left to go home to shower and change clothes. Vince and Charles stayed behind to have a few beers. It would be a long while before either could be productive.

With the massacre of his father, along with the responsibilities now handed down by him, understandably, Charles wanted to hide from the world. Getting shit-faced blotto with Greg may take his mind off reality for a while.

Although Vince did not have the newfound responsibilities of his brother, he knew he could and would cover up his bereavement temporarily by getting sloshed. Charles and Vince wished Carol were there to partake in the soon-to-be drunken salute to Joseph.

"Guys, I'm gonna take a little nose candy break." Greg winked.

"Greg, don't be stingy. Share," Vince begged. Greg retrieved all the paraphernalia.

"I haven't done coke in so long. I don't know if I should." Charles thought for a few seconds. "Oh, what the hell."

The three of them were wasted in no time.

Carol came home and decided to play catch-up to her husband and cousins. The rule of not smoking in the house was in full force, and all congregated in the garage due to the cold temperature outside.

Charles and Vince had children, so any drugs were forbidden in their households. Because Vince lived so near, he went home and retrieved a portable heater and brought his wife. Charles telephoned his wife, and a babysitter was set up for all the Giovelli children. Lawn chairs and boxes made for comfortable makeshift seating. Soon everyone was trashed, and for the moment, the visions of missing body parts on Joseph had given way to loud, riotous laughter. Thoughts of dead fathers, uncles, father-in-laws, and a best friend's father had been replaced by loud music, seafood linguini in white cream sauce, wine, beer, mixed drinks, cocaine, and marijuana. All was right with the world.

The telephone rang, and they deliberated not answering it. Vince turned the music down and answered.

"Hello," Vince answered, laughing.

"Who is this?"

Vince recognized Willie's voice. "It's Vince, Willie."

"Are you guys having a party or something?"

"It started as a business meeting at noon. Now it's a party in Dad's honor," Vince replied. He glanced at the oven clock to see that it was only four o'clock in the afternoon.

"I called to tell this to my daughter, but I guess I'll tell you. You'd better sit down, Vince."

Vince could hear Willie sobbing. Vince waved Carol off and motioned for everyone to quiet down. The younger Sandra Giovelli turned the stereo completely off.

"What is it, Willie? What's wrong?"

Struggling to get the words out through the tears, Willie spoke.

"Sandy killed herself this morning." The alcohol-and-drug-induced smile suddenly changed into a solemn stare. Everyone knew it was bad news when Vince unintentionally crushed his half-full can of beer with his mammoth hands. He needed a whole two minutes to let that sink in. Vince took a few deep breaths.

"Are you sure?"

"No, Vince, she might have just been sleeping in the hospital morgue when I identified her body. Yes, she's quite dead."

"I'm sorry, Willie. It just shocked me. How, I mean, where?"

"She hung herself from the stair railing in the front hall at the house."

Vince could hear Willie crying. It took Vince a minute to think of something to say.

"Who found her?" Vince asked.

"The maids or the cleaning women. One of them called the cops. I guess an ambulance and fire truck went there also."

Vince remembered the sirens from earlier and thought those must have been the ones tending to the already deceased Sandra Giovelli.

"I'm sorry, Willie, I don't know what to say. Would you like to talk with Carol?" Vince blankly handed the telephone to Carol. She did not say one word before the waterworks started.

Vince told the remainder of the crew about the suicide of the elder Sandra Giovelli. The party atmosphere reversed drastically, yet no one—with the exception of Carol—shed a tear. Vince and Charles had a silent discussion, while Sandy and Sally helped clean.

Greg sat at the kitchen table drinking a bottle of tequila and chasing it with beer. Carol reluctantly hung up the telephone, and everyone went in the garage to smoke. Greg brought a bong and his dwindling bags of cocaine and marijuana into the garage. Everyone looked at him as though that was in very poor taste. Yet as soon as he lit the bong, everyone, except Carol, joined in.

"Honey, I need to go to Mom and Daddy's now," Carol said as she stood, and he continued sitting.

"I'll go with you if you want."

"I don't think that would be a good idea right now in your condition. Sandy was his sister. Daddy would go berserk. Sandy was his sister. I'll just tell him you're consoling Vince and Charles. I need to drive the Thing. The streets were pretty slippery today. Daddy doesn't drink at all. Sandy was his sister."

"Am I obviously that wasted?"

"Not to other people that are stoned, but to Daddy you would be. Sandy was his sister. I need to clean up and desmellify a little myself. Sandy was his sister. Daddy doesn't drink. Or rarely I guess. He'll be able to smell the booze, but pot he won't tolerate. Sandy was his sister."

"Carol, you're jumpy again. You keep repeating yourself. Do yourself a favor and take some downers before you go. Are you gonna stay there tonight? It's still officially our honeymoon," Greg said as he put a hand in her back pocket.

"No, I just need to go over there for an hour or so. Sandy was his sister. This has been a memorable honeymoon. I love you. Sandy was his sister."

"I love you too. I think I understand that Sandy was his sister," Greg said, laughing.

Greg and Carol kissed for a few minutes and drew the attention of the two other couples in the garage. Carol did a quick cleanup, took some downers, and drove away.

"Carol is going over to her parents' house now. Are you guys all right?" Greg held the tequila bottle like a microphone. Sandy, Sally, Charles, and Vince sat on the makeshift seats and grinned as they snorted more cocaine.

"Greg, we can pay for some more if you want," Charles said.

"Don't worry about it. Consider this my condolence dish."

Greg did not intend for that to be comical. Because of the condition of his guests, they all began laughing hysterically. Greg could not understand the laughter. He did not want to appear foolish as if he missed something of great humor, so he laughed with them.

"Greg, I'm sorry, but we're laughing at you," Vince confessed. "You're holding the bottle like a microphone. You're even laughing into it."

Greg stood up and sang "My Way" into the bottle. He had an excellent singing voice. He hit all the high notes with ease. His drunken actions and stumbling around were hilarious. At the end of the song, he bowed and fell on the floor, while they applauded. Vince stood up and questioned Greg, who was facedown on the floor.

"Are you all right?" Vince asked, laughing.

Greg began to speak, then took a big swig of tequila and spoke into the bottle to say, "I'm fine." Everyone laughed harder, if that was possible. Vince assisted Greg to his feet. Greg walked to the table then stumbled and fell backward into a trash can. Greg struggled again to stand up and eventually sat down on a box. He lined up two lines of cocaine on his mirror and snorted it. Quickly, he seemed to sober up.

Sally began speaking of the tragedy of the past week. The others begged her to drop the subject. After a half hour, they finished the blow. Sandy hinted that they should get more. Charles and Vince disappeared for what seemed ten minutes. Sandy and Sally stayed behind to help clean. Greg attempted to clean some of the mess between falling and stumbling. In the midst of his attempt at cleaning, he opened another pint bottle of tequila. The Giovellis arranged for the babysitter to stay the night. When Charles and Vince returned, Greg glanced at the clock and realized they had been gone for nearly two hours. They had purchased nearly two ounces of cocaine and an ounce of marijuana. Carol came home and immediately wanted—no, *needed,* more. Soon, Greg was most in control.

What started out as a business meeting at noon the day before had turned into a full-fledged party still going strong at ten o'clock the next morning. By two o'clock in the afternoon, Greg and Carol were the first ones to call it quits and go to sleep. The Giovelli brothers and their wives reluctantly agreed to call it quits also and drove home.

24

Another funeral. Two in less than one week. This one without the great number of people. A modest turnout at best. The elder Sandra Giovelli also elected to be cremated and buried in an urn close to her children that passed away nearly half her life ago.

Now it was up to Charles and Vince to sell the property. They were determined to keep some of the nicer automobiles, including a 1937 Silver Cloud Rolls-Royce. They actually had no difficulty dividing the valuable assets. All the items were paid for, and as executors of the will, they fairly distributed the remaining cars and cash to relatives, with Willie receiving the majority: three cars and an undisclosed amount of cash. To make things appear legal, trifling checks were fashioned so they could be subjected to inheritance taxes.

Willie was intensely glum to see his sister die. However, he had no complaints about the cars and cash granted him.

The brothers retained some of the more elegant jewelry, both male and female. Charities were to be granted virtually all of the clothes after certain relatives selected some garments. The only items that presented problems were the items that no amount of money could purchase: pictures, mementos, and woodworks Joseph had crafted with his own hands.

Gerald had expressed interest in the house, so it was determined that he was the only person who desired it and could afford it without going through the hassle of a traditional sale. When the cash would come in from the casinos in Las Vegas, the Giovelli brothers would deduct an additional amount as a mortgage payment.

Greg was granted the first opportunity to purchase his brother's home. No interest. Carol beat the odds and was as happy as could be in their small home. Greg would also never live in a home without the master bedroom on the first floor. Carol assured Greg that there was no need to search for another home until they began a family. She spoke too soon.

25

Carol knew she was late. Without telling Greg, she scheduled an appointment with a doctor. She was very pregnant. She was too excited to continue work that day. Besides, with the money Greg was made of, her working was totally unnecessary, although she enjoyed it. She quit smoking immediately.

That night, Greg telephoned and asked her to join him and some friends for drinks. She knew he wanted to party all night, as he so customarily did, so she went. She could not drink alcohol, so she quietly asked the bartender to bring her a club soda with lime. There were too many people around that night to announce to her husband that she was with child. The announcement would need to wait until the next day. She needed to wake up early, so she exited the saloon, as Greg was already sloshed by nine o'clock. Greg's drinking and partying had never disturbed her until that night.

Greg's drinking problem escalated quickly to hazardous levels. Carol understood that Joseph's dying fueled the escalation. She remembered her pledge to him when she first moved in about not lecturing him in regard to the drinking. She promised herself never to go back on her word. She would tell him she was pregnant in the morning. But, more than likely, it would not be until he woke up.

Greg stumbled from the bar and drove home at three o'clock in the morning. He drove his red Corvette and must have fallen asleep on the wheel. Driving south on Ward Parkway Boulevard, he smashed head-on into the Meyer Circle Fountain.

In the middle of upper bracket mansions, the city constructed a majestic fountain in the center of the boulevard. There were three lanes of traffic in each direction. Drivers are to slow down considerably to maneuver their automobiles around this fountain. Scenic yes. Practical no.

What the fuck was that? Oh shit! A fountain. The glass idn't broke. Just back

138

out and go home quick. Won't back up. Hmm? Get out and see. Door won't open eider. Hmm? Oh that's the fuckin' window thing. Here's the door thing. Ouch! Oh, fuck, slipped on somethin'. That's gonna bruise. Car not stuck on anythin'. Hmm? Somebody dropped a bag of weed here. Shut de door. Strait de wheels and punches it, man. Out of dat. Well, now I not sure where I live. Dat way. Soon I get home. Smokes, where is dey? Oh, here dey is, man. Go home fast. I fuckin' drunk, man.

Greg pulled in the driveway and parked the mangled car right in front. He stumbled and collapsed two or three times while weaving his way to the front door. He was anything but quiet opening the door, and Carol could not avoid hearing him. She came out of the bedroom to find Greg a blood-covered mess. It was apparent that someone had beaten him badly. She panicked. There was a gash above his right eye and his upper lip. His nose continued to bleed profusely. He was, by far, much more intoxicated on alcohol than she had ever seen him. He noticed the blood and sat down. She wet down a kitchen towel and started cleaning his face.

"Oh my god! Greg, what happened? Who did this to you?"

"The dumb shits who put that fountain where I was drivin'."

"You didn't get beaten up? You wrecked your car?"

"I thing so. I mean, I think so."

"I thought someone hit you." She exhaled.

"The damn fountain did. Go kick its ass." He laughed. She could not hold back and started laughing also.

Carol did a sufficient cleaning and sauntered out into the bitterly cold night to look at the new Corvette. The windshield was not busted, but the entire front end was crumpled like an accordion. She immediately moved it to the garage.

"Greg, the front license plate is gone. That's like leaving your name and number at the scene. Go get in the shower quick and clean up. I imagine the police are gonna be here soon."

As late as it was, Carol instantly telephoned Anthony "the Ant" Gilante.

She communicated quietly so Greg would not hear whom she was speaking with. Greg stumbled to the bathroom to do as instructed. Sure enough, the police knocked on the door while Greg was passed out, sitting in the full-blast and stinging shower.

"Carol, I take it Greg left his license plate behind at the scene to make it easy on us." It was Kenny Bondano, the guardian angel hovering over Greg in the police department. "Ant just radioed me. Is Greg OK?" Kenny smiled.

"Yes, he's just banged up a little bit," Carol responded, visibly embarrassed.

"Here's the license plate. When you get Greg sobered up, have him call me at home. But quick. He didn't hit any other cars, but the Meyer Fountain might as well be a lawn sprinkler now. As far as we know, it wasn't witnessed by anyone. Nobody has called and reported anything."

Carol gave her brother Paul's widowed wife's fourth cousin a kiss. What a close family.

It was next to impossible for Carol to wake Greg. She did the next best thing. She turned off the water in the shower and placed a pillow behind his head, as it was evident that he intended on spending the night naked on porcelain. If not for her, he would have used the ceramic wall as a pillow. Greg had done a respectable job of wiping off the blood.

She realized there was no point in attempting to go back to sleep. It was Ash Wednesday, and she was supposedly a devout Catholic. It was necessary for Carol to go to the cathedral, then return home to wake Greg and demand he telephone Kenny immediately.

By the time she returned home, Greg had made his way to the bed. He heard her enter the room and, of course, had no recollection of his automobile accident a few hours before. He only had a few bruises. His cuts were minor and would not require stitches. He did not look to have a broken nose. She leaned over his bruised face and kissed him as he came to.

"Honey, you really messed up last night. Do you remember anything?"

"Not really. I remember you cleaning my face. Who beat me up?" He slurred.

"You did, honey. You had a car accident last night. You need to get it together fast and call Kenny. You crashed into the Meyer Fountain on Ward Parkway."

Greg's eyes bugged out. "What happened to your head? You've got shit on your forehead!"

"Cut it out, Greg." Carol laughed. "You know I'm Catholic."

"What does that have do with having shit on your forehead?"

As Greg attempted to raise his arm to wipe her forehead, Carol tried hard not to laugh. She could not resist and fell on the bed laughing.

"It's Ash Wednesday, Greg. I'm Catholic, get it?"

I guess on Ash Wednesday, Catholics smear shit on their heads.

"Where's the car?"

"I moved it to the garage. It's trashed. Call Kenny quick." Carol flashed her brilliant smile. "Greg, I was gonna tell you something last night, but you were surrounded by all those drunks."

"Carol, stop. I asked you never to call me that."

"I didn't say you were. I don't think you're a drunk, just some friends. I'm sorry. That was way out of line. Anyway, I need to give you some news that I think, or should I say I hope, is gonna make you happy." Carol gazed affectionately at Greg to see that he tried to pay attention.

For the first time, she wondered if this pregnancy was a mistake and if she should make up something else to announce. Deep down, she knew it was not a mistake. They had talked about children several times.

"Honey, look at me please. I was late, so I went to the doctor yesterday. I'm pregnant. You're gonna be a daddy."

Any shred of a hangover immediately vanished—mentally anyway. His face brightened up with a smile. He leaped out of the bed and fell on the floor. Major rug burn on his elbow did not keep him from jumping back up and shouting for joy. He jumped up and down on the bed like a child. He hit his head on the ceiling and collapsed beside her. He kissed her entire face. He ripped open her blouse and kissed her stomach.

"Carol, this is,"—he could not find the right words—"you're incredible. Call in sick today. You can't go to work like this. Quit."

"Greg, hold on. I can't quit. I own them." Carol laughed.

"At least today then. Please, please, please?"

"OK, today only. And only if you'll call Kenny when I get off the phone and take care of the fountain."

I'm a man now. She's more beautiful than ever before. I didn't think it was possible, but I love her more now. Look at her. God, thank you. She's an angel.

Greg telephoned Kenny. Greg then made a generous tax-deductible donation to repair the fountain as a gift to the city that had been so generous to him.

141

26

Carol desperately wanted to keep the pregnancy silent until she started showing. Greg began notification of seemingly all mankind in two days. Willie was angry with Greg initially. Then he realized how happy Carol was and actually started liking Greg. He would not admit it publicly. Willie was not sure, but he may have started to love Greg for the bundle of joy Greg implanted in his Carolyn.

Greg remembered the advice from Joseph Giovelli and immediately quit smoking. He absolved doing drugs for the most part. However, quitting drinking proved a much more difficult task. Overall, he was very well behaved.

They purchased a larger home on the Kansas side of State Line Road. They continued to live in the smaller home while the larger house was being renovated. The new home was basically a shell. Greg was unquestionably not as hung up on appearances as his brother, but he wanted the new home to be extra special.

There would be no swimming pool for now because of the likelihood of an infant or toddler drowning. A four-car attached garage would be sufficient at the moment. The master bedroom would need to be on the first floor with a connected nursery. After the baby was old enough, it could become a sitting room. All the other bedrooms were on the second floor. The company owned the smaller house they were living in. However, in order for the company to continue owning it for visitors, they would compensate Greg for it.

Carol defied what Vince had told Greg about the increase of a pregnant woman's temper. She did display an unusual craving for extra spicy food. Very unnatural cravings. Jalapenos straight from the jar. Crushed red peppers on everything, including the jalapenos.

The next few months were a living fantasy for Greg and Carol. At the time, doctors were able to accurately predict an unborn child's sex by the heartbeat. By August, when they moved into the larger home in Mission Hills, they knew they were going to have a boy. Again, they discussed names.

"What if the doctors are wrong and we have a girl?" she asked.

"Then she gets the most beautiful name ever—Bertha Crow." They laughed because an extremely rude elderly waitress in a breakfast diner they frequented was named Bertha. "Seriously, Carol, I would love it if we named her Carolyn."

"No, I wouldn't do that any more than you would want a boy to be named Gregory. I should probably name her after my mother, but I don't think Margaret Crow would be a very nice name. I really like Amber."

"I like it too, but there's already an Amber close to us. Amber is out. What about Robyn with a *Y*?"

"Robyn Crow. You've gotta be kidding. Why not just call her Bird Girl?" They started laughing. "Greg, I've got it . . . Candice. Candy Crow. That would be cute and memorable. Candice Cassivano Crow."

"Candice Cassivano Crow. I'm sorry, Carol, but Cassivano isn't a middle name. Candice is good, though. I'll tell you what, let Carolyn be her middle name. Then her initials would still be CCC. I think that stands for something in Roman numerals." Greg shrugged his shoulders and sipped his beer.

"OK, that's fine. But what if the doctors are right and we have a boy? I know you said Gregory is out. What about naming him after your brother?"

"No, I don't like the name Gerald any more than I like the name Gregory, first or middle."

"What's Gery's middle name?"

"Are you ready for this?" Greg smiled. "Alvin."

"No good. What about naming him after my father?"

"You wanna name our kid Rat? Rat Crow? Imagine what it will look like in the phone book: Crow Rat. Sounds like a new fuckin' species." He laughed. She tried not to laugh, but failed.

"Look, if we can give a girl the middle name of Carolyn, then your middle name is only right for a boy."

"Matthew is fine. I don't mind that at all. I actually started trying to use it as a first name when I was a kid. I tried too late—everyone already knew me as Greg." Greg sipped his beer.

"OK, something Matthew Crow. You know, my father's middle name is Daniel. Daniel Matthew Crow. That would be a good name. An honorable biblical name."

"I didn't know your father's middle name is Daniel. My father is

Gerome Daniel Crow. We name him Daniel Matthew Crow and tell both fathers that the kid is named after their middle name and my middle name."

On October 22, 1973, the most beautiful child in the world, Daniel Matthew Crow, was born.

On December 7, 1973, Victor Spelo was found murdered and stuffed in the trunk of his car. He was in the parking lot of his newly founded Spelo Development Company. Victor had been missing for two weeks. He had been shot five times in the head.

BOOK 2

27

The Giovelli faction of La Cosa Nostra activity gradually slowed down to nothing. Almost. Charles Giovelli relayed a message to Nicholas Cibella that he and others were no longer interested in anything, except the real estate and construction industries.

In early 1975, Kansas City had just completed construction of the Bartle Hall Convention Center. The center faced the notorious Kansas City Strip. The notorious Kansas City Strip was not a steak; it was a haven for gambling, prostitution, pornography, and narcotics trafficking, along with many other widespread vices. Because those vices were an embarrassment to the city convention bureau, and due to the inability to shut the particular businesses down unless they were caught in the act, the city came up with an elementary alternate plan: relocate the businesses to an area that would cater to the patrons. Essentially, institute an unwritten "red light" district. River Quay!

The business owners on the strip agreed with the munificent grants given them by the city. Owners of family-oriented businesses in the River Quay were not happy when the relocated adult businesses began destroying their businesses because of the proximity.

Peter Cassivano had recently quit college and desperately desired to open a strip club. However, new businesses that were not in the relocated nightclub district would have trouble receiving the proper zoning.

Willie the Rat would take care of it for his son. Willie would communicate with David Vasallo, a made member whose son, infamous chef and restaurant owner Fred Vasallo, carried substantial weight in the district with city councilman Robert Martinez.

After several discussions, the Vasallos were not interested in working with Willie and Peter unless they received a substantial sum of the profits.

Willie summoned councilman Robert Martinez to his mechanics garage. Anthony "the Ant" Gilante and Willie's friend, Missouri state representative Alex "the Mouth" Ferrino, also went along. When Robert arrived with his unarmed bodyguard, Anthony, Peter and Alex greeted them. The attendance of an important representative such as Alex the Mouth relaxed the tension. When Robert walked in, Peter slammed the garage door shut. Robert and his unarmed bodyguard were frisked and ordered at gunpoint to sit in chairs facing Willie. Alex "the Mouth" Ferrino immediately sped off. His presence was used only to lure Robert.

Robert was stripped and tied to the chair, which was anchored to sheet metal that was fastened to the floor. A wooden box with greased-down interior walls was placed around Robert, while the bodyguard had been taken to another room where earmuffs and a black stocking were placed over his head. Robert was sprayed on the legs with a sticky substance.

"Robert, I'm gonna make this real easy for you, spick—or should I say, Roberto?" Willie laughed. "Is it Robert or Roberto, spick?"

"It's Roberto," Roberto said, freaked.

"Just to show you that I'm a man of serious intent, here are a few friends." Willie dumped three large rats on Roberto's lap. Because of the sticky substance on his legs, the rats moved extremely slowly. Willie slapped Roberto teasingly on the top of his head and his back. "I just wanted to see if your back is really wet." Everyone laughed hysterically. "My son wants to open a strip joint in your district. Are you gonna have a problem with that?"

"I won't, Willie." Roberto's voice was of great composure. Nevertheless, his eyes expressed horror.

"What are you gonna do to make sure he gets zoned for this?"

"Anything I can," Roberto said.

Willie dumped three more rats onto Roberto's lap when he could not help notice that Roberto had a generously endowed erection.

"Good answer. Is this turning you on, pervert?"

"No, I'm nervous."

"Good god, beaner! That's what I call a dick and a half. Peter, Ant, you've gotta look at this spick's dick."

Anthony laughed and said no. Peter walked to the wooden cell to gape at the huge penis. When Peter saw it along with the rats, he stuck his finger down his own throat and purposely vomited in the cell and on Roberto. Peter walked to the bathroom to wipe his face, laughing. With all of his attributes, Anthony Gilante was intensely fearful of mice and rats. Even hamsters.

Willie pointed a gun with a silencer down at the face of Roberto. "My son does whatever the fuck he wants down here. He can run whores out of the Quay, and no one better stop him. Anyone who gets in the way will die.

148

I'll kill anyone I need, including politicians. Understand?" Willie shouted. "Do you understand me, Pablo, taco?"

"Yes, Willie, I understand. I'll do whatever it takes," Roberto said, extremely calm.

"Boys, clean him up. I think, or at least I hope, for his and his family's sake, that this Mexican understands."

Anthony and Peter elevated the jail cell from around Roberto. The two rats not stuck to his legs scurried away. Anthony jumped back and then ran outside. Peter laughed at Anthony. Peter wore rubber gloves and pried the four remaining rats off of Roberto's legs. Peter placed the rodents in a paper bag and threw it into a metal can. The rats were driven five blocks to the base of the Missouri River and given their freedom.

Roberto was untied by Anthony and supplied with a rag containing a cleaning substance and shown to the washroom where the door stayed open. Roberto was given back his clothes and an unopened can of beer to prove it had not been tampered with. His unarmed bodyguard came out of an adjoining room, smiling. The two were granted permission and drove away. Not one block away, the driver spoke.

"Well, I didn't know what to think. I was scared to death at first, but that was all right."

"What are you talking about? I feel like I just left a scene from one of *The Godfather* movies. What happened to you?" Roberto asked.

Roberto and his unarmed bodyguard compared stories. It turned out that after the unarmed bodyguard had been blinded, deafened, and immobilized, he'd been given a blowjob, straddled, then screwed by an unknown girl.

"She might have been fat, though. I could feel her tits and stomach next to mine." The bodyguard giggled.

Roberto wanted to slap his unarmed bodyguard. "Maybe you're the one who's fat then. I would take getting screwed by a fat chick any day over being barfed on, having six rats gnaw at me, and having a gun pointed right between my fucking eyes!" Silence.

Roberto wished he were not a city councilman. He decided that when his term expired, he would go back into the private sector as a lawyer.

Within two weeks, the city denied Peter Cassivano's application for a strip joint in the location he favored. Roberto explained to Willie that he'd voted for it. That was all he could do. Roberto would keep working on it. Roberto suggested to Willie that they open a jazz club and gradually change the atmosphere. Then the zoning could easily be manipulated as a "grandfather clause." In the meantime, Roberto could use some cash to begin bribing people in the liquor control and entertainment divisions of city hall. Likewise, the zoning commissioners could easily switch the zoning to CX in any location they wanted. Everybody had a price.

Once again, Greg was called upon. Greg issued his usual plea of "Don't tell me anything." The cash was not that important to him. It quite simply was not that much money to Greg. Willie publicly admitted now that he loved his son-in-law.

Within months, Peter was granted CX zoning to open a strip joint. Because Peter was so fond of his status as an uncle, the club would be named Uncle Peter's Tavern. Peter had already begun constructing the joint to open as a jazz club. Giovelli Construction was hired.

Charles and Vince had an insignificant number of their men build the club without an advertisement sign. The design embarrassed them. The building was constructed cheaply and quickly. Cement block construction textured with stucco paint. The building, inside and out, took less than thirty days to construct.

When Uncle Peter's Tavern opened, it was not the smashing success Peter and Willie expected it to be. The principal reason for the lack of success was too much quality competition. The Warehouse Inn, a four-star restaurant with scantily clad waitresses and opened by licensed chef Fred Vasallo and his father, David, was less than two blocks away. It contained an after-hours nightclub and strip joint that illegally operated in the basement. Considering the reputation the Vasallo family had, authorities looked the other way. The Vasallo family already owned one restaurant in the River Quay that had a very respectable clientele. They had a mini casino with every game, except slot machines in the basement of their original restaurant.

Peter always had a decent crowd of men who were not hungry. Nevertheless, Willie and Peter knew it could and would be better.

Less than one week later, the Warehouse Inn was severely damaged by a fire during closed hours. A city engineer who accepted a bribe from Roberto Martinez determined that the Vasallos could not reopen without a complete teardown and rebuild. The engineer subsequently condemned the facility.

David Vasallo knew the person who was responsible for the fire that put the Warehouse Inn out of business. David was an out-of-control made member of La Cosa Nostra who needed revenge. David announced to reporters that he knew Willie the Rat was responsible for the fire. David announced to reporters and police that if he or his adult son and daughter were ever murdered, they should suspect Willie the Rat. David announced that the Warehouse Inn would be rebuilt and would open again as soon as possible.

150

28

The money Crow Brothers Real Estate Company created legitimately was phenomenal. Shopping centers, office parks, and hotels across the nation were lawfully acquired or constructed. Most of the money could be attributed to Gerald. However, Greg overwhelmed his brother by exhibiting immense knowledge in the world of real estate investment and development.

Crow Brothers became so affluent by early 1976 that four additional small casinos were purchased in Las Vegas. The process would remain the same, with the Giovelli brothers putting up half the money as "straw men." The skimming operation worked so successfully on the three previous casino purchases that nobody could see a need to adjust perfection and attach the Giovellis as legal owners to the general warranty deeds. Charles would simply make the necessary adjustment to the "lettuce sandwiches" to cover the taxes paid on the justifiable money made by Crow Brothers.

Candice Carolyn Crow was born April 18, 1976. After her birth, Greg and Carol decided to halt childbearing temporarily. Carol needed to go back on birth control pills to clear up the acne that had returned.

Fourteen additional Italian delis, along with two additional floral shops, opened throughout the metropolitan area. Carol and her partner, Patty, had designated in each deli a person they trusted to assist in the accounting and skimming operation. Greg invested his own cash to assist in expanding the deli chain. A portion of the skimmed cash was used to refund Greg's generous investment. Greg did not desire to own the deli chain. He only wanted to make Carol happy. Although Carol was half owner of the deli, Patty controlled the majority of the day-to-day operations. Carol was engrossed in raising two beautiful children and briskly attending college.

151

29

July 21, 1976

Crow Brothers Real Estate and Giovelli Construction teamed up to sponsor a "Night at the Royals." The Crow and Giovelli brothers insisted that none of the workers or independent contractors or members of their families paid for tickets. Over seven thousand people had reserved seats to the sold-out Kansas City Royals game against the Boston Red Sox.

Greg made a drunken ass of himself again at this annual affair. Carol wanted to beg him to slow down tonight, but she promised she would never do that. If people did not know Greg, they would swear he just tried to be funny and lead cheers along the way.

Vince was in no condition to help. Greg and Vince proclaimed this the night to get drunk with the common man. Carol Crow and Sally Giovelli decided to let their husbands make fools of themselves again tonight. They sat away from their husbands and talked.

Greg and Vince were playfully arguing trivia, as they did at all sporting events. As a self-proclaimed baseball expert, that night would live in infamy because of a prophetic statement by Gregory Crow.

"Vince, that's the fourth hotdog you've shoveled down your throat tonight."

"I didn't know you were counting."

"I'm just saying that's a lot for somebody who's already fat enough to fit in a clown suit without any padding."

"You're a drunk, Greg."

"You're a fat slob, Vince."

"You know me better than to call me a slob. I could throw your ass down these stairs, over the railing, onto the first deck, and I'll swear, none of my people would see a thing," Vince said, laughing.

152

Just at that instant, a wicked line-drive foul ball bounced off the facing of the second deck.

"Holy shit! What a sweet swing. That was hit as hard as any baseball I've ever seen. Forget me talking about your fatness for a while and look at this kid batting."

The very next pitch was hit. A screamer into right center field that would have ripped the arm off any player who dared catch it. A double.

"Lucky hit. Who is the guy anyway?"

"Number five. George Brett."

"You really are drunk, Gregy. I've never even heard of this guy. Who is he?"

"He's a kid."

"I guess I don't follow players I've never heard of."

"Write down the name. George Brett."

"Why should I write the name down of a player that's never done anything? One lucky hit, and you're already putting him in the Hall of Fame. I've never heard of him, Gregy. You don't know what the fuck you're talking about." Vince waved his hand in a sarcastic motion at Greg.

"He's a kid. That kid is gonna be a superstar."

"You're gonna need a ride home. You're very definitely a drunk," Vince said.

"Are you saying that I'm a drunk or that I'm drunk right now?"

"Both! You're a drunk that's drunk. I'm pretty drunk too."

"That's a mouthful. Someone your size getting drunk would need to consume a million times as much alcohol as someone my size."

"It's not my fault you're a skinny little wimp."

"Sticks and stones may break my bones, but you are a fat fuckin' wop."

When the game ended, Charles Giovelli and Gerald Crow were shaking the hands of employees and contractors as they exited. Gerald was understandably embarrassed by his brother's behavior. Charles lectured Gerald not to make a public scene and to "let it go." Charles's own brother was an enormous embarrassment. After the game, just as before, a party in the parking lot ensued. After the party, everyone drove home safely.

Sally and Vince permitted their children to stay at Charles and Sandy's home that night with their cousins. After over two hours in bed asleep, the telephone rang, and Vince answered. The babysitter said that Charles and Sandy had not shown up yet, and she needed to go home. The babysitter assured Vince that Charles and Sandy were never late without calling. Vince and Sally had no choice but to sit with the children. Because of the drunk condition he was in, Vince sat with the children, while Sally drove

153

the babysitter home, then drove back to her own home. Vince passed out on the sofa.

At approximately three forty-five in the morning, Sally returned to Charles and Sandy's house with tears in her eyes. The police had approached her house with the tragic notification that Charles and Sandra Giovelli had been killed while they were getting in their automobile in the parking lot of Paglissi's Bar & Grill, a tavern near their home on the northeastern side of Kansas City. Each of them had apparently been shot several times. Kenneth Bondano had been promoted to homicide detective and would be working the case. Vince or Sally needed to make the official identification.

Vince knew Charley and Sandy would patronize Paglissi's Bar every time they went out for the evening. Vince knew they would have a maximum of one cocktail then leave. Vince knew someone else knew that information also. Vince had not cried yet. He remained in shock. Vince already ran an entire catalogue of names in his head.

Sally telephoned Carol Crow to have her stay with the children while she drove Vince to identify the bodies.

Being the daughter of Willie the Rat never hardened Carol to the point that she would not cry; she did. Greg was absolutely hysterical. Carol needed to leave so she could stay with all the Giovelli children, Vince and Sally's children, Amber, Sarah, and Vince Jr.; and the two suddenly orphaned girls, Trisha and Tina.

Carol could not quiet Greg down. She had seen him sad or angry before. Compared to what she was accustomed to with men in her family, Greg's temper was mild to the point of being comical. This time, she quickly became gravely frightened.

He yanked the clock radio from the night table and threw it through the bay window in the bedroom. The noise woke three-month-old Candice. Carol picked up the baby and brought her upstairs to a second-floor nursery. Greg tried to apologize through his tears. She understood. His grip while hugging her for comfort was so severely tight that she could not breathe. He unknowingly bit through the strap holding her purse. He cried so violently that she feared he would dehydrate himself again and pass out. His breathing was so labored that she worried he would have a stroke. The expletives flying out of his mouth would have been offensive to a sailor. She was finally able to calm him down by pouring him a tall glass of bourbon and water. He promptly finished it and threw the glass against a wall. He promised her he would not break anything else while she was gone.

Please, no, Charles. God no. More bourbon. No, just a beer. Where are you at, Charles? I hope you're up there. I don't want you to be down there. I know

154

you are, though. Well, I'm usually wrong. I hope I am now too. I need to know you're up there. There's no way to let me know. I think maybe you are up there. Excellent father. Great husband. Great son. Great friend. I hope you've seen one of those Catholic priests. I believe you are up there. I love you, Charles.

Greg telephoned his father and told him. Greg then telephoned his brother. In minutes, Gerald loudly pulled onto Greg's driveway. Gerald poured himself a glass of vodka and asked Greg if he had any tranquilizers. They sat at the table, crying.

Carol came home by dawn and joined them after she checked on the babies. She hugged Gerald. She had obviously done her share of crying in the past few hours.

"How are Vincey and Sally?" Gerald asked Carol.

"Sally said Vince was still in shock or didn't really believe it until he viewed the faces. Then he lost it. Sally didn't look at the bodies, but she said one of the guys there told her that Charles had been shot four times in the chest and once in the side of the head. I think she said the guy told her that Charles was stabbed ten or eleven times. Sandy was shot three or four times and stabbed several times. Vince was wearing dark glasses when he came back. He took them off when he came in." Carol began to cry hard again. "He hugged me, then he fell on the floor. Sally said the only thing Vince said on the way back to the house was he didn't think he could tell Charley's daughters. Sally told him she would tell Trisha and Tina."

After several minutes of crying, Greg said something Carol and Gerald had not thought of.

"Vince told me one night about, I don't know, maybe a couple of weeks ago, that Charles smoked so much, he expected him to die of cancer before the girls grew up. He worried that then he'd need to give Sandy money all the time to raise the girls. I don't think Vince ever thought that Charles and Sandy would die together. If Vince and Sally can't take the girls, then we should."

Carol gazed at her husband affectionately, with tears rolling down her face. "Greg, that's the nicest, most generous thing I think I've heard anyone say . . . ever. We'll do it. If they can't take the girls, we will."

Gerald began crying again at the surprising fact that he had not thought of that before his unmistakably intoxicated brother did.

Gerald also knew it could present a problem, having two awkward-aged boys living with two girls of an equally awkward age.

As they wrapped up, Gerald informed Greg that he would cancel all appointments for the next week and would not be going into the office until after the funerals. As Gerald was leaving, he and his brother had a conversation on the driveway.

"Gregory, I'm scared. How we ended up being wrapped up in this mess is something I still don't believe. At first, I thought it was an honor. Now it scares the hell out of me. Does Carol know?"

"We've never talked about it, but she knows. I'm sure her father or the Ant told her. I still don't know what benefit it brings. The only thing I've gotten from it is total paranoia. I'm constantly looking over my shoulder. I can't believe I need to carry a gun everywhere I go. What about Sherry, does she know?" Greg swayed back and forth. There would be no doubt to anyone driving by that Greg was wasted.

"Yes. Not less than a week after the ceremony, I told her. She didn't understand it because I never told her that it's a license to kill by the Italians."

"Gery, it's not a license. In case you didn't know, murder is still illegal. You know as well as I do that your friend Nick Cibella did this. I'm sure that one or two of his men murdered Charles and Sandy, and you know it too," Greg said, pointing at his brother.

"First of all, Nick is not my friend. He never was. He just had this appeal to my business sense because of his money. When Charley and Vincey told me a few years ago to stay away from Nick and the reasons to stay away, I obeyed. Everyone, including Vick Spelo and the police, knew Nick killed Joseph because of us. I'll bet you anything that the payouts from the casinos start coming to Nick instead of Vincey. I'll bet your father-in-law told Nick that Charley was receiving the cash. That's what has to be behind this."

"I'm not taking the bet because I think you hit the nail on the head. I'll tell you now what I've been holding in for a few years. I know you spoke to Nick about borrowing the money to buy me out if I didn't go along with the fraud loans and original casino purchases."

"How did you know?"

"I just know. Everyone knows we own the casinos, but no one knows about the skimming. I'll guaran-fuckin'-tee that Willie had nothing to do with Charles and Sandy, though. Willie may have told Nick about the casino skimming, but I know he wouldn't do this because Willie knows how honest Charles is, or was." Greg hesitated. He could not believe Charles had really died. "Willie knows the share I'm getting is benefiting his princess daughter and grandchildren, and sometimes Willie is benefiting himself. The only person who knew for sure we were skimming the money was Joseph. Unless Joseph told Willie way back then. Carol would've never told her father about that."

"Sherry knows about it too. And think about it. How many people could have told Nick? Joseph wasn't the only person who knew. The runners, the accountants in Vegas, Jacob Rosenstingel knows, Anthony knows, Vick Spelo knew more than anyone. There are so many people who know and are making no money compared to us. God only knows how many people everybody involved has told and how many people those people have told. On and on. If our share of the cash starts shrinking, then we should sell to someone else. Have the accountants stop the skimming for a long while to increase the book value. Sell it to the highest bidder. That would fix him. If we can't sell them to someone, then Nick has to go."

Greg could not believe what he just heard. His own brother recommended the murder of another human being. Worst of all, Greg knew Gery might be correct.

"After Vince calms down, we need to talk about this with him." Greg swayed. "I can't believe I agree with you, Gery, but I think you're right."

"I know I'm right. Vince can set someone up to do this if we need to. Let's see what happens first. It'll need to be up to Vince if we sell the casinos. I need to go, Gregory. Sherry tried to control herself, but she was in pretty bad shape when I left. She has class in a few hours."

"Is she still taking this photography thing?"

"That's just a hobby. She's taking classes to be a doctor."

"I didn't know that. What kinda doctor does she wanna be?"

"Just a family doctor. Who knows? She may wind up being a cardiologist or a neurosurgeon for all I know. It keeps her from complaining about, you know, me!"

"Well, congratulations, Mrs. Doctor's husband. Mr. Mrs. Doctor, that's great." Greg laughed. "I'll just call you Mr. Mrs. Doctor."

"She already had her degree in nursing. I couldn't very well say no. She doesn't do anything all day anyway, so it seems like an OK idea."

"When did she start this?"

"You are truly a dimwit dunce drunk. Sherry started medical school over two years ago. Everyone paid attention, except you, I guess." Gerald smiled.

"Well, tell her I said good luck."

"I think she's way beyond that, Gregory. Good-bye."

The two of them hugged briefly and shed a tear one more time. The entire neighborhood awakened and went through their weekday morning rituals.

Greg whispered, "I know you were in on the Trafficanly hit. Charles told me. I begged him not to tell me, but he threw it in the middle of a sentence." Gerald did not say a word. He simply nodded his head yes one time. "Tell me, Gery, were you also in on the Spelo hit?"

"No. I ordered it, though. Nick may need to go. Vick had to go. He knew too much about the skimming. He wouldn't keep his mouth shut. We had no choice."

"Not *we*, bub. It was you, totally. I should've never asked. Now I'll need to get drunk again so I will forget it. From now on, that's my plea. Don't tell me anything." Greg looked around and opened a beer. Gerald shook his head in humorous disgust. "Vick's brother Carl vowed revenge on the killer's head. Carl was in prison when Joseph was blown to bits, so he couldn't have done it. He's not the type who'd order it. He's a maverick. He would've done it himself. Willie told me that they can't keep Carl in line for even a week. When Willie says someone's crazy, you have to believe it. Carl's a time bomb. Hope like hell he never finds out," Greg warned.

Gerald slowly drove away. Greg walked back inside and turned on the television. It was only ten minutes till seven o'clock in the morning. Greg was sitting on the sofa, drinking a beer with a blank look on his face when the local news started. As expected, the murders of Charles and Sandra Giovelli were the top story. He could not bear it and turned the television off.

Greg drank several more beers and took a Quaalude. Carol walked him to the master bedroom before he passed out. Carol believed Greg to be one of the children at times. She actually needed to undress him. Greg slept the entire day.

When he woke that afternoon, he stumbled into the kitchen to see Carol sitting at the table, crying and smoking a cigarette for the first time since she'd announced she was pregnant with Daniel years earlier. He presumed she was upset because of the murders of Charles and Sandy. He knew it would not be the right time to ask her to smoke outside. He hugged her from behind and said he loved her. She assured him that she would only smoke tonight. Greg agreed and lit a cigarette. It tasted too good, so he extinguished it. The tears and the whimpering grew louder as Greg opened two beers. "Thank you."

They heard Danny acting like he could read—reading to his little sister. Carol and Greg looked at them and smiled to the point that they laughed and then began crying yet again. Carol instructed Greg to watch the evening news. He turned on the television, and the top story was, of course, the murders of Charles and Sandra Giovelli.

For some reason, this time the story had been mixed in with the story of another murder. Greg sat baffled. Apparently, "David Vasallo has been shot twenty-seven times and shoved in the trunk of his car. The body was discovered at approximately one o'clock this afternoon. Authorities believed the two acts of violence are related, as David Vasallo was the father of Sandra Giovelli. Her maiden name was, of course, Sandra Vasallo."

As the Crow Falls

Greg sat speechless. He immediately remembered his father-in-law had been labeled the murderer of David Vasallo a year earlier by the eventual victim himself. The evening news made certain everyone would remember, as they played the tape of David saying that. Greg sat stunned. He knew he still had a hangover and a bit tired from the Quaalude, but he knew this would not make sense to him absolutely stone-cold sober.

Greg knew his father-in-law was not stupid enough to have killed a made man who had predicted publicly that Willie would kill him. Greg knew he could not see Willie tonight because he was sure the booze could be smelled by anyone. Greg wanted to think about this for a few days beforehand anyway. Then he would be comfortable discussing this with his father-in-law. When he did, he wanted it to be private. Greg would send a message to Willie that night to let him know he was with him.

"Carol, your father didn't do this. I'll guaran-fuckin'-tee it," Greg said.

"I know." Carol sighed.

Greg had Anthony Gilante deliver the handwritten note to Willie that night from him and Carol. They loved him. If he needed anything, just call.

The next three days were intense for Willie. Local police and federal agents searched his mechanics garage and residence, looking for clues or evidence. No pieces of evidence were found, or ever would be. Willie the Rat was innocent.

The funerals of Charles and Sandra Giovelli were closed to the general public. It was a private ceremony with approximately thirty people present. A double funeral. Both Charles and Sandra had been shot in the head and chest and stabbed with a serrated blade.

The autopsy on Charles revealed lung, liver, and stomach cancer. Likewise, there was a golf-ball-sized grade-four malignant myeloma formed in the marrow of the top of his spine and at the base of the right cerebellum. The tumor had tentacles weaving through the brain and reaching as far as his right ear. Had Charles not been brutally murdered, he would have experienced a long, painful death within the next two years. It was difficult, though, for Vince to be thankful.

Trisha and Tina Giovelli would stay one week, maybe ten days, with Gerald and Sherry Crow, then permanent custody would be granted to their Aunt Sally and Uncle Vincey. Vince did not think it would be tolerable for Carol and Greg to have the girls stay with them while they had their hands full with an infant and a toddler.

30

When the first payout of the Las Vegas skim arrived following the death of Charles, the cash came directly to Vince. The cash was usually divided four ways, with Gerald and Greg receiving the majority. When Vince asked the courier why the three individuals were still receiving the same amount as before instead of the larger amount expected, the courier responded that Nick had already taken his tribute. Nicholas Cibella received one-fourth of the cash from the casino skim. For what? Vince knew who murdered his brother and father beforehand. This statement alone confirmed it. A brazen, nearly public, statement like this showed some big balls.

Vince did not trust in himself enough to meet with Nick personally. The hostility Vince had bottled up toward Nick may blow at any time. Vince also knew that he could be hit at any time. Vince summoned Anthony to his office to deliver a verbal message to Nick.

"Anthony, tell Nick I'm out. I want the money, but I'm out. Tell that prick that he won. I'm writing down this number. Take it to Nick and let him know that's my price for being bought out of all seven casinos. That price is more than fair. If he pays, then he'll just need to deal with Greg and Gery Crow. Legally, they own the casinos and can stop the cash anytime they choose. I could be gone tomorrow, and Nick wouldn't receive a dime. Both of them could pull a moral prick on Nick and they could make tens of millions legally every year. If they're gone . . . either one of them, or me, or any more of my relatives, then Nick is fucked!"

Anthony "the Ant" Gilante did not fear anyone physically. Despite his size, Anthony was strong, quick, and agile. Anthony was also devious and smart, and loyalty meant nothing to him. Anthony knew being aligned with Vincenzo Giovelli was far more lucrative and lawful than being aligned with a hard-core criminal like Nicholas Cibella. Anthony organized several hits for Joseph and Charles Giovelli and the Spelo hit for Gerald Crow.

The fact that a lovable mentor such as Joseph needed to go hurt Anthony emotionally to no end. However, he received in excess of six figures for the hit.

Everyone knew Nick ordered the hits on Charles, Sandy, and David. Anthony wanted Vince to give him the permission to execute Nick. If not, Anthony would assassinate Nick without permission. Anthony was a master at organizing the clueless homicide. La Cosa Nostra bosses in other cities always paid Anthony well for his services.

Anthony relayed Vince's message to Nick. Ever so cool and calm, Anthony returned the message back that everything was fine the way it was. Nick was perfectly happy with his quarter of the pie. When the message was relayed to Vince, he immediately telephoned Gerald and Greg.

31

The only major change to the interior of the Giovelli estate was to the second floor. Gerald kept most of the furnishing that had not been inherited and moved the furniture to a storage unit or his new vacation home in Tempe, Arizona. He had the entire first floor and basement wallpapered, repainted, and carpeted again in roughly an identical fashion. Cleaning alone would not get rid of the cigarette smell. Gerald also had a photography contractor construct a darkroom in the basement for Sherry, as she was now interested in photography.

The only alteration made to the exterior was a security necessity. Facing the street was a seven-foot-high decorative stone wall complete with an electronically controlled wrought-iron entrance gate. A copper plaque on the stone wall said it all: "Chateau Crow." The same wrought-iron fence surrounded the remainder of the estate. A wooden privacy fence now surrounded the outdoor pool.

It broke Vincey's heart to see the house that his father designed occupied by another person. This was the first time Vince had seen the interior since his father was murdered three and a half years earlier. This was his friend Gery, though. If anyone had to live in the house, Vince was glad it was Gery.

"I told Nick that I no longer wanted to be involved in this casino thing. I gave him my price, and he sent the message back that, basically, I should go fuck myself. He liked receiving his quarter. That prick! Nick the Prick. From now on that'll be his name. The Prick!"

"You spoke with him personally?" Greg asked, confused.

"No. Hell no. I had Ant running his verbal messages." Vince had trouble fighting back the tears.

"Vincey, don't you think that Gregory and I should have been consulted before you sent a message like that to Nick? Or, excuse my language, to Prick?" Gerald asked.

162

As the Crow Falls

"I knew he wasn't going to buy it. Nick doesn't have that kind of money. Besides, I told him that you guys officially own the casinos and could stop the skimming tomorrow."

"Why would you send that kind of message?" Greg asked, still confused.

"Just to see if he would make an offer to purchase, or in some way admit that he had Charley killed. He did just that. That prick! I can't believe he admitted it to Ant," Vince said with a broken voice.

It had been more than two weeks since Charles was murdered. Vince did not think he had any more tears in storage. He was wrong.

With all his shortcomings when it came to business, the lights suddenly clicked on in Gregory Crow's mind.

"Guys . . . Ant killed Charles," Greg said.

Vince and Gerald looked stunned.

"What are you talking about, Gregory?" Gerald asked abruptly. "Nick admitted, or I'm sorry, Vincey the Prick admitted it."

"Prick may have ordered it, but I'll guaran-fuckin'-tee it. Ant was there. What were, or as close as you can remember, Ant's exact words?"

"That Nick is happy receiving his one-fourth. I just told you that," Vince said, frustrated.

"Why would Prick say that to Ant? You need to give Nick the Prick some credit. Don't you think Nick is smart enough not to admit conspiracy of murder to a verbal message runner? Unless the message runner was there at the murders."

Gerald got goose bumps. A shiver ran up his spine.

Vince knew that was an asinine question for Greg to ask.

"Greg, people know Ant everywhere. He and Charley were friends. Good friends. The runner from Vegas told me before I saw Ant today that Nick was keeping his tribute."

"Gregory, think about it. Vincey must be right. Anthony would never do that . . ."

"Gery, stop. I haven't said anything to you since we were kids, but now I'm telling you. You're the only person still alive who calls me Vincey. Let me say it this way, you're the only person alive that I care about or like that calls me that. Stop calling me that right now. Every time you call me Vincey, I'll call you faggot. Maybe fudge pounder or bologna smoker. Don't call me that again. Just Vince. Sorry, go ahead."

"Mellow out, Vincey!" Greg could never pass up a wide open door for a joke.

It had been weeks since they laughed together. This was exactly what they needed. Gerald turned on the light behind the bar. He pulled out three frosted glasses from a cooler and pulled the lever for the beer tap.

Charles should be laughing and drinking with us. I know you hear us and are laughing with us, Charles. Have a drink on me. This is for you.

Greg chugged his beer in one swallow and asked for another. Gerald rolled his eyes.

"Vinnnccce! I just thought about it. Gregory may be right. Why else would Nick admit it specifically? I doubt that Anthony even met with Nick today. If Nick knew Anthony was with us and he told Anthony that he was happy, I don't know, I guess."

"Ant probably thinks one of us is gonna kill Nick. Or pay him to do it." After Greg said that, he finished his beer and reached over the bar to pour himself another one. Gerald and Vince sat in stunned silence for an everlasting minute. "Break it down. Ant was at the baseball game that night with us. He works as a part-time laborer for you, right?" Greg asked.

"No, he did that for one summer for us. Told us he hated it. He has a painting and drywall company now. We use him on small jobs. Send him referrals. He does all right with that. Where most of his money comes from is he's a spotter for us."

"Explain?" Greg asked.

"I'll explain this real quick. Gery, can you pour me another beer? Ant has people through our connections in unions everywhere. Thanks, Gery. Anyway, he finds out who's doing the check of union IDs on small- to middle-sized commercial jobs. He tries to get his own people doing the checks, and if he fails, he fails. But it works like a charm, I'd say, at least one out of every ten times he tries it. He has the guy checking union IDs move like a turtle, checking every truck, every piece of equipment very slowly after part of the apartments, office, or strip shopping center is built. When the developers or the general contractor call and bitch about it and say shit like 'You're killing me. I budgeted it with my investors for, say, two million over the next sixteen months. At this rate, you guys are going to take six years to build it.' Ant, or whoever is working the gate, says, 'Well, it would go faster if you would hire ABC Electric out of St. Louis or DEF Excavating out of Chicago,' meaning us. The general contractor, then, fires the subs and hires us unknowingly. The job still moves too slow, so the main developer fires the general contractor and ends up hiring Giovelli Construction from Kansas City or one of the Friends of Ours companies from that city. Then we only take a small fee. I actually like that the best. No paperwork, easy cash. Anyway, every truck moves in and out of the site quickly after that because the guy checking union cards has been given what is to him a big cash payday. So he never says anything."

164

"How does it benefit you, though?" Greg asked.

"The companies. The first general contractor can't put a lien on a commercial job because if he tries, we make sure it gets publicized that he did a lousy job and now wants his money. He'll lose credibility in that city. So if he's smart, he forgets it. More than likely, he has already received an advance anyway. We have the job, so we hire the same subs, plus a few more, to make sure it's completed quick and way under budget. After the frame and the exterior are done, we hire nonunion contractors to work around the clock to make sure the interior is completed quickly under budget. We'll usually get the next big job that developer has. Then we're sitting pretty in that city under another name and assign us the job under our real name, and we start getting jobs from developers all over that city. So if we lose a little money on the first small job, it's OK. We just make sure we lose the money on the books."

"You've done this to us?" Gerald asked, offended.

"We don't do it in KC at all, or to you guys anywhere. Dad specifically warned us not to."

"How long have you been doing this?" Gerald asked, smiling and fascinated.

"As far as I know, Dad thought the scam up more than twenty years ago, when Giovelli Construction started to get big. Not once have we needed to use any muscle. If they don't do it for cash, we move on. It's really simple. There really isn't anything illegal either. Someone could make a stink about us hiring nonunion workers, I guess. But usually it's the union guys. They just work extra hours for cash. That's what we've been using some of the cash from the casinos for. Or just me now."

"Vincey—I mean Vince, don't say it," Gerald said, which immediately caused Greg to laugh.

"Dick breath!" Vince shouted.

"We need to get back to the subject of Anthony. If he does that, then how much do you pay him?" Gerald asked.

"Percentages. It varies job to job. But here's what I've been wondering. I know it sounds trivial, but Charley went to Paglissi's Bar every time he and Sandy went out at night. Without fail, he and Sandy would have one drink and go home. Who else knew that?" Vince asked.

"It's so close to his house. Who knows who all knew?" Gerald replied, a little helpless.

"Vince, do you have a list of people who went to the game with us that night?" Greg obviously enjoyed playing detective.

"I can check. We had to have some kind of list. There were so many

165

people we needed to buy tickets for. It has to be in the office somewhere. I don't know where it would be."

"Let's go to your office." Greg and Vince chugged their beers.

"Vince, Gregory, I know exactly where the list is in our office. You guys find that and come back here. I'll go get ours."

Once inside the car, Vince said, "I'm sure you know, Greg, but Charley swore me to secrecy years ago. Gery told Charley when they were teenagers that he's gay. You're the first person I've ever said anything to. I never even told Sally."

"Vince, I know. He told me a couple of years ago. I've always known, though. I've never told Carol, but she already knew. Gery and I talked about it a few times. The only time I bring it up is when we're completely alone and he says or does something to piss me off. I'd never tell anyone or even threaten him with it. I just call him names sometimes. He's my brother, and I'd never do anything to hurt him, or the boys, or Sherry. I really don't give a damn what he does." Greg took a break and opened another beer. "Since about the time your dad died, and Carol and I got married, Gery has been a terrific father. Before that, he was never around. I've never seen Sherry happier either."

"You think it had something to do with the house?" Vince asked.

"I don't think so. It was about the time Carol and I got together and your dad died. Maybe it was the house or, I don't know, but something changed his personality overnight. Gery has always been obsessed with money and appearances. I think with the casino money coming in, he would've built a big house anyway. Even without the casino money, he would've eventually found a way. You have to admit, when it comes to business, Gery is pretty smart."

"Yeah, you're right, he is that." Vince cocked his head. "I never really thought about it, but he never was with the boys until Dad died."

"No, it was before that. But around that same time. I don't know what happened, but one day he was just different. He still gets a little snooty at times, but he's easier to get along with now than ever. So if I were you, I'd lay off the faggot comments. Unless it's just the two of you, then let them fly. If it's just the two of you, he couldn't care less. I think that he thinks the jokes are funny. Just expect him to make fat jokes to you at the same time. He makes drunk jokes to me. If anybody is around, including me, then don't do it."

Greg and Vince went into the corporate office of Giovelli Construction. There were withering flower arrangements everywhere. From all across the country, people had sent beautiful arrangements mourning the deaths of Charles and Sandra Giovelli. Hundreds of arrangements had already been delivered to area hospitals. Amid all the models of larger office buildings, apartment complexes, hotels, or stadiums that Giovelli Construction had built nationwide, there were flowers.

Every desk and file cabinet needed to be searched. Charles's private secretary's desk had been searched by local police and then moved into Charles's office, which had been padlocked by Vince. Charles's private secretary had been assigned other duties since the murders and had not cleaned out her old desk. In the top left-hand drawer of her old desk, in a manila file folder labeled "Company Functions," were several lists. On top was the list of employees and family members who attended the baseball game on the night of the murders. Sure enough, the name Anthony Gilante was on there. Vince made copies, and then he and Greg closed up Giovelli Construction and drove back to Chateau Crow.

Gerald was there with his list. The boys and Sherry were already home. Greg was given a bruising hello and tackled to the floor by his nephews. Sherry gave Greg a wink and a hug. While Sherry hugged Greg, she pinched his butt as always. This time she whispered something to him that was sexually graphic because he hurried down the stairs.

What the hell was wrong with me?

Gerald was in the basement and had already gone through his list and came to the conclusion that it was meaningless. Gerald drew all three a beer. Greg and Vince scanned each roster and determined the same.

"Well, we're not gonna solve this tonight. You know, Carol and me took a bunch of pictures that night out in the parking lot. I look at the pictures from that night just to see Charles's face. When I get home, I should look at them again," Greg said.

Gerald, Greg, and Vince turned and were mildly shocked.

"Uncle Greg, my mom took pictures of us and Uncle Charley that night. She has them in her bedroom. She cries when she looks at them." Michael had wandered down the stairs silently and accidentally eavesdropped.

"Michael, what did I tell you about listening to other people? It's not a nice thing to do. Let people know that you're here. I was just getting ready to say that Sherry has pictures also. I'll go upstairs and get them. What did you need, Michael?"

"Mom told me to tell you dinner is ready."

Always feeling the need to impress someone, Gerald took the elevator up to the kitchen.

He probably forgot Vince's dad built this house. What a dick.

Inside the elevator, Gerald asked his son how much he heard.

"Just Uncle Greg saying Aunt Carol had pictures."

"Did you hear anything else?"

"Uncle Greg said he looked at pictures to see Uncle Charley's face."
Gerald let Sherry know that he needed to tend to business.

"Greg, why don't you go home and get those pictures tonight then come back? After we look at Gery's pictures," Vince requested.

"I will," he said, pouring a shot of tequila and a beer.

Gerald walked out of the elevator and tossed one package of photographs across the card table where Greg and Vince were sitting. Greg turned up the lights as bright as possible. As they thumbed through the pictures, they set aside every photograph that had Anthony in it.

The night of the game, they sat in the upper deck behind home plate and had taken the pictures at an angle down in order to get the scoreboard in every photograph. Royals Stadium did not allow flash photography. However, Sherry had been taking classes part time as a photographer. The photographs she took with a professional camera did not require flash under the bright lights.

"Vincey—I mean Vince, Gregory, my eyes must be going bad. Here, look at these too." Gerald handed them the photos.

Greg and Vince sifted through the photographs again.

"OK. We have forty-eight pictures here, and eleven of them have the Ant in them. I don't see anything different about him." Vince said as he and Greg were studying the photographs closely. Then Greg noticed something strange.

Strange for Greg because he was positive beer was served in a clear plastic cup at Royals Stadium. Greg then looked at any photographs of himself to be positive.

There I am, clear plastic glass. Maybe I really do have a problem. Who else would think someone not drinking was strange? Strange maybe, but Anthony always drinks with us. Look at the scoreboard behind us, shit. Put these in order. I need a scorecard from that night.

"Gery, go upstairs and see if Michael still has the scorecard from that night," Greg ordered.

"Scorecard, what do you mean?" Gerald asked.

"Scorecard, you twit! In the Royals program, there's a scorecard. Mark and Michael keep track of the scores as they come." Gerald did as ordered.

Mark and Michael kept track of the score right down to foul balls at every baseball game. Greg taught his nephews how to keep score. Gerald returned with the program. Greg went to the scorecard section and studied it. He went to the scorecard to see if there were many foul balls hit in the bottom of the sixth, the top of the seventh, and after the seventh-inning stretch in the bottom of the seventh inning. Many, except the bottom half of the seventh inning. Three fouls by Amos Otis. One two three inning. Quick half-inning. Greg then looked at the first photograph again.

"Guys, look at this picture. Do you notice anything strange?" Vince and Gerald looked at the photograph. Neither of them perceived anything unusual and shook their heads accordingly. "Now, look at the picture of me with Ant. He's suddenly holding a beer. I remember now. I took this next picture of Carol and Ant, Charles, you Vince, you Gery, Sherry, Sandy, and Sally's arm. So I'm not the best photographer in the world. Look at the scoreboard. The lyrics from 'Take Me Out to the Ball Game' are there . . . 'duh duh to the old ball game.' The last line of the song. Now, look at this picture again and pay attention to the scoreboard. Now look at this picture with all of us that somebody took and look at the scoreboard again. Then look at the next picture of you and me, Gery. Sherry must have taken it of us and accidentally got Ant in the picture. Look at the scoreboard."

"I don't get it. They're pictures, Greg. What are you seeing?" Vince asked, perplexed.

"What do you see, Gregory? I don't get it." Gerald asked.

"Look at all the pictures in succession. The clock is in the bottom left corner of the scoreboard. Five of the pictures that Ant was in are obviously during the seventh-inning stretch. You can tell it's the seventh-inning stretch because there's nothing but zeros in the Red Sox score box in all but one inning, the top of the fifth. The scoreboard is blank for the Royals half of the seventh, no zero, blank. Ant is holding a red paper cup for the first picture. Look now at the second and third pictures. It proves they're the second and third because of the time. He's holding a full beer in the second and third pictures. Look at the time on the scoreboard. Then look at the next picture. He has a red cup again. There are two guys sitting with him when Ant doesn't know a picture is being taken. Now look at the next three pictures. Here they are posing. Here's another picture of Ant and the other two guys walking up the stairs. Look at the time on the scoreboard. The bottom of the seventh had just ended because there's suddenly a zero in the Royals box."

"I need to look at my list to see who they are, but I still don't see what you're getting at, Greg." Vince had an intensely confused look on his face.

"That guy on the right looks familiar. I don't know," Gerald said.

"Wait a second, he's the guy who brought the payout a few weeks ago. The last one before Charley died. Tim, Tom, something like that," Vince said.

"All this proves, Gregory, is that Anthony wants to look sociable in pictures," Gerald whined.

"Look at the scoreboard time in the last picture of Ant. In less than eight minutes after the song, he drank a Coke, then a beer, then a Coke, and ordered another beer. Look at the time in every picture. Then look at the one of Mark and Michael. Mark and Michael are keeping score, and they're sitting in the seats in front of Ant the whole time. The picture of Ant's empty seat is less than eight minutes after the last picture of the seventh-inning stretch. It was a quick half-inning. Ant's beer is full, he sets the beer down, and he just walks out. You guys know Ant doesn't leave even a drop of beer, ever!"

"Greg, Charley was my brother, but, man, this is too much. This doesn't prove anything," Vince said, obviously wanting to believe Greg.

"Maybe not, but it still looks kinda fishy. How do you explain the fact that one minute he's laughing and drinking a beer with all of it going down his chin and none in his stomach? Whenever he was aware of a picture, he's holding a beer. When he doesn't know, he has a Coke. Look. Ant faked being drunk that night. He needed to stay sober so he could think straight." Greg smiled.

Gerald took the beer glass away from Greg and then set it on the bar. "I wish you would leave full beers now and then and fake being drunk. Vince is right, this says nothing," Gerald said.

"We need more pictures," Vince said.

"If I'm right, then Carol has one roll of I think twenty-four. Let's roll." Greg pulled out four bottles of beer and handed Vince one.

"I need to check in with Sally. So, Gery, do you not want us back here?" Vince asked.

"No, come back, but be extremely quiet. We need to tone it down when you come back. I don't want anyone upstairs hearing whatever it is you guys are talking about," Gerald said, pointing upstairs.

Greg and Vince drove separate cars with the agreement that Vince would pick Greg up at home, then drive back to Chateau Crow. Greg brought the photographs of Ant with him.

When Greg walked inside, Carol was obviously angry with him for not telephoning to inform her he would not be home for dinner.

"Carol, do you know the two guys with Ant in this picture?"

"Why? And where in the hell have you been?" Carol did not make eye contact. "Here's your dinner." Carol took the plastic wrap off of a plate and slid it onto the table.

"Because I wanna know. And I've been over at Gery's with him and Vince."

"That's Sonny Brown on the left. I think that's Tommy Branato on the right."

"You don't know for sure or that's what you remember?"

170

"Greg, I'm telling you what I said. I know it's Sonny. I think it's Tommy T Boy."

"Tommy T Boy, huh? What did you say his last name was before you called him a pet name?" Carol smacked Greg. It wasn't the first time, but it was the first time she struck him out of anger. "Thanks, Carol. What did you call him before you called him one of those silly little wop names?" Carol smacked Greg again, this time soft and seductive, as she always did. "Carol, I'm sorry. Let me have a rain check for later tonight. This is really important." She looked at Greg and then tried to wipe the tipsy smile off her face. "Carol, I might need to speak to your father."

"I'm sorry, Greg. I didn't wanna hurt you. That first smack was kinda hard. Make it up to me. I'm sorry. I wanna show you how much I love you right now." She placed his hand on her crotch.

Greg smiled and laughed. "I love you too, but this is some serious shit here. Carol, I might need to talk to the Rat later. Are the babies in bed yet?"

Carol looked at Greg and then studied the photographs harder.

"Yes, they're in bed, honey. Why were they at the baseball game that night? I thought that was just employees of Crow Brothers or Giovelli Construction."

"And relatives. Or friends, I guess."

"They may be friends of Ant, but I doubt it." Carol sipped her wine. "And they can't be related to Ant. Ant doesn't have any relatives. At least not here."

Completely blindsided by that statement, Greg sat down.

"What do you mean?"

"Just what I said. Ant killed his parents when he was eleven. Burned down the house. Investigators said it was an accident. Everybody knew he did it on purpose. Ant is one of those guys who loves fire. Neither parent had relatives, just friends. Ant was raised in foster homes until he was fifteen. Then none other than David Vasallo took Ant under his wings. Vasallo gave Ant a place to live and forced him to go back and finish school. Ant got a huge insurance settlement when he was eighteen. David got a big cut of the insurance settlement."

Greg grabbed his head as if it were going to explode.

"Do you know what do they do for a living?" Greg asked.

"Sonny works at a used-car lot east of the Quay. Quality Motors. I don't know what Tommy is doing now. Whatever it is, you can be sure it's a cover for whatever he makes his money at. He's a bum."

"Carol, where are those pictures you took in the parking lot that night?"

"In the drawer of the end table," Carol said.

Greg walked to the living room and opened a drawer, and there were the photographs. He pulled out the pictures and sat down at the kitchen table. He thoroughly studied all the photographs as he ate his lukewarm roast.

Vince drove up excitedly and waddled to the front door. He did not bother knocking and just walked in. Vince had a total of twenty-four pictures with him also. Vince smiled and had changed into a pair of shorts.

"Hey, Carol. Greg, you're not going to believe this. I guess Sandy had taken a bunch of pictures that night in the parking lot before and after the game. She gave them to Sally that night as they were leaving because she knows Sally goes by a photo place every day. Sally had them developed a week or so ago. She didn't look at them or let me look at them because she knew it would upset me."

Greg began studying all the pictures. He went through the photographs Carol took and did not see anything of significance. Greg started studying all of Sandy's pictures very cautiously, as Vince and Carol were talking. Twenty of Sandy's photographs had been taken after the game.

"Is that who I think it is?" Greg asked with a smile.

There was a picture of Charles and Sandy kissing in front of his new Lincoln Town Car. In the background, at least ten car lengths away, Anthony sat in the front passenger seat of a car. Vince went to the table to look at the photograph.

"I don't know, Greg. It's pretty small. How can you tell?"

"You're looking at the wrong picture, fat ass. Look at this one."

Vince studied the photograph thoroughly. It may have been Anthony sitting in the front passenger seat of an automobile. Vince could not see as well as Greg.

If the photograph had been taken in daylight, no image would have been distinguishable at all. Because it was an evening photo, the image was clear, but very small. This particular photograph would need to be magnified. Apparently, something had obstructed the glare of the flash because Charles and Sandra's eyes were red, but the background was clear, including the windshield of the car Anthony sat in. The license plate was not visible in that photograph. In another photograph, the license plate was visible, but it was still too small to be seen without magnification. Greg began to search the house for a magnifying glass when he remembered that Gerald constructed a darkroom for Sherry. Immediately, they drove back to Chateau Crow. Greg brought three more beers for the road. In the automobile, Greg told Vince the names of the other two men.

"Familiar names, but I don't know them."

"Carol knew who they were instantly. She knew they didn't work for us or you," Greg said with a tipsy grin.

"Greg, don't get too carried away with this. We still don't know for sure if Ant had anything to do with Charley."

"I know, Vince. But here's what we do know. One, Ant was at the game. Two, Ant left the game early. Three, Ant faked drinking that night. Four, he's sitting in a fuckin' car waiting for Charles to leave. Five, one of the guys with Ant brought the payout at least once. Six, and I just found this out, Ant killed his parents, and David Vasallo helped raise him. David Vasallo is murdered the same night that Charles and David's daughter Sandy are murdered. Here's what I think. Ant is pretty stupid or brilliant because he thinks if David and his daughter are murdered the same night, then everyone thinks naturally it has something do with them. Charles was just an innocent bystander when we established the casino money is behind this. Ant knows that senile loudmouth David Vasallo told everyone a year or so ago that Willie the Rat would kill him. David Vasallo was killed as a diversion to take the heat off Nick the Prick and crush my father-in-law's balls. Willie might be a bit of an asshole at times, but I don't believe he'd do something so incredibly stupid as to kill somebody who predicted to the press and police, mind you, that he would. The television stations made sure everyone remembered. Every station ran that old tape again of David saying that the day after the murders."

Vince listened intently. Each one of the points Greg made was totally unsubstantiated. Vince gave careful consideration to each point Greg made and decided not to label Greg as insane just yet. For some outlandish reason, Greg and his eccentric theories began to make sense.

"Gery, Carol knew who those guys with Ant were. That's Sonny Brown on the left and . . ."

"Tommy Branato, he worked for Vick Spelo." Gerald smiled.

"I thought you didn't know who he was?" Greg asked.

"I knew I had seen him before, but I didn't know where from. After you guys left, I was in my study looking through something else. It occurred to me then that I recognized him as somebody at Spelo's company. I went through the roster and knew it was him," Gerald said, smiling.

When Greg and Vince walked downstairs at Gerald's home, they saw something they believed was a sign from above. Sherry had been in the darkroom in the basement the entire time Greg and Vince were gone. She was blowing up certain negatives of the photographs she had taken at the baseball game the night of the murders. Greg handed Gery the important negatives. Sherry told them that it might take a few hours. She would do a good job, but she was not an expert yet. It was just after ten o'clock. Mark and Michael were already in bed.

"Gery, do you have a magnifying glass somewhere so I can see the license plate in this picture?"

Gerald returned from the darkroom with a magnifying glass and a microscope. Greg placed the photograph in question under the magnifying glass and was able to read the license plate. A dealer tag.

Immediately, Vince called Kenny Bondano and asked him to run the plate. Kenny could not run the plates. He had run too many license plates for friends and had been ordered to stop. There were no new leads.

Vince telephoned another friend in the Kansas City police. The officer was not an associate. He was not a detective either. He was just a desk jockey and occasional parking violations cop. This guy was a member of the overweight individuals' clinic Vince had been attending. The only thing Vince and this police officer had in common was the love of the same kinds of food. All kinds. In just minutes, the officer telephoned with the owner's name: Quality Motors, the car lot Sonny Brown worked in. They looked at one another deviously, grinning.

"Greg, I might sound crazier than you now. Let's go to Paglissi's. They might be busy tomorrow, but since it's Thursday, we should go."

"Go ahead, guys. I'll just help Sherry if she needs any. Call before you come back. I may go to bed soon," Gerald said, while Greg went behind the bar and took a six-pack for the road. "You're very welcome, Gregory," Gerald said sarcastically.

Vince and Greg drove to Paglissi's Bar & Grill. They drove into the immense parking lot. Vince recognized the automobile of the owner, Vito Paglissi.

"Vince, I don't like the looks of this parking lot. One fuckin' car. Forget it. Let's call it a night."

"C'mon, Greg. Vito's the only one here, obviously. Let's go on in."

"Screw you, Vince."

"Greg, are you carrying a piece?"

"Yeah, but forget this. This is scary."

"Look, just walk in casually. If it makes you feel better, I'll carry a snub in my shorts."

"I don't care if your dick is snub. Let's go."

"I'm going in, Greg. Stay here if you want."

"All right. I wanna go at the first feeling I get that's bad."

"Deal."

Greg and Vince walked in Paglissi's without incident. Sitting at the bar and watching television was Vito Paglissi. Vito and Greg shared a brief introduction and hello. Vito kissed Vince on the hand.

Vito was in his late sixties and had opened Paglissi's Bar & Grill as a hobby. Vito had retired from the United States Postal Service and did not care if he profited a dime. The saloon just kept him occupied. The two main goals Vito wanted to accomplish were to break even and keep out of the prison he named a house and away from the warden, his wife of forty-one years. Vito's house and wife were less than three blocks away.

If I live that long, I hope I look half that good.

"Vincey, I'm so sorry about Charley. Sit down, you boys are gonna have a drink on me." Vince and Greg ordered a tap beer and were happily served.

"Thanks, Cheato. Greg, when Vito was young, they called him Cheato Vito. Dad said it was because he used to pick up ladies all the time. And he was married!"

"I still do, you punks. I could pick up your wives if you had the guts to bring them 'round me." Vito smiled and pointed at them.

"Vito, we need to ask you some questions about the night Charley died," Vince said.

Vito immediately turned up the music, although there were no customers except Greg and Vince. Vito put one finger to his lips. Vito whispered to Vince. All of a sudden, Vito began going through the motions of closing for the night. Greg was instructed by Vince not to talk. Vito would follow them to Chateau Crow and tell what he knew. Vince let Vito know it was Joseph's old house they were going to.

When all drove back to Chateau Crow, the lights were still on. Gerald met them at the front door with a grin. He did not recognize Vito and stopped himself before he revealed what he'd obviously discovered. Gerald told Vincey and Gregory that Sherry had snapped an additional partial roll of film the night of the murders. She was developing the photographs as they spoke. They walked downstairs and sat at a card table. Gerald made Vito a scotch and water. He poured Greg and Vince beers. Gerald drank coffee.

"Vincey, I shouldn't care if anyone finds out I told you this, but it's still probably a good idea if you boys don't tell anyone." All shook their heads. Vince assured Vito that any information Greg and Gery were told would remain confidential. Gerald laughed that Vito had used the forbidden name, Vincey. "Vincey, nobody with the police asked me a damn thing. Charley and Sandy never came in that night."

Vince jolted his head backward as though the words spoken by Vito were a billy club swung to his forehead.

Greg and Gerald may as well have been identical twins. The brothers opened their mouths and appeared as if their jaws were locked.

"I'm sorry, Vito, it sounded like you said the police never talked to you," Vince said.

"They talked plenty, but they never asked me nothin'. They started takin' pictures of the inside of my joint for some reason. Then the outside. If they would've just asked me, I would've told them the truth. Charley and Sandy didn't come in tonight. They never asked, so I didn't tell them nothin'."

"Have you talked with anybody about this at all?" Vince inquired.

"Absolutely not. It isn't that people haven't asked me. I just don't say nothin'. Charley gave me a few bucks to open the bar a few years after I retired. I wasn't gonna say nothin' to no one, if not to you. I wanted to tell the police. This thing has ruined my business. I bet since it happened, what, two weeks ago, I've had maybe thirty customers. I've got no choice but to shut down the beginnin' of next week."

"Excuse me, Vince. Do you mind if I ask a few questions?" Greg asked.

"That's up to Vito," Vince said with a faraway gaze.

"That's fine. I don't care. Can I get another scotch?" Gerald brought Vito another scotch and water.

"Mr. Paglissi, did anything unusual happen to you that night?" Greg asked. Vince and Gerald looked at Greg like "What a stupid question."

"Well, people dyin' in my parkin' lot is kinda new."

"Other than that." Greg smiled.

"Well, the cops told me I'd need to shut down the next day. Routine, they said. If I wanted to open, they couldn't stop me. I know that much of the law." Vito had an annoying habit of pointing his finger at people. "If it would've happened inside, that'd be another story. I'm not much on arguin' anymore, so I just didn't say nothin'."

"Who talked to you?" Greg asked.

"I have his card. Irish Italian guy." Vito rummaged through his wallet. "Here. Kenneth Bondano. He's supposed to be leading the investigations."

Gerald, Greg, and Vince looked at one another. The three of them had all reached the same conclusion: Kenny the Cop was covering for someone.

"Vito—I'm sorry, Greg—why did you turn the music up at the bar earlier?" Vince asked.

"'Cuz I don't know the cops on the scene that night. 'Cuz I'm Italian. I bet they have a bug in my bar. That might be why some regulars which includes a bunch of cops are not comin' in."

"Vito, nobody's going to bug you," Vince said, laughing.

"Look, I know what it's like to be Italian in this city. The cops here wanna arrest everyone who's Italian. Not me. I just wanna be left alone. *Basta!*"

"What does 'basta' mean?" Vince smiled.

"That's Italian for 'enough!' They're a bunch of bigots. Every time somethin' illegal happens 'round here, they look to arrest a greaseball. That's their word for people like me—'greaseball.' I'm Italian."

"Mr. Paglissi, have you spoken with anyone since the murders of Charles and Sandy?" Greg asked.

"Yes, of course, I've spoken to other people." Vito looked at Greg as if he were really thickheaded.

"Have you spoken to anyone regarding Charles and Sandy?" Greg asked the revised question.

"No way. I was waitin' for you guys, or Vincey at least. Here's somethin' I don't get. I'm not a cop or a scientist, but it seems as if there should have a lot of blood. Right? I mean, when two people are stabbed like that, it seems like blood would be everywhere. Right?" Vito continued pointing at Vince. "There was hardly any. When I went to clean up the parkin' lot, I expected a bunch of blood. I was gonna go to the hardware store and get wire brushes, bleach, everything. Then I figured I'd just burn the mess away. I got a gas can and pulled a garden hose outside. I got ready to burn it when I saw very little blood. I was able to wash it away. I bet I didn't spend five minutes cleanin' it with a push broom."

"Mr. Paglissi, or Vito—may I call you Vito?" Greg asked.

"Sure. Can I get another scotch?" Vito did not seem to pay attention to Greg.

"Is it possible the police cleaned it up?"

"No way! I didn't leave the bar the whole night. I was worried about someone robbin' the joint. I even tried to sleep there that night. I couldn't sleep because I was so upset. Boys, I can tell you that even if the cops had cleaned it up, there still would've been more dried blood than there was. I enlisted in the Army durin' World War II. I was stationed in Turkey. I didn't need to fight. I was a cook, but I saw a few guys shot. There would've been blood everywhere. Charley and Sandy were parked at the edge of the lot. Half of Sandy was on the grass. No blood on the grass. Not a drop. From what the paper said, Charley and Sandy had been butchered. The paper said Charley had been stabbed eleven times," Vito said.

Vince reminded Vito that Charley was his brother. Vince could not handle hearing any more graphic descriptions of the homicide scene.

"None of the customers saw or heard nothin'. And the place was hoppin' that night. There are eyes on that parkin' lot all the time. There's a 7-Eleven right down the street now, two doors down. You saw how busy that place was tonight. It's like that twenty-four hours a day. Somebody drivin' by would've seen somethin'."

Greg had already reached another theory. After some small talk, Vito Paglissi drove home. When she heard him leave, Sherry urgently called out to Gerald, Greg, and Vince to come into the darkroom. She clamped three enlargement photographs to a wall outside the darkroom—pictures that Sandy had taken.

The first photograph was supposed to be of various people partying in the parking lot before the baseball game the night of the murders. Ant and Charles were lifting a cooler out of the trunk of the Ford Fairmont that Sonny Brown drove. Charles's underwear showed a little. The next photograph was of Ant and Charles setting the cooler down. Charles's underwear showed a bit more. The next photograph was intended to show nothing but hilarity of Charles showing most of his underwear as he bent down and opened the cooler. On the original photograph, the subjects were, of course, Charles and his underwear. Sherry cropped the main subjects out in the enlargement to show that the cooler contained sandwiches already made and wrapped in clear plastic, soda pop, and, for some reason, a large kitchen butcher knife. Very tired and not wanting to rush to judgment, Gerald said that the photograph proved nothing. Greg and Vince were already judging.

"Charley always carried a gun. Look, he's wearing shorts that night, he couldn't have." Vince tightened again. This time, he found himself capable of holding back the tears.

"Guys, it's almost one o'clock. I've got to go to bed," Gerald said, whining again.

"Vince, let's go before Gery sics his pet goldfish on us. Gery, we're gonna take the pictures."

Gerald motioned that it was fine. Greg took another six-pack for the road. Gerald and Sherry said good night as Greg and Vince left.

"Greg, this has been one hell of a day. I don't think I'll need a downer to sleep tonight. First time since Charley and Sandy were killed."

"Vince, I know we can work on this tomorrow. Where's Charley's car?" Greg asked, smiling.

"It's still in the impound lot. Why?"

"I'd love to see it."

"We can go look at it tomorrow."

"No good. Then we would need permission. And who are we gonna get that from? Not Kenny Bondano, I'll guaran-fuckin'-tee that. If we get permission from anyone, Kenny would find out. Let's go there now and just cruise by. We'll need to break in probably."

"How can we do that, Greg? I'm not going to climb any barbed-wired fence."

"Just go back by my house. I'll get some cash and see if the guard will let me in for a few thousand bucks. Do you have the keys?"

"No, but if there are any, they would be at the office. The parking lot is so small, we need to move cars around all the time."

Following the brief stop at Greg's to get $5,000 and allow Greg to change into dark garments, Greg and Vince drove to Giovelli Construction to retrieve the keys to Charles's Lincoln Town Car. Employees of the main office routinely hooked their spare keys to a pegboard next to the back door. The keys to Charles's car were there.

Greg and Vince drove past the police impound lot. To their amazement, there was no need to bribe anyone. Greg walked right into the impound lot unnoticed, hiding behind a tow truck towing a crashed automobile.

Greg discovered Charles's automobile and searched the interior. Other than the stale aroma of cigarettes, there were no clues, except one tiny alteration that Greg noticed.

The driver's seat had been moved up considerably. The automobile had been towed from the parking lot of Paglissi's Bar the night of the murders. Unless someone had driven it since the murders, the seat was way too close to the steering wheel for a man of Charles's height to be comfortable. Greg would have not been comfortable, and he was two, possibly three, inches shorter than Charles. Greg crawled out of the impound lot beneath a section of the fence, not touching the ground. Greg was able to twist the chain-link fence enough with his gloved hands to allow an expeditious yet scratchy crawl. Back in the automobile, Greg told Vince about the seat.

Greg then had Vince drive to Quality Motors in case the automobile that Sonny Brown had driven the night of the murders remained unsold. It had not been sold. Greg used a wire coat hanger to unlock the automobile and searched it. He did not want to break the glass for fear of being caught. Besides, if the glass were broken, it would send a message to Sonny that someone may know.

While inside the automobile, he noticed a new-car smell. Odd. He noticed the front seat had old interior. He looked at the backseat closely to see it was the same color but substantially newer, in perfect condition, hence, the new-car smell. Greg shined his flashlight on the carpet to see that it, as well, had been replaced. To eliminate any noise, he stayed in the car and climbed over the front seat to sit in the back. He looked at the back of the front seats. Greg then sneaked back to Vince's automobile to obtain a knife or razor.

"What the hell do you need a razor for?" Vince asked, visibly paranoid.

179

"The backseat has been replaced. The front hasn't. I'm just gonna cut along one of the seams," Greg smiled.

"You're carrying this way too far, Greg." Vince looked in the rearview mirror.

"I'm on to something, Vince. Do you wanna find out who killed Charles, or don't you?"

"Greg, it's almost three in the morning. We have to call it a night. We're gonna get caught here, breaking into cars." Vince turned his head every three seconds.

"Look, drive around the block. Come back in five minutes. That should give me enough time."

"Whatever. There's a razor in the toolbox in the trunk. Look for a zipper before you cut into it. Check the side of the seat." Vince handed Greg the keys to the trunk. Greg opened the toolbox. Next to the toolbox, he noticed office supplies, including a stapler. He slammed the trunk shut and threw the keys to Vince.

At that second, Greg heard police sirens coming toward him. He knew he was bound to have some serious explaining to do. A wealthy drunk guy breaking into automobiles of a used-car lot in one of the roughest, poorest neighborhoods anywhere. This would be like signing his death certificate. After he was arrested, the hit men he'd decided to investigate would kill him, his wife and kids, definitely his brother, and probably everyone he had ever associated with.

There's Vince, going the other way. At least I can just sit down and act civil. How did I get into this? Oh, fuck, the gun! If they see the gun, I'm dead for sure. Just walk to the other side of the car and drop it. They aren't stopping. Two cars. Three, four, five. An ambulance, a fire truck. Somebody else. Shit, look under the seat quick and get the hell out of here.

Greg hastily sat in the backseat of the automobile again. The vinyl-covered front seats had perforated vent holes. The new-fashioned backseat did not. He did not detect a zipper, so he lifted up the headrest and made an incision along the seam down toward the floor. He saw what he expected: blood drops on the foam. He cut a small quantity of foam to show it to Vince. This was adequate evidence for now. He pulled the seam as tight as possible and slammed the headrest. He used one staple in a discreet piece of the seam. He casually walked out of the lot. Vince was driving down the street. He saw Greg and stopped.

"Let's go. I've got it."

"Hold on, Greg, there's a cop behind us." The police turned on his cherry lights. Vince pulled over, and the police sped by. "Greg, that was scary. Don't even speak until we hit highway."

Less than two minutes later. "Vince, one of us needs to buy that car tomorrow. The backseat is brand-spanking new. I'm almost positive these are blood drops. Send someone they don't know to buy the car tomorrow and take it to Gery's. We can park it in that detached garage."

"Greg, I was positive you were gonna get busted by those cops."

"So cops scare you, but an empty parking lot where your brother was dumped doesn't?" Greg asked jokingly.

"I guess not. Are you sure they were dumped?"

"Vince, I'm almost positive now. I don't think Charles and Sandy were killed in the parking lot. I'm pretty sure they were killed in that car and dumped at Paglissi's. Vito was talking about no blood. The backseat and the carpet in that car have been replaced. There are a few drops of blood that—excuse me, I know you don't wanna hear this, but a few drops of blood were splattered on the back of the front seat. They replaced the backseat and just cleaned up what little blood there was on the front. Morons! I need something to write on."

"There's a notebook in my briefcase," Vince said, yawning.

Greg began writing down every piece of evidence he had discovered, no matter how trivial. He also made a checklist of suspected evidence he had not found.

"OK. We need to buy the car in a few hours. It's not much. They didn't have the price on the window, but give me like fifteen hundred. I'll put up another fifteen. That should be more than enough to buy it. I'll get this girl I used to bang to buy it. I buy pot and coke from her and her husband all the time. She and her husband are cool. I'll give them another grand. They won't say anything to anyone." Greg again began looking at the photograph of Charles and Sandy's Lincoln Town Car the night of the murders to see a section marker in the parking lot of the sports complex. "Vince, is there any way we can get the autopsy report without Kenny finding out?"

"Probably not. Just go ahead and ask me. I pretty much know what was in it. I can take it."

"Stop me if you don't think you can make it through." Vince nodded. "Charles was shot in the chest, right?" Greg asked.

"Four times in chest. Once in the right side of the head, above his ear."

"We know he was stabbed. Do you know for sure how many times?" Greg asked.

"Eleven. One guy in the coroner's office told me in private after the funeral that he knew it was with a serrated blade because the knife left blood prints on his shirt that, uh . . . I don't remember the medical term, but that were left by a serrated blade. Also he said the cuts on the bodies were jagged, or something like that. Remember, I was in a daze for a week

181

or so. I was on tranquilizers constantly. The whole thing is like a dream to me now. A real bad dream."

"And Sandy?"

"Sandy was shot twice in the head, twice in the chest, and stabbed four times with a serrated blade."

"Were the shots basically on the side? Or were they in the back of the head?"

"I'm sorry to say this, but I don't really remember with her." Vince shrugged.

Greg studied the enlargement picture taken of Charles and his underwear opening the cooler to see that the knife was indeed edged with a serrated blade.

"Vince, we don't need to blow this picture up anymore—that's a serrated blade. Did they say how long the blade was?"

"They might have. I don't remember."

"I'd say that the blade on this knife in the picture is probably eight to ten inches. Is there any way we can find out what caliber bullets they were shot with?"

"Not without Kenny finding out."

"It doesn't matter, I guess. OK, are you ready for my theory?"

Vince knew this was not a question. "Go ahead."

"For some reason, Charles and Sandy got in that car that night and sat in the backseat. Probably to smoke a joint or something. Wait for the traffic to die down. Both Charles and Sandy are shot in the chest while they sit in the backseat. A gun with a silencer is used so the few people in the parking lot don't hear anything. The windows aren't covered with blood because Charles and Sandy are shot in the chest. They aren't shot in the back of the head because the shots come from the front seat. Tommy or Sonny is in the backseat with them and stabs them, probably Tommy, because Sonny, more than likely, is driving. Ant isn't back there because he needs to stay clean. Everything in back is covered with blood. That's done, so Ant drives the Lincoln to Paglissi's. He's so short that he has no choice—he moves the seat up and forgets to move it back. They look for a break in the crowd at the parking lot of Paglissi's. Ant pulls the Lincoln into a safe, inconspicuous spot. They dump the bodies out, and one of 'em pumps in the headshots. A gun with a silencer so nobody hears anything, or nothin', as Vito said. I know even with a silencer there's still sound, but that area is pretty loud. There's very little blood at Paglissi's because all the blood was already gone from the bodies into the backseat. It's about, what, a twenty-minute drive from the stadiums to Paglissi's? Then the whole thing at Paglissi's didn't take one minute. Kenny is on duty that night and gets the case. End of story."

"Greg, if Kenny is in on this, then he must have received a shitload of money." Vince rubbed his fingers together.

"He doesn't need to say shit to anyone except the canned response: 'We are searching every lead, every tip. Please call this number if you can help.' I'd love to see pictures of the scene, but I don't think that's necessary after what Vito very innocently told us. Besides, Kenny would freak if he knew we wanted to see 'em. Someone else with Kenny is in on it too. Somebody takes pictures of the inside of the bar to keep Vito occupied. Kenny covers up the scene in the parking lot. You don't think Vito would just make all that up, do you?"

"No. No way. He'd have nothing to gain and everything to lose by telling us there was no blood. I'm worried now that if anyone knows Vito talked to us about this, then he'll get knocked off right away."

"Well, we're almost to my house. I'll tell you. I might try to sleep for a couple of hours, but that car needs to be purchased right away. Then, later, I'm gonna go out to the sports complex to see if there are any traces of blood anywhere around where they parked. I'll go out there early so I can take pictures of the parking lot. I'll just make sure my nephews are in the stadium, and I'll disappear in the parking lot. My nephews love baseball anyway. If there's blood there, then it's open and shut. If we can figure this out in one night over two weeks after it happened, then a trained detective like Kenny should have. And he could've figured it out that night."

"Greg, it was you that figured it out. So far, every hunch you've had since yesterday afternoon is right. I don't know if you're right about the order, but it all makes sense." They pulled onto Greg's driveway.

"It all might be in the wrong order, but it all adds up the same. They changed the seat and carpet. That's obvious. We also know there was no, or should I say very little blood at Paglissi's and that Charley and Sandy never went in there that night. This whole thing stinks," Greg said, as he pinched his nostrils.

"What do we do if the car shows the blood?" Vince asked, as he fished $1,500 from an envelope in his brief case and handed it to Greg.

"I don't know. I'm being totally serious when I say this. We should just plant it in Carl Spelo's mind that Sonny Brown and Tommy Branato killed his brother Vick for somebody—namely, his cousin Prick. Let Carl start a war. Let them all blow each other to bits, and we'll stay out of it. Just start planting rumors," Greg said.

"Good idea!" Vince laughed. "What about Anthony and Kenny?"

"I've thought about it. As of yesterday, Ant knows we think Prick did this. As far as he knows, we don't suspect him at all. Besides, Ant would kill any of us if he thought we knew." Greg opened another beer. "Prick needs us, so I'm confident we're in no danger with him. In fact, what we should do is give the accountants and runners in Vegas instructions to keep bringing him money. But instead of 25 percent, just give him, say, 1 percent of the payout next time. Then 5 percent. Then 1 percent. Mess with his mind. I'll have Gery pass it along to Prick that we bought you out and we're stopping the skimming."

"What about Kenny?" Vince yawned again.

"That I don't know. He might just be a terrible cop. I doubt it, though. It was so easy to figure this shit out."

"Greg, I've been amazed at your detective work in the past day."

"It was easy for us. It should've been easy for Kenny." Greg yawned. "Your yawn must be contagious."

"Greg, I've gotta get to bed. Ya know, just to be safe, don't have them bring the car to Gery's. I don't wanna see him hurt. We have a storage warehouse down in Olathe. Call me when you get it, and we'll take it out there."

"No problem. I know a lake out there we can drive the car into. Nobody will ever find it. I'm gonna sleep for a few hours, then have this friend buy the car. I'll call you later."

During the drive home, Vince looked at the empty beer bottles and realized that Greg had drunk at least fifteen beers out of the nineteen in the car, and he forgot how many others from last night through early that morning. Nevertheless, Greg could still function. Fascinating, yet abnormal. The more alcohol Greg consumed, the braver he got. Greg never would fight. Interesting.

Vince flashed back to younger days with Greg. Although he never fought, Greg was always brave when he was drunk. His ability as a marksman and his ability to act foolish when drunk somehow needed to intertwine.

Vincenzo Giovelli knew Gregory Crow was correct. Vince would force the issue.

The war was about to begin!

32

An emergency meeting had to be called. A strange place? Inside the barn on a farm in Pleasant Hill, Missouri.

"They're on to you."

"What are you talking about?"

"The car was purchased this morning, with cash. Some woman bought it."

"You wanted it to be sold, remember? That's why I needed to drive all the way out here to the boonies? Because the car was purchased with cash? Big deal. The car is probably gonna have kids in it on the way to school. Then the mother goes to a sleazy motel and turns tricks all day. Then she picks up the kids in the afternoon. It's no big deal. We see it all the time."

"They must have purchased it."

"Who are you talking about?"

"Gregory Crow and Vincey Giovelli. Gregory figured it out, along with help from Vito Paglissi and my wife." Gerald Crow looked at the ground.

"Do they know about Joseph and David too?" Kenneth Bondano asked, alarmed.

"No. They think Nicholas Cibella ordered all the hits. I was floored when Gregory figured the majority of this out. I watched him do it as he consumed twenty or so beers. Gregory figured out that you helped cover it up. Gregory figured out that Anthony, Tommy, and Sonny did it. I thought about attempting to dissuade his theories and eventually pretended to agree with him. It was eerie. Gregory kept nailing it, except for Nick. You must have done a real lousy job if an idiot drunk like Gregory can figure it out," Gerald said in an accusatory tone.

"I did an excellent job, twerp. Even the other detectives don't know. They all think Nick ordered it too. Nick is freaking out right now. The detectives on the Vasallo case think Willie did it because David was killed

185

the same night. From what I've gathered, Willie thinks Nick ordered it, Nick thinks Willie did. It's hilarious."

"What do you think of Vito Paglissi?" Gerald asked.

"Probably harmless, but we shouldn't take any chances. He needs to go."

"What do you think of Vincey?"

"Scares me. He needs to go."

"So you think everyone needs to go?" Gerald asked, smiling.

"Gery, calm down, you twerp. I didn't say anything about Greg, did I?" Kenny responded sarcastically.

"No, you didn't. Are you saying you think Gregory needs to go also?"

"I don't think so. If he begins flapping his mouth, he'll need to be shut up, though. I'd leave that to you."

"I'll never permit anyone to get rid of Gregory. He's my brother. I would never permit anyone even touching him. My boys absolutely adore him. Gregory has two children now. I could never do that to the kids or my dad."

"You were supposed to be Charley's best friend. If you cared so much, then why do it? Charley's daughters don't have a mother or a father now."

"It was necessary." Gerald smiled.

"The autopsy said those girls wouldn't have had a father in a few months anyway. My gramps died of cancer. Believe me, Charley is better off if he never had to go through what Gramps did."

"Kenny, I don't care about your gramps. Gregory and Vincey think I'm only getting a quarter. Tommy Branato and Sonny Brown have no idea what it was done for or who ordered it, but they were there. So they need to go. I'll wait, though. I think Vincey will order it. I think, for now anyway, everything should stop, except for Vito Paglissi."

"I'll do it myself tonight."

"Well, I think we've wrapped this up. Vito Paglissi goes." Gerald crossed the barn to lean on a post. "I hope you're right about this, Kenny. You've managed to screw up a few times too many. One of the main reasons Victor Spelo was hit was to try to help you get promoted, and you found a way to screw that up. I know you can be trusted, but I seriously wonder if you're smart enough. It took you two years to get promoted to help me. Still, you're so brain dead that you're of little or no help. I've paid you nearly three hundred grand over the past few years, and you could have received upward of a million if you would have just done what I said and pinned Joseph Giovelli's murder on Nick. You did it wrong, so you needed to pin Victor Spelo's murder on Nick. You fucked that up. You do everything the opposite I say, and Nick has to be charged with gambling illegally.

Boo-fucking-hoo. Now no one knows why Victor was killed or who did it. I wanted you to pin it on Nick. You're such a moron, Kenny."

"I thought you wanted Vick killed because of the casino money?"

"You're an idiot, Kenny. He didn't know anything. That was an excuse to get that pain-in-the-ass Nick out of the way. Willie should have been so easy for you to pin Charley's, Sandy's, and David's murders on. You're definitely a poor detective. Nick can't be killed because of the surveillance. I wanted him sent to prison. Willie is just such a character that I figured almost anything could be pinned on him. You had two chances to pin murders on Nick and three on Willie and you fucked it up. I guarantee now, Nick won't extort money from me again. If he knows that I can get him sentenced to prison for gambling, it should send him the message to stay away from Gregory and me. I could get him sent to prison for anything I want. No thanks to you."

"What the hell are you talking about, twerp? You, Greg, and Vincey have benefited directly because of me."

Gerald Crow then pulled out the gun that had been taped to the post he had been leaning against and ended the life of Kenneth Bondano.

Officer Kenneth Bondano of the Kansas City Police Department was quite dead. Two men then entered the barn and chopped the body of Kenneth into easily disposable pieces.

The men, Eric Brenington and Patrick Rutledge, were enlisted in the Air Force Reserves and stationed at the once full-service base of Richards-Gebaur Air Force Base in Belton, Missouri. Eric Brenington and Patrick Rutledge then disappeared.

The bodies of Kenneth Bondano, Eric Brenington, and Patrick Rutledge have never been found.

33

After tearing the Ford Fairmont apart, Gregory Crow and Vincenzo Giovelli determined that it was exactly as Greg predicted. Blood.

"Well, they did a lousy job of cleaning it up. I know you don't wanna look, Vince, but that's dry blood underneath the carpet." Greg removed the rubber gloves he wore. He was a bit nauseous because of his weakness for blood.

"What do we do?" Vince asked with another tear in his eyes.

"Nothing. We plant rumors in Carl Spelo's mind, then we wait. If Carl doesn't take out Sonny and Tommy, then we find another sucker."

"What about Ant, though? He must have masterminded killing Charley."

"Sandy too. And his father figure, David Vasallo," Greg said while opening a beer. "I can't believe Ant would kill David just to confuse everyone."

"Ant is smart. I want him and Nick the Prick gone also. Somebody needs to shoot them from a hundred yards away. In public, probably, send a message that I know."

"I know what you're getting at, Vince, and forget it. I couldn't live with myself if I killed somebody. Even on accident in a car wreck."

"Greg, you have a gift. How long do you think it'll take for Nick to kill you or Gery if you don't kill him first? Hmm? It's just like when you got drafted. You almost convinced me to enlist. I stayed in college and got married instead. What if you hadn't failed the physical?"

"But in a war you don't go to prison." Greg smiled.

"You said you couldn't kill anyone. What if you would've been sent to Vietnam? Are you telling me that you wouldn't kill some gook that had every intention of killing you?"

"Vince, that's totally different. I don't wanna go to prison."

"Greg, how is this any different from giving the order to Dad to

188

kill Harold and Rebecca Trafficanly? You could have gone to prison for ordering that."

"I didn't give the order. I only gave permission."

"That's splitting hairs, Greg. It's the same thing. You can't tell me that you would rather be killed yourself. Or me. Or even Gery, for that matter. You know damned well that one of the three of us is going to be murdered. Probably two of us. Nick Cibella will never be happy until he receives three-quarters of the pie."

"Probably the whole thing," Greg said knowingly.

"No, he needs one of us alive to make sure the skimming continues. It'll more than likely be Gery alive because he's the one with the brains and he's a legal owner. You and I are as good as dead," Vince said.

Greg gave that proclamation serious consideration before speaking.

"Vince, there's no way I could do it. It doesn't need to be done right away. Gery could do it with an easier conscience than me. He's also a better shot than I am. Maybe I'm not real religious, but I don't wanna go to hell."

"Greg, you're not going to hell. If you are going to hell, then you already punched your ticket because of Trafficanly. If you could do this, you would be taking out an evil man. It may be God's work that would be done."

"From what it sounds like, Prick is probably going to prison for his gambling conviction anyway. If he doesn't go to jail on that, then maybe he should go for something else. We could just set him up for something else."

"That's pretty good. I'll bet if we slipped $100,000 to the sentencing judge anonymously with a note that said, 'Sentence Nick Cibella to the maximum, and a million dollars will be yours,' the judge probably would. Nick is so old-fashioned, he would never squeal on anyone."

"He's such a prick that I wouldn't mind planting some hard evidence on him for something. He never does any of his own crimes, but the public or the police don't know that. That would be hilarious if Prick got sentenced to prison for a crime he didn't commit." Greg laughed.

"What kind of evidence, though, and what kind of crime?"

"I don't know. Something with gambling, probably, that would at least send him the message that we know. I think the sentencing for Prick is next week. Let's find out who the judge is and slip him a couple of hundred Gs. Hopefully, he's sentenced to at least a year. Then we see how soon he needs to report for prison."

"What then?"

"Give me some time to think about it."

Less than one minute later. "Greg, I know this guy, Gary Porter, that'll do anything I ask of him. For some reason, he wishes he were Italian."

189

"I know him too. He's an imbecile. Always wearing that stupid pinkie ring. What a doofus. How in the world can he figure into this?"

"Plant some things in his head that he gives to Carl Spelo. Give Gary enough praise, and he'll do anything. He's close to Spelo. Believe me, Gary will keep his mouth shut."

"Let's give Gary some money to plant it in Spelo's mind. Sonny and Tommy will be gone soon if Spelo thinks they even double-parked in front of his bar." Greg laughed. "I never thought of Gary Porter. Porter is an unknown. Worry about Gary, though—he doesn't have it upstairs."

"I know." Vince smiled. "His brother-in-law is Jeff Lorzani, isn't it?"

"John Lorzani. Carol knows Lorzani because he owns a bar down in the River Quay right next to the original Italian Deli. Carol is going to school right now with his daughter, Jennifer. Carol would absolutely freak out if she knew I had about a one-week stand with Jennifer before Carol and I got together. She always says she doesn't care about women in my past. But if she knew about Jennifer, or a few other women, she'd freak."

"Gary and John would make a perfect team to set some of this up. Lorzani is aligned with Nick the Prick, but he absolutely hates him. He didn't like my dad much, but that was just financial stuff. We could give Gary Porter and John Lorzani a few bucks, and they could start a war."

"Let's do it, Vince. It would eliminate us getting involved. Keep us secret and out of it. This whole city would freak, and we wouldn't know anything. Let's do it!"

That afternoon, Greg and his nephews went to Royals Stadium. Greg pulled his Volkswagen Thing close to the scene of the crime and saw that there were indeed small drops of blood in the parking lot. Greg took pictures.

The same night, Vito Paglissi was shot point-blank in the back of his head inside of Paglissi's Bar & Grill. Money and additional valuables were stolen. Vito was killed with a .357 caliber.

It was widely reported that Officer Kenneth Bondano was missing. Kenneth had been known to be unfaithful to his wife. Rhonda Bondano had been detained and questioned by police and federal agents, then released.

Gerald, Greg, and Vince were convinced that Kenneth Bondano murdered Vito Paglissi and took off. It was then widely reported that the gun used to kill Vito Paglissi was legally registered to Officer Kenneth Bondano. In addition to Vito Paglissi, the FBI was now investigating Officer Kenneth Bondano for the murders of Joseph, Charles, (the younger) Sandra Giovelli, and her father, David Vasallo.

In an unrelated missing-person story, Eric Brenington and Patrick

190

Rutledge of the Air Force Reserves were believed to have crashed a small twin-engine airplane in the snow-covered mountains of Alaska. The flight pattern of the rented plane showed that Kotzebue, Alaska, was their destination. The equipment malfunctioned, and no recordings of the flight were available to the Federal Aviation Administration.

34

Nicholas Cibella had been sentenced to thirty-six months in prison for running a mini casino in his club known simply as The Hall. He would be eligible for parole in nine months. His brother, Corky, was believed by Greg and Vince to be receiving the skim money from the Las Vegas casinos.

Greg met with Fred Vasallo and explained to him that Anthony Gilante was responsible for his sister's and father's murders. Greg did mention the fact that Nicholas Cibella was behind all the murders and a few reasons why he knew that. Greg did leave out more of the graphic reasons and the casino skimming, but Greg's ability as a salesman had Fred sold.

William Cassivano and Fred Vasallo were stunned yet satisfied. Fred hesitated for weeks and then went along with Greg, although at first he was leery to believe anyone, except Willie, was responsible. Fred relived some childhood memories involving Anthony and soon apologized to Willie. Fred gradually understood that Willie was smart enough not to have killed his father when David had announced that Willie the Rat would. Greg had Willie hand Fred enough cash to cover expenses incurred last year, when the Warehouse Inn was damaged by fire. At Greg's insistence, the two would not reconcile publicly. Only Vince and Greg knew what was transpiring. Willie knew certain aspects. Other higher-ranking members, including Anthony Gilante and Gerald Crow, were oblivious.

Gerald supposedly had no idea his brother and Vince were pulling the strings of this battle by planting beliefs in other minds. Gerald read the daily paper and watched the television news, laughing as the violence slowly escalated.

It had been determined by Greg that Gerald concentrate on building wealth, while Greg made his token appearances and rehearsed bad decisions. Gerald despised his brother's appearance in the office anyway.

Vince became uncommonly absorbed in running the construction company.

35

The next major problem was the fact that Greg slipped again after not receiving the necessary discipline of being required at the office daily. Greg and the booze had slowed considerably for a few years. At that moment, his drinking escalated once more. This time, it was not only hazardous but also a suicide waiting to occur.

Carol thought she would never renege on her pledge. She needed to maintain her promise to Greg, but she met with a female student psychiatrist at the University of Missouri-Kansas City that Carol attended to air her concerns.

The woman, Jennifer Lorzani, already had her degree in psychology and was studying to become a psychiatrist.

Carol began smoking again. The one cigarette the night after the murders had led her back to full addiction.

"He never gets violent or anything, but at times I'm worried that he drinks so much, he won't wake up one day," Carol said.

"You say he never gets violent to you, Carol." Jennifer wrote in a notebook as she and Carol talked. "Does he ever get violent toward the children or anyone else?"

"Absolutely never. Greg is a picture-perfect father. He's so affectionate to the children. Other than what he's doing to himself, he's perfect. I've been told that he's never raised his hands to anyone, ever. He doesn't have a mean bone in his body. He normally never gets sad or angry either. When my cousin, his friend Charles Giovelli, was murdered last summer, he went hysterical—breaking things, throwing things. He cried so hard, I thought for sure he'd pass out."

"I hate to say it, Carol, but I think that's probably normal." Jennifer smiled.

"That wasn't normal by any standard, for Greg at least. Jennifer, it was scary."

"Is he losing his appetite?" Jennifer asked as she continued writing.

"No. We eat at home more now than we used to. He still eats out most of the time. Because of school, three or four days a week, I pick something up at one of the delis and bring it home. Candy is only six months old, so she's still on baby food and breast milk."

"Are you sure he's eating, though?"

"No doubt. When he doesn't eat out, he eats at home with the babies and me. I know he eats because I know him that well. I see the dirty dishes in the dishwasher. I know the places he goes for lunch and have driven by. Believe me, he's eating fine."

"Is he letting himself go at all? Not staying as clean? Not showering? Always leaving dishes out and clothes?"

"No, not at all. He's so clean and organized that, at times, it's aggravating."

"Do you know how he's performing at work?" Jennifer inquired, although she already knew the answer.

"I'm sure he's fine. Believe me, his brother runs the company and doesn't want Greg around. I guess the little that Greg is there, he's of very little help. He's done some things that are pretty profitable. Gery told me that Greg is real smart about real estate when he applies himself, which is rare. Gery makes a lot more money, but Greg still makes millions yearly. I don't know exactly how much. All I know is that as a girl, I never pictured being around this much money. I never even pictured Greg being this stinking rich when he and I got together. The way he invested in the deli is making my partner and me wealthy now. Greg has given Patty and me advice on purchasing apartments and condos."

"Is he avoiding you when he has been drinking?"

"No. We see each other now more than ever before. I'm sure that's because of the babies. That's how I know he's been drinking so heavily. It doesn't matter what day of the week either. He's always enjoyed partying. I have to say that I do too. His drinking is out of control now. He's drinking as much as twenty to forty beers a day. He also mixes in wine, champagne, bourbon, scotch, tequila, you name it. Not to mention, he does drugs all the time."

"What kinds of drugs?"

"All kinds. Drugs enter his body frequently, if not on a daily basis. Pot, cocaine, speed, and downers. I don't know if he does things like acid or mushrooms anymore, but I'm pretty sure I could tell if he did. He does hallucinate and laughs uncontrollably sometimes, so maybe he still does," Carol said, wiping the tears from her eyes. "I'm sure some of the drugs allow him to drink that much without getting sick."

"Carol, how about the sex?" Jennifer asked, grinning.

"It's still great." Carol blushed. "I've talked to Greg's sister-in-law, and she said there was a time when she and Gery were complete strangers. After their second child was born, she said they never did it. Thank God Greg isn't like that." Carol laughed.

"Does his brother drink?"

"Rarely. Sometimes, though, Gery drinks enough that he and Greg start arguing trivia. Movie trivia, music trivia, it's hilarious."

"What do you think can be done, Carol?"

"I have no idea. That's why I'm talking to you. If I knew, I wouldn't be here. I can't believe you psychiatrists get away with asking that. If that's what they teach you in school, then you're getting ripped off."

"Well, I can't give you any advice on how to deal with another person who isn't physically harming you or your children." Jennifer stood and walked to the coffee machine and continued talking to prevent her next statement from being detected as a blatant lie. "Except to say that I would enjoy meeting him and talking about this in the open."

"He'd go berserk if he knew I talked to anyone about his habits."

"Carol, keep in mind that I'm still a student. I'm closing my notebook now. I'm speaking as a friend, not a student." Jennifer leaned against a file cabinet. "Just talk to him. Tell him you're concerned."

"I promised him years ago, before we were married, that I wouldn't lecture him once about partying. I can't go back on that promise," Carol said, crying again.

"I never said you need to lecture him. You need to talk with him, unless you plan on losing him permanently, and very soon. Even if it hurts you a little to speak about it. I don't care who it is. I don't care what size a person is. How tall, how fat, or thin or muscular. A human body can't tolerate half of what you just described. Human bodies aren't made to absorb that kind of abuse. You need to think of the children also. If he doesn't die from an accidental overdose or alcohol poisoning, he'll die in a car wreck. Think about what could happen if one of the babies is with him in the car. If not a car wreck, then he'll freeze to death because he passes out outside somewhere. Carol, if what you describe is close to being accurate, then you or his father or one of his friends need to say something soon. It may be painful, but if you really care about him, something drastic has to be done."

Carol began to cry harder. She could not imagine life without Greg. She knew Jennifer was correct.

"I really love him. I don't have any idea how to confront him, but I know I need to. Maybe I could get his best friend Vince to say something to him. Vince is my cousin too—Charley Giovelli's brother. Vince isn't much better, though. He might not drink as much, but he eats like a pig."

"Do both of us a favor and don't mention my dad. My dad and Joseph Giovelli didn't get along too well. I think my dad's intelligence had something to do with it. It couldn't have been that big of a deal, though. They still talked all the time. Went out together with your father all the time. I'm sure it was just business stuff."

"You know, it might be a good idea to have Greg's sister-in-law say something to him. She's a nurse and now she's studying to be a doctor. I guess she helped him a few times before I was around. If she talked to him privately, then he wouldn't suspect I had anything to do with it."

"I'm never going to suggest anything to you or anyone else in the least bit deceiving. She could just speak some medical mumbo-jumbo. Also, I can go ahead and tell you that these sessions help me prepare. I need to accumulate so many hours of counseling for credit. This helps me enormously. As I said, Carol, if you ever want the two of you to talk about it in front of someone, I would really like to meet him. I want to do anything I can to help." Jennifer secretly yet desperately desired to see Greg again.

"I don't see it happening—Greg coming. There's no way Greg could ever come this soon. At this point, I can't tell him I spoke with anyone about my concerns. I'm gonna have a private word with his sister-in-law. The sooner the better."

"Call me anytime, Carol. I think I can help." They hugged good-bye.

During the embrace, Carol whispered, "Greg told me one night when he was trashed that he did it with you, so don't worry." Jennifer blushed and smiled.

After Carol walked to the parking lot, the professor of psychology and psychiatry spoke with Jennifer. He had been listening.

"I need to know how well you know Carol before I can allow you to see her as a patient again."

"I really don't know her that well. I've known of her my whole life. I've seen her over the years."

"You've never met her husband?"

"No. I've heard of him."

"Everyone around here has heard of him. Crow Brothers, right?"

"I believe that's right. I believe they're some real estate company or something."

"Big company. They're into everything. They have offices and property everywhere. I've never met him either, but only money can buy that attractive of a woman."

197

"I really need to go, Ron. If you weren't my professor, I would say that's the most sexist thing I've ever heard." Jennifer abruptly walked out.

Carol telephoned Chateau Crow to talk with Sherry. Carol informed Sherry that an urgent meeting was necessary. They agreed to meet at a restaurant in the River Quay. Sherry was already there when Carol drove up in her new Ferrari. The normal pleasantries were exchanged as the two sat down.

"Indian summer. Sixty-four degrees in November. Only here. Tomorrow it's supposed to be thirty-eight," Carol said, visibly apprehensive.

"So what did you need, Carol? I think I know, but tell me. I don't think it was to give a weather forecast. By the way, next week, snow and ice." Sherry smiled.

"Can we order first, Sherry?" Carol asked, paranoid. She looked at all the patrons in the restaurant.

"Sure, but tell me what's going on," Sherry replied.

The Crow wives ordered burgers and iced tea.

"Sherry, it's Greg. The drinking and drugs . . . it's too much. I'm seriously worried now."

"Carol, I don't know what you think I can do. I know Gery, Vince, and Gerome are worried too. I assure you, I can do nothing. Also, that was not what I thought you were going to bring up."

"What did you think this was gonna be about?"

"The murders last summer. You and I have never talked about it. That's why I thought you called. Gery is looking over his shoulder everywhere he goes. He's putting bulletproof glass in every car. He's wearing a bulletproof vest everywhere he goes. He's so paranoid of getting killed himself. You know, the night before Vito Paglissi was killed, he was at our house," Sherry said quietly.

"Greg told me that they talked to Vito the night before, but he didn't say anything about seeing him at your place."

"Carol, I swear that was one amazing night." Sherry realized she was talking too loud and quieted down to a whisper. "Gery said that Greg and Vince figured out that Ant killed Charley and Sandy for Nick Cibella."

"I gathered that. Greg didn't talk about it, but I could see that he and Vince had figured it out."

"Carol, it was amazing. Greg could understand things in pictures that no one else could see. The whole scoreboard at the stadium was the key to him. I confess, I eavesdropped on some of it, and Greg kept seeing and understanding things that no one would ever consider. It seemed like it took forever for him to convince Gery and Vince, but eventually they came to the same conclusions."

"You know, after David Vasallo was killed, when the stations started running the tapes of David saying that my Daddy would kill him or his kids, Greg came right out and said he knew Daddy didn't do it."

"I hate to tell you this, Carol, but Gery thought Willie did kill David until Greg convinced him otherwise," Sherry confessed.

"No, that's completely understandable." Carol spoke in an assuring voice. "I'm sure everyone thought that. Probably still does. I knew in my heart that Daddy couldn't have done it, but the media convicted him right away. The police and feds tore Mom and Daddy's house apart. Greg knows Anthony did it, and he or Vince won't go to the cops. It's been rumored that Nick had Anthony do it. I know Greg is feeding this to people somehow. The worst part of it is that Anthony doesn't have any idea that Greg and Vince know. He came over last night and had a few beers with Greg while they talked about a painting job at our new cabin down at the Lake of the Ozarks. I know Anthony isn't long for this earth."

"I know. I've never trusted the little shit." Sherry snickered. "So what about Greg and the drinking?" Sherry needed to change to another subject.

"Greg knows you're studying to be a doctor. If you just talk with him, he'd listen," Carol begged.

"Carol, I'm sorry to tell you this, but I've been going to medical school for over two years now. Gery told me that Greg doesn't even know."

"Sherry, he knows. He either forgets or he plays dumb for Gery. I honestly think he forgets. He forgets almost everything. Or, I should say, he has a selective memory."

"That's a classic sign. I'll talk to him if you want me to. But I really don't know what good it would do."

"Someone needs to talk with him soon. I can't. I promised him years ago I never would. He'd respect your opinion medically. I don't think he has given consideration to his health."

"I don't know how to approach him without him knowing you talked with me about it. If I told him Gery asked me to talk with him, he would just drink more to spite Gery."

"It would be nearly impossible for him to drink more. I don't know this, but you could talk to Gerome first. Gerome has questioned me about how frequently Greg is drinking right now. If you talked to Gerome and had him call Greg to his house, then he'd think it was his father's idea. Greg is still a kid when it comes to his father," Carol said with a smile.

"I know. So is Gery. You have to admit Gerome is a fox, even at his age."

"He is that. Have you ever seen pictures of their mother, Ruth? She was absolutely gorgeous," Carol smiled seductively. Sherry could see something in Carol she had never seen prior to now. "She was only twenty-two when she died."

"That's where Greg and Gery got their blond hair. They both seemed to have inherited the best of their mother and father. Greg a little more of Ruth, though." Sherry tried to conceal her smile.

Carol could not resist. "Sherry, look. Greg was so drunk one night after we first got married that he told me he had sex with you," Carol said.

Sherry smiled and, as if on script, choked on a bite of her hamburger. "You've known this since then?"

"When Greg gets rip-roaring drunk, he tells me everything. I don't even pry him for information. He just starts talking. Sometimes it's really scary or hilarious. He starts hallucinating when he does drugs. Or a combination of drugs along with the booze. Talking to people who aren't there. He starts taking orders from these imaginary people. Push-ups, sit-ups, jumping jacks, he starts saluting them. You wouldn't believe it. He'll sit at the kitchen table and carry on a conversation with some invisible guy named Alfred. Sometimes he starts talking to Spock from *Star Trek*. He walks around holding his right hand up, like a Nazi saluting Hitler, and shouts 'Spock!' Sometimes Greg says that the Skipper from *Gilligan's Island* gets inside his brain and forces him to call everybody 'Little Buddy.' I have to admit, it's cute sometimes. Lately, it's been getting worse. The next day he won't remember anything." Carol took a deep breath. "Anyway, when you and Greg did it, that was before he and I got together. It was none of my business."

"Carol, when it happened, I was stone-cold sober and Greg was wasted. I'm really sorry, but it was after the two of you had been together for a little while. I didn't know you at all. I'm really sorry. Gery hadn't touched me in months."

"Sherry, I swear, there's nothing to apologize for. We'd only been together for a few days. We didn't really have a commitment to each other yet. If it would've happened after the commitment, I probably would've been pissed. At the time, I was just infatuated." Carol smiled that unintentional sensual smile. "Believe me, Sherry, I was well aware of Greg's past before I decided to move in with him. Even after we got married, there were women calling at all hours of the night, coming by the house unannounced to fuck Greg at three o'clock in the morning. Greg would usually blush or something, and I'd casually inform them I was his wife now. I didn't mind. In a sick way, I guess, it turned me on. It didn't even stop when we moved out of that little house. It slowed down, but very little. Three different times, two girls showed up together. I actually got used to it after a while."

200

"God, whatever you do, don't ever let anyone know, Carol," Sherry whispered. "If it ever got back to Gery that I had sex with Greg, he would just die. I shouldn't care if he knows, but that happened before Gery and I had our deal. Somehow, Greg seems a little different," Sherry wondered aloud. Suddenly she realized that no one other than her or Gerald were supposed to know about the deal. Men she had sex with just thought she was cheating.

"Sherry, I'd never say a word. I know that Greg has never told anyone, except me. Not even Vince. I know for a fact that Greg has been 110 percent faithful to me since the day I moved in with him. Believe me, Greg never talks to anyone but me when he gets drunk. He starts avoiding everyone but me when he goes on these binges, which are soon becoming every day and night. His drinking might be the reason women, even just his friends, aren't coming around anymore."

"I would go absolutely bonkers if women came around the house for Gery."

"You mean men, don't you?" Carol displayed a devilish grin as Sherry turned bright red.

"Greg told you that?"

"No. Charley did. He told me before we got married. I asked him once. Charley swore me to secrecy. I was the only one other than Vince that he ever told." Carol smiled again. "I've talked to Greg about it, though,"

"I thought I was the only one who knew for sure. I mean, I figured Greg knew, and the other men, of course. But I never talked with Greg about it," Sherry said, perplexed.

"Greg said he's known since Gery was in high school."

"Gery said he's known since he was a little kid. When Gery and I talked about it one time, he said the first time he had a homosexual experience, he was already twenty years old. He had already been with twenty or thirty girls by then. He told me that he and Greg shared a girl one time. Greg skipped school one day. He was home with this girl in the middle of the day, and Gery walked in not knowing. Gery said it wasn't one minute before he was doing it with them."

"Sherry, we need to stop talking about this. I'm starting to get flushed," Carol said. They blushed and giggled together as though they were two schoolgirls.

"Carol, I can't tell you how many times I wished I were that girl." Carol and Sherry looked at one another, smiling as if they read one another's minds.

"Sherry, just do me a favor and talk to Greg about the drinking and drugs. I'll do what I can to make sure your fantasy comes true," Carol said with twinkling eyes. It was the first time Sherry realized how spectacular Carol's eyes were.

"Carol, there's no way that you could make that happen."

"How much do you wanna bet? I'll bet I can put it together so Gery doesn't get mad or anything."

"I don't care about Gery getting angry now. Maybe with Greg he might. He and I have a deal that we can both have sex with any men we want. It just can't affect appearances, and the boys can never find out. I'm worried about you. I don't want you getting mad at me."

"I've told Greg before that I wouldn't get mad at him ever if he was with another woman as long as I'd be able to watch," Carol said.

Sherry looked shocked. "You've talked about me having a threesome with Greg and Gery?" Sherry realized she was speaking too loud.

"No, no, no. I've talked to Greg about him having another woman, with me watching,"—long hesitation—"or sharing."

"You're right, Carol. We need to stop talking about this in public. I'm getting ready to pass out just talking about them." Sherry closed her eyes and smiled. "God, what a fantasy that would be. With everything that can be said of Gery, his sexual endurance is incredible. Of course, usually he's alone, but I hear him." Sherry laughed.

"Greg has incredible endurance too. He jacks off when I ask him to and I'm doing it too and we're watching each other. When I'm out of town, I always tell him to make notes so he can show and tell me when I get home. He doesn't do it very long before I'm part of it. I'm getting hot talking about this. I'll make you a deal. You run into Greg accidentally tonight or tomorrow and talk about the drinking and drugs, and I'll make sure your fantasy comes true."

"Sold!"

"Sherry, my fantasy too." Carol seductively touched Sherry's hand.

Following the tab being paid, and Carol adding a little extra for the tip, Carol and Sherry stood at Sherry's Jaguar, plotting to confront Greg. They briefly prattled and hugged one another good-bye.

Seemingly, the light traditional hug deviated into a tight embrace. The tight embrace evolved into a trivial kiss on the cheek. The brief kiss on the cheek turned into a peck on the lips. The peck on the lips evolved into a hand exploration. The hand exploration started lasting for more than just a few seconds, accompanied by an open-mouth kiss. The open-mouth kiss quickly became full-fledged passion as Carol began delicately and discretely tonguing Sherry's neck, face, and ears.

"Carol, we're in public. We can't do this here," Sherry said with closed eyes.

"I know. I can't help it. Follow me to these apartment buildings Patty and I just bought." Carol continued kissing Sherry's neck. "There's a vacant apartment that the agent holds open on weekends as a model." Carol reached her hand up the front of the light jacket that Sherry was wearing and began touching her breasts.

"It's you who should be the model. You're the most gorgeous woman I've ever seen."

"I can't wait, let's go. My mom is watching the babies all weekend."

Sherry followed Carol to the apartments. In less than five minutes, they parked in a private garage attached to one of the amenity-filled apartment buildings. Carol and Sherry went into the furnished model unit and dead-bolted the door.

After nearly three hours, one missed class for Sherry and three for Carol, the Crow wives went their separate ways.

36

The telephone rang that night at the modest Cape Cod–style home of Gerome Crow. It was Sherry telling of her concern over Greg and his drinking. In medical school, the students met someone suffering from cirrhosis of the liver. The man was only a few years older than Greg and appeared healthy other than the jaundice he now agonized through. The man did not exist.

It was very important for Gerome not to notify Carol or Gerald. Sherry quickly convinced Gerome that it needed to be his idea only. Gerome agreed and summoned his son to his home.

"Gregy, you and I need to talk. Sherry has been working with someone who's dying from cirrhosis. She'll be here soon."

At that moment, Sherry pulled onto Gerome's driveway in one of her and Gerald's two Rolls-Royces.

"Dad, there's no way I'm gonna listen to this shit. It's absolutely nobody's business what I do." Sherry entered without knocking. "Did my brother put you up to this, Sherry?" Greg asked.

"No. I've been seeing a patient at the hospital that's dying now. He drank himself to death." Sherry spoke with her eyes wandering.

Greg picked out her body language at once. "You're a fuckin' liar, Sherry. Either Gery put you up to this or Carol did."

"Neither of them did. Gerome and I have talked about it several times recently. What would you say if I told you I can smell alcohol on you now—from this distance?" Sherry smiled.

"Let me think, hmm . . . I'd say fuck you. It's none of your business. I'm leaving." Greg stood up.

"Gregy, please don't leave. I've never said anything to you. You have children now. What about them? You're going to leave them without a dad soon if you don't straighten up. You remember what it was like growing up without a parent. Do you want to put them through the same hell? Maybe

204

it's selfish, but think about me too. I lost my wife from an accident, and more than thirty years later, I still can't deal with it. I think I would kill myself if I lost you or Gery. I couldn't take it," Gerome said with a sigh.

"Greg, Carol didn't put me up to this in any way. I called Gerome and spoke with him about it. Gery and Carol don't know I'm here now. I will say, when I've asked Carol about it, she has never given details. All she says is that she's scared of losing you. Greg, Carol worships you. She thinks you're a god. Not to mention how much you mean to so many people. Everyone around you is scared right now. Greg, I'm scared right now. If it weren't for what I've learned in medical school, I wouldn't know how dangerous this path you're on is."

"Gregy, no one is mad at you. We wouldn't have called you if we didn't think it was a matter of your life or death," Gerome pleaded.

"Please, Dad! That's such an old cliché. You can certainly do better than that. And, Sherry, if Carol didn't put you up to this, then what were your cars doing in the City Market today down in the River Quay?" Sherry opened her mouth, stunned. "Yes, I know your cars were there. If the two of you were gonna plot against me, then you should have driven cars that don't stick out. A Ferrari and a Jaguar, give me a break. You must really think I'm stupid. You don't think I have eyes and ears all over this city. Fuck you, Sherry. Carol was supposed to be in class today. Someone from school called. You're really a terrible liar, Sherry."

"Greg, I'm not lying to you. She had to check on something with Patty down there. I was down there to go to a craft shop. We saw each other and had lunch," Sherry said, attempting to trivialize her actions.

"Then you plotted against me." Greg smiled.

"That's awfully egotistical, don't you think? I asked her about the drinking and drugs. She said she was scared. That's it. I told her about the man at the hospital. Carol wouldn't talk to you because she promised she never would. I swear, all she said to me was that she's scared of losing you. Done."

"Gregy, you can do what you want. But if you keep this up, you're going to isolate yourself."

"Why, Dad? I'm never violent. I'm never nasty. I'm never abusive to anyone. I'm always clean."

"Gregy, I know that's all true. Do you have any idea what it's like to be around someone who's constantly slurring their words? Someone you love more than yourself who's killing himself fast?" Gregy shook his head no. "What would you do if someday when Danny grows up—presuming you're still alive, which is doubtful at the rate you're heading to death—and he abused himself the way you are? I'll guaran-damn-tee you'd step in."

"So why don't you just get me out of the company and let Gery the wuss run it if I'm such an embarrassment?" Greg asked sarcastically.

"I can't do that. And you're anything but an embarrassment. Gery has told me he needs you. Even if I still had that power, I wouldn't do it. I love you. I love my grandkids and I love Carol. I'm scared too. If Sherry hadn't called me tonight, I would've never thought of confronting you about this."

"Call me any names you want, Greg. Be mad at Carol if you want. Just please do something to stop this now. We all love you. You're way too nice for me to just sit by and watch you kill yourself. You know how Mark and Michael feel about you. When Michael said one night he didn't want to be with you because of the way you were talking that night, I broke down and cried," Sherry whined.

"All right, I'll clean up my act. I'm sorry. When Charley and Sandy were killed last summer, I started drinking heavily again. Sometimes drinking is the only way I can stop the nightmares. I'll cut down."

"That's all we're asking, Gregy. Cut down. If you can't cut down, you need to stop completely."

"That won't be necessary. I can cut down."

Gregy hugged his father and walked out instantly. Sherry's Rolls-Royce blocked his Volkswagen Thing. When she came outside to drive away, Sherry forced a hug on Greg that he obviously did not have any interest in.

"That's the same perfume Carol wears. I've never noticed that on you before. She tries to cover up the cigarette smell with it. She thinks I don't know she smokes again. I do know. I just have enough courtesy not to talk with her parents and brother about it. See you later. Hopefully much later. You have sixty seconds to move your fuckin' car, or I'll back it out with force. Sixty seconds, starting *now!*" Greg bounced in his Thing and began revving the engine. He started backing up till he touched the bumper of the Rolls-Royce.

Sherry cried, shaking with wide eyes, as she backed out rapidly and sped away. Until his turn to go home, he stayed right on her tail. He even nudged her bumper a few times at stoplights.

It was the first time Sherry had ever been afraid of Greg. It was the first time she'd ever witnessed an evil temper in her brother-in-law. Greg thought the whole thing was funny. He was not mad. He genuinely thought it was funny.

He drove on and stopped at a neighborhood bar. For some reason, Carol was there. He then walked in the backdoor and entered. He saw Carol and Sherry immediately.

How the hell did Sherry get here before me? I turned away from their house.

She must have followed me and come in through the front door. They're gonna gang up on me. How in the world did they know I was gonna stop here? Habit, I guess. I guess I stop here every night. Drink the shot real quick and order another one. That'll show them. God, Carol is beautiful.

Carol and Sherry charged him at once.

"Just couldn't resist, could you?" Greg asked while continuing to drink and talk. "So I suspect this is gonna be a lecture on everything I've done wrong since I was eleven."

"Not at all, Greg," Carol whispered with twinkling eyes. "Everything you do well is more accurate."

"So did you prompt Sherry to lecture me tonight, Carol?" Greg stared directly at Sherry as he addressed Carol.

"In a way, I guess. I told her I was worried about you. I love you. If I didn't prompt her at lunch, then that would say I didn't care. I would let you drink or drug yourself to death," Carol said, hugging Greg. "I can't watch you do it. You mean too much to me."

"Greg, asshole, you scratched my car!" Sherry shouted.

"Then paint it, bitch! It's not like you don't have the money." Greg took a big swig.

"That's not the point. You could have seriously injured me, rear-ending me like that."

"Don't be so melodramatic, Dr. Bitch. It was just a little love tap." Greg laughed.

"You really rear-ended her, Greg?" Carol asked, surprised.

"It was nothing, honey. Sherry is probably becoming like my brother. She probably enjoys being rear-ended." Greg laughed and ordered another beer. Two customers near them chuckled.

"Greg, please don't say that so loud," Sherry whispered harshly. "I don't want people hearing that about my husband. Everyone knows who your brother is."

"I'm sorry. So if the two of you aren't here to gang up on me, then what are you here for?" Greg asked.

"Greg, I'm here to see you and have a few drinks. The babies are with Mom and Daddy this weekend. We have all weekend together," Carol said suggestively.

"Then what are you doing here, Dr. Eagle Nose?" Greg asked, laughing. He knew he was going to receive a nasty comeback.

"I suppose that's directed at me. I'll tell you, Mr. Moon Chin. I'm here to party with you. Carol and I ran into each other today and talked about everything."

A glance of disbelief came across Greg's face as he looked at his wife. Carol smiled brightly and nodded her head yes.

"Greg, you're the one who told me years ago one night when you were wasted. Sherry had no idea that I knew until I told her I did." Carol laughed.

"Am I wrong to think this is an invitation?" Greg smiled as he eyed Carol.

"No, Greg. I told you that I'd love to watch you with another woman. You didn't believe me. I never had sex with another woman in my life. Until today," Carol said. Greg's jaw dropped, and he adjusted himself. "This is my fantasy, honey. Let me live it."

Greg was understandably shocked, and Sherry was understandably embarrassed as people in the bar watched when Carol planted a kiss on Sherry's lips. Carol then guided her husband's hand to Sherry's breasts.

"Carol, stop it. There are people watching," Sherry said, grinning as she pushed Greg's hand away.

"Does my brother know?" Greg looked directly at Sherry.

"Absolutely not. I will tell him unless you do exactly what Carol orders."

Greg looked at Carol, confused, as she smiled with one arm around her husband and the other arm around her sister-in-law.

"What a terrible position to be in. I guess I owe you an apology, Sherry." Greg smiled.

"You don't owe me an apology, Greg. Just stop this self-destruction." Sherry kissed Greg on the lips. "Stop for everyone. Please."

"Let's go," Greg said, clapping his hands. He whispered to the stocky bartender and slipped him $200 as an advanced tip.

Customers in the bar were unaware of what transpired. There were murmurs from two men sitting near the wives and Greg in the dark and gloomy smoke-filled room.

"Rich freaks."

"That guy has all the money in the world. What a lucky jerk."

"Isn't he married to Willie Cassivano's daughter?"

"Yeah. That was her acting like a drunken slut."

"Good-lookin' lady. What a lucky jerk."

The bartender stepped up to the men. "Gregory Crow told me to buy every drink for you guys all night. Only as long as you keep your mouths shut. Said to put it on his tab. Order up." The two men were given their cocktails.

"He's a nice kid, though."

"Yeah, he spreads the money around. Nice kid."

208

Sherry telephoned her husband at the office to let him know that she would not be home until late, hopefully. Gerald understood.

Carol directed the entire scene. When she did participate, she paid equal attention to her husband and sister-in-law.

At about midnight, Sherry drove home to find her husband sound asleep on the sofa of the sitting room inside the master bedroom. Folders and papers, real estate contracts, and blueprints littered the sitting room floor as usual. Sherry quietly washed up, douched, and slipped into the sexiest negligee she could find. She nudged her husband and woke him to suggest he get undressed and come to bed.

"I'm sorry, honey. I guess I fell asleep working again," Gerald mumbled.

"You keep complaining about your back. Sleeping on that rock of a couch is why. It's for sitting, not sleeping."

"You're so sexy in that. Was it anyone I know?" Gerald asked, obviously jealous.

"Gerald Alvin Crow, you know the rules." Sherry smiled.

"I'm sorry. You are sexy tonight. I love you."

"I love you too. Get cleaned up so you can go to sleep."

After Gerald cleaned up, he went to bed, holding Sherry in his arms. Within minutes, they were making love. This had been one incredibly sex-filled day for Sherry. Her sex life was only beginning.

37

On Monday morning, November 15, 1976, it was an unseasonably violently cold and frozen day in Kansas City. Gary Porter had an easy mission: connect a bomb that explodes the millisecond Sonny Brown ignites the engine of the dealer car he would be driving. On Sunday evening, Gary attempted to do as he had been instructed. One colossal problem, Gary was a true imbecile as he wired the wrong automobile.

Because of the glacial conditions, an automobile driven by the father of a soon-to-be-sixteen-year-old boy, looking to help his son purchase his first car, slid into the explosive-wired vehicle. Sparks flew as the father attempted to unlock the bumper of his vehicle from the left front wheel well of the sloppily dynamite-wired automobile. A detail technician watching came to assist with a floor jack to elevate the wired car. Insignificant sparks flew as the automobile was sufficiently jacked, then the father and the boy spun the tires on the icy, unsalted pavement. A mechanic from the garage next door volunteered to the use of his tow truck at no charge. Following the two automobiles being safely unlocked, the detail technician lowered the wired automobile too quickly. The teenager, his father, the detail technician, and the mechanic from next door were accidentally instantly murdered.

Boom! Another vehicle exploded. Two more onlookers were killed. The explosions shattered the window of the business shanty shared by Sonny Brown and fellow salesman and owner, Chad Thompson.

Sonny was completely oblivious to the fact that the booby trap had been intended to annihilate him. Owner Chad Thompson was puzzled. Chad had been handsomely compensated to be positive Sonny took that particular vehicle that evening. The wrong vehicle exploded. An automobile wired that unprofessionally may not have exploded on ignition. The automobile would have exploded without reason.

The explosions were seen and heard miles around. Ambulance, police,

As the Crow Falls

and fire departments barricaded the streets surrounding Quality Motors as a precaution. The bomb squad began searching neighboring houses and vehicles. Bomb-sniffing dogs confirmed no explosives nearby. Although the main purpose of the explosion was unsuccessful, the second purpose of the explosion was effective as a diversion from what was transpiring in a secluded garage in Gladstone, Missouri, near Kansas City International Airport.

Gary Porter was already well aware that his car bomb did not work properly. He would refund the money used for the explosives, as any traditional stand-up guy would. This hit would need to be done the old-fashioned way. Gary and his brother-in-law, made member John Lorzani, had been informed that torture would be necessary prior to this hit in order to gain information about the murders of Charles and Sandra Giovelli. Gary was assured that if this assignment were carried out properly, the failed bombing would be overlooked, and he would receive his status as a member.

After being lied to, Tommy "T Boy" Branato was convinced his expertise in the area of firearms and explosives was desperately needed. Tommy was convinced his presence would be necessary because of the insufficient knowledge Gary and John held in all subjects. Tommy was given $1,000 to supervise the purchase and pickup. Tommy volunteered to drive. Once inside the garage, the real purpose of his presence was evident.

Gary sprayed Tommy in the face with an aerosol household chemical that did not burn. John shot Tommy in the buttocks. The gunshot from the .22 caliber legally registered to John penetrated Tommy's wallet.

"Grab him, dumb shit!" John yelled, as he and Gary grabbed Tommy and his gun before Tommy had the chance to pull it out. Tommy fought back too aggressively for comfort and was lightly hit in the head with a shovel. Gary retrieved some rope and chains that he used to insufficiently tie Tommy's hands and legs. Once dragged inside the house, John retied the chains and rope securely.

The torture method Gary rehearsed was unsatisfactory to John. The man supposedly being tortured looked confused. It was a glove made of masking tape and thumbtacks. The problem was that the tape kept falling off with every smack because Gary decided to push the thumbtacks through the tape that was not fastened to his hand because the sticky side was out. When Gary realized this method of torture was not working, he went to the basement to get a baseball bat.

"Damn, Gary. We need to get information from this guy. You can't beat him unconscious," Idiot Lorzani shouted.

"I never thought 'bout that. Let's just stab him," Imbecile Porter said.

211

"Gary, you stay out of the way and let me handle this. Don't do anything but watch." Idiot Lorzani walked back out to the garage and did not see anything that would work sufficiently.

Imbecile Porter actually had an idea. "Let's just use a knife to cut little tiny pieces of him. That should be painful enough," Imbecile said.

"Forget it, Gary. We're not leaving tiny bits of blood in my daughter's house. That might get noticed. Let's take him into the shower and scald him with hot water."

Imbecile and Idiot dragged Tommy into the hall bathroom. They violently threw him in the porcelain tub and turned on the water as hot as possible. After steam started rising, they were ready to begin asking questions and forcing answers.

The goof Imbecile and Idiot made had Tommy faking pain. It was uncomfortable enough, but it was not painful at all. Tommy was fully clothed. He had taken his bulky coat off in the car and seriously wondered if these guys would have been smart enough to remove the heavy coat had he continued wearing it. At times, they would push his face under the hot water. Tommy convinced himself that it was no more uncomfortable than dunking his head in a hot tub. Nevertheless, Tommy found that he was a good actor as he could fake pain visually and audibly. Imbecile and Idiot laughed at the man in obvious pain. Tommy knew his life was in grave jeopardy, but he wanted to laugh also. Tommy was nearly out of his makeshift shackles as false answers were given to the bathroom guards.

Imbecile and Idiot were not aware that the hot water was running out. Idiot noticed the homemade handcuffs slipping off and quickly secured them again. Imbecile plugged the drain and forced Tommy to gulp massive amounts of water, as he would hold Tommy's head underwater for long periods of time. Then Idiot had a great idea. Idiot pulled out a lighter and used it to burn marks on Tommy. Now the torture was real. The screams let Imbecile and Idiot know this method worked.

"So tell me one more time—who killed Charles and Sandy Giovelli?" Imbecile Porter asked.

"Anthony!"

"Anthony who?" Idiot Lorzani asked.

"Anthony Gilante!"

"We know Sonny Brown helped. What was his job?" Idiot asked, as he noticed the lighter held to the bottom of Tommy's chin continued to lose its flame. Idiot realized that the water extinguished it. He wiped Tommy's face dry and held the lighter back under Tommy's chin again. Surprisingly to Idiot and Imbecile, the flame did not extinguish itself when dry.

"Sonny drove and shot 'em. Anthony shot 'em, too. I stabbed 'em."

The flame burned Idiot's finger and forced Idiot to drop the lighter in the water. Imbecile went to retrieve another lighter. When Imbecile walked back to the bathroom, he flicked the lighter under Tommy's earlobe and asked a meaningless question.

"Why did they do it?"

Tommy could have been under any torture method available and could not have answered that.

"I don't know. Anthony wanted it done," Tommy said, moaning.

Imbecile lit the other earlobe.

"Why?" Idiot asked.

"I don't know! Gary, please," Tommy begged with a blood-curdling scream.

"Was Anthony saying why?" Idiot asked.

"He just gave us money to do it," Tommy said.

Idiot picked up a towel and wet the tip of it and snapped Tommy in the face. Imbecile lit Tommy's left cheek. Imbecile then lit the right cheek.

"Gary, please stop. What else do you want?" Tommy screamed in obvious pain.

"Do you know if anyone else gave Anthony orders?" Imbecile asked as he lit Tommy's chin again. The screams were chilling to anyone who would have been smart enough to recognize human suffering.

"I don't know if anyone did. If anyone did, it would have been Nick Cibella." Tommy moaned.

"What about killing David Vasallo?" Idiot asked.

"Just me and Anthony. That was for Nick too, I think. I don't know who. Anthony just paid me. Gary, please don't."

"I think he meant 'please burn me again,'" Idiot said.

Idiot took the lighter from Imbecile. This time, Idiot held the flame from the lighter under Tommy's nose. Tommy could not take the heat and bit Idiot's right index finger all the way to the bone. Idiot was furious. They held Tommy's head under the water for almost a minute until Idiot noticed his finger bleeding profusely. The tip of Idiot's index finger, including half of the fingernail, was gone. Idiot wrapped his finger in toilet paper and searched his daughter's home for Band-Aids.

When Idiot walked back into the bathroom, Imbecile was sitting on the toilet, smoking a cigarette. Tommy sat in the tub, shackled, burned, and totally dumbfounded at the stupidity surrounding him. Worse, Tommy Branato was amazed that these two clodhoppers had duped him. Idiot took off his belt and strangled Tommy "T Boy" Branato. Idiot killed him dead. Just to make sure Tommy was dead, Imbecile took off his own belt and killed that motherfucker again.

Thomas Branato had been reported missing after the customary forty-eight hours. Twelve days later, police found his partially frozen body in his very own car, with his very own license plates, in the busiest parking lot of the busiest terminal of the Kansas City International Airport. Three warmer days prior to the body being discovered, people passing by the car complained of the stench.

It was obvious to any layman that Thomas had been tortured before he was strangled to death. Torture in a mob killing is unusual unless information needed to be obtained. If the police knew at the moment who was responsible, they would have seriously wondered, "What order?"

Smeared fingerprints were found. Blood was found on the exterior of the trunk and on the steering wheel.

38

Gregory Crow and Vincenzo Giovelli met at Giovelli Construction after police found the body of Thomas Branato.

Greg had been sober for over two weeks. Sobriety for Greg meant that no more than twelve beers could be consumed daily. Marijuana and downers were smoked or consumed in multifarious fashion by Greg every day. Carol actually preferred it this way. It eliminated Greg stumbling around in front of the babies. Besides, Carol loved pot.

"I found out Lorzani has never been arrested, but his fingerprints are on file with Liquor Control." Vince breathed deeply. "Greg, it's only a matter of time, maybe just hours, before the police finger him. I asked Gary what happened. After about twenty minutes, I finally got a nonretarded answer from the guy. No offense to retarded people, they're much smarter than Gary Porter," Vince said with a grin.

"Vince, what do you think we can do before this gets out of hand?" Greg asked.

"For starters, we need to get a message to Lorzani never to say one word to anyone if he's picked up. Let him know his bail will be taken care of. I'll just call Willie now and have him deliver the message." After Vince used his telephone ring code at Willie's garage, Willie called him back from a pay phone. The two talked for more than twenty minutes with Greg absent from the room. "If the police don't get to Lorzani first, we need to. I never thought I'd say this, Greg, but he's gotta go."

Greg's head was hanging low. "Vince, you know I don't wanna hear that. I will say that you're running out of people to do this."

"What would you think about meeting Ant and having him get rid of Lorzani?"

"I'm not gonna meet with him for that. Why do you keep asking me or telling me things that you know I don't need to know? And things you know I'm not gonna answer?" Greg asked.

"I'm sorry, Greg."

"Even if I did want to be part of it, Ant is gonna figure out—if he hasn't already—that we're on to him. I don't know what happened, but he probably knows the bomb was meant for Sonny. And with Tommy Branato gone, Ant is probably looking over his shoulder in our direction." Greg mimicked looking over his shoulder.

"I know. Let's get Gary to take care of John," Vince said, only for the purpose of receiving Greg's direct response.

"I'm seriously wondering if he's smart enough. I'm really scared that he'd mess this up and get all of us caught. John is Gary's brother-in-law. How's he gonna react if you order him to kill his wife's brother?" Greg asked.

"What other choice do we have?" Vince asked with a hint of anger in his voice.

"Just you, Vince, not me." Greg slapped his chest.

"I know. After Willie takes care of this message, just give Willie a whole bunch of money and a list of names. He'll figure it out."

"I'm not gonna meet with Willie for that. I don't want him to think his daughter is married to a person capable of ordering the murders of people. I'm not ordering them to be killed. I should have just let it go back then. I'm so confused. I'm seriously getting scared now."

"Me too. I'll tell you what. Since you don't want to know anything, as usual, I'll meet with Willie. I'll give him whatever he asks and leave you out of it. Willie doesn't need to know you're involved in the least. Just make sure that somehow I get my money back."

"I've never given you any reason to doubt me when it comes to money," Greg protested.

"I know, just bear with me. I'm really not mad at you at all," Vince replied.

"You sound like it." Greg voiced the obvious.

"I'm not, Greg. I'm just nervous right now. Plus I'm so overloaded with work right now. I need to hire someone to help with this shit. I can't tell you how much business I'm losing out on because I just can't keep up," Vince said, frustrated.

"Just hire some people," Greg said, as if it should be so easy.

"I've never hired anyone but secretaries in my life. I need to find a vice president, but I have no idea how. The foremen do all the hiring for the crews through the unions or subs."

"Go to a headhunter. Or executive placement. They can help," Greg said with a hint of assurance.

216

"I need to find someone who can be trusted with this other money and stuff."

"I'll ask Jacob Rosenstingel at our office. He might be able to help find someone. And he knows almost everything."

"That's a good idea. I don't want to sound racist, but I would prefer for it not to be someone Italian."

"In case you haven't noticed, Vince, you're Italian," Greg replied with a smile.

"That's exactly why I don't want someone else who is. I also don't want to hire a woman. So many bad things can happen. If you don't pay them double or triple, they scream sex discrimination. I actually thought about hiring my wife. If she weren't my wife, she would be the only woman I would hire."

"Do you know how ridiculous that sounds? She's a woman and she's Italian. The very two characteristics you said you didn't want." Greg laughed.

"Sally is so smart, though. And she's a structural engineer too. I guess you're right. My mind is turning to mush from all this work."

There was a knock on the door. Greg's courier from his own office dropped off a blueprint tube from Crow Brothers.

"Hey, kiddo. Have you ever met Vince Giovelli?" Greg asked as he looked up.

"No, sir," the kid said.

"Vince Giovelli, this is Brian Nivaro. Brian Nivaro, meet Vincenzo Giovelli." Vince and Brian shook hands.

Vince was astonished. This was the first time Vince ever shook a hand larger than his.

Brian Nivaro was a towering, muscular, yet awkward-looking kid with severe acne on his chin and nose. By the look on his face, this kid could not have been older than seventeen or eighteen. His body looked like he was a seasoned lumberjack. Not only did this kid's biceps fill his shirt, but also, more noticeably, his arms filled the raggedy winter coat he wore. Light-brown hair and bright-blue eyes. When the acne cleared up, this kid was destined to be wildly in demand by every woman on the face of the earth. He was taller than Vince, yet more slender and muscular than Vince at that age. With the exception of the acne, Brian had better looks than Greg at his best.

I can't remember what Brian's situation is.

"Brian, sit down. We hardly know each other," Greg said, as Brian took off his coat and displayed the nicest male physique either Greg or Vince had ever set eyes on.

"I can't stay long, I've got a bunch of deliveries to make," Brian announced.

"So, Brian, what grade are you in?" Greg asked.

"I'm out of school now. I graduated last May. I want to go to college, but I can't until I can afford it. I'm taking two classes, or six hours, at the community college. But you can't earn a degree there, so I'm living at home and saving."

Greg and Vince looked at one another and grinned.

"What do you want to study?" Vince questioned.

"I'd like to be an architectural or structural engineer."

That was the nicest answer Vince could have received.

"Mr. Nivaro, or Brian—is it OK to call you Brian?" Vince asked.

"That's my name, so, of course, I don't mind." Brian shrugged.

"That's exactly what my degree is in. Structural engineering. Minor in business. How much do you know already?" Vince asked.

"Not much, really. That's what my dad did before he died. I want to make my mom happy."

"I'm sorry, Brian. Vince and I both lost our mothers when we were young. I'm truly sorry," Greg said compassionately.

"No, it's all right. He died when I was two. I don't remember him."

"How old are you now?" Greg asked.

"I turned eighteen in late August. Look, I really need to go, Mr. Crow. Mr. Giovelli, it was nice meeting you."

"Wait a minute, Brian. Have you ever thought about grants or loans?" Vince asked.

"Student loans, yes. They're a joke. Since I'm still living at home, they won't loan me the money. I only applied for three loans. I got frustrated and stopped applying. One of my friends lives at home and he got a loan. As for grants, I don't know. My mom and stepfather make just enough money that they turned me down. I really need to go."

"Were you ever in football?" Vince asked, smiling.

"Yes. I played briefly. I could hit pretty hard. I was good in the games, but I hated practice. I played basketball and baseball too. I wasn't very good at either of them. People ask me that all the time. I really don't like sports, except wrestling. I was real good at that. I play drums and piano. If I ever get to college, music will be a minor. I need to go."

"If Gery gives you any trouble about running late, I'll take the blame." Greg pointed at himself.

"Mr. Crow, I hate to be rude, but I need to get to two banks before two o'clock, so it's not just your brother. I have to go." Brian shook Greg

218

and Vince's hands again and began to put his coat back on. Greg noticed there was a gun in the pocket of Brian's coat.

"Brian, I noticed there's a gun in your coat pocket. Do you wanna explain yourself?" Greg asked sternly.

"Am I fired, Mr. Crow?"

"No, I'm just asking." Greg smiled with assurance.

"I had a few problems with muggers following me from the office. For some reason, people think I carry cash on me because of the stupid magnetic signs that are on the delivery van."

"Take the damn signs off!" Vince shouted.

"Nothing is worth your life," Greg added.

"Mr. Rosenstingel won't allow me that common-sense privilege. I told him about the muggers, and he said I had to leave the magnets on the van," Brian said, obviously frustrated.

"Tell him you take the signs off or you quit," Greg said loudly.

"I can't do that. With all respect, sir, some of us aren't born with money. When I use my own car, they pay me twenty-two cents a mile. I would use it all the time, but it doesn't want to run that often. Mr. Rosenstingel lets me drive the van home at times. When he doesn't, I hope my car starts or I go home with my mom. Look, I really need to make it to the banks."

"What does your mom do again?" Greg acted as though he had a temporary memory lapse. The fact was, he never knew. Or did he?

"She's a secretary for you," Brian said, unsurprised that Greg forgot.

"That's right. She works in our acquisitions and mergers," Greg recollected.

"I need to leave," Brian said with visible offense.

"I understand, Brian. Take the damn signs off the van right now. I'll tell Jacob and Gery to lay off. It's my order. I'll tell them that." Greg smiled.

"I appreciate it, Mr. Crow."

"Brian, don't call me Mr. Crow again. Just Greg. You make me feel old."

"Yes, sir."

"Or sir. I know you're very polite, but that's as bad as mister to me. Just Greg."

"Greg, thank you. Nice to meet you, Mr. Giovelli."

"Same rules. Call me Vince."

Brian walked out with Greg and Vince smiling.

"Vince, wipe that shit-eatin' grin off your face. I know what you're thinking, and I am too. Let me pull up his file and do some background checks on him."

"Greg, I'm thinking you need to do the checks quick. The new semester

219

starts in about three weeks. One way or another, that giant youngster is going to college. Italian name too!"

"You don't trust other Italians, remember?" Greg said sarcastically.

Vince and Greg made some diminutive talk about Brian Nivaro. Greg agreed that the background check on Brian would be done quickly. Vince opened the blueprint tube from Gerald with Greg present.

"You know, Gery isn't like any other developers in the country, to me at least. He sends me these prints before he has even acquired the land to build on. I wonder how many other contractors he grants that privilege to?"

"Hell if I know. He does something right, though. Honestly, I think you might be the only one. I know for a fact he doesn't send prints on jobs out of town."

"Greg, do you have any idea how expensive it is to have architects draw up plans? Some of them are outrageous. I'll look at it at home tonight or whenever I get around to it. It looks like a hotel here. Crown Regency. I don't have the time to look right now."

"So I guess blowing off the rest of the day and getting drunk is out of the question."

"Leave, Greg, before I'm tempted to act like you," Vince said, laughing.

"I'll go do the background check today."

Greg went into Crow Brothers to obtain the personal information on Brian Nivaro. Greg telephoned a friend who did background checks on the employees of the casinos in Las Vegas. Greg gave the friend Brian Nivaro's social security number and birth date.

The following morning, the friend called Greg at home. Brian Nivaro had two arrests as a minor for pranks and one arrest for misdemeanor assault on a member of a rival high-school wrestling team. Three arrests with no convictions; minor crimes. No fingerprints, no mug shots. One speeding ticket. Mother: Marilyn Davis. Probably her second or third marriage. No father on record. Greg asked the man to check on the father a little further. In minutes, the man called back. No father on record. Greg went to pick up the file on Marilyn Davis. She had indeed been married to a man named Angeto Nivaro. Greg called his friend again. In minutes, the man called back and told Greg that her husband was killed while conducting an elevator inspection for a real estate developer in Englewood, Colorado. Following his death, Marilyn changed back to her maiden name. Nothing illegal, just a second marriage. Davis is her second husband's name. Her son retained his birth name. Greg telephoned Vince to notify him.

Over the next few months, Greg and Vince became as familiar with Brian as possible. They had stand-up private detectives doing in-depth

220

background research. In addition to his minor crimes, Brian had been suspended from school three times for fighting—once for ripping a wooden door completely off its hinges and throwing it at another student.

Greg, Vince, and Gerald had it arranged and staged so Brian was pulled over for speeding. After the officer searched the delivery vehicle and found the gun, he began to place Brian under arrest. Seemingly, out of nowhere, another police officer drove up and informed the first officer that Brian was with Crow Brothers. Brian was free to go.

Brian thought working for Crow Brothers was a good job. Now he realized it meant power. Brian had been employed at Crow Brothers for over two years as a delivery boy and as a heavy box and furniture mover.

Greg, Vince, and Gerald told Brian that they would fund his college tuition for him. During the current semester, he would need to go to a community college. In the autumn, he would transfer to a university of their choice. He would need to do some work for them off the clock. In return for the favors, they would remove dollar amounts from his student loans. They purchased a new company car that Brian was allowed to keep at all times along with a company gas charge card.

Because tuition was highly visible, the money loaned needed to be on the books. They could arrange loan payments to be paid back off the books.

Brian started at Longview Community College. In the afternoons and early evenings, Brian worked at Crow Brothers, making routine deliveries and bank deposits, picking up or dropping off dry cleaning, washing cars, and other monotonous duties.

Greg confidentially set an appointment with a dermatologist for Brian to see regarding the acne. Within weeks, the acne cleared.

39

Sherry had her fantasy come true one evening. Greg said that was it. Never again.

Gerald and Sherry were wild about their new young friend, Brian Nivaro. Sexually, Brian did everything and anything Gerald or Sherry asked him to do to them or have done to him. Tuition money was always reduced.

Sherry would spend much of her free time with eighteen- to twenty-one-year-old boys. Brian's friends loved Sherry. Sometimes, as many as five boys would love her simultaneously. Sherry realized she was growing addicted to group sex. Mark and Michael would never find out, and Gerald knew he could not say a word, or else. The reputation of Sherry among young men was filled with respect.

40

Gary Porter killed another six innocent people trying to perfect car bombs meant for his brother-in-law. Yet because he was not Italian, the Kansas City Police Department never suspected him of anything. For some reason, Gary's stupidity actually worked to his advantage.

The police had fingerprints and blood evidence from the automobile owned by Thomas Branato for months, and nothing had come to pass. The usual suspects were questioned: William Cassivano, Anthony Gilante, and Carl Spelo. Two bungled attempts to kill John Lorzani had the police wondering if maybe Lorzani was part of the long list of underworld crimes that had been getting longer.

John Lorzani had never been suspected—that was, until an armed robbery at his nightclub on Sunday, February 13, 1977. A homeless man entered at closing time with a water pistol that looked real. John stood in the storage room doing his weekly inventory when he heard the man ordering the two remaining patrons to empty their pockets and lie down. John was ordered to empty the safe in back and the cash register behind the bar.

Like many small nightclub owners, John had a gun hooked underneath the cabinet holding the cash register. John fired one shot to the head of the water-armed gunman and crippled him. John then emptied his legally registered .22 revolver.

Police questioned the patrons and John Lorzani separately. All three stories were exactly the same. Although this was obviously a justifiable homicide, John went into the police station for routine questioning. While at the police station, an officer noticed the relatively old scabs and new scars on the end of Lorzani's right index finger. When asked how he cut his finger, John replied that he cut it trying to fix a blender at the club. When asked if he had ever been fingerprinted, he told the truth. Liquor Control had his prints on file. His gun was seized as a matter of routine. One officer knew that John Lorzani was part of the underworld. The ballistics from his gun matched the bullet pulled from Thomas Branato's wallet. The fingerprints matched those on the trunk of the car. During the autopsy on Thomas Branato, human skin was found behind his front teeth.

At approximately 1:00 p.m. on Valentine's Day 1977, John Lorzani was arrested for the murder of Thomas Branato. Keeping to his promise, John never said a word to the police. At the arraignment two days later, the bail was finally set at $50,000.

Brian Nivaro delivered $5,000 cash to Janie Lorzani, who would then give it to a bail bondsmen, and John would be released.

41

Greg was once again called into an emergency meeting at Giovelli Construction. Greg presumed it was concerning the bail of John Lorzani. If only. Apparently, Anthony Gilante had also been arrested on an unrelated crime.

"We have a serious problem, Greg." Vince closed the door and instructed the receptionist to hold all calls. "Ant got into a fight last night at a bar. He was arraigned this morning for felony assault and is playing mute. Ant set it up with some Friends of Ours and me, so he would be arrested for misdemeanor assault so he could get to Lorzani." Vince smiled. "Felony assault, even though the guy he supposedly fought with never went to a hospital. Somebody with power and bucks is seriously fucking with Ant." Vince shrugged his shoulders sarcastically. "He'll do a couple years for assault. No bail bondsmen will touch him because of his reputation as a bad dude. His bail is twenty thousand. He won't communicate with anyone."

"If he won't communicate with anyone, then how did you know?" Greg asked.

"You remember Doug Chandler?" Vince asked. Greg nodded his head yes. Douglas Chandler went to college with Charles and Gerald at the University of Kansas. "Doug went back to school and is a lawyer now. A prosecutor. He called me and told me that Ant is in jail. Doug saw him in court this morning. Ant wouldn't say a word. Doug told the judge he couldn't prosecute Ant because of their friendship. Doug called not more than two hours ago, after the hearing."

"What does Doug care if Ant is in a county lockup?" Greg asked, confused.

"He thought it was strange for Ant to be in jail overnight with nobody coming to the rescue." Vince rubbed his eyes.

225

"Are you sure Ant didn't talk to Doug?" Greg asked, with the color gone from his face.

"From what Doug told me, Ant hasn't said one syllable to anyone." Vince shook his head accordingly. "Doug is cool, though. He's on the payroll with Barbara Percival."

"Let's bail Ant out and see if he'll talk to us."

"Greg, I will not, under any circumstances, see Ant. If he thinks we know, then we're both dead," Vince replied, making a gun with his fingers, mimicking pulling the trigger. "You have an unknown go and bail Ant out."

"I don't have that much with me. I've got the cash at home."

"I've got it here," Vince said.

"Let me think about it for a minute. Who to bail Ant out?"

Greg suddenly had a headache. Vince pulled a bottle of vodka from his desk and poured two glasses.

"Maybe we should wait until at least tomorrow to bail him out. Ant won't say a word to anyone. That'll be enough time to set some things up to scare Ant."

"I don't wanna know anything, Vince."

Vince opened his briefcase, pulled out $20,000 cash, and handed it to Greg.

Greg slammed his vodka and walked out. On the drive home, it hit him.

Brian Nivaro can bail Ant from jail and bring him home.

Greg took Vince's advice and rehearsed his speech overnight. He would speak with Brian tomorrow afternoon.

42

"Brian, what I'm gonna ask you can make you a wealthy man as soon as you complete your degree. And very legitimately." Greg smiled.

"I'm listening."

"I remind you that we've already agreed to pay your tuition whether you agree to this or not. So this in no way obligates you." Brian nodded. Greg continued. "Brian, I'm gonna give you $21,000 to bail a friend of mine out of jail. Do you have a problem with that?"

"No, sir!" Brian shouted enthusiastically.

"Please. I know you're a polite young man, but I've asked you to just call me Greg. Call everyone else sir or ma'am if you like, but I'm just Greg. Sir makes me feel like I should be in an old folks' home." Greg smiled. Brian's face gleamed, obviously nervous. "His bail is twenty thousand. I want you to have the other thousand. After you bail him out, take him to this address. That's his home." Greg handed Brian a note. "After you drop him at home, go to Giovelli Construction, their main office. At that point, you'll be given further instructions and another $5,000," Greg said.

Brian had a very surprised expression on his face. "With all respect, Greg, do you have any idea what the other instructions will be?"

"That'll be determined by Vince Giovelli. It's extremely important to me that I don't know anything. Just keep in mind that we'll make you a wealthy man when you graduate," Greg reiterated.

"I understand that and I can't tell you how much I appreciate it. For now, though, I would like to know who I'm bailing out. What crime is he in for?" Brian asked.

"Fair enough. His name is Anthony Gilante. He's in jail for assault, like you." Greg smiled.

Brian looked bewildered. "I've heard of him. Mafia guy." Long hesitation. "How did you know I was arrested for assault?" Brian asked, perplexed.

227

"Relax, Brian. We do background checks on all employees nationwide. We have to do them for the casinos in Las Vegas."

"They sign a waiver. I never signed anything that granted you permission," Brian said, irritated.

Greg was not surprised that Brian knew much more of the law than he did. He knew Brian Nivaro could break him over one of his massive legs, like kindling. Greg knew the solution to this problem. He took an envelope from his briefcase, counted, and gave Brian $5,000.

"That's my way of saying I'm sorry."

Brian was obviously nervous or offended. Greg could not read him. Brian then stood up and stuffed the cash in his pocket.

"Tell me what to do again." Brian suddenly smiled.

I got him. I thought when he stood up, he was gonna pound me.

"Just what I said. Bail him out. Take him home. Tell him your name if he wants it. Ant won't say a word. Then go to Giovelli Construction. I won't be there. Brian, most importantly, never say a word to anyone, including me." With the look on his face, Brian could see Greg was very serious about not knowing.

"How big and strong is this guy?" Brian asked, as though he may have actually been concerned.

"Good question. I would say he's maybe five-foot-four, and that's doing him a favor. By looking at you, I don't think you'll have any problems." Greg grinned.

"I don't know, sometimes short guys are awful tough," Brian said, smiling.

"I seriously don't think you'll have any problems. In case you're worried, bring this with you." Greg handed Brian the same 9 mm automatic pistol Joseph Giovelli gave him years earlier.

I'm just like Joseph now. This is wrong. What am I doing?

"No thanks. I've got a .44 in my car. I prefer it." Brian looked at the 9 mm and shook his head no.

"Well, keep it in your car."

"I'm not stupid. What did you expect me to do? Bring it into the jail?"

"No, I just wanted to make sure you have something to protect yourself."

"Thank you. I guess I need the bail money now." Brian put his huge worn coat on to show he was ready to leave.

"Here you go. Just remember to keep your mouth shut to anyone. Don't even talk to yourself about it, and, most importantly, never talk to me. Then go to Giovelli Construction." Greg handed Brian an envelope with $21,000 in cash.

Brian handled $5,000 in cash for Vince Giovelli yesterday. Brian was stunned yet again. If Brian performed his job correctly, he would have $11,000 in cash by the end of the night. All his. He thinks he knows what the other money will be for. Brian does not care. He killed another kid with his bare hands at the age of thirteen just for fun. He wanted to see how it would feel to kill another human being. Killing another human being made Brian feel so alive. This time it was for money, not fun. Brian can get rich off these guys. As Brian walked out, Greg stopped him and whispered, "Tell Ant some friends of his bailed him out."

Greg telephoned Vince to notify him of their new partner. Vince notified a Friend of Ours in the police department to handle this expeditiously. Vince called a relative to make sure everyone and everything was in place.

43

Brian walked into the Jackson County Detention Center and bailed out Anthony Gilante. The two men were a sight to see as they walked to the parking lot where Brian had parked his personal wreck. Anthony looked like a true midget walking next to this skyscraper and muscular specimen. For the first time in nearly two days, Anthony spoke.

"I guess you know I'm Anthony Gilante. Who're you?"

"I'm not at liberty to say," Brian said, stone-faced.

"You'll have to tell me who you are before I get in your car," Anthony said.

"Brian Nivaro," he said as he showed his driver's license. "You can take a cab if you want. I was instructed to make sure you get home safely."

"To whom do I owe this gratitude?" Anthony asked sarcastically.

"I'm not at liberty to say." Brian had difficulty remembering what Greg whispered to him.

"A stranger came up to you and gave you $20,000 cash to make sure I get home safely."

"Something like that." Stone-faced again.

"Who was it?" Anthony backed away. "Tell me or I am taking a cab."

"Some friends of yours," Brian said.

"Not a Friend of Ours?"

"No, some friends of yours," Brian said, confused.

"All right, let's go." Anthony grinned and jumped in the jalopy vehicle. In minutes, they pulled in front of Anthony's home.

Brian drove away, having completed his secret mission, and looked forward to picking up the remainder of his jackpot and other instructions.

Anthony gazed up and down the street with suspicion. He lived modestly for the money he had accumulated in the last few years. The neighborhood he resided in never complained about the junk car sitting on cement blocks in his front yard. No engine, no backseat, no carpet. The

230

junk car was a prop. Ever the expert and paranoid as Anthony was, a gun had been bracketed to the inside of the front passenger-side wheel well. Cautiously, he walked to the front door. As he slowly approached the door, he heard one of his cats meowing. Suddenly, he relaxed and shoved the gun in his pocket. He remembered his two cats and one little schnauzer must have been starving.

"Daddy couldn't feed 'em when he was away, ooh, poor babies. That's so selfish of me not to have someone come by and take care of my babies. I hope their water is OK. Ooh, poor babies. Daddy's home now, hold on."

He turned on the light and opened the door to shock as he saw twenty or thirty rats scurrying from a cage. Anthony jumped. The cats were destined to have a field day instantly. Anthony now knew who the jerk was behind this: "Willie the Rat." The rats and mice were in a small cage. One side of the cage was spring loaded and wired with fishing line tied to the doorknob. As scared as he was of rodents of any kind, Anthony looked down at what he thought was going to be another rat bumping his foot. If only it were a rat. It was his calico cat Poochy being choked by a fifteen-foot-long boa constrictor. He opened the door quickly. Out of the corner of his eye, he glimpsed at least seven other boa constrictors. As he jumped outside and slammed the door behind him, he had no idea where to turn in the cold twilight. Big ugly snakes choking their own food, rats, mice, and his precious Poochy the kitty, Doggy the kitty, and his old schnauzer Hippie. "Take me, but not my buddies." Snakes in complete control on one side, probably a hundred bullets close at hand on the other side.

Anthony noticed the porch swing. Not because it moved but because there was a legal-sized envelope in the swing that he convinced himself was not there when he entered his home. Once again, he gripped the gun tightly, expecting another rat inside the envelope. He nudged the envelope four times before picking it up. He carefully opened the envelope. He noticed it contained a huge wad of cash, along with a note sealed in a smaller envelope. Before he opened the small envelope, he counted the cash—$25,000. He opened the envelope and examined the typed note.

Dear Anthony,

Please take this money and go to the pay phone at the Laundromat on the corner. We are watching.

Anthony did precisely as the note directed, knowing he could not enter his home. Although he could be considered an explosives expert, he could not inspect his own automobile in the garage because of his undeniable fear of rats. He heard the pay phone ringing. An obviously disguised, intensely deep male voice.

"Anthony, how are you?"

"I'm fine." Anthony could not recognize the voice. Yet.

"There are two jobs for you tonight if you want to stay alive. How are the pets I sent you?"

"They looked fine, Willie. You killed my kitties and my dog." The anonymous voice released an evil, deep, very fake chuckle. Anthony fought back tears of rage for whoever was responsible for those precious little lives.

"It's not William. I'm sorry about the cats and dog, but you know as well as anyone, 'ya do what ya gotta do.' If you want more despicable pets, then piss me off one more time."

Anthony tried desperately to figure out who this voice belonged to. "What do you want?" Anthony was shaking not only because of the cold but also because his nerves were vicious.

"If you'll go to the third dryer on your left, the one with the 'out of order' sign taped to the outside, and lift the lid. Your instructions will be taped to the lid. There will be another great deal of cash if you do your job well."

"Is my car OK?" Anthony asked.

"As far as I know."

"Will I have any more snakes or rats in my garage?"

"Absolutely not!" A long eerie hesitation.

Anthony could see a homeless man with filthy long hair sleeping under the table for folding clothes in the rear of the Laundromat. He was familiar with all the homeless people that frequented his neighborhood. This man was not one of them. He looked outside to see familiar-looking homeless people loitering in a running automobile.

"How do I know that I'm in no danger?" Anthony asked, frightened.

"Oh, you are, my short little friend. If you don't do exactly what I've explained, you will be in grave danger." Mystery chuckle.

"You can't tell me what to do!" Anthony shouted.

"I am telling you what to do. I'll tell you one thing, if you see Brian Nivaro again, remember he's only there to help you."

"The kid that bailed me out this afternoon?"

"Correct. Don't touch him."

"If I do this, I'll still have to stay at a hotel tonight."

"That would be an excellent idea. Unless you enjoy sleeping with snakes wrapped around your fucking neck!" Another deep, mind-piercing chuckle. "Besides, Anthony, you have the money now."

"I know, but when can I go back to my house?"

As the Crow Falls

"After you get the instructions, call the police and tell them about the inside. Break your own windows in order to get inside the garage for your car. When the police get to your house, they'll block off the area. Be honest and tell them you just got out of jail and are going to stay at the Muelbach Hotel for a while, maybe just the night. Check in at the Muelbach, where you will be given further instructions for the evening." The mystery caller hung up.

Anthony walked back home and broke a few glass panes on the garage window and crawled in. He inspected the entire vehicle and determined there were no bombs. Although he was an explosives expert, he could feel his heartbeat inside his throat as he turned the key. He pulled the auto outside and hid the gun and cash under the seat. He then walked two doors back to the Laundromat and telephoned police. The homeless man with the disgusting long hair had disappeared. Police blocked off the area and radioed animal control.

"Do you have any idea who could have done this, Mr. Gilante?" the police officer asked.

"No way. I was in jail for the last two nights, so I don't know."

"What were you in jail for?"

"That's between me and my lawyer."

"Where can we reach you tonight or tomorrow?"

"Muelbach Hotel, more than likely, tonight. I'm sure I'll stay in hotels, maybe for weeks. After you guys get the snakes out, I'm gonna have the house searched with a fine-tooth comb. Whoever did this must know about my feelings for mice and snakes. The damn snakes killed my kitties and dog. I'm fine now, but I thought I was having a heart attack."

"I'm sorry about the cats."

"I had a dog too."

Anthony registered at the Muelbach Hotel, where he was given another envelope instructing him to set his things in his room and leave. He had no luggage or clothes. Immediately, he drove to the parking lot of the boarded-up and deserted Paglissi's Bar & Grill. The parking lot was now used by a neighboring church and was completely occupied.

Brian Nivaro waited eagerly in a brown Oldsmobile Cutlass. He gestured Anthony over to his loaner car. Once inside the car, Brian handed Anthony an empty sawed-off shotgun. Anthony thought of jumping from the moving vehicle until Brian sped up and automatically locked the doors. Anyone attempting to spring from a vehicle moving that fast would be dead the second he touched the frozen pavement. On the way to work, Anthony Gilante and Brian Nivaro had a discussion.

"Nice to see you again, Ant. Here, put these on." Brian handed

233

Anthony a pair of black rubber work gloves that obviously did not belong to Brian. The gloves were Anthony's size.

"Brian, I think I should know a little more about you before we do this."

"I'm not at liberty to tell you anything," Brian said, stone-faced.

"You can't tell me who sent you to do this with me?" Anthony was visibly enraged.

"I'm not at liberty to tell you anything."

"Tell me who sent you, now!" Anthony shouted.

"What, will you kill me if I don't, Ant?" Brian asked, laughing. Brian had a handgun pointed directly at him. "I think you better stop asking questions. If anyone wanted you dead, I would've killed you already. They want you alive. They told me I could learn from you."

"Who is this for?" Anthony asked, pointing at the shotgun.

"John Lorzani and any witnesses."

In minutes, they were at the home of John and Janie Lorzani.

Anthony was given another gun, a loaded .380 with a silencer, and verbal instructions from Brian. Anthony was ordered by this immense specimen to try all the doors and windows on the house, while Brian worked only on the garage door. Brian had a modern gun with a silencer in his cumbersome winter coat.

A woman sat on the living room sofa. The doorbell sounded and prompted her to answer the front door. She recognized Anthony instantly and opened the door to allow him entry. Janie and Anthony hugged. Janie Lorzani was killed by a single shot to the back of the head as soon as she turned her back. Anthony delivered three more shots just to be safe.

Anthony searched all the rooms of the three-bedroom dollhouse on a crawl space and exited through the back door. Anthony and Brian convened at the back of the garage where Anthony was given the sawed-off shotgun again, loaded this time. Brian also had a sawed-off shotgun. They waited for over an hour with just a few trivial words being spoken.

When John Lorzani came home, he always parked in the garage. When the garage door opened, Anthony hid behind a storage cabinet, while Brian squatted behind a garbage can. When John Lorzani emerged from the car, he was shot four times by them. Brian delivered the two nearly decapitating headshots, Anthony the two pulverizing body shots.

Anthony could not wait to drive away from this imposing stranger. They drove back to Paglissi's.

Anthony was positive he would be unable to sleep that evening. On the drive from Paglissi's back to the Muelbach Hotel, he stopped at a convenience store and bought a twelve-pack of beer, cigarettes, and some over-the-counter pain relievers.

Once in the hotel room, he dialed for room service. A gourmet meal, complete with a bottle of red wine. He watched a little television, wondering who this mystery voice could be.

Gerald Crow had only spoken with him a few times since last summer. Never did any conversation between them have any substance. Gerald was the only person he knew who talked with perfect grammar, as did the mystery voice. He did not think Greg or Vince knew, even though Greg and Vince were the only two people he knew who would have this quantity of expendable cash, except Gerald.

Anthony intentionally landed in jail for fighting so he could threaten John Lorzani. He was paid handsomely to do so. If the opportunity presented itself, he would have massacred John in jail.

His arrest was arranged with Friends of Ours in the police department to be a misdemeanor. All Anthony did was accidentally bump into a guy on Valentine's Day evening and caused himself, the guy, and the girl to fall down. The guy and girl were in on it. Anthony purposely cussed at them loudly, acted drunk, then apologized and bought them replacement drinks. Twenty minutes later, he was arrested for drunk and disorderly conduct, as planned.

The following morning, he found out he was being charged with felony assault because of his vast arrest record and one lengthy prison stay. Anthony would not be able to figure this out tonight.

When the evening news came on, Anthony blasted the volume on the television. The murders of John and Janie Lorzani were the lead story. Police were not commenting, other than to say, "Family has been notified." Neighbors heard the gunshots and called police. Reporters came to their own conclusions.

"John Lorzani had been released from confinement yesterday for the murder of reputed mobster Thomas Branato." The reporters declared this to be the latest in a long list of violent crimes and murders committed lately by the Kansas City underworld.

Anthony was about to phone the front desk to request a wake-up call, when his telephone rang. He debated not picking it up, but he knew it may have been the police.

The mystery voice, "Hello, Anthony."

Anthony could barely speak. He gently rubbed his eyes. "I don't suppose you can tell me who you are?"

"Of course, I can. I don't want to, though, so just do as I say and no one will hurt you." Mystery laugh.

"What do you want me to do now? I'm almost asleep."

"You will go see a lawyer tomorrow. Her name is Barbara Percival. She's a tax and corporate lawyer. She and Douglas Chandler will take care of the case. You will need to give her twenty thousand cash."

"Why so much?" Anthony sounded outraged.

"Don't complain, Anthony. We made sure you had it. Did we not? Besides, you were charged with felony assault. That is an expensive crime to buy your way out of."

"It must have been expensive to get me arrested for a felony anyway. That was supposed to be a misdemeanor."

"No, it was really serious. I may have saved your life. Some people want you dead." Another deep sardonic laugh.

"Why is that?"

"I will let you figure that out for yourself. It shouldn't be that difficult. I will give you instructions on when you can go back to your home." The mystery man hung up.

Anthony called the front desk to request a wake-up call at 9:00 a.m. He seriously wondered if he would ever be capable of going home again. His only friends had been murdered and consumed there. He began to cry again. Soon they would be digested and eventually become snake poop.

Anthony made a list of names, crossing them off one by one. He crossed off the names Greg, Gery, Vincey, Willie, Nick, Corky, Brian, and Gary. After an hour, the Ant passed out. He passed out with the question in his head. 'Who was the owner of the mystery voice?'

Fred Vasallo! Anthony woke up in bed. It had to be Fred. That may have sounded like Fred attempting to disguise his voice. He struggled to make sense of it all. Gery, Greg, and Vincey had the money to throw around. However, it could not have been any of the three speaking, although one, or all three of them, may be the money behind the mystery voice.

Anthony considered Greg to be a wimp, though. Greg never wanted to know anything. He contemplated calling Fred at home to determine if it was indeed his voice that controlled his life today. Then he thought it better if he did not. He drank the remaining beers and went back to sleep.

At 8:00 a.m., the telephone rang.

"Mr. Gilante, this is your wake-up."

"What time is it?" Anthony answered, groggy.

"It's eight o'clock, sir."

"I wanted the wake-up call at nine."

"No, sir, Ant. I wanted it at eight." The mystery man.

"What am I supposed to do now?" Anthony asked, frustrated.

"First, you may take a shower. Then take the twenty thousand I asked you to over to Barbara Percival by eight forty-five. Follow her to court, and your case will be thrown out. The police who arrested you will see you in court. Also, one of the police officers that were at your jungle last night will be there. That should give you an excellent alibi. Then eat lunch somewhere and check into the Crown Center."

"Alibi for what?"

"You should know me better than to ask stupid questions like that. Especially after all we've been through together. Alibi for last night, you midget. You need to get it together soon."

"I guess I better get ready then, huh, Gery?" Anthony tried to hear any semblance of familiarity.

"No, it's not Gerald or Gregory."

"I think it is you, Gery."

"Well, you're wrong. If not for me, you would be dead wrong. I'll tell you what. To prove it's not Gerald, call him at home or the office. Knowing Gregory, he's probably just going to sleep, but you should call him anyway. Wake his ass up. That should set in nicely."

"I believe you, Gery. I'll take a shower. Where is this lawyer's office?"

"Fine, call me Gery if you like. Look up her name in the phone book. Barbara Percival. Walking distance from the Muelbach."

"I wrote her name down last night."

"Then we have nothing else to discuss. Right now, that is." The mystery man hung up.

Anthony showered and walked two blocks in the freezing rain to the two-room office of Barbara Percival. He told his name to the thin and gorgeous secretary with light-brown long hair. The dazzling secretary was Barbara Percival. She assured him she was not a police officer. Nevertheless, she needed to search him for weapons. To prove she was not a police officer, she flashed him a nipple.

Barbara had been an exotic dancer in college. Her job as an accountant did not pay the bills as well as being a dancer. Her stage name was Shelly. She had been doing special favors for La Cosa Nostra bosses since she was a teenager. Dancing allowed her the time and money to go back to law school. The gorgeous lawyer patted Anthony down. Anthony counted out $20,000 and handed the cash to Barbara. The two took the waiting taxi to district court.

In the empty courtroom, Barbara took her briefcase inside an adjoining room. Rows of men in shackles and chained together were brought by several correction officers through a door on the right side of the courtroom. The officers loudly instructed the prisoners to sit.

The police officer at Anthony's home last evening was there and approached Anthony to whisper that animal control had not cleared his home for occupancy. Anthony let the officer know that he would be staying at Crown Center this evening. Two of the officers present at Anthony's felony arrest walked out of the witness isolation room. After over an hour in the counselor's conference room, Barbara emerged and pointed to the back door.

Anthony followed Barbara to the curb, where another taxi was hailed. Anthony and Barbara did not say a word to one another during the eight-block drive. After she unlocked the office door, she spoke to Anthony without looking at him.

"Case dismissed. You're free to go." She turned and began working on something else.

"That's it?"

"Afraid so, Ant. Please leave now." Barbara would not make eye contact.

Anthony obeyed. It was already almost 11:00 a.m. He walked back to his car at the Muelbach Hotel and drove toward Crown Center. While in court, he confirmed to himself that Fred or Gerald had to be the mystery voice. He walked into the lobby of the new hotel to check in. After a quick purchase of new clothes, he changed in his room and went to lunch. He was ready to sit down, when he heard the unmistakable voice of Gerald Crow.

Gerald sat at the head of a table of at least twenty other men and women. Between the suit-and-tie-clad men, Greg was present. Due to the size of Vince, he was difficult to miss. Many of the other men and women looked familiar. Many of the men and women owned or operated construction companies and/or real estate companies in the metropolitan area. Anthony knew a little about real estate and easily convinced himself that the meeting was probably illegal. Collusion among real estate companies is not greatly approved of by the general public.

At that second, a waitress walked to his table to ask if he was indeed Anthony Gilante. There was a telephone call for him on one of the house phones. Anthony knew it had to be the mystery man. Correct.

"Well, well, well, Anthony. Are you satisfied now that it isn't Gerald?"

"I guess so. How did you know I was here?" Anthony asked, with all the color suddenly gone from his face.

"Let me say, I would be very disappointed if you were not. Crown Center is where I ordered you to stay. Is this the first time you have ever been there?"

"You mean you don't know?" Anthony asked sarcastically. "Yeah, it's the first time I've ever been in here. But how did you know I'd be in this restaurant?"

"I thought you were smarter than that. There are only three restaurants

238

currently open. One of them doesn't open until evening. That leaves two. I knew you were going to be in one of them."

"So you're not watching me?" Anthony looked around the lobby, paranoid as usual.

"No, I'm not watching you now. I will always let you know when I am."

"That's so kind." Anthony did not trust the mystery man, so he looked around him in all directions. He did not see anything unusual.

"You will need to stay there for a few days, maybe a week."

"I'll have to move into something cheaper tomorrow. Even with the money someone gave me, I'll go through it quick staying here."

"Stay in the Crown Center! That's an order!"

"I won't be able to afford it very much longer. I need to buy meals every day and clothes, basically everything in my house."

"The expenses will be taken care of. Move into a smaller room if you like, but stay in that hotel. If you need to go to the grocery store, go between the hours of seven and nine tonight. There's a kitchen in your suite."

"I don't know. You killed my kitties and dog." Anthony fought back tears at the thought of his buddies. "I'm pretty pissed off at you right now. I might stay somewhere else, since you made sure I can't stay at home." Anthony tried to see if audible anger would assist in dropping the obviously disguised voice.

"If you fuck with me, Ant, you'll be joining your pets soon."

"You think I care anymore? Fuck you! You've made my life a living hell. So do it." Anthony hung up the telephone. He sat back down at the table to order a sandwich and a beer.

He looked at the table of interest. Gerald and Vince smiled and waved to him. Gerald and Vince acknowledged his presence, but they looked consumed with business at the moment. Greg did not acknowledge him. Greg never looked away from the woman now addressing the group. He was almost positive now that Greg had to be the money behind the voice. But without the brains of his older brother, he had serious doubts. Nevertheless, as soon as he was sure, Gerald and Gregory Crow would need to go.

The waitress informed Anthony that the tab had been paid. He motioned thank-you to Gerald and Vince. Vince tapped Greg on the elbow as he drifted in and out of slumber. Greg waved.

As Anthony walked to the elevator, he saw three bellboys and a security guard harshly escorting a vagrant from the lobby. He studied the man harder and realized that it was the same homeless man from the Laundromat last evening. Weird. What would a homeless man be doing in the lobby of a new hotel? Almost ten miles away in distance and a world away economically. Maybe his physical appearance was the reason the homeless man was being escorted from the building?

Anthony went up the elevator to his suite and realized he was much more paranoid now than ever before.

As he approached the door to his suite, he saw an envelope wedged between the door and the jamb. He sat down and opened the envelope. Instructions on where to eat tonight, along with another $500. Somehow, the supposedly homeless man played a role in this hell. Maybe he was a spy faking being homeless. When Anthony closed his eyes to visualize the man, he did not see anything. If he saw the homeless man again, he would pay special attention.

Anthony had not slept well last evening, and attempting to sleep in jail did not agree with him. He unplugged the telephone. Sleep came within two minutes.

At 9:00 p.m., Anthony was awakened by a knock at his door. Paranoid as usual, he grabbed the gun from his jacket and looked out the peephole. A hotel security guard knocked on the door again. "Can I help you?" Anthony shouted through the door.

"Mr. Gilante, we needed to make sure you're OK."

"I'm fine. Why?"

"Someone tried to call you. We couldn't ring your room."

"I unplugged the phone. I needed sleep."

"I understand." The security guard walked away.

Anthony plugged the telephone in and began to get dressed. Almost instantly, the telephone rang. Again, he knew who it had to be. The Ant was growing impatient with the mystery voice.

"What the hell do you want now?" Not a voice of mystery this time.

"Anthony, it's Gerald. I need to talk with you immediately. I'm in the lobby bar." Gerald hung up the telephone abruptly. Although Anthony was well rested, he was extremely grumpy. Not absolutely sure he could trust Gerald, he concealed the automatic pistol in his sweater.

Gerald sat at a corner table nursing his vodka and tonic. The Ant was jumpy and frustrated. Anthony did not intend to give any information regarding his new accomplice, Brian, or the murder of John Lorzani or the mystery voice. But he did not hesitate to accuse Gerald or Gregory of killing his buddies, as it was already public knowledge on the news.

"What would I be doing here talking to you if I had killed your pets?" Gerald looked perplexed.

"If not you, then your drunken brother," Anthony snapped.

"Gregory is a drunk, that's quite fair. Gregory isn't a killer. He could never do that. He doesn't have the aptitude for anything involving animals."

"Do you think I'm stupid, you faggot? Someone ordered all this. Someone with a lot of cash is making my life hell for the last week. Someone is spending a lot of money on me. You, Vincey, and Greg are the only people I know with this kinda throwaway bucks."

"I guarantee it isn't Gregory or me. I can't speak for Vincey." Gerald raised his eyebrows.

"Do they know about, ya know?"

"No." Gerald smiled. Gerald was not as convincing of salesman as Greg. Anthony picked up hesitation and nervousness immediately. The Ant would pry a little further.

"Who do they, ya know? Still Nick?" Anthony whispered.

"Yes. Nick 'the Prick' Cibella is what they call him. Someone in his crew. Anthony, let me buy you a drink."

"Just a bottle of beer." Anthony thought swiftly. "They need to open it at the table."

"Why?" Gerald asked, mystified.

"Because I don't trust you, Gery."

"Have I ever given you a reason not to trust me?"

Anthony looked down his nose at Gerald. Gerald did not realize having your best friend, his wife, and both their fathers murdered, then trying to frame it and blame it on your brother's father-in-law and another boss may institute a little mistrust. A waitress came to the table. Anthony did not hesitate to make his special request.

"Gery, do you know a guy named Brian Nivaro?"

"The name sounds familiar. Why?"

"Just wondering." Anthony viewed Gerald carefully.

"So tell me, Anthony, do you need any money?"

Now Anthony was almost positive Gerald had no participation in the mystery voice. Money was always the key. He needed to take it one step further.

"Gery, that's nice. If you can loan me a few grand until I get home, I'll pay you back then."

"Whenever. I can give you a thousand now. Tell me how much you need. I know I have it at home or in my briefcase."

"My invisible helping hand isn't making paying for this too easy."

"Just tell me how much," Gerald said.

Anthony closed his eyes, acting as if he were giving the expenditures careful thought. He wanted to blurt out a disgusting sum to Gerald.

However, he was not sure how much money it would take to offend a rich smart guy like Gerald. He decided to just roll out a low round number.

"I think another thousand would be OK. I don't know if I'll need any more, but check on me tomorrow. I might need another ten thousand, unless I can go home."

"I'll give you fifty thousand tonight. Gregory and I purchased a plane. We need to go out to Las Vegas tomorrow."

"Who all is going?" Anthony knew for that kind of money, Gerald needed a high-profile hit.

"Everyone. Gregory and Carol, Sherry and me, two officers of the company and their wives, my father and a date, everyone."

"What about Vincey?"

"Strangely enough, no. He and Sally are staying here. I'll just give you fifty now. Is that OK with you?"

"How long will you be gone?"

"Until Monday the twenty-first, at night. I can only give you fifty. I can give you another fifty after I get back."

"OK. I just need to know—what's gonna happen to the kids?" Anthony showed obvious interest in the children.

"Don't worry about it. I'm sure they'll be fine."

This disgusted Anthony. Gerald smiled, showing no concern for the Giovelli children in the least.

"The price just multiplied by at least ten times then."

"I will double it."

"Make it even—250 now, 250 when you come back."

"That's steep, don't you think?"

"Find someone else then. Vincey and Sally are too noticeable and high-profile. Tina and Trisha don't have a mother or father anymore. Now all five kids will be orphans. Screw it. That's what it'll cost."

"All right. Just Vincey, then. I'll give you a hundred now and a hundred when I get back."

"No deal. Same price—250 now, 250 later."

"I'll give you 250 now, Anthony. A hundred when I get back."

"Three now. Fifty when you get back, Gery. No more haggling."

"Deal." Gerald and Anthony shook hands. Gerald drove home to get the remaining cash. In about forty-five minutes, Gerald handed Anthony $300,000 cash.

Anthony ordered room service and went to sleep. He would periodically check in with police over the next two days to find out his home had been clear of rodents and reptiles. The mystery voice staged a robbery. The police notified Anthony then that his home had been burglarized.

242

Anthony hoped and prayed he would be afforded the opportunity to leave town permanently with the cash from Gerald along with the $1.6 million he had stolen and saved over the past ten years. He desperately needed to leave before Gerald and Gregory returned from Las Vegas. If not, Vincey would need to go as payment dictated. As it stood now, Anthony had no intention of murdering anyone else, except the person behind the mystery voice and maybe the mystery man himself. Revenge for Poochy, Doggy, and Hippie.

44

On Saturday morning, February 19, 1977, the mystery man telephoned to let Anthony know that he only had a few measly jobs remaining.

At midnight, the mystery man called back. Brian Nivaro waited in a lounge in the lobby of the hotel. Anthony was instructed to stay one more night at the hotel and make a drunken scene at the exact same lounge when he returned. Anthony walked into the restaurant, where Brian handed him an envelope with $10,000 and gave him verbal instructions. Brian drove away so he and Anthony could complete their assignment.

During the drive, Anthony loaded three guns, his .380, an old-fashioned twelve-gauge shotgun, and Brian's 9 mm. Anthony's instructions said they were to empty their weapons completely.

Anthony was impressed with Brian. Every time he saw this moose of a kid, he drove a different car.

Paddy O's nightclub would be the scene. This is where Sonny Brown had been working since Chad Thompson at Quality Motors fired him.

Anthony screwed the silencer onto the .380 and killed a bouncer outside. Anthony and Brian walked in the back door after closing time. Two waitresses and a bartender were present. Anthony would make sure he enjoyed these hits. Because of the insidious difference in height between the two men, there could not be any witnesses.

Anthony fired the shotgun at Sonny. Brian followed with the two pistols, as he and Anthony killed both waitresses and the bartender. Anthony walked into the women's restroom and executed two female customers. One girl fell flat. The other girl gurgled before Anthony shot her one more time in the throat and twice more in the head.

Brian went into the men's room and killed three men with ten bullets. Brian clipped a full magazine onto both pistols, as he and Anthony turned Paddy O's into a bullet-riddled bloody grave. Sonny Brown was the original target. Now he looked identical to all the other bodies. Bloody.

Spotless. Both of the men were virtually spotless. They enjoyed one another's company as they drove away.

"That was cool as hell, man," Brian said with a grin.

"I admit, that was definitely better than Lorzani. And I don't think hell will be too cool. So, Brian, do you wanna get a drink?"

"I'm not twenty-one yet."

"I knew you were young. We can have a drink at the hotel if you want. They won't card you or anything," Anthony said.

Brian then whispered to Anthony. Crap! Anthony reloaded all the guns, as he and Brian headed toward Grandview, Missouri.

During the thirty-minute drive, they talked about cars, women, sports, anything and everything, except the murders they just committed, nor the job that awaited them.

"So are you ever gonna tell me who this guy is that's calling me?" Anthony asked, smiling.

"Probably the same guy who's been calling me." Brian shrugged his shoulders.

"You expect me to believe you don't know who this is?"

"I think I know, but I'm not sure yet." Brian hesitated. "Who do you think it is, Ant?"

"I thought maybe it was Gerald or Gregory Crow. I mean, the money behind the voice," Anthony said.

Brian looked confused. "Who the hell are Gerald and Gregory Crow?"

"Don't worry, it's not them. I just don't know anyone else that has this kinda money to throw around,"—Anthony smiled broadly—"except one person."

"Who is that?"

"Vincey Giovelli."

"That's possible, I guess. I worked as a laborer for them last summer," Brian said, cool and calm.

"It's him then. That's exactly what I did for them a few years back."

"I'm just going to shut up and not say a word. The money is too good." Brian rubbed his fingertips together.

"I hear ya." Anthony smiled, knowing that he had been granted a huge down payment to execute Vincey. Now he knew he would do it. He had been paid, and now he hated the lard ass. After Vincey was gone, bye-bye to Kansas City.

"Is everything loaded?" Brian asked as Anthony handed him the shotgun.

"Most definitely. Let's get this over with. We shouldn't be out on the roads this late."

The lights were bright. The music blared as they passed the house. Too many cars for a little two-bedroom house. It was obvious these people were not alone. Brian and Anthony were not, under any circumstances, going to waltz in and murder these people not knowing for sure how many people and how many guns.

"So, Ant, what do you think we should do?" Brian asked.

Anthony needed to play tough. "We do what we were paid to do. Let me go up and look in the windows. If need be, we break a window and make some other noises and wait for people to run out," Ant said.

"How do I know what to do?" Brian asked innocently.

"Just follow me. We have the firepower if they don't have any guns. If they do, we leave immediately."

Anthony peeked in as many windows as he dared. At least five people doing nothing except sitting around getting stoned, laughing, and joking. How many people in the other rooms?

One of the men may have been Peter Cassivano. What if it was Peter? Good! Anthony could never stand that guy. Suddenly, he remembered that Peter had been trained as a veterinarian for years. The snakes. It was Peter. Peter had pet snakes. Peter was an artist and always painted snakes killing their prey, boa constrictors. Peter always handled snakes when he was a kid.

Anthony broke the glass portion of the door with a rock and attempted to barge in. Immediately, Brian pulled a .45 automatic with a silencer from his jacket and fired two shots point-blank at the back of the head of Anthony "The Ant" Gilante.

Peter Cassivano took a gun with a silencer from his jacket and shot Chad Thompson and his wife, LeAnn. The innocent bystander couple in the midst of this bloodshed were assassinated as soon as they began to scream. Brian and Peter shot Todd Nixon and his wife, Gail, four times each. Brian and Peter shot Anthony several additional times each. Neighbors did not hear anything.

Brian walked into the two bedrooms to find the baby crying loudly. The baby boy was in a crib. Peter begged Brian not to harm the baby.

"It's not like the baby can identify you. Forget it, Brian," Peter begged, "you don't wanna get a reputation as a baby killer."

Brian huffed and decided to leave the baby unharmed.

At that point, Brian fished the hotel room key out of the pocket of Anthony "the Corpse" Gilante along with the $10,000 that Brian and Peter divided equally. Peter drove toward home, stopping first at the home of Fred Vasallo.

Brian drove to the Crown Center Hotel. It was difficult for a man of Brian's stature to enter a hotel incognito. Brian was able to accomplish that.

He searched the room of the recently deceased Anthony Gilante and found the $300,000 that belonged to Gerald Crow. Gerald would receive every dime that was his. An additional $5,000 found by Brian was kept. Brian drove back to his bedroom at his mother's home.

Peter Cassivano met with Frederick Vasallo at Fred's home in order to split the $500,000 that Fred found in a fireproof safe under the hot water heater in the garage. After just a few minutes, Fred busted the lock on the cheap safe with a drill.

As a teenager, Fred spent a few years with Anthony and knew Anthony kept a safe in the eighteen-inch-high wooden support box under the water heater in the garage.

"OK, let's each put in fifteen thousand to give to Brian. He doesn't need to know there was a half a million in here." Fred chuckled.

"That's fine. One of us can tell him that's his third." Peter agreed. At the time, Peter was unaware that the safe contained another $1.1 million.

"I can't imagine how Ant was able to save five hundred thousand bucks." Fred did a poor job of concealing his transparent lie.

"Look how he lived, Fred. Look what he drove. The guy obviously didn't spend very much on his lifestyle. I actually figured he'd have more than this," Peter said.

Fred continued sweating profusely in the early morning hours at the end of February.

"I wonder how he got this much, Pete." Fred failed to hide his lie.

Peter smelled a rat. "Ant was paid well. How did he react? Did he ever say he thought it was you?"

"Never. He had no idea. I scared him to death. Gery or Vincey would call me all the time and give me instructions on what to say and when or where to call. Anthony thought someone was watching him. I tried to improve on the grammar thing, but I was scared shitless."

"I thought for sure he was gonna recognize me at the hotel. I thought the security guards were gonna rip that stocking cap and wig right off. I knew I couldn't fight back. I shaved that itchy beard off that day. After that, I called Gery and Vincey and told them to forget it," Peter said.

"I really worried that Ant was going to find out that Vincey knew he killed Charley. But the little shit got what he deserved. I wish I had pulled the trigger, since Ant killed my dad and sister." Fred bit his bottom lip.

"Remember, he tried to frame all this on my dad. I couldn't believe how long it took for Gery and Vincey to organize this," Peter said, shaking his head.

"Gery volunteered to see Ant at the hotel. Vincey didn't want to see him. He was afraid Ant would kill him. Greg doesn't want to know what's going on. He just gives cash to his brother or Vincey. Gery was the only one who wasn't afraid of Ant."

"Would you have brought Ant that kind of money?" Peter wanted to somehow get back to the subject of money.

"No way. I'm going to be worried handling this much cash. We handle cash at the restaurants every day, but this seems to be different. Most of that is legal," Fred said as a joke between club owners.

"Greg is hilarious. He gives money to Gery or Vincey all the time," Peter said with a smile.

"I know. You try to talk to him about anything, and he puts his hands over his ears and runs out of the room."

"Fred, I don't think all the money is here. I think Ant must have had a bunch of money. Buried it somewhere." Peter looked directly at Fred as he spoke. Peter's bullshit detector went sky high.

"I don't know. Maybe, I guess." Fred could not look at Peter.

Peter decided to drop the monetary subject and take matters into his own hands at a later date. He needed to be assured beyond any shadow of a doubt.

"All right. I need to get home. Call Brian tomorrow. Or later today. Tell him you've got something for him."

"Will do, Pete."

Peter walked out with the undeniable feeling that Fred had more cash. Peter would need to think about how to detect if Fred did indeed hold a greater treasure.

45

Throughout the next week, police and federal agents dusted Paddy O's, the home of Chad and LeAnn Thompson, the home of Todd and Gail Nixon, the home and garage of John and Janie Lorzani, and the home of Anthony Gilante.

Ballistics tests showed that some of the bullets from the three recent murder scenes were of the same caliber and fired from some of the same guns. Police formed the opinion that reputed mobster Anthony Gilante committed several of the murders and was then assassinated by an unknown number of assailants. Police needed to question Fred Vasallo because his fingerprints were found in Anthony's home.

Police and federal agents commonly knew that Anthony and Fred were friends. Frederick Vasallo answered all their questions easily. There was nothing to detain him for.

Peter Cassivano explained to Vincenzo Giovelli that he did not believe Fred Vasallo could be trusted and the reasons he believed that. Before any information was obtained from Fred, he would need to be sent a message to keep his mouth shut. Brian Nivaro had the solution, therefore the assignment.

After the school day ended on February 28, 1977, two masked men broke into the home of Fred Vasallo. A staged robbery similar to the staged robbery that Fred and Peter performed at Anthony's home was carried out. Fred's sixteen-year-old son, Wayne, was severely beaten on the legs with a baseball bat after a pillow had been placed over his face. Brian was the person holding the pillow, while Gary Porter swung the bat. Wayne Vasallo had two broken legs and one broken rib. One leg was broken in four places. If Brian had been the batter, the injuries would have assuredly been worse. The only message Fred received was a message of hostility and rebuttal.

Within one week, an obvious arson occurred at Uncle Peter's Tavern.

The damage was minimal. The fire damaged the carpet, which needed to be replaced anyway, a few ceiling tiles, some chairs, tables, and a section of the stripper's stage. Uncle Peter's Tavern only closed for two days. The bad blood shared between Peter and Fred instantly worsened. Publicly, both men were becoming an embarrassment.

Willie telephoned his son-in-law and told him to communicate with Fred, while Willie spoke to his son. Both men were acting juvenile, and Willie was determined, as boss, to stop this immature behavior. At the time, Willie did not understand that his son was responsible for beating Fred's son, nor was Willie aware that more than $1 million in untraceable legal tender was the motive. When Peter told him, Willie quickly became furious at Fred. After Greg met with Fred privately, Willie notified Greg of the money. Greg let all three men know that he was fed up with them. That afternoon, Willie set up a meeting with Greg.

Because Greg did not trust his father-in-law, the meeting needed to be held in the offices of Crow Brothers. His preferred .38 revolver was under a stack of magazines toward the front of his contemporary desk. Just in case.

"I told you, Willie. There's nothing I can do," Greg said, visibly hostile.

"I understand that. Fred respects you and Gery. I hoped you could convince him to meet you, then bring him to my garage." Willie smiled devilishly.

"How in the world can I pull that off, Willie? The second we pull up, he's gonna bolt. What's so important about Fred Vasallo anyway?"

"He stole a bunch of money from me."

"We may have a different definition of what a bunch is. How much are we talking about?" Greg asked.

"I think it had to be somewhere between five hundred and a million."

"You're right, that is a bunch. But something I don't understand is, if he stole it from you, why don't you know a narrower range of how much it is?"

Willie moved in closer to Greg. "Greg, it was Anthony's money. We think Fred took it before he split the remainder with Peter."

"Then it's not your money. You don't even know for sure Ant had that much. This is weak, Willie. I don't want any part of this. I don't know what happened, but let's assume Fred did take extra money. He and Peter should settle it without breaking an innocent kid's legs."

"I know. I'm disgusted with that too. I lectured Peter about it. But that's way too much money to ignore."

"Consider it a prepayment for that kid's medical bills. I found out the kid is gonna be OK, some broken bones, but that's serious shit. Whoever did it for Peter ought to be sued. Peter too. Peter is a good guy. I think the world of him. But that was as wrong a thing to do as anything I've ever heard. I'll tell him that. No painting he's ever done is worth that. What if someone broke his fingers so severely, he couldn't paint again? Peter should consider that money a judgment. He paid in advance. That's only a fraction of what he could lose if he was sued in civil court. Plus all the money he would spend on legal fees if he was charged criminally."

"Greg, don't you agree that it's too much money to ignore?" Willie asked.

"Maybe it is, maybe it isn't. I think ignoring it now would be wise."

"I'm not gonna ignore it," Willie snapped.

"Then I don't wanna know anything." Greg waved a hand in frustration. "Why did you come to me anyway?"

"Because Fred likes you." Willie displayed another devilish grin.

"And you expect me to lure him under false pretenses to your garage so you can beat the money out of him? Maybe you wanna see if rats can gnaw the money out of him—that is, if Fred has it. If Ant ever did. I'm out of this, Willie. This stinks."

"You know, I'm sick of you and your rich spoiled-brat attitude." Greg had returned to smoking recently, so he lit a cigarette and blew the smoke in his father-in-law's face. "That's a lot of money for me." Willie waved the smoke away.

"Calling me brat doesn't help, you fuckin' rat! You've benefited by god only knows how much money because of me. I could've put it all on paper, and you'd owe me everything you've made in your entire smelly life." Willie witnessed a rare display of anger. Greg began shouting, "Instead, I have given you, not loaned you, and Peter so much money because I love my wife. Do you realize, Willie, that if I'd never met Carol, you wouldn't receive one thin dime?" Greg usually held his temper in check.

Willie suddenly realized that Greg was about to come to blows with him and backed away. "What do you want me to do, Greg?"

"I don't give a fuck what you do. You're the boss now of this moronic Thing of Ours. Just leave me and Carol and our children out of it."

"Carol is my daughter."

"Fine, then try to get her to counsel you." His shouting reached a peak volume. "Do you even come close to understanding me, Willie? I hate this. I don't want anything to do with this Thing of Ours. I never did. I'm not even Italian. I've had it with you guys." Greg knew he needed to calm down. He could not.

"So what should I tell Peter?" Willie asked.

"Are you deaf, you rank son of a bitch? Tell him whatever the fuck you want. Do whatever you want. Leave me out of it. Don't ask me how to talk with your son. Don't try to tell me anything. You handle this however you want." Greg wanted to turn his back to Willie. He thought better of it. "Why in the world would Peter need to give you anything, you dirty, smelly rat?"

"Because I'm his father."

"Thank god my father isn't like you."

"I don't take any money from Uncle Peter's Tavern." Willie flashed a dazzling white smile. It did not match his other filthy features.

"You're losing me. I didn't ask that. If Peter had any of this money— that is, if the money exists—why would he need to give you a dime?" Greg had a look of confusion and anger on his face.

"Because Peter is honorable." Willie smiled.

"Whatever, Willie. This sounds like another silly goombah wop tradition."

"Don't ever say that again, you immature drunk."

"Willie, get the fuck out of my office. I didn't call you a name personally. Don't ever come here again. Move your fat, dirty, stinky, worthless, disgusting body off my property now. *Now!*" Greg shouted so earsplittingly loud that shocked employees and clients stood outside the office door, wondering who he was yelling at.

Brian Nivaro was making the afternoon interoffice mail delivery. Brian knew that Greg always carried a gun. If, for some reason, he did not have one now to protect himself, Brian would unfailingly protect Greg.

"I'm going to Carol's house now. I'm gonna ask her, or tell her, to leave you."

"You rat, Willie. Carol would never leave me. I'll call her right now, and she can arbitrate this." Greg picked up the telephone and dialed. He placed the call on the speakerphone.

"Carol, I need to ask you a question. Would you leave me if your father, the Rat, asked you to leave?"

By the tone of his voice, Carol could hear Greg was furious. She also did not think her father could be present with Greg loudly referring to him as the Rat.

"Of course not. I could never leave even if you asked me to." Carol laughed.

Greg smiled sarcastically at Willie. "Now, say your father, the Rat, killed me. What would be your reaction?"

Willie clenched his teeth together.

"I'd kill him. Honey, what's wrong? This is scaring me." Carol hesitated. "Daddy didn't threaten you, did he? Please tell me he didn't threaten you."

"He didn't threaten to kill me, yet. He threatened me with you leaving me." Greg laughed. "By his request, of course."

252

"He doesn't speak for me, Greg, you know that. Why in the world would you ever think I could leave you?"

"Maybe he could force you?"

Willie wanted to jump over the desk and punch the smart-ass smile off his son-in-law's face.

"How could he do that? By forcing me to smell him?" Carol laughed.

Willie turned bright red. His heartbeat was dangerously fast.

"Carol, what if I told you your father is standing here in my office?" Greg asked, looking at Willie, grinning.

"Daddy, are you there?" Carol asked over the speakerphone.

"Yes, Carolyn." Willie had his eyes closed, understandably embarrassed.

"Daddy, what makes you think you can order me to leave my husband?"

"I just got angry, Carolyn. I'm sorry."

"Why are you there, Daddy?"

Simultaneously, Greg and Willie answered, "Business."

"I've told you before. Now I'm warning you. Never ever touch my husband. In fact, if anyone ever touches Greg, I'll hold you responsible. Even if Greg is in another country and something happens, you're responsible. If one hair on his head is ever touched by anyone, I hold you responsible."

"I understand, Carolyn."

"I don't think you do, Daddy. If you did, you'd make sure no one ever touches him. You'd go out of your way to make sure he's never touched." In the background, Candice screamed and cried loudly. "Honey, I've gotta go. Danny is teasing Candy again. The babysitter is coming in an hour."

Greg picked up the handset and had a private chat briefly.

"You may have brainwashed Carolyn." Willie looked at the ceiling as he spoke. "But you don't fool me."

"Brainwashed, that's good. That's original. Get out of my office now, Willie. I don't know how a smelly rat like you was able to raise a goddess like Carol. She must take after her mother."

"At least she had a mother to raise her."

"That was a brilliant comeback, Rat. Get the fuck out of my office. *Now!* Don't ever call me again. Don't ever call the house again. Consider yourself very lucky to have known me. Consider yourself out of debt to me. Carol knows tonight how much money I've given to you over the last few years. She'll never wish to talk with your dirty mug again."

"Greg, please don't tell her about the money. I'll pay you back."

"I'll tell you what. Only pay me back if you wanna talk with her again. If you don't care, tell me now. Believe me, if she finds out how much, she'll never talk to you or Peter again. I just need to give her a number, and you're out."

253

"Do you really not remember how much?"

"Figuring conservatively, I'd say about two hundred grand. You know what? I'm not gonna tell her about the money. Forget the money. Just promise me you never call me again. I never wanna see you again. That's worth the money. From now on, other arrangements are made for you to see the babies. Margaret is allowed to see them whenever she wants. I don't want you in my house ever again. Every time you're there, it takes three days to get your stench out of the air, the furniture, everything you touch. You reek. Have you ever noticed that Danny can't stand your odor? He tells us every time we see you, 'Grampa stinks.' You used to scare me. Now you just piss me off. Get the fuck out of my office. Now. *Now!*"

"You need to watch what you say on the phone. Carolyn does too."

"I have the phones swept twice a month. There's no danger." Greg's face was six inches from his father-in-law as he continued shouting, "Get out now!"

"I'm leaving. How many of the Friends of Ours know about the money?"

"Willie, no one is a Friend of Ours, especially a friend of yours!" Greg shouted and then stopped himself. He brought the volume of his speech lower as the intensity increased. Greg was less than an inch from Willie now. "Friends of Ours is a bullshit code line for this stupid secret society that everyone knows about. Unless people are afraid of you, they don't like you." Greg used his hands as a makeshift megaphone and shouted, "You stink too much!"

"Can you just tell me?"

"Two. Other than you and Peter."

"Who?"

"Guess! Vince and Gery. Don't worry. They're too busy with respectable business to think about it. Leave now!"

Willie walked out as employees stood with mouths open, staring at the person that was capable of raising the voice of Gregory Crow.

No one knew Willie, except for Brian. Willie noticed Brian at once. Brian was eighteen years young and already a legend to high-ranking La Cosa Nostra members. Greg instructed Brian to escort Willie out of the building without touching him. Willie did not doubt that Brian could tear out his thumping heart in one swift motion. For the first time in his life, Willie feared another human being.

How could Willie come up with that kind of money? Why was he interested in knowing who knew about it? Oh no! Not Vince or Gery. Willie is my wife's father. Could I do it? Forget it. I couldn't do that to Carol. Someone else will probably order it anyway. Forgive me for thinking that. I'm sorry.

Gerald heard the entire conversation on the basic tape recorder he placed above the ceiling in Greg's office. When Gerald wanted to hear what Greg said in a meeting, he simply placed a tape recorder in an air vent in his office and plugged the recorder into a microphone strung from his office and ending above Greg's office in another vent.

Gerald decided he needed the money. With all his millions, Gerald was nearly broke. Almost completely cash poor.

Gerald had borrowed $20,000 cash from his brother just days ago. Greg was shocked that Gerald laundered all the money and would not keep some cash for a rainy day.

His spending was out of control. In addition to the vacation home in Arizona, he purchased homes in San Diego, California; Padre Island, Texas; and an apartment in Manhattan. It would take more than one week to set this up. Gerald would need to contemplate how he could pin this on someone else. Bingo.

Willie communicated with his son and told him what Greg recommended. Willie and Peter agreed with Greg. Ignore it.

46

Although Fred Vasallo was married, he could never say no to women. His reputation was well known. A prostitute named Kathy seduced him at one of his nightclubs. Kathy brought Fred to a dive hotel where she turned tricks. Kathy drugged Fred's drink. After he passed out, two men took him to a barn north of the city. When he awoke, Fred became aware he had been stripped and tied to a chair that was anchored to sheet metal that was fastened to the floor. A heavy sheet of plastic was underneath the entire contraption. Fred knew what was coming as soon as his entire body was sprayed with a sticky substance. He knew they were going to kill him, so he had no intention of cooperating. He was wrong.

In addition to his personal predicament, his son Wayne was screaming his name, "Dad!" Wayne had also been sprayed with a sticky substance and stripped of not only his clothes but also the casts on his broken legs. The looks of terror and sorrow on Fred's face let everyone present understand who controlled the power. A wooden box with greased-down interior walls was placed around Wayne. This time, a glass patio door was used as one wall so Fred could witness the torture before him.

Fred wanted to close his eyes or move his head. He could do neither. His head was immobilized, and his eyelids had been sloppily surgically removed while under the influence of the prostitute's anesthesia. He was still able to look down occasionally and avoid the visual holocaust. Fred could not be certain who the man standing in back of him was. However, hands that large and strong could only belong to one person he had ever met.

Twenty rats were thrown into the cage with Wayne. A strange man stood there wearing a red stocking cap that hid everything apart from his eyes. Fred knew he had seen the eyes before. The walk. There was something distinguishable about the man's walk. The man with the walk reached down over the back wall of the cell and punched Wayne in the back of the head. The screams were deafening. The same man walked around to the right side and punched Wayne in the side of the face. He walked around and punched Wayne on the other side of his swollen face.

A wooden box was placed around Fred. This box also had a glass front wall for viewing the familial torture. Fred wanted to cry, but his eyes were deprived of tears. Wayne suddenly fell silent. A black blanket was placed over the glass wall of the cell containing Fred. After a brief time-out from the visual torture, Fred heard his son mumbling again and then screaming. The gag was gently untied.

"Fred, I know you can hear me. I'm going to ask you some questions. Every time you don't answer me, you and your son will have a few friends," Brian said.

The man with the eyes and the walk lifted the blanket off Fred so he could see his son clearly. Wayne could barely hold his own head up, yet he screamed as the man with the walk dropped a concrete block down on his already broken leg.

"Please, Brian, leave him alone. I'll tell you whatever you need to know. Just don't hurt him."

"Bad news. I'm afraid you're a little late." Brian laughed. "Does he not look hurt already?"

Fred saw the man with the walk drop another concrete block down on the other previously broken leg of his son. The screams were gradually quieter because of Wayne's voice. He quickly became hoarse.

"Where's the money?" Brian asked.

"I'll tell you. Just promise to let him go."

"OK. We can do that."

"Promise on your mother's life that you'll let him go."

On his mother's life was pretty severe. Brian hesitated, closed his eyes, and eventually made the promise.

"I promise I won't hurt him," Brian smirked.

Fred thought fast. "Promise on your mother's life that no one here hurts him."

"I promise," Brian said, as he held up his right hand. He gave instructions to the man with the eyes and the walk to allow Wayne physical peace.

"It's in a safe under the sump pump in my basement."

The man with the eyes and the walk left immediately.

Wayne had a stunned look on his face. His own father was responsible for this. He thought maybe it was possible. Now a confused look of disappointment, anger, and terror ran across his swollen face in just a millisecond.

Fred kept yelling, "I'm sorry!"

"How much is left?" Brian asked.

"One million, one hundred thousand." Fred sighed.

"How much did you spend?"

"None, until Wayne's medical bills. Then I spent a few thousand."

Brian opened a box containing twenty rats and dumped them on Fred. The rats were an aggravation to Fred. Nevertheless, at that second, he showed more interest in the ill health and well-being of his oldest son.

"How much was in there to begin with?"

"The money Peter and I split and $1.1 million."

"Where is your part of the money that you and Peter split and ripped me off of?"

"In the safe at Warehouse Inn?"

Brian sat down to wait for the man with the eyes and the walk to return.

After more than an hour, he returned with the safe. The silent man with the eyes and the walk told Brian that Connie Vasallo and the remaining children were not home. No one else needed to be killed.

"OK, now tell me what the combination is."

"Right three times to forty-one, back to the left once around, then stop at sixteen, then back to the right, stop at twenty-four."

Brian opened the safe immediately. Brian counted the cash and confirmed to the man with the walk that it was there. Brian then went to the prison cell containing Wayne and shot him five times in the head. Fred screamed and cried hysterically immediately.

He looked at Brian and swore. "I'll see your mother in hell soon. Then you." Brian took another gun from the man with the eyes and the walk. In an instant, before Brian fired his gun, Fred looked at the man with the eyes and the walk again. Before Fred was able to speak the name, Brian fired his revolver five times into the head of Fred Vasallo.

After the money was divided, with the man with the eyes and the walk receiving the majority, the barn was set ablaze. Intentionally, they had not disposed of the bodies. The old barn was consumed with flames in a hurry. A neighbor could see the flames and called emergency. Before emergency vehicles arrived, the neighbor was able to write down one of the two license plates.

Firefighters were able to extinguish the flames. The bodies of Fred and Wayne Vasallo were barely burned at all. Police were supplied the license plate number and immediately traced it to Fred Vasallo. Police went to the door of Fred and Connie Vasallo to interrogate Fred. Connie let them know she was worried. Her husband and son were not home yet.

Within hours into the following day, coroners had positively identified the bodies of Fred and Wayne Vasallo. Fred's wallet was found in a hotel room. The hotel was a commonly accepted favorite of prostitutes, considering the management rented rooms by the hour.

Before any arrests were made, someone with the police leaked to local newspapers that the bodies appeared to have been tortured. Rats and mice were found in the makeshift cells. The rodents died of smoke inhalation.

Police and the special RICO task force of the FBI wanted to question Willie the Rat. His new lawyer, Barbara Percival, did not need to be present when they interrogated Willie, although she was. Willie had trouble breathing the night of the murders and spent the night at a local hospital. Police knew Willie was responsible and, as usual, had nothing on him. Anthony Gilante was dead. Nick Cibella was in prison. Most of the well-known soldiers in Kansas City La Cosa Nostra were dead or in prison. Whoever did this had a personal vendetta with either Fred or Wayne Vasallo. Wayne had obviously been tortured with his father watching.

Greg and Carol hired three bodyguards for her father and three for Peter because of death threats. Willie and Peter were aware of the bodyguards. The bodyguards for Willie and Peter watched in shifts, twenty-four hours a day. Greg had one bodyguard protect his father without Gerome's knowledge.

Greg did not think of hiring a bodyguard for himself. Carol did. Three off-duty police officers guarded him without his knowledge, in shifts.

Following only thirty-six hours of silent protection, Greg had Brian Nivaro approach one of the officers and ask why his boss was being pursued. The bodyguard never intended to lie. He announced that it was only protection for Gregory Crow. His wife employed the security guards. Greg immediately telephoned Carol to question her. She had them tailing him silently because she knew he would refuse a traditional bodyguard. Greg feared that having bodyguards this dreadful at undercover surveillance would send the wrong message. Greg did not want people to think he was guilty of something. Everyone knew who his father-in-law was.

Greg informed Vince that he and his wife were nervous and would leave town for a few weeks with the children. Following their return, they would go on hiatus at home. They would stay at home for an undetermined amount of time until things calmed down.

Despite having his own plane, Greg and Carol took a commercial flight to Chicago. Chicago was far enough away to be peaceful, yet close enough to keep abreast of the news.

47

Graduating from college this spring was Carol's goal. Now the dream of a college degree would evade her. Graduating next fall was more realistic. She did not want to pay bribe money to earn her degree. She wanted to earn the degree with good attendance, hard work, and integrity. With her business booming, taking care of two babies and a childlike husband, it was truly amazing that Carol achieved nearly perfect grades.

On the national news that Friday evening, there was a story of "mob activity" in the United States. This particular network had been running a weeklong special during their evening broadcasts. This was the last episode of the segment. Greg and Carol watched assiduously. Thankfully, Danny was napping.

During the segment, the larger cities of New York, Chicago, Los Angeles, and Miami were barely mentioned. Small town "Mafia-infected" metropolitan areas such as Cleveland, Kansas City, and Milwaukee were the focus of the special segment tonight. The reporters recapped violent crimes and loan-sharking convictions of the past few years.

When the reporters got to the story about the escalating violence in Kansas City, Greg and Carol hoped and prayed her father would not be mentioned. They not only mentioned William Cassivano but also showed his picture. Not only did they spend more time on Kansas City than other small metropolitan areas, but also they named more people. Deceased people, incarcerated people, missing people, and a whole list of other violent crimes and arsons that remained unsolved. The deaths of kingpin Joseph Giovelli and his son, Charles. They mentioned there was a warrant for the arrest of Officer Kenneth Bondano, who disappeared after four murders last summer. They reported on the murders of the Vasallos early this week and the conditions the bodies were found in. As the story wrapped up, the reporter smiled and made a humorous remark about the nickname of William Cassivano—Willie the Rat.

As the Crow Falls

Danny was awake. "Grampa da Rat."

Greg immediately turned off the television and tickled Danny. Carol wiped tears from her eyes in the bathroom. They had been in Chicago for three nights. Now they never wanted to go home. Greg gave Danny some crayons and a coloring book to steer his attention away from current events. Carol came out of the bathroom, smiling as if nothing were wrong.

Greg requested that they talk at dinner of nothing more complicated than *Sesame Street*. Following dinner, Greg purchased two cases of beer along with a cooler and various baby supplies.

Greg always amazed Carol. She could never believe that her husband always brimmed with positive words and probably positive thoughts. She occasionally wondered if other people's desire to mask reality by getting wasted was real. It appeared to work beautifully for Greg. After the babies were asleep, they sat on the balcony of their hotel suite, smoking.

"Carol, we need to talk about this." So much for forgetting reality. "We've avoided talking about it for a week now. You know I'm not gonna beat around the bush with you. I'm not trying to sell you anything. Do you think your father killed Fred and Wayne Vasallo?"

"I don't think so. I honestly don't know anymore. Are you ever gonna tell me what he was doing in your office that day?"

"I didn't want to until you asked. Now that you've asked, I'll tell you. He talked about the money Ant had that Fred supposedly stole. He wanted me to lure Fred to his shop because I was friends with him. I wasn't really that close. Fred just liked me."

"That says it, I guess." She began crying again. "But Peter told me that Daddy thought about it and decided they shouldn't pursue it. Peter said that it wasn't worth it, since they didn't know for sure if Fred had any money."

"That's almost verbatim what I told your dad. Do you think he repeated what I said to Peter or that he came to that wise decision on his own, with Willie knowing that information would be relayed to you?"

"I don't know, honey. I don't wanna believe that Daddy had anything to do with this. I don't know what to think anymore. If I find out he did, I never wanna talk with him again."

"He's your dad, though, Carol. This goes back to last summer, somehow. I don't think Willie would have ordered Fred killed after that old tape ran on TV over and over. After David's murder last summer, the whole city looked at Willie. Your dad really pisses me off sometimes, but I can't believe he'd do something so incredibly stupid for the second time. Every station ran that old tape again of David saying that after Fred and Wayne were killed. Someone is really trying hard to frame your dad."

"Who do you think did it?" She hoped to witness him playing detective.

"I don't have any idea. I don't think Kenny Bondano is back in town, but I wouldn't doubt that somehow he's involved in this. Or, more than likely, Nick."

"Nick, I can see. But why would you think Kenny is in on it?" she asked, genuinely fascinated that he mentioned that forgotten name.

"I don't know. A gut feeling, I guess."

"If Kenny was in on Charley, Sandy, David, and Vito, like the news says, he would be incommunicado now," she said.

"It's gotta be Nick, then. Maybe we shouldn't talk about this. I wanna get blotto drunk and forget this. That's why we came up here. Just to get away. I love you so much."

"I love you more." She wanted him to get ripped so she could ask him about Anthony.

He consumed eighteen beers and a joint in no time. Greg and Carol played a drinking game. They laughed and joked all night. A satisfying human emotion they had been deprived of the last few months. When she brought up the murder of Anthony, he flat out denied it. He did admit to having a friend bail Anthony out of jail, but that was it. He never gave her a reason not to believe him. She phoned the front desk and requested no phone calls until 11:00 a.m.

March 12, 1977

At nine thirty, the telephone rang. She answered.

"Hello."

"Carol, it's Gerald."

"Greg is asleep. I don't think he's gonna wake up for a long time. I'm not sure I wanna either." Carol giggled.

Greg mumbled that he was awake.

"Carol, I need to talk with you."

Carol knew by the tone of his voice that it was bad news. Nerves sobered her up quickly.

"What is it, Gery?"

"Last night in the River Quay, four buildings were destroyed by bombs . . ."

"Is the deli gone?"

"Yes." Gerald sounded very sad. "Carol, I'm sorry."

"If no one was hurt, then we don't have anything to worry about. We lost one out in St. Louis last year from a flood."

"Carol, there's something else." She thought her heart was going to stop. "Now, keep in mind there were not that many people hurt for the kind of destruction it did. Carol, your brother was arrested for it." Carol dropped the phone immediately.

Greg picked it up. "Gery, what happened?"

"Gregory, her brother was arrested last night, or this morning, for blowing up the River Quay."

"Fuck! Hold on." Greg held the telephone lower and gripped his temples as if they were about to blow up themselves. After twenty seconds, "What happened?"

"Gregory, four buildings blew up down in the Quay last night. One of them was Warehouse Inn. It was the only business other than Italian Deli not completely leveled. I think they said on TV it may take five days to recover all the bodies."

"What other buildings?"

"Vasallo's place, the Warehouse Inn. Everything in that building, what, six businesses and four apartments. Reporters said as many as twelve people were in there. Paddy O's. Italian Deli was damaged but not as severe as the others. And the building with that new club, The Judge's Bench."

"So when did this happen?" Greg asked. Carol cried loudly.

"I guess after everything closes. What, like four in the morning is when people leave down there? It must have happened after that. Gregory, I'm really sorry. I can hear Carol. What else could I do?"

"How did you find out?"

"Vincey called me. He couldn't talk. All he could do was cuss. Sally got on the phone. She was able to get the words out."

"Did Vince give you my phone number?"

"Of course. He told me to call you and tell Carol. He couldn't even talk. He was swearing up a storm."

"Does everyone know already?"

"No. I had the television on, and they didn't give names, but they were giving the names of the businesses."

"How do they know Peter did it?"

Carol shook her head no repeatedly.

"From what I heard, they were evacuating all the buildings near there. They evacuated Uncle Peter's, and Peter left with some girl. Police were searching every car and truck around there as people were leaving. Peter had plastic explosives and dynamite in this toolbox in the bed of his truck."

"How did you find all this out?"

"The arrest was on television."

"You mean the station showed him getting arrested?" Greg asked loudly.

"No, no, the lady on the news just said what they found on a suspect. I already had Peter's name from Vincey." A long hesitation. "Gregory, it doesn't look too good right now. All the businesses surrounding his were destroyed. And his sister's business was barely harmed."

"Saying it doesn't look too good is the understatement of the year. Are you at the office?"

"No, Gregory. It's Saturday."

"Please, just call me Greg, you dickhead." Greg chuckled.

"Anyway, Greg U. Dickhead, I'm leaving in a few hours to go to San Diego. I'll be there for a week. Do you have my number there?"

"Yeah. Gery, look, I'll call you later. Carol and I need to talk."

"I understand. Let me know if I can do anything."

"Thanks, Gery." Greg went into the other room of the suite and changed Candy.

Carol used her ring code to telephone her mother and father. Willie would not talk on the phone, but Margaret would. Peter Cassivano had been arrested for possession of explosives without a license, possession of a controlled substance, and driving while intoxicated.

Peter remained in the police station, answering questions for hours with his standard answer: "I'm not speaking to you without my lawyer." When Peter called his father, his mother informed him that Dad was not going to bail him out of jail. The press would kill him. Peter could only think of one person in town that he knew well with the kind of cash necessary to bail him out.

Vincenzo Giovelli sent his personal bodyguard to the police station with enough money to bail Peter out. After Peter was bailed out, he was taken by one of his own-armed bodyguards to his father's house. Willie and Margaret did not want to see their son because the press was everywhere. There were television cameras on the street in front of their home. The bodyguard brought Peter to Vince and Sally's elaborate estate. One of Peter's bodyguards telephoned Vince.

Three bodyguards had been watching Peter nonstop for six full days going on seven. All three bodyguards gathered at Vince and Sally's home. Two of the three were employed as police officers, working for extra money part time. The other one was a retired police officer.

They agreed that Peter was not allowed out of their sight the entire time. The only time they were not with him was when he went to the bathroom and when he was asleep. When he was asleep, the bodyguard on duty remained inside his fourth-floor apartment. The one night when Peter had a female spending the night, the bodyguard watching the apartment

264

As the Crow Falls

waited across the street. This protection was at the request of the people paying for bodyguard services: Gregory and Carolyn Crow.

Vince summoned the new "house counsel," Barbara Percival, to his estate. Barbara spoke to Peter in front of the other witnesses. After being informed of the details, Barbara asked several routine questions of the bodyguards. A tape recorder ran. The retired police officer was the designated spokesman. The other two shook their heads yes or no.

"There's no possibility that Peter Cassivano escaped from his apartment without us seeing him."

"Could he have gone out the back?" Barbara asked.

"No. The apartment building is on a hill. To go out the window, he would have to climb a fifty-to sixty-foot rope or ladder. Then go back up without anyone seeing."

"Is that possible?"

"No. The back of his apartment building faces a busy street."

"What about the back door?"

"There is no back door."

"What about the elevator? Taking it down to the basement? Going out a window?"

"There is no elevator. There are no doors or windows in the basement. It's a very old building," the number-one bodyguard answered.

Barbara could not believe how robotic his answers sounded.

"You scouted the basement?" Barbara smiled at the monotonous tone of his voice.

"Yes. On a body job, we always do. On a property watch, we rarely do."

"What about the sides?"

"No side doors. No side windows."

"How do you guys think the explosives got in his truck?"

"We don't know." He stared straight ahead when talking. Barbara grinned.

"Is it possible that someone planted it?"

"It's possible. We weren't able to watch his truck all the time. We were instructed to watch him and stay with him, not the truck. Only one of us watches him at a time."

"Who instructed you?"

"His sister and brother-in-law."

"What are their names?"

"Crow Brothers."

"You have been ordered by a company?"

"No. We were ordered by his sister and brother-in-law to protect Peter at any cost."

"Where does the company fit in?"

"Crow Brothers is sent the bills."

"What are the individuals' names?"

"Carolyn and Gregory Crow."

"You have only been watching Peter for one week. How many bills have you sent?"

"We send them individually. We are friends or coworkers. We coordinate this with each other and bill them separately. We have all watched buildings for Crow Brothers."

"Have you talked to anyone other than Gregory or Carolyn Crow regarding Peter Cassivano?"

"No."

"Who pays you?"

"We haven't been paid yet. We send three individual invoices. I send them weekly. My partners send them daily. The bills go to the accounting office directed to Jacob Rosenstingel."

"So people in the accounting office know that Peter has bodyguards?"

"Yes, I work security for them all the time. Some of them would know."

"You have not talked to anyone about Peter?"

"No. Except Gregory and Carolyn Crow. We only talked to them the day they ordered surveillance and protection for Peter."

"I need your names and phone numbers in case I need to talk with you. Write them down or give me your cards. You have not been paid?"

"We just answered that."

"That's all I have. Thank you." The three men gave their cards and walked out of the room. The spokesman bodyguard stayed behind to complete his shift. Vince and Peter returned. Barbara spoke. "We need to wait until you're arrested." Barbara looked directly at Peter. "If you are. Did you tell the police that you have licensed bodyguards?"

"I never said a word to any of them. I only said I'm not speaking to you without my lawyer."

"Good. If they don't know you had bodyguards, then we wait until they arrest you. Again if they do, which they more than likely will, I'll have somebody at one of the news stations interview those bodyguards and listen to the tape."

"If I get arrested, they're gonna hold me forever. I was there for nine hours this morning."

"I don't want to give the prosecution any time to dispute the authenticity of this tape or the bodyguards until right before discovery conference. Believe me, that's what prosecutors do. The only other thing I can do is tell them you had bodyguards and I interviewed them. Then they might think it's a bluff and arrest you promptly."

"When do you think they will arrest me?"

"Actually, without knowledge of the tape, anytime. This is a multiple homicide with special circumstances. They won't mess around."

"That doesn't tell me when."

"More than likely today."

"What do you think I should do, Vincey?"

"You do what Barbara says." Vince shrugged his shoulders.

"This is unbelievable." Peter sighed. "Someone is seriously trying to frame me." Peter's hands trembled. "Will you bail me out, Vincey?"

"Pete, that depends on how much the bail is. I believe bail bondsmen only take 10 percent. And that's nonrefundable. If it's not that much, I'll just pay the whole thing. Then when you go to court, I would get that money back."

Barbara scratched her head. "I'm sorry, Peter and Vincey, but if the prosecutor's office adds special circumstances to the warrants, and I believe they will, then there is no bail. You would be in jail until trial."

Peter closed his eyes and clenched his teeth to keep from crying in front of Barbara. He could not hold back.

"So do I just go home and wait for them to arrest me?" Peter asked, blubbering.

Barbara and Vince could not look at this pitiful, honest display.

"I can call a friend in the DA's office and see if they'll drop the special circumstances from the warrant. That can backfire, if they haven't added it prior to a phone call. That just reminds them again to add it. So it's up to you if you want me to call them or not. I think it would be wise for me to wait until Sunday night to call."

The telephone rang. Barbara and Peter continued their conversation, while Vince answered. It was Carol, asking if they should come home now.

"I'm sorry to interrupt right now," Vince said. "Pete, your sister and Greg want to know if they should come home."

"I'd like somebody with bucks to be here to bail me out," Peter whined.

Barbara interrupted. "Vincey, tell them absolutely not. They should definitely stay away. Peter, before they arrest you, I'll be informed. I can register as your attorney today. I'll tell them you didn't let me know where you'd be. Then I'll disappear for the rest of the weekend. It's much better if you surrender at the police station without them coming after you. I can accompany you to jail. This is high-profile, Peter. Your father and brother-in-law are both high profile, and you just joined the club. I can accompany

267

you in the middle of the night. We go in silently, with no press. It's much better if we can keep the press away."

"I feel like I should just take off now." Peter attempted to fight back tears.

"That's brilliant, Peter. If you do that, I'll never represent you. If, by any chance, they have a bail hearing on the warrant instead of special circumstances, then, believe me, they'll add it then. You don't want to be seen by police or, worse, by the media driving down the highway in your truck, fleeing arrest. That'll prompt them even more to revoke bail. If they label you a flight risk, forget it. You'll never get bail, and good luck getting a fair trial."

"Stay there. I'll call you back," Vince told Carol and hung up the phone abruptly.

"All right. Tell me what to do."

"Nothing. Can he stay here, Vincey?" Barbara asked Vincey.

"As long as no one knows you're here, Pete. I'm sorry, but I don't want cameras out here."

"No one knows you're here, except the bodyguards. Unless you told someone? I certainly don't know where you are." Barbara smiled.

"Nobody will talk to me. Not even my mom and dad." Peter cried again.

Barbara did not want him to be alone. She was afraid he would commit suicide or attempt to escape.

After Barbara was gone, Vince called Carol and told her Peter was with him. Peter spoke to Carol and reminded her to keep his location silent. He knew as much of what was transpiring as she did.

"I'm swearing to you, sis, I'm innocent. Someone is after Dad and me. Dad wouldn't talk to me. Press was all over him. Don't come back home now. I'll have someone call you later. Mom is worried Dad might have a heart attack. *I love you.* I love you too. *Good-bye.* Good-bye."

It would be the last time brother and sister would ever speak.

Peter telephoned his attorney on Sunday evening. There was indeed a warrant for his arrest. After Peter was gone, Vince called his buddy Doug Chandler at home. Vince smiled and then telephoned Greg and Carol to tell them the good news. "Everything is fine."

Two bodyguards and Barbara escorted Peter to central booking, where he was formally charged with six counts of arson, fourteen counts of intentional destruction of property, and sixteen counts of involuntary manslaughter.

Barbara knew what district attorney had drawn this warrant: Douglas Chandler. Involuntary manslaughter meant no special circumstances. A bail hearing was scheduled for nine o'clock the next morning. The bail would likely be high, but Barbara considered this development a major victory. She would not tell Peter of the good news for fear he would blab.

At 9:00 a.m., Peter went into court unshackled, in a new suit and tie. Douglas played the part beautifully when his mistress, Barbara, made the argument that her client was a local business owner, he could not afford expensive bail, and keeping him in jail was morally reprehensible. Douglas argued that he wanted bail of at least $1 million because of the reputation of the defendant's family. Douglas knew full well he could not say that in court. Douglas said it on purpose to help his mistress and his buddy Vince. Douglas was on the payroll.

Peter entered a plea of not guilty. The presiding judge, the Honorable Harold L. Amaro, set bail at $50,000. Barbara expected bail of at least $500,000. The discovery conference was scheduled tentatively for Thursday, May 12. A bailiff escorted Peter back to a jail cell with a telephone.

Sally Giovelli delivered the $5,000 necessary to bail out Peter. After Peter was officially released from jail, he went to his tavern and reimbursed Sally the $5,000.

Uncle Peter's Tavern was closed on Mondays. Instead of going home, Peter bought new clothes and agreed to stay at Vince and Sally's for a few days. Vince took off work early, as his new vice president, Sally Giovelli, wanted to work late. Sally had been working part time for two and a half months and had recently moved to full time. She loved working for her husband. Vince actually began working for Sally. She knew the industry better than Vince.

Vince had lost over thirty pounds and was back down to a respectable 280. Peter and Vince spent the afternoon drinking in a neighborhood dive bar where nobody knew their names.

The next two days were pleasantly uneventful. Vince talked to Carol, while Peter worked at his strip joint on Wednesday evening. Peter would stay at the home of a female dancer that evening.

At closing time, Peter had a drink with a dancer and performed the closing accounting, when four explosions inside of Uncle Peter's Tavern disintegrated the bodies. Peter Cassivano, dancer Melanie Bertanali, and bodyguard Timothy Glaholt were gone, and so was the building.

Suddenly, seven additional massive explosions rocked the city for miles, shattering windows from buildings and vehicles for up to five blocks away. After the area was blocked off, six more buildings housing eight businesses were declared destroyed in the River Quay.

After four days, the rubble had been cleared, and fifteen additional innocent people were found dead. Materials inside Uncle Peter's Tavern had all been destroyed or disintegrated, and the safe inside the office had been stolen. Someone had taken revenge on William Cassivano for crimes he never committed by killing his only living son and stealing the safe.

Small remnants of the bodies of Peter Cassivano, Melanie Bertanali, and Timothy Glaholt were found. The small remnants were seized and studied by the county crime lab.

Peter's funeral was only a memorial service. There could be no casket. There were no cremains in an urn. A humorous self-portrait caricature that Peter painted was the centerpiece, surrounded by other paintings and drawings he completed. Among the one hundred paintings at the service were drawings that Peter sketched as child of five years old. The paintings were arranged chronologically to show how Peter was drawing at an early age through painting in his later years of life. Horses, dogs, snakes, and cars as a child. As an adult, paintings in every category were attempted to perfection. Several paintings of the most beautiful creature he had ever seen: his sister.

She had no idea he had ever painted her. Tears were absent when Carol and Greg saw them. They were stunned.

The final painting Peter completed before his murder was of Greg and Carol kissing while they held Danny and Candy. No photograph like that was ever taken. Peter painted from the heart.

I never met my one uncle, Peter. He died before I was born. I never met my one aunt. She died when I was only four. Gery has never been an uncle. You were the way uncles should be. When the babies were born, you stayed in the hospital on a cot until Carol was able to go home. Every Christmas, you played Santa for Danny. He'll never know how much you loved him. Candy will never know either. Someday we'll tell them. I wanna be an uncle like you. I love you, Peter.

48

Greg coached his eleven-year-old nephew, Michael's, baseball team that spring and summer. Michael benefited unjustly by extra time spent after practice with his coach/uncle. Michael quickly became a lethal hitter and precision pitcher. Michael wanted desperately to have his uncle teach him how to throw a curve ball like the pros. Greg would never do that until Michael grew older. He was afraid Michael would hurt his arm permanently, learning junk pitches at an early age. Greg would teach Michael and other pitchers how to throw fastballs and off-speed pitches accurately.

Greg took the team and their families to professional games four times per month on days when it did not conflict with the team game and practice schedules.

The boys loved him, and the parents loved him. Greg would bench his star players for displaying the slightest hint of temper. Kids that would have normally played very little for other managers played equal time to the stars. By the end of the Little League baseball season, every player on the team had played or sat on the bench an almost identical amount of time. The boys that did not show any interest or talent at the beginning of the season were close to all-star talent by the end of the season.

Greg persuaded his brother to install a batting cage in the basement of his estate. All winterlong, Michael practiced hitting in his new batting cage. Michael practiced pitching or just plain throwing at the targets in his father's shooting range.

An obsession for Greg is what Carol and Sherry hoped for. They got it. The hidden plan worked like a charm. Greg did not drink nearly as much.

271

49

The violence in the River Quay slowed drastically. It had to. The violence had nowhere to go except down. Businesses not destroyed by the March bombings and murders closed or relocated. Throughout the remainder of the year, there were nine additional murders of innocent people. Once or twice per month, an explosion would destroy a business or two.

One morning, Gary Porter attempted to wire a car for practice. He tried to start the car to see if the bomb would work this time. He scattered himself over a two-square-block area.

No one came to the River Quay because of the negative publicity. Stubborn business owners refused to close or relocate. To add insult to injury, the remaining businesses were severely damaged or destroyed by a flash flood in September of 1977. River Quay was a ghost town.

Nicholas Cibella had been released from prison. Although he had not completely relocated, he spent little time in Kansas City. The La Cosa Nostra violence in the area scared him away because he knew if it continued, it would be him that would be the prime suspect.

Federal, Missouri State and local law enforcement agencies considered that Kansas City La Cosa Nostra had become virtually extinct.

Not quite.

50

Greg had no intention of partnering his brother in the $150 million hotel and office park Gerald broke ground on. Several contractors refused to bid on the job because of the blueprints. Several major flaws in the design were the reason Greg did not want to invest. Greg had been warned about the poor design, and, even with the finest construction crews in the world, the hotel was an architectural disaster waiting to occur.

Gerald may have been spending $150 million on the project, but most of that money would be invested in visual stimulation: fountains, waterfalls, suspended skywalks, and restaurants—the finest decor money could purchase. The more expensive, the better. The construction itself was less than half of the budgeted price. After over thirty general contractors refused to bid, a construction company out of Albuquerque, New Mexico, was granted the contract for the job.

Because Gerald did not want to borrow the entire amount himself, and because Greg refused to have anything to do with the hotel and office park, Gerald had to accept other investors.

Greg finally agreed to invest $13 million after constant haranguing from his brother. He would invest the money under the following conditions. He would invest only as a "straw man." No one could know he had invested in it. He would only invest the money as an installment loan, and only if Gerald gave him $13 million of equity in the Las Vegas casinos as collateral. When the money was fully paid, Gerald would pay $14 million back in principal only if the loan was paid back over the course of fifteen years. The interest was not included.

In addition to the inflated principal and interest, Greg would pocket $1 million in cash from the Las Vegas casino skim regardless of when the loan was paid back. If Greg ever wanted to be bought out as a "straw man," he could call the loan due and payable. If Gerald did not have the money, then Greg would keep the equity in the casinos; $2 million and

273

change for Greg if the loan was paid over the course of the silent partner covenant, $1 million and change on the books. The remainder was just between brothers.

Gerald thought this was an absolutely brilliant idea on Greg's part, especially for a drunk. Little did Gerald know that new college graduate Carol was the brains. Her degree was in finance. Because of name recognition, Gerald had no trouble selling investors across the country. The brief mention of his name was all developers needed. The money to construct the hotel and office park, plus a $15 million cushion, was raised easily. With everything budgeted correctly, the majority of the hotel and one-office building would open in the fall of 1979. The goal was to have the main corridor of the hotel opened in time for the beginning of the new decade. The remainder of the hotel and park would open gradually over the following five years.

To prove his confidence in the design, Gerald planned on putting the Crow name on the project: Crow Regency Hotel. Greg told his brother this was a breach of contract and called the loan due. When Gerald told him it was a joke, Greg was not amused.

Gerald took the idea he believed Greg formulated on the hotel and park and applied it to projects nationwide. Gerald discovered a way to improve on perfection. Although Crow Brothers had become a commercial development monstrosity since Gerald and Greg became partners, nobody, including the brothers, was emotionally prepared for the financial windfall about to take place.

Gerald, Greg, and other officers of the company were traveling on one of the company's two private airplanes every week for meetings across the country. As brothers, Gerald and Greg were able to do any deal between one another financially, and it did not necessarily require to be written on paper. With investors around the country, every detail needed to be in print.

Crow Brothers always added special clauses in the contracts at the time because of the economy—anything to make the investors breathe a little easier. The only stipulation was that Crow Brothers would need to approve the sale if the partners were ever to sell to an outside interest. Crow was always given "Right of First Refusal" to guarantee the partners could always count on having money if the market were to get worse.

Partners on projects would be supplied three offers to purchase simultaneously. One was a handsome "contract for deed" proposal near the original purchase price with little or no down payment. The second offer to purchase would be an equity exchange on property elsewhere. The third offer would be a cash offer worth considerably less than what the partners were asking. Pennies on the dollar. The market was so poor in the late 1970s that the majority of real estate investors could not wait out the storm and would usually settle for the pittance of immediate cash.

If the investors were a little braver, the partners would counteroffer with a combination of the three previously mentioned propositions. If ready (reportable) liquid money was not available, then Gerald, Greg, or officers of the company would obtain a loan based on the appraisal of the subject property. Commercial banks and appraisers on large properties would usually grant the loans. If not, equity on property elsewhere would be used as collateral in order to obtain the loans.

It was a thing of beauty for Gerald. The company was quickly acquiring valuable property everywhere. Patient, practical, and wise partners in property all across the country would phone Gerald if a large commercial property could be purchased inexpensively because of the financial condition of a developer or investor. In just over a year, they acquired property, along with minority owner partners, valued at over $300 million in addition to the property they already owned.

Greg refused to be a partner on some of the more-extravagant properties. Carol called the shots behind the scenes so Greg would not need to rely on his brother's advice. She translated finance for her hubby.

Although the company was growing at an extraordinary pace, Greg and Carol added little to their lifestyle. They remodeled the home they lived in and added a swimming pool with strict rules for the children and babysitters. A hot tub outside the master bedroom and three fountains were also professionally installed. Greg and Carol absolutely loved the home and did not comprehend the necessity to move into a larger residence. *This house is too big anyway.* They decided to remodel because a little change would be nice. They never had a maid or cleaning service because of Greg's privacy fixation.

Greg remodeled his vacation cabin himself for recreation. He overhauled his Volkswagen Thing with help. Travel was strenuous with two toddlers, but they did go on modest junkets occasionally. Rarely did Greg and Carol go on vacation without the children.

Gerald's spending was more out of control than ever. Three vacation homes were not enough. Two private jets were not enough. Gerald loved the areas of the vacation homes, but the homes were not colossal enough and expensive enough for the appearance Gerald needed to portray. He would sell the smaller homes and purchase mansions. Although he was usually able to steal the properties for prices nothing compared to what they were actually worth, everyone knew he was still going overboard.

One Rolls-Royce would eventually be transported from his base home for every mansion, along with one small Mercedes. A Porsche was parked in a garage for his use when in New York.

With assistance from his comptroller, Gerald was able to launder the cash being skimmed from the Las Vegas casinos to make the extravagant purchases. Sherry was the only person ever to explain to Gerald that he was nuts for not saving more than he was. She handled the saving of some cash from the casinos behind Gerald's back. Jacob Rosenstingel would always bestow some cash back to Sherry so she could retain it in a safe that Gerald had no knowledge of.

51

Greg needed to get ready for his real job to start: Little League baseball. While Gerald accumulated wealth, Uncle Greg attempted to draft as many boys as possible from last year's team. Fourteen boys were on the team. A total of eight players had been on the team the year before, including Michael. Michael did not need to be drafted. He was granted son status for Uncle Greg. This year, 1978, the team was more than outstanding. They were nearly perfect, 19–1.

Every player learned how to play every position except pitcher or catcher. The team had two catchers and three pitchers. Michael played both positions. Twelve years old and as a catcher, Michael could throw other boys out on the bases regularly. As a pitcher, Michael never pitched a no-hitter, but he also never gave up more than four hits in a single game. Granted, in a condensed twenty-game season, he only pitched ten games, but Michael was the talk of the ballpark by big guys, fifteen to sixteen years old.

Uncle Greg would not teach Michael how to throw junk pitches, so Michael learned by asking older guys and watching the pros on television. He pitched with revenge. He hit with a vengeance. The kid was awesome. Fences as far away as 250 feet could be cleared with ease. Trees over twenty feet beyond the fence were no problem. Michael could clear the trees. Big guys were noticing his hitting. Some of them were ancient, as old as seventeen.

When the regular season ended at the end of July, only one three-game series would decide the championship. Michael pitched a one-hitter in the deciding game.

The league had so many talented players that two all-star teams were selected from the ten teams. Michael was the star of the A all-star team. The A all-star team in the dream league was undefeated going into the final game of the state championship.

During a morning practice, Michael threw up on the mound. Greg, of course, thought the worst. *The kid must have a hangover.* Coaches, including Greg, benched Michael for the remainder of practice. All the other coaches presumed Michael had a hangover until one of them felt his forehead. Michael was burning up.

Uncle Greg took Michael to the hospital that very day. Summer flu was the diagnosis. Michael was sick as a dog. He stayed at home during the final two practices to rest before the big game only two days away.

Michael had seen a commercial for an over-the-counter medicine that helped people suffering from nausea. He was determined to pitch in the championship game.

Gerald was out of town again, and Sherry stayed home for the big game by request. Michael did not want his mother at the games anyway. She was his mom, and she made him nervous. He always tried so hard to impress her. At times, she would go to the ballpark incognito and sit at another baseball field to watch her son. Gerald had only seen one game this year.

His brother did not like baseball as much anymore. Mark never thought he was that good at baseball anyway. He did watch his brother, though. Mark was a football guy now. He played football the past fall and loved it. There was also a hint that Mark may have been into partying. No one could see the signs with the exception of Uncle Greg.

Uncle Greg looked at Michael the day of the game and decided to let him to pitch. For some reason, the flu bug agreed with him. Michael was on fire. Little League games were only seven innings. In the top of the sixth inning, a teammate hit a rocket-like bases-loaded triple all but ending the game. Michael struck out two players and attempted to pitch to the last batter of the sixth, when the nausea was more powerful than the medicine his mother bought him. Michael stepped off the mound and threw up again. Again and again. Several coaches from both teams rushed out to assist. Parents of children on each team showed genuine concern when Michael started heaving blood. Michael suddenly passed out.

Uncle Greg helped his nephew to his feet. Michael begged the coaches to let him finish. *No way.* It took some begging from Michael for them to let him stay at the ballpark at all.

Michael was allowed to sit on the bench and watch his team squander an eight-run lead in the last half-inning and lose. Not only the players cared that they lost.

Picture for a moment the worst ballpark parents ever. Now multiply it by a hundred. There were parents screaming profanities at the coaches.

278

Michael should have never been pulled from the game. Blah, blah, blah. Uncle Greg was not thinking about the game. Michael.

I'm taking him to the hospital tonight. It's just a game, you fuckin' idiots. Throwing Cokes and Seven-Up at each other now, how mature. Adults are worse than my players. Jerks.

Uncle Greg took his nephew to the emergency room only to hear one more time that it was nothing but the flu. He was getting pissed off now. Michael was being probed and prodded by these doctors. Greg called his sister-in-law and told her of the problem. Michael had been eating peanut butter with pickles lately. That did not explain the fevers or the dizziness.

Michael spent the next few days feeling fine, then suddenly passing out or throwing up or both. He never told anyone, with the exception of his uncle. Finally, on August 11, the day after his thirteenth birthday party, Uncle and Mom took Michael to a children's hospital this time.

Michael checked in as an inpatient. Two days of tests were administered. Every test was given at least twice. If the results on a particular test were inconclusive, the tests were administered repeatedly until the results were conclusive. Positive or negative. Uncle Greg stayed with his nephew the entire time. Dad was out of town as usual, and Mom was serving her residency as a family physician. A doctor met with Greg alone and notified him of the tragic results.

Greg could not tell Michael right away. He tried desperately to remain quiet for Michael's benefit, but he was crying hysterically. Uncle telephoned Mom and told her. Mom began crying and announced she would take unlimited absence from her residency immediately. She could not telephone Gerald. She was too upset. Greg had Gerald's secretary put an immediate page. There was an emergency at home. His brother needed to speak with him. Gerald did not call back. Greg had the secretary page Gerald again with the information that it was a medical emergency concerning Michael. Gerald called immediately. Gerald knew when he called his home and his father answered, it was serious. Gerald immediately flew back home from New York. Michael knew. Something was wrong.

Michael had been diagnosed with acute leukemia. The leukemia was in an advanced stage, and the diagnosis included the dreadful word: terminal. The doctors did say there was a chance of remission, but it was a very slim chance. The doctors could not explain the queasiness. Nausea is not an atypical side effect of leukemia prior to diagnosis and treatment.

Michael was intuitive. He wondered why none of the adults were telling him anything. He could see his mom had been crying. She spent little time in the room. His grandpa was able to mask his tears, but Michael could see his grandpa had been crying also. His dad came into town after having been away on business. That was very strange. Michael became fed up with the adults and started screaming.

"If somebody doesn't tell me what's goin' on, I'm gonna walk out o' here!"

The adults elected Uncle Greg to speak with his nephew. Not because of the undeniable fact that everyone was too emotional. It was primarily because Greg had this uncanny ability to speak with Michael and with kids in general. They were not kids to him. Maybe they *were* kids, but he was also.

"Mike, the doctors told us that you have a blood disease."

"Tell me what it is."

"Leukemia. It's a kind of cancer."

Michael had heard about leukemia before. He was not naive. He knew it was a bad-blood thingamajig.

"How long before I get rid of it and go home?"

"Mike, that's kinda hard to say. One, you're not gonna get rid of it. Two, I don't know when you'll go home."

"I'm not gonna get rid of it ever?" Mike asked, surprised.

"No. Mike, I'm afraid I don't know how to put this. They're gonna start giving you all kinds of medicine and stuff. They have this thing called chemotherapy. There's this thing called radiation that they need to do on you also."

"I saw this guy on TV, and he had that radiation thing. It made his hair fall out." Michael laughed. Uncle faked a smile when he wanted to cry.

"Well, Mike, it's probably gonna make your hair fall out too." Uncle Greg looked to see if he could read Michael. The kid did not pay close attention. He just fidgeted in the bed.

"I don't care about that. The guy said it grew back a different color. Gray. He didn't have very good hair before the radiation thing. He was pretty old. I'll just shave mine. I wanted to shave it anyway. Mom wouldn't let me do it before. Now she has to say yes. It'll make me look mean." Uncle Greg knew he could not tell Michael the bad-blood thingamajig was gonna make him die. "All the other guys want long hair. Mom won't let me do that either. I'll just shave it."

"I'll tell her to bug off then," Uncle Greg said, smiling.

Michael could see this smile was bogus as a tear streamed down Uncle Greg's cheek.

"Why are you so sad?"

"I just don't like seeing you in the hospital. I think I'd rather be in here than having you here."

As the Crow Falls

"I don't think so. I know you and Aunt Carol go out to eat all the time. The food in here sucks." This time, Uncle Greg's laugh was really cool.

"From now on, Mike, just say the food isn't very good. I don't think your mom or dad would be happy hearing you say that."

"Why? They hear Mark say it all the time. This sucks, that sucks, everything sucks. Can I go home today and just come back for the medicine and that stuff that makes your hair fall out?"

"I'm afraid not, Mike. See, some of the things they do are gonna make you sick and weak. Real, real sick and real, real weak. They need to put this thing like a big needle in your back to get some of the marrow from inside your bones. It's gonna hurt real bad."

"What's marrow?"

Uncle Greg labored to think of the best way to explain it. Even understand it.

"It's like when you're eating chicken or a steak with bones. If you look inside of some of the big bones, there's this red stuff, that's bone marrow."

"Why do they take it?"

"Well, Mike, it's real complicated. But leukemia is like when your white blood cells take over and eat all your red blood cells."

"I cut myself the other day, and my blood was red, not white."

How the hell can I get out of this?

"Regular people can't see the white blood cells. Everyone has white blood cells. You just have too many. Only doctors and scientists can see it, and they use all kinds of machines and microscopes and stuff to be able to see things that even they can't normally see."

I hope that's OK. I can't explain it any better.

"I get it."

"Then they also need you to be here so they can do things at night and monitor you while you sleep."

"What's monitor?" Michael asked, as computers were not in the hands of seemingly all youth then as they are now.

"That means they're gonna hook you to machines and stuff. People can't watch you all the time, so the machines do." That was as good of a definition as Uncle Greg could think of, and it worked.

"Whatever. Could you get me some things from home for here so I don't feel like such a tool?"

"Sure, just make a list. I'll make sure I get it all. I'm gonna go out there and talk to them."

"Why did they have you to talk to me?"

How can I answer that? He doesn't know how bad it is.

"Just because they all think you suck," Uncle Greg said. Michael

281

laughed loudly enough and long enough that every member of his family in the lounge down the hall heard. What a beautiful sound. "No, just because they know that you're my best friend. Plus, they wanted to see if I can make you understand how sick this is gonna make you."

"I can handle it." After a brief hesitation. "Greg?" Greg turned his head, trying desperately to hold back the tears for one more second. "I needed to tell you that I know you had to pull me out of the game, so don't worry about the way some of the guys moms and dads acted. I play in the bigger league next year. We can do it again."

"Thank you, Mike. That makes me feel better." Once out of the earshot of Michael, Uncle Greg raced down the hall and fell to his knees. Gerald and Gerome helped him to his feet. "He doesn't realize how bad it is. I couldn't tell him. If he thinks he's gonna die, he might not fight it. If he doesn't know, he might. I want him to fight it." Uncle Greg cried. Carol, Sherry, Gerome, and Gerald joined in again. "We can talk to the doctors, but I don't think he should know it's terminal. None of this goes beyond any of us. I don't want him to find out from anyone. I don't even want Mark to know." They all looked at one another and agreed. "The poor kid tried to comfort me for the team losing the game. I haven't even thought about that once in the last week. Go in there and talk to him, but don't let on how upset everyone is. Sherry, when do they start the treatments?"

"They already have. Today or tomorrow they probably start the chemotherapy and radiation. I don't know if they start everything, but the sooner, the better." Sherry was too weak to stand. She put her head in her lap, sobbing. Carol put an arm around Sherry and placed the side of her face on Sherry's back.

"This is because of me. I'm a terrible father." Gerald sobbed.

Gerome slapped his son on the face. "Don't ever say that! You're not a terrible dad. You never have been. If anything, you take after me. You provide for your wife and kids better than I ever could've provided for you. I've seen you with them. You're a natural, wonderful dad. Don't you ever say that again. No one is to blame for this. It happens. We all need to get through this together. And we all need to be strong for Michael." Gerome was the best of the bunch at fighting back his tears.

"I'm sorry. I just know I've been spending too much time away," Gerald said, weeping.

"Guys, look,"—Greg needed to be the voice of reason—"get it together and go in the room. He's making a list right now of things I need to pick up at home for him. Talk to him and then go home. Tell him you have things to do. I don't think if you say you're gonna leave, he'll know how serious this is. Get the tears out tonight and come back tomorrow rejuvenated.

He knows me too well, so I'll tell him I'm gonna go out, get drunk, and eat a chimichanga tonight. Please, he doesn't find out how serious this is."

Everyone looked at Uncle Greg as a certified lunatic. They knew it was lunatic speak, but they also knew Uncle Greg was right on the money again.

They all took turns washing their faces and went into the room and attempted to look positive. Michael could see right through them. His hair was gonna fall out, big donkey balls deal. Michael asked Greg to bring the list of stuff back to the hospital tonight.

"Will do, Mike."

Greg accompanied his brother into Michael's bedroom to get the items Michael requested: a *Playboy* he had hidden under his mattress, a local paper's television section, a generic scorebook and, most importantly, his baseball glove and a baseball. When Uncle Greg returned the golden find, Michael had one question.

"Greg, am I gonna die?"

"You are. So am I. So are your brother, your mom and dad, Aunt Carol, and everybody you've ever met. We all die."

"I'm not a kid anymore. Is this leukemia cancer thing gonna make me die soon?"

"I don't know, Mike. I was hoping you were still a kid so I could bullshit you a little longer. You have a good chance of beating this thing if you fight it. If you act like a girl or, worse yet, a kid and cry and feel sorry for yourself and give up, then you won't."

"You cried a little while ago."

How the hell do I get out o' this now?

"Yes, I did, Mike. I'm just using that as a poor example. Just fight it and you'll be OK. Baseball season next summer should be your goal."

"I wanted to play football like Mark."

"That's something you're not gonna be able to do." Greg thought fast. "At least not this year. Maybe next year."

"Whatever. School starts the week after next. Am I gonna go?"

"I never thought about school. Hell, I never thought about it when I was twelve . . . I mean thirteen, so why should I think about it for you?"

Michael could hear that the laugh Uncle Greg let out this time was really cool.

"Whatever. I'll see you tomorrow. Good-bye, Greg, you suck." Michael laughed at his own funny thing he said.

"I'll see you later, Mike. By the way, I forgot to tell you—you suck." Uncle Greg ran out of the room. He pressed his face against the window into the room and stuck his tongue out at Michael.

Michael tried to hide his laughter and yelled, "You suck!"

Uncle Greg was gone for the night. After his evening meal, Michael turned out the lights and cried. And cried. And cried some more. And cried himself to sleep.

Sherry decided to do as Greg suggested and only took one week off her residency. This was the last semester of her residency.

During the evenings, Gerald and Sherry were always at the hospital together. It took a serious illness in the immediate family for them to realize how much they still loved and hated one another. This was a normal marriage again.

Gerald made a point to stop by in the mornings and evenings and occasionally afternoons. He did not travel as often. When he did, he desperately attempted to structure the meetings to last no longer than one day. The other officers of the company had more authority and were immediately handling more big business decisions. Gerald would, of course, have the final say.

Gerome visited the hospital frequently.

Aunt Carol would meet with Michael privately and answer his questions about girls. She did not volunteer information, but she was amazed at his knowledge of the female psyche.

Carol and Greg went to eat at restaurants near the hospital daily. At night, they would eat at home with the kids or hire a babysitter and go out as usual.

Mark could drive now, so he and a few of his and Mike's friends would visit frequently.

A private tutor was hired to keep Michael up-to-date with the eighth-grade curriculum. At times, he was too tired or queasy to pay attention. He was seldom allowed to leave the hospital. When he did, he wore a baseball cap to cover his balding head and long-sleeve shirts and sunscreen to protect his now severely sensitive skin.

In months, Michael went from a moderately hefty 130 pounds down to a scrawny ninety pounds, and still going down fast. None of his old clothes fit him anymore. Friends of his were starting to shy away from him; they were not scared of him. They had no idea what to say. Soon, the only visitors he had in the hospital were the aforementioned adults. Mark and a few older kids were the only visitors of a relatively close age.

Michael was released from the hospital on the condition that he would receive treatments five times per week and could receive them on an outpatient basis. He went back to school in November and picked up right where he left off: A's. Occasionally, kids would tease him. To show

As the Crow Falls

it did not bother him, Michael would take off his cap, pull out a clump of hair, and blow it toward the name-callers.

Michael lectured his mother about his brother smoking pot all the time. She did not know how to stop it. It was important that Gerald not find out.

"When I have kids, they'll never do anything like that."

Sherry did not have the heart to explain to her son that the medication and therapy had made him sterile. He would never father a child. When he found out, Michael was about to take another turn for the worse.

On Christmas morning, Michael was too weak to unwrap his gifts. He complained he was tired and needed sleep. The whole family was there and understood. He was too weak to walk. Dad and Uncle Greg picked him up to take him to bed via the elevator. Everyone in the room heard a bone snap. Michael started screaming and crying. They did not waste another second and rushed him to the hospital in a station wagon that allowed him to lie down. After he was safely in the hospital, X-rays were taken. He must have hit the leg on something because the leg was severely broken below the kneecap. Michael told the doctors that he tried to swim in the indoor pool yesterday and hit his leg on the diving board. He would only need to stay in the hospital for a brief time, maybe two weeks.

The treatment, along with the drastic weight loss, made his bones intensely brittle, and the doctors were concerned. After the leg was set and placed in a cast, Michael was wheeled back into the hospital room that he had become so familiar with. Doctors, nurses, and orderlies were on a first-name basis with Mike.

Gerald went home and retrieved all the gifts. He brought them back to the hospital and left again as Michael went back to sleep. Greg stayed behind because he did not want his best friend/nephew to be alone on Christmas. Carol agreed and promptly drove to the hospital. Gerald and Sherry watched Daniel and Candice and were not very adept at hiding their emotions. Besides, Greg and Carol did not talk to Mike like a kid.

Four hours later, Michael woke up long enough to have Greg open one gift. Michael then went back to sleep for twelve hours.

Greg and Carol slept in shifts and stayed in the hospital room. The following day, Michael woke briefly for twenty minutes, and four more gifts were opened. Another eighteen-hour slumber. Greg talked with doctors about his obvious concern.

"He is severely depressed. The medicine does make him tired. However, rather than expressing his feelings through typical behavior, Michael sleeps."

It did not seem possible for Michael to lose more weight. He did just

285

that, losing over twenty pounds in the next few weeks. He was now being fed intravenously. Greg would spend days and nights with Michael, leaving only when it was necessary to take a shower or eat. At those times, Carol would sit in. Gerald and Sherry would, of course, make daily appearances, but were always too emotional. Greg warned them that tears would only upset Michael further.

One morning, at approximately three, after over five weeks in bed and another twenty-pound weight loss, Michael woke to ask a very poignant question from his skeleton-thin face through his dry-encrusted lips.

"Greg, you lied to me last summer. I'm gonna die." Uncle Greg had been able to mask the tears for months. Now he did not try to hold back. The tears were immediate.

"I didn't lie to you. No matter what they said, I knew you could make it. You still can. You just can't give up now."

"I think I'm gonna need to. This hurts too much."

"Please don't give up. There are so many people that care about you so much. Think of them. Think of me and Aunt Carol." Uncle Greg could not stifle the tears anymore.

"If Dad cared so much, he'd be here." He did not cry. He had a look of analytical brilliance on his sunken face.

"He does love you. I told him not to come around when he's crying. He cries all the time, and I thought the crying would upset you."

"But you're crying." Michael looked at his uncle with no emotion on his face.

"Yes, I am, but I'm not fighting it now. I'm crying because I love you so much. Not just because you're my nephew, but because you're my best friend. I wish I could be the one who's sick, not you. I don't like seeing you asleep all the time. I like it better when you're awake and you talk to me."

"I still don't know why Mom or Dad is never here." This was of great concern to Uncle Greg now. Michael showed no signs of typical human behavior or emotions. "If they cared so much, they'd be here."

"Mike, they have been here. They're here every day four or five times. Almost every time they're here, you're asleep." Michael reached out to comfort Uncle Greg. Uncle Greg needed to do the rest of the reaching, as Michael was too weak.

"Mark is never here."

"He cries when he sees you. That's all. And I hate to tell you, but Mark kinda smelled like pot one day. I told him to leave before a doctor got a whiff of him. I didn't say a word to your mom or dad, so I don't want you to squeal. I'll talk with him. Anyway, I just don't want you to be sadder.

I'm kinda checking people out when they come in to make sure they're not gonna make you more sad."

"I'm not really sad. I just hurt real bad." Greg could certainly understand why. It would hurt anyone to be in this condition, let alone a thirteen-year-old boy. Having doubts about supposed loved ones and friends loving you. "Especially my broken leg and both of my arms."

Shit, the kid is talking about physical hurt. Not emotional.

"Look, Mike, remember how bad you hurt when you were hit in the mouth with your own foul ball last year? Busted your own lip and three teeth. You cried like a baby. But two days later you played again. You were tough. You need to be tough again and fight this."

"OK, I'll be all right. But why does Dad never stay until I'm awake?"

"I'll tell you that your dad has to keep making money. You know he and I work together. It's pretty complicated, so I don't know how well I can explain it. Hell, I'm not even sure I understand it. Your dad is a lot smarter than me. He makes the money, and I just take care of other stuff. I need him to work so I can stay here with you. If I did all the work and he stayed here, we'd be in big trouble. We'd be broke. Don't ever tell anyone I said this, OK?"

Michael attempted to nod his head. He could not. He tried to smile like Uncle Greg. He could not.

"OK."

"I'm not a real smart guy when it comes to business. Your dad isn't real smart when it comes to people. I take care of people, he takes care of business." Michael was able to smile faintly because he understood. "Are you hungry at all, Mike?"

"Not really. Tomorrow I'll eat something."

"Mike, you need to start eating regular foods. One of these tubes is feeding you through your veins."

"I'll eat tomorrow. I don't feel like it now. Greg, I've gotta go to sleep."

No good night, just immediate eerie silence.

Greg prepared himself to sleep. One of the night doctors made her hourly rounds. Greg stopped her and asked for the current prognosis on his best friend/nephew. She told him that the primary care physician would be able to answer his questions more thoroughly than she could.

Greg slept in a cot beside Michael as usual. As he attempted to sleep, Greg spoke a silent prayer that was becoming a frequent ritual.

Several times during the morning hours, nurses entered the room to check the various monitors a great deal more frequently than usual. This was scary. This was the end. It was obvious to Greg that Michael would not live through the day.

Michael slipped into a coma and was taken to intensive care. Uncle Greg telephoned Mom and Aunt Carol to notify them. Greg walked to the nondenominational hospital chapel. After he sobbed with his head in his hands on a chapel pew for over an hour, a pair of lips kissed him on the cheek. He looked up to see his sister-in-law. They sat speechless, holding hands and crying for what seemed an eternity.

Gerald had been notified and promptly left the office so he could join his wife and brother. Gerome was next. Then Carol. Then Mark. Vincenzo and Sally Giovelli and all five of their children were next. Brian Nivaro appeared with a river of tears streaming down his face. Officers, accountants, and salespeople from real estate companies citywide came in and obviously declared work over for the day. To everyone's utter surprise, William and Margaret Cassivano were next. All day, people came in and stayed. Many of Michael's friends came with their parents. Teachers and students in Michael's classes arrived on a bus. Several local celebrities and professional athletes came to pray for their hero. Friends of the family entered for their own solace.

The chapel did not have space for another person to sit and seemingly nowhere to stand. People kept coming in anyway. Over three hundred people were crammed into the small chapel. The only sounds were of unbridled whimpering and low-volume prayers. Conversation did not need to exist. After nine hours of virtual silence, Greg was the first person to address the congregation with words that he was barely able to speak:

"Thank you. I need to check on Michael." The news was as expected. Uncle Greg begged the doctor to speak in terms that a layman could understand. "Sherry is a doctor, but that's her son. She's a wreck, as you can imagine. If you tell her in some medical terminology, it'll scare her to death. Please, just tell me so I can understand and let me relay it to her."

The doctor had become a friend to Uncle Greg in recent months. He knew he needed to drop the medical terminology.

"Michael slipped in and out of a coma until about one o'clock. Some of it can't be explained. Now he's not slipping out. He's in the coma. I hope not permanently, but he may never come out of it. I'm sorry. The longer he's in that state, the more likely he'll never come back. If he lives another couple of days, it would be a surprise. I'm sorry. We're doing everything we can."

"Do more!"

Greg returned to the chapel to see people he had never met sitting or standing in silent prayer. He sat silently and joined. Mom and Dad tapped Greg on the shoulder. Greg walked out with the two and his own wife. Gerald looked as unhealthy as anyone had ever seen. They needed to know.

"He said Michael slipped in and out of a coma for a few hours. Now he's not coming out of it. He's in a coma. Hopefully not to stay, but that's the way it looks. They're doing everything they can."

Sherry and Carol hugged one another, crying. After several minutes, the hold was broken. Sherry and Carol walked back in the nondenominational chapel to pray.

Gerald and Greg embraced tightly. This particular embrace could not be broken.

"Forget everything I've ever said bad to you. You're a wonderful person, Greg."

That's the only time he's ever called me Greg. Always Gregory. That must be more of an act than I thought.

"We gotta be strong, Gery. Not just for Michael, but for Sherry too." *What am I saying? He's in much worse shape than she is.* "There's nothing we can do. We can only hope and pray." *Listen to me. I know I'm not religious, but I've always believed. Please, God, help that little guy. I don't wanna lose him.* "There are so many people in there that I've never seen," Greg said as the embrace lightened yet stayed strong.

"I know. It's incredible. Sherry said Michael went into the coma about six this morning. She got here at eight, after you called. It's after seven now, and I haven't seen one person leave yet. More people just keep coming. It's incredible." Dad wiped his eyes. They were immediately flooded again.

"I only called Sherry and Carol. I called them about seven this morning. I can't imagine how everyone found out so soon."

"Let's go back in. I love you. You're the best friend Michael could ever have—that anyone could have. I mean that more than anything I've ever said to you or anyone else. I'm never ever gonna forget this."

Uncle Greg and Dad walked back in together and sat together again on the front pew. The first person exited at nine that evening. A guest register sat on a podium for people to sign as they exited. At the top of the list were instructions to leave a private note for Michael. Every person exiting the chapel signed the register and wrote a private note for Michael and sealed it in an envelope. The notes and envelopes were supplied and sitting there for that sole purpose. Someone had taken the initiative to have *Michael Darryl Crow* monogrammed on stationery notes of the thank-you note variety. After the notes were sealed, they were tossed into a velvet-lined basket.

By eleven o'clock, everyone had left without saying a word to Mark, Gerald, Gregory, Gerome, Sherry, or Carolyn, who were the only parishioners remaining. They were all determined to stay in the chapel forever. After a brief discussion, Carol, Gerome, and Mark were elected to retrieve clothes and toiletries for the others. Uncle Greg, Mom, and Dad would not leave the chapel. Carol took the notes and gave them to Sherry. Absolutely no one was allowed to read them. Except Michael.

Greg, Gery, and Sherry would not leave the hospital. When they were not eating or showering, they were in the chapel, praying silently. Only one of them would leave the chapel at a time. When biology told them it was time to sleep, they fell asleep on the pews.

Carol had two kids and could not stay at the hospital continuously. Mark begged not to go to school, but his mom and dad insisted. He did not go anyway. How in the world could he concentrate? Instead of skipping school in the traditional way, Mark would stay at home, crying for his little brother. At night, he would drive to the hospital chapel.

Gerome tried to get back in the swing of business and attempted to run the company. Symbolically, Gerome remained chairman of the board. Gerome knew the company was big, but he was flabbergasted. It was the first time he realized the monster company his sons had turned it into. Gerome was lost, so he went home or to the hospital.

People from everywhere came by the hospital chapel to sit in silence with them. Mom, Dad, and Uncle would not accept a single phone call.

After the long four-day coma, the physician in charge recommended they elect to turn off life support. Mom and Dad had the final say. Uncle begged them not to touch Michael's life. They did not.

After the sixth-day of the coma, the physician asked again. This time with a strong recommendation. No.

During the eighth-day of the coma, a nurse ran into the chapel to notify them that Michael came out of it. They were not allowed to see him yet, but he came out. Uncle stayed in silent prayer. Mom and Dad were anything but silent.

After another two pivotal days, Mom, Dad, and Uncle were allowed to see him through the glass. His immune system had been shattered by the medication. Michael was definitely awake. He drifted in and out of sleep, which, the doctors assured them, was only induced to prevent seizures. Michael had some brain damage from the coma. Doctors were not sure how bad the damage would be. Only time would tell.

Michael could not hold food of any substance down. The doctors increased the amount of liquids both intravenously and orally. Michael was dangerously underweight. He only weighed fifty pounds.

He had at least twenty hours of sleep per day to begin with. Eventually less and less sleep. There was a problem.

Michael tried hard to speak, yet he could not form words. He attempted to write requests and could not. Michael was aware of the difficulty and wanted to cry himself back to sleep. He never let anyone see his tears.

Greg could not stay at the hospital continuously. When Michael woke and did not see any relatives or friends, he would sleep. When he did see visitors, his uncle was always among them.

Finally, one month to the day when Michael slipped into the coma, he was able to speak. Mom and Uncle were present to hear the glorious words that Michael labored to say at a whisper.

"Can I have a sandwich now?"

Uncle and Mom hugged. The tears were of joy. Uncle thought he was sure to pass out.

Thank you.

"Can you write what you need honey, or can you talk?" Mom asked, crying.

Michael still drifted in and out of sleep. He motioned Mom to him. "Peanut butter," he whispered.

The two sweetest words that Uncle or Mom had ever heard.

Greg ran up and down the hospital halls in quest of peanut butter. He saw someone who looked like a doctor. The doctor brought Greg to a nurse's station. Greg breathed like he had run a marathon.

He screamed at a nurse. "Peanut butter! We need peanut butter. He talks now. He needs peanut butter."

A nurse that was quite familiar with the situation retrieved a peanut butter sandwich. Michael could not sit up or raise his arms to his mouth. Mom tore tiny pieces of the sandwich until Michael finished all he was able to, nearly half. Uncle and Mom were overcome with emotion once again. Uncle smiled while he looked to the sky, mouthing the words over and over: *Thank you.*

Mom sat once again with her head in her lap. Michael could barely see his mother and motioned Uncle Greg to the bed.

"More."

Greg tore the remaining portions from the thin sandwich. Michael was able to finish the whole, very skimpy sandwich. For Uncle and Mom, this was a monumental event. Mom wanted to phone everyone, just like she did when Mark or Michael took their first steps.

"Drink." Greg moved the Styrofoam cup to Mike and allowed him a little sip from the straw. Michael motioned Greg toward him again. "I told you I could eat today." Michael smiled and fell back to sleep.

The little guy doesn't know he almost left us. Thank you.

Now the exhaustion hit like a bolt of lightning. Uncle and Mom used telephones immediately. Gerald, Gerome, and Carol were instructed to relay the messages to as many people as possible. They did. When Carol became aware that people thought she was nuts for calling to say a thirteen-year-old boy had eaten a sandwich, she stopped the phone calls and drove to the hospital. Gerald followed. Then Gerome. Then Mark. Then others.

The hospital administration had to order the people flooding the hospital with rules. There were too many visitors. Michael had come out of a coma. He remained a very ill boy.

Over the next two months, Michael gradually slept less. Gradually, he became a little stronger and was able to feed himself. He was not as nauseous as previous months, but his progress was too slow for comfort. He had been meeting with a dietician regularly. Minor physical therapy had him walking under his own power again.

When he was finally told he had been in a coma, he did not cry. He simply said, "I don't remember that."

Radiation had taken what remained of his hair, eyebrows, and eyelashes. Slowly, he regained some weight, but not nearly enough for comfort. Michael had gone back up to a whopping sixty pounds. He always asked for the seemingly only food that he could keep down—peanut butter. At times, he requested his favorite, peanut butter and pickles. Anything that would help him put the weight back on.

For weeks, doctors did not notify family of something that concerned and baffled them. This was not supposed to happen. Many more tests were administered.

Finally, on April 30, 1979, with the prognosis confirmed, doctors hesitated but made the announcement. For some reason, Michael achieved remission. After another week or so, he may be able to leave. "We want to monitor him closely. He needs to start eating better. That's the main concern." Sherry promised she would stay at home and tend to Michael if he could be released. Michael needed to be home.

On May 4, 1979, Michael Darryl Crow was released from the hospital.

At home that evening, Greg asked Carol the question that haunted yet pleased him, something that he never spoke about once: the notes.

"Carol, did you put the notes there the day Michael slipped into the coma?"

"I was there all day, how could I?"

"Who did that?"

"Daddy lined it up with a printer. After he met Michael a few years ago, he just loved him. When he found out Michael had leukemia, he talked to a priest. As far as I know, he called the printer when Michael went back into the hospital on Christmas. When he went in to visit Michael one day when he was asleep, before the coma, he had the printer get the notes

292

ready. Then he had a priest deliver them to the hospital that day. He said he could see something special about Michael when he met him."

"I owe Willie the biggest apology ever."

"A thank-you might be OK, but from what you've told me, Daddy doesn't deserve an apology for the way he has always been to you."

"I still need to send him a big thank-you."

"That would be fine, I guess. I had a long talk with Mom after Peter was killed. Daddy needs people to fear him, so he never lets anyone know he does nice things. Whenever he does something charitable or nice, he does it anonymously. He doesn't want anyone to know he can be a nice guy. Keep it silent that Daddy can be a nice guy." Carol shrugged her shoulders.

Greg wanted to laugh. He drank twenty beers and smoked a joint instead.

52

Michael continued sleeping for long hours. Gradually, the sleep became less. A private tutor would assist him through the summer to make sure he would be able to begin ninth grade on schedule.

Michael was practical enough to realize he could not play baseball that summer. Greg would coach his son, Daniel, at tee ball that year. Michael begged and pleaded with his mom and dad to let him coach. Greg convinced them that Michael would be an excellent coach. He desperately needed something to bring him back to reality.

He was more than wonderful. He helped the little kids tremendously, and, in turn, they loved him. The parents loved him. He never talked with anyone regarding the leukemia. When adults would ask him how he was feeling, his response was:

"Well, I'm disturbed about the Middle East and the economy sucks. Other than that, I feel fine." It was obvious he paid closer attention to the news than other kids his age. Everyone close to the family believed Michael to be a walking miracle.

By the end of the tee ball season, Michael was up to an even eighty pounds, and he sported a very neat flattop. He thought he might keep it that way. All the other guys were trying to grow long hair. He may, just to see if his hair would grow, but the flattop seemed a little rebellious.

One day, after the ten-game tee ball season ended, Uncle Greg drove Michael home from the ballpark. Michael thanked his uncle for everything. Uncle Greg reversed the thank-you.

"Thank you, Mike. You've been great. I actually think you might be able to play ball again next year."

"I don't know if I will or not. I'm still kinda of weak. My arms, especially. We'll see."

The illness had matured Michael—just three weeks shy of his

fourteenth birthday and speaking as someone who believed the life in him had been worn down. He actually did have a hint of arthritis.

"Mike, now that you're OK, I'll tell you. I was seriously afraid a few times that we were gonna lose you."

"What do you mean? I really almost died?"

Greg looked at Michael and realized he had just broken his promise to himself.

"Yes, Mike. You almost died a few times. But you're here now. You being here has brightened so many lives. Did you ever read the notes that all those people wrote for you when you were in the coma?"

"I've got them, but I didn't look at them. It would probably get me real depressed. I just thought I was real sick. I didn't realize I almost died. Someone may have told me that, but I don't remember anything for a few months. Bits and pieces, I guess, but not much, really. What's a coma?"

"I don't know how to answer that. Your mom probably would." Greg almost cried yet again. "It's kinda like, when someone is in a coma, the body is there, but their mind isn't. You were just a stone lying there for a couple of weeks. We were all scared."

"It seems like I slept a minute. Then, at times, it seemed like I'd sleep for a week. I couldn't get enough sleep. I don't remember anything. It's just like—boom!—three months were gone. I slept through it."

"Well, Mike, we're almost to your house. I can't tell you how much you mean to so many people. Your mom and dad, Mark, Grandpa, me, Carol, everyone. Don't tell anyone, but Carol's dad, Willie, set up the notes for you. So forget what you hear about him on the news." Greg and Michael laughed. "He's really a nice guy. You really need to read those notes and thank him. There were a couple of hundred people in the hospital when you went into the coma. People that I've never seen before. So many kids from school you wouldn't believe it. Professional ball players. It was the most beautiful thing I've ever seen. People sitting there, not talking. Just praying for you."

Michael began crying. It was the first time since he was diagnosed nearly one year earlier that he wept in front of another human being. Michael and Greg shared a hug in the old Volkswagen Thing before departing.

I can't tell what the poor kid's brain damage is.

Greg went home and looked with feeling at his wife and kids.

Gregory Matthew Crow had truly been blessed: money to burn. Everything anyone could possibly desire or crave was his. When he got ready for bed, he kneeled by the side of his bed and prayed. This was the first time his wife witnessed him praying when he thought no one could see him. He prayed for everyone. His kids, his father, his brother, his sister-in-law and nephews, his friends, a special prayer for Michael, and a special prayer to the mother he never met.

His deepest and most heartfelt prayer was a thank-you for the angel he believed was sent to watch over him—his wife.

Gregy believed that only he and the *man* upstairs that he always believed existed heard the prayer. Greg needed to believe *he* existed.

Carol did not think it was possible, but she loved her husband even more today.

Book 3

53

The majority of the first phase of Crown Regency Hotel opened in autumn of 1979. It was by far the nicest hotel either Gerald or Gregory had ever been involved with—cosmetically anyway. A high-powered investment group based in New York purchased the existing construction loans on the project. All sixteen of the original investment groups were also granted payment. The company from New York assumed all construction loans and future liability from the date of closing.

Greg pocketed $1 million in cash and the original $13 million, plus interest he earned as a "straw man." Gerald would simply structure adjustments in the casino skim to assure he did not lose the $1 million.

In the Las Vegas area, the couriers who knew too much about the skim were winding up dead. Because of the high suicide rate in Las Vegas, the majority of the deaths were assumed to be self-inflicted gunshot wounds, suicidal automobile accidents in the mountains surrounding the city, or drug overdoses.

Vince had no adverse feelings in permitting Gerald to supervise the skim. Vince was Italian, and since his father and brother were long gone, the FBI naturally believed Vincenzo Giovelli must be the boss. Therefore, federal agents had continual surveillance of Vince; although they had several good reasons to believe the majority of Kansas City La Cosa Nostra members had blown one another away. Nevertheless, Vincenzo Giovelli and William Cassivano were targets of blatant racial discrimination by the RICO task force. Vince had no choice other than to turn the spotlight away as much as possible.

Giovelli Construction had become so reputable and dependable that no spotters from unions were needed. Other than the casino skim and occasional personal marijuana or cocaine use by Vince, nothing he was involved in was remotely illegal. Vince went down to 240 pounds.

Gerald and Greg continued their innovative real estate investments.

Partners continued to be given the clauses in increasing complex contracts that guaranteed a buyout if they wanted one. Crow Brothers continued buying out the majority of partners for pennies on the dollar.

Greg knew Gerald was getting too big much too quickly. Greg refused to partner with his brother on several projects he had a feeling were not destined to be profitable. Several of the properties Greg refused to partner on came back to bite him at Gerald's profit.

Carol always coached Greg on finance. She would accompany her husband on business trips to cities around the Midwest, yet, because of the children, she would never stay away for more than two nights per month. Day trips were all she would usually tend to.

As the deli business continued to flourish, Greg often pondered leaving real estate and partnering his wife. He wanted to remain partners on the Las Vegas casinos and a few other lucrative properties, but he seriously considered arranging an installment plan for Gerald to buy him out of the real estate company. Carol insisted that as soon as the economy turned better, he could organize a much more lucrative proposal.

Greg really wanted to become a househusband. He wanted to partially retire. Carol reminded him that he had always been partially retired by having Gerald as his brother. Financially, Greg and Carol were more than set for life. The sole reason Carol did not approve of Greg leaving the real estate industry was the fear that with too much idle time, he would drink himself into oblivion daily.

Carol's deli chain had grown to fifty-two stores strategically placed throughout the Midwest. Patty was tired of the business, so she asked for a buyout from Carol. The buyout was minimal on the books because the continued skim had devalued the chain. The cash given to Patty was beyond adequate. The three floral shops that did succeed were sold to an outside interest. The delis required minimal overhead and provided immediate cash that Carol held alongside of the Las Vegas cash.

Greg never understood how the Las Vegas skimming operation worked. Not because he was incapable of understanding but because he knew it was illegal, which, of course, meant he begged not to be informed. Carol explained how the deli skim worked so easily. Greg was fascinated. If the deli business continued to flourish, the skim would be larger than the casino skim in another seven or eight years.

There was a definite beauty to both businesses. With the economy so poor, people gambled as much, if not more, money than ever. The deli stores were a basic fast-food business, and people always need to eat.

54

In the summer of 1980, the brain damage Michael suffered in his coma became apparent. His speed and depth perception were extremely disagreeable for someone who loved to pitch a baseball. His hitting ceased to exist. His bones remained too brittle; although his muscular and orthopedic problems continued to improve. His baseball career moved in another direction at the age of fourteen. Because his depth perception and vision remained subpar, Michael decided to be an umpire.

He was a very good umpire in the field. He would often shower the other kid/umpire with false praise to persuade the kid to work the plate, while Michael stayed in the field. After practicing umpiring in his private batting cage, he was able to work behind home plate near the end of the season. With practice throughout the winter and much more weight gain and strengthening, he knew he could play any position the next year, except pitcher or catcher. He loved playing in the outfield anyway. At times, he could showcase his throwing arm. He practiced tapping the ball lightly in the batting cage and convinced himself he could hit with force again eventually.

He assisted Uncle Greg with the second-year tee ball team that finished in first place. He watched games of guys his age and convinced himself that he could do it again the next year. At the tender young age of fourteen, he vowed to live life to the fullest. Michael loved baseball, and, mostly, he loved life.

The following spring and early summer, his sophomore year of high school, Michael made the junior varsity team as a right fielder with a rocket arm. After only three games, the coaches promoted him to the varsity squad. As the only sophomore on the varsity squad, they gave him absolutely no playing time in the first two games. He demanded to be sent back down to junior varsity so he could play. The coaches hesitated to play

300

this skin-and-bones sophomore (110 pounds), yet Michael started the next game in left field.

He went four out of five. Two singles, one double, one triple, two stolen bases, four runs batted in, and three runs scored. He started every game for the varsity team the remainder of the season. He led the team in batting average, stolen bases, and runs batted in. He was no longer able to hit for power, but the kid could fly. The kid was awesome again.

55

July 17, 1981

Candice Carolyn Crow had a routine tonsillectomy scheduled in a local hospital that morning. At only five years old, she would heal quickly. Mommy checked her into the hospital the previous afternoon. Candy would need to stay in the hospital for only one, possibly two, additional nights. She was awful scared, so Mommy and Daddy needed to stay with her. Not just Mommy, but Daddy had to sleep in her room too.

Candy came through the tonsillectomy with ease, but her throat hurt real icky. Candy coughed up stuff that looked really yucky. Danny spent the night with Grandpa Crow.

Mommy and Daddy had been invited to a tea dance at the Crown Regency Hotel, the same hotel Gerald began construction on and sold. Candy came first.

Grandpa Willie and Grandma Maggie have just walked out of the room. Mommy and Daddy are holding Candy to the window so she can wave to Grandma and Grandpa. Mommy and Daddy can see several ambulances and helicopters leaving the hospital at the same time.

Must be a bad car wreck near here.

Mommy and Daddy set Candy down and looked out the window at the other hospitals on Hospital Hill. They could hear and see ambulance and fire truck sirens everywhere. Life flight helicopters swarmed the sky.

There must be a big fire downtown. I can't see any smoke.

Suddenly, a breaking news story came on the television. Two suspended skywalks at Crown Regency Hotel have just collapsed. The top skywalk hit the one below it and caused the lower skywalk to collapse to the floor, crushing an undetermined number of people.

Mommy and Daddy are watching in terrified horror. No one knows how many casualties there may be at this time. Police barricades are

302

holding reporters back, and no reporters are going to speculate at this time how many casualties may occur. Mommy and Daddy look at one another frightened as soon as they hear. If not for Candy having her tonsils out, Mommy and Daddy would have been in the hotel tonight. Trying desperately not to wake or scare little Candy, Mommy and Daddy walk out into the hall after only five minutes of the live coverage that would last for days, possibly weeks.

"Greg, we were almost there," Carol said through clenched teeth.

"Gery and Sherry are there!"

Without saying another word, they walk back in front of the television. The television is mounted to the wall above their heads. Mommy and Daddy are struggling not to cry in front of little Candy as she sleeps off and on. They are hoping and praying that Gerald and Sherry are OK.

The reporters on each television station are saying the same thing. They are not saying anything; they are only recapping what everyone else already knows: nothing.

After over one hour, a female reporter said, "In addition to the skywalk collapse, there is deadly flooding in the lobby. Apparently, the force of the crashes has ruptured water mains and set off the fire sprinkler system."

Mommy and Daddy are too terrified to look away. They are watching the helicopters coming and going from the very hospital they are sitting in. Mommy and Daddy are automatically thinking the worst.

Reporters let viewers know there is no hope of the general public getting anywhere near the hotel. Only trained paramedics and doctors are allowed. It is obvious this is a national-scale disaster as national news networks break in on local coverage. Medical emergency volunteers from all over the country are converging on Kansas City, Missouri. Military personnel from Whiteman Air Force Base in Knob Knoster, Missouri, are arriving via helicopter. Reserve units stationed at Richards-Gebaur Air Force Base in Belton, Missouri, arrived immediately. The military personnel are present not only to help with the hundreds of rescues but also to keep the many screaming crowds in control. National Guard units are policing the entire metropolitan area to prevent the looting that has been reported in suburbs. It is, without a doubt, the most dramatic event many people have ever seen on television.

All people are being evacuated from other sections of the hotel. Several exits have been blocked by the collapse of the skywalks. Mommy and Daddy are fixated on the television, while helicopters swarm outside the hospital window above their heads.

Then, as the first people in the ballroom are escorted from another section of the hotel, Greg is hoping to see someone he knows. Preferably

303

his brother or sister-in-law, but neither Greg nor Carol can remember what friends attended the dance this evening. Emergency workers lead out person after person. Greg and Carol cannot see a soul they know. Even if someone they know is among the evacuees, it will be almost impossible to recognize them. Almost everyone being evacuated is drenched in other people's blood.

Greg attempts to use the telephone to call his father. A recording on the telephone makes the announcement: "Due to an increase in activity, the telephone network you are using is full. Please try your telephone call again later. Thank you." Greg and Carol are watching the television helpless, hopeless, and intensely scared.

After over seven hours of nonstop glaring at the television, Greg can see someone he believes may be his brother. The person is obviously conscious and sitting up but is covered in blood. Greg and Carol are not saying a word. Sherry. All Carol can think of is Sherry.

Over another hour passes. Cameras are showing photographs of the exterior of the hotel from every possible angle. Hysteria abounds. Reporters who are normally very levelheaded are screaming. Suddenly, the person resembling Gerald emerges from one of the several hundred ambulances, wearing a T-shirt, a pair of oversized gym shorts, hospital slippers, and clean of almost all blood. It is indeed Gerald. He is visibly shaken and dazed. Greg joins Carol and is now praying for Sherry.

Within minutes, a person on a stretcher is carried from the catastrophic lobby. One of the people carrying the stretcher is covered with blood. Sherry. She steps into a military ambulatory truck after helping the nearly dead person on the stretcher into a civilian ambulance. In minutes, she reappears from a military truck cleaned off and wearing a white gown. Her hair remains matted with blood. She picks up a hard hat from emergency crews and reenters the rear entrance of the hotel lobby that is, by now, assuredly a massive grave. Greg and Carol are relieved that Gerald and Sherry appear to be OK for now. They are worried about Sherry reentering the hotel, but they understand doctors are needed. Greg's respect for his sister-in-law instantly rises to almighty status. This is going far beyond any oath she has ever taken.

Greg attempts to use the telephone again. When the result is the same tape recording, Greg hangs up.

Occasionally, Candy wakes up and struggles to speak. Mommy is trying to tend to her tonsil-and-adenoid-amputated daughter without letting her own fear be seen. Candy loves ice cream, and today is a perfect excuse to eat all she can eat.

Finally, at seven thirty in the morning, Greg is able to pick up an outside telephone line. Danny answers the telephone at Grandpa's home.

"Danny, it's Dad. Are you being good for Grandpa?"

"I'm OK. Can I see Candy today?" Danny begged.

Dad can hear Grandpa in the background.

"Yeah, you can see her. I need to make sure with the doctors. I need to make sure they'll let anyone besides me and Mom in here." This was easier for Dad to explain than the hospital staff is overrun with emergency patients. "They might not let you see her if Candy gets to go home today. Let me talk to Grandpa."

"She comes home today?" Danny said, really excited.

"Maybe. I need to talk with the doctors. Let me talk to Grandpa." *Dad sounds real weird.* Danny hears it. *Dad must be worried about Candy.*

"Grandpa said when I got my tonsils out, I got nothing but ice cream. I'm making Candy a ice cream smiley face with chocolate chip eyes." Danny laughed.

"Danny say 'an' instead of 'a' if the next word begins with a vowel. But forget it for now. What you're doing for Candy is pretty cool, Danny. Can I please speak to Grandpa?"

"When you had your tonsils out, did they give you ice cream?"

"Yes, Danny. Can I please speak to Grandpa?"

"What about ice cream when Mom had her tonsils out?"

"Probably, Danny. I didn't know Mom back then. Can I please speak to Grandpa?"

"How old were you when you and Mom had your tonsils out?"

"I was a big guy already, probably fifteen. When you're old, it hurts for a long time." Greg laughed. "I don't know how old Mom was. Can I please speak to Grandpa?" Mom motioned to Dad that she never had her tonsils out. Dad rolled his eyes and smiled.

"How old was I when I had my tonsils out?"

"Three. Maybe four. Can I please speak to Grandpa?"

"What kinds of ice cream did you get?"

"All kinds. Can I please speak to Grandpa?"

"Grandpa and me are gonna go fishing later."

"Daniel Matthew Crow! Put Grandpa on the damn telephone right now!" Dad can hear Danny shouting for Grandpa.

"Hello, Gregy." Gerome could not conceal his laugh.

"Dad, I couldn't get an outside line until now. After going through an anal examination about ice cream from my son, I wish I hadn't. Jeez!" Greg laughed. "I saw Gery and Sherry on TV last night, or this morning, I guess. Have you heard anything?"

"I finally spoke to Gery about an hour ago. I couldn't get through either. Just luck one time, I guess. He said it was impossible for him or Sherry to sleep. She cleaned up, then went back down there to help. I guess they've set up a few mobile blood banks down there." Gerome sighed.

"So Gery's at home now?"

"Yeah. But he's not much on conversation right now. I've never heard him so at a loss for words before. All he said was he couldn't believe how many people are dead in there. I tried to ask him some details. He just kept saying, 'Not now.' He's pretty shaken."

"Do you think I should try to call him?" Greg asked.

"I think probably not. He forgot Candy is having her tonsils out. I didn't think it was necessary to bring it up."

"The TV said at least two, maybe three hundred people are dead in there." Greg tried to avoid visualizing the horror. "What did Gery say?"

"He didn't. I didn't ask. Gregy, you need to understand he's in major shock right now. He said he's pretty sure he broke a few fingers and maybe his arm, but compared to everyone else, he has nothing. I don't know if he's on a tranquilizer or anything now, but he's slurring his speech real bad. I'm worried he might have a bad concussion or something."

"He and Sherry were both covered with blood."

"Think about it, Gregy. Two skywalks weighing God only knows how many tons crushing all those people," Gerome said. Greg sat silently, thinking of the horror Gerald and Sherry must have witnessed. "That's like a sledgehammer slamming down and crushing an egg. A big sledgehammer crushing hundreds of eggs." Greg got nauseous at his father's words. "I'm holding my breath, hoping there wasn't anyone I know down there," Gerome said, accompanied with another sigh. "I know that's not realistic, though."

"Dad, you're not gonna believe this." A long hesitation. "If Candy didn't have her tonsils out yesterday, Carol and me would've been there last night." A longer hesitation.

"Thank God she had her tonsils out, then. I guess the day she had her tonsils out will never be forgotten."

Greg looked at his beautiful little daughter. His gorgeous wife struggled to stay awake, while she remained glued to the television.

"I'm so glad that Gery and Sherry ore OK. Man, what are the odds? Dad, is Danny giving you any trouble?"

"Of course, he is. He asks all kinds of questions about you when you were his age. No, he's fun. We're going fishing this afternoon." Gerome whispered, "I gave him some things to do out of the range of the TV so he wouldn't hear. How's Candy?"

"She's fine. We might go home today." Greg faked a smile for Candy's benefit. "I'm sure she's gonna set a world record for the most ice cream eaten ever. She can't talk right now, but she'd probably love it if she could listen to her Grandpa talk like a duck." Greg handed the telephone to Candy. Mommy and Daddy watched as Candy laughed at everything Grandpa said like a duck. Grandpa did a wicked Donald Duck impression. Greg took the telephone back so he could call others. "Dad, I'll talk to you later."

Greg began to telephone his brother and then thought he should abide by his father's advice. Greg and Carol attempted to phone other friends all morning. When the generic recording did not play, they heard a busy signal. Reporters on the television let viewers know telephone lines in the calling area were full. "Please eliminate all telephone calls unless completely essential."

By one o'clock in the afternoon, the otolaryngologist that removed her tonsils and adenoids gave Candy medical clearance to go home. The otolaryngologist lost a colleague in the disaster. The confirmed death toll was at twenty-seven. And rising.

Curiosity would normally have prompted Greg and Carol to drive toward the disaster. Because of Candy, they could not. After they were safely inside the home, he turned on the television in the bedroom. Nothing new, except the confirmed death toll had risen to thirty-eight. And rising.

Greg decided to drive over to Chateau Crow to check on Gerald and Sherry. Mark was home from college for the summer and answered the door.

"Mark, I need to talk with your dad," Greg said.

Mark held one finger to his lips and whispered, "I don't think he can talk right now." Mark shrugged his shoulders. "He's just sitting in his bedroom, staring straight ahead. He tried to turn on the TV earlier and turned it off when Mom said she was going to go back down there to help."

"I'm gonna try and talk with him." Greg walked up the stairs to see his brother lying faceup on the bed, staring at the ceiling. "Gery, are you OK?"

"I'm fine." There was little volume and absolutely no emotion in Gerald's speech.

With only two syllables being spoken, Greg could hear the slurring.

"Gery, can you talk to me?"

"I probably can." Gerald sat up and leaned against the headboard. His left arm was badly bruised, and four fingers on his left hand were braced in splints. "What's goin' on?"

"Gery, you need to go to the hospital. You're slurring your words something awful."

"Like you sound most of the time." Gerald grinned slightly.

307

At least saying something smart-ass shows he's not out of it.

"At least I know you're still a pain. Do you wanna talk about what happened?" There was a hint of morbid curiosity in Greg's voice.

Gerald closed his eyes to speak. "I didn't see it at first. I heard a crash, and somethin' wet was on my neck. I turned around, heard a big crash, and got hit in the face with somethin' wet. It knocked me to the floor, and I heard screamin' and yellin'. I tried to wipe my eyes with my sleeve, and it was wet too."

Greg knew what "the somethin' wet" must have been. "Gery, do you realize how bad you're slurring? I've never heard you talk this bad before."

"Sherry said I'm fine. She gave me some painkillers." Gerald smiled. "Now I know how you must feel half the time." Both chuckled. "She said I got a concussion, but nothin' to worry about. Believe me, I wasn' slurrin' this bad before the painkillers." Gerald held up the water glass. "Straight vodka."

Greg realized that he, of all people, had no business asking how much his brother had to drink today.

"Did you know anyone there last night?"

"I don't remember. I'm not even sure what the order. I just tryin' to remember like a movie I saw years ago," Gerald muttered.

Greg could relate with that easily. "Well, as long as you're positive you're gonna be OK. I probably need to go back home to stay with Candy." Greg frowned. "We were sitting in the hospital watching all the helicopters and ambulances coming and going. It was weird."

"Where were they goin'?"

"Gery, they were going to the hotel. Are you sure you're OK?"

"Pretty much. I kinda tired now. How's Michael?"

"Gery, that's it, I'm taking you to the hospital now!"

"No. I'm fine, I just need sleep." Gerald grinned.

"How many painkillers have you taken?"

"A bunch. I won't take any more."

"Do you know how many pills you've taken?" Greg asked forcefully.

"Maybe five or six. Two or three glasses of vodka."

"I'm taking the painkillers away then. No more vodka either. Your system isn't accustomed to this."

"Whatever. I too tired to argue with you." Gerald passed out, snoring loudly.

Greg looked in the bottle of painkillers and could not determine how many his brother had taken. Greg gave the empty bottle to Michael. Greg went into the kitchen and mixed up a potion assured to make his brother vomit: mustard and water.

Sherry walked in the front door. It was obvious she was not in shock or denial when she put her arms around Greg and immediately began crying.

"Greg, I've never imagined anything like it. It was horrible. I turned around after I heard the first crash. Then the second crash covered me with blood. I was in shock, so I didn't know what happened. I cleaned off my eyes with the bottom of my skirt." Sherry closed her eyes, trying to revisit the horror. "A man's arm with a Rolex was right next to me." Long pause as Sherry tried to gather the words. "Greg, there was no body attached to the arm. The arm was just lying there on the floor beside me when I fell. The man was under the skywalk fifty feet away." Greg held Sherry up as she began crying harder. "I shouldn't talk anymore now. One of the guys helping was in Vietnam. He said he never saw anything like it there. I tried to do anything I could to help. People walking around in shock, covered in other people's blood or their own. People dead or screaming and dying all around me. People drowning in two feet of water. I was fucking helpless!" Sherry's eyes expressed she had seen more graphic terror than she described.

"Sherry, we need to worry about Gery now. I think he's overdosed."

"No, he couldn't have. I only gave him five Demerol. He has a mild concussion. I gave him some neurological tests before I drove back down there. He does need to go to a neurologist, but he can't right now. It's Saturday, and every neurologist in the metro is overrun with emergency patients."

"I think he has taken a few more than five."

Sherry looked at Greg holding the mustard and water and ran upstairs. Gerald snored unbelievably loudly. She looked in the prescription bottle and realized Gerald had taken all of the five Demerol she gave him, along with five that he was given from Mark for a minor back problem he had. Ten Demerol, not a fatal dose.

"He might be a little sick. He'll be fine." Sherry assured Greg with a pat on the shoulder.

"Sherry, do you realize he's had two or three full glasses of straight vodka?" Greg asked Dr. Crow.

Sherry's eyes grew larger quickly. She checked the water glass Greg had brought to the bathroom and raced to the wet bar in the bedroom suite. She opened the cabinet to see only half of one bottle of vodka remaining. Gerald had consumed at least one and a half liters of vodka along with the ten Demerol.

Greg immediately forced Gerald to drink his potion of mustard and water. It worked. Greg and Sherry grabbed Gerald and forced him to walk. Mark and Michael heard the commotion and raced upstairs. Gerald vomited again on the carpet and quickly appeared to sober up. Sherry attempted to telephone emergency only to hear for the first time that telephone lines were full. Gerald assured them he did not need to go the hospital as he vomited again. Again and again. Gerald hugged his wife as she broke down.

Greg, Mark, and Michael walked from the room, while Gery and Sherry talked. After more than fifteen minutes, Greg entered the room again to find his brother and sister-in-law hugging one another vigorously. Gerald and Sherry were letting the tears and emotions fly, while much of the city remained in shock.

Greg finally drove home from his brother's estate after three hours and watching Gerald drink a few cups of coffee. Greg heard on the radio that the confirmed death toll was now at fifty-five. And rising.

Greg was home in minutes and told Carol about the scene at his brother's house. Carol had not spoken to anyone, as Candy would never leave Mommy alone. Greg turned on the television in the bedroom with the door closed. He also had the radio on the rock-and-roll station he usually listened to, which was now an all-news station. The confirmed death toll had risen to sixty-three. And rising.

Greg would not turn off the television all night. He did turn off the radio, as it would repeat what he had heard on the television three minutes earlier. Carol brought him dinner in the bedroom. He drank beer after beer in the bedroom. Finally, at two o'clock the next morning, he went to sleep for a few hours with the television on. Carol slept upstairs with Candy that night.

He could not be positive because he was sleeping, but he may have heard a few familiar names of deceased people being read by the dogwatch television reporter. He woke and opened another beer while he waited for the list to be read again. The confirmed death toll was at seventy-eight. And rising.

At five thirty in the morning, the confirmed death toll was at eighty-seven. And rising. At seven o'clock on Sunday morning, July 19, 1981, the television station ran the list of the confirmed deceased again. The printed names were running up the screen very slowly, accompanied by elevator-type music of a sad variety. Among the deceased that Greg knew were:

Randolph and Marilyn Davis
Brian Nivaro's mom and stepdad.
Connie Vasallo
Fred's widow.
Amy Rosenstingel

Jacob's daughter.
Tammy Summerall
I used to bang her.
Jennifer Lorzani
Ditto
Vincenzo Giovelli
No, no, no, no, no, no, no, no, no!

No, Vince, please! Fuck me! No, Vince, please! It can't be!

Carol had been watching the same newscast in the guest bedroom upstairs. She came downstairs silently to see if her husband was awake. He was glued to the television with his mouth open. He could not believe what he just heard. He was startled at the name he had seen a moment ago. It can't be. It was. Greg had a best buddy since the age of five. Now his buddy is gone. Greg and Carol held one another for hours.

56

When all the bodies had been uncovered, there were 106 people dead on the scene. Another eight would die from massive injuries within the next week. Over two hundred people were traumatized by injuries as severe as amputations of major limbs or broken necks. Gerald only had a cast on his arm.

The funeral for Vincenzo Giovelli was no more a public spectacle than any other funerals in the area that week. Vince was no longer an individual. He died as a number.

Several candlelight vigils for the victims mentioned his name. Greg shouted the correct pronunciation when people mispronounced his buddy's first name at those vigils. Vincey had gone to his death as a victim of shabby architecture. A hotel he personally refused to bid on because of major flaws in the design. The design killed him.

One radio station told a bad joke about reputed mobster Vince Giovelli being the target and 113 people being innocent bystanders. Greg threatened to sue the radio station that told the joke. They apologized on the air.

Widow Sally Giovelli accompanied her husband that morbid evening. Sally suffered two shattered hips and massive leg injuries. She was stranded only feet away from her husband as she watched him drown. Sally tried desperately to reach her husband as the water continued rising on his body. Only his feet and shins were trapped in the rubble, but Vince could not raise his torso off the floor. He screamed for someone to help his wife, not him. When the water reached his chin, he panicked and suffered a heart attack. Then his final few breaths were of water.

After nine months of intensive physical therapy, Sally was able to walk with the assistance of a quad cane. Sally was instructed to continue physical therapy, and within two additional years, she would be able to walk without assistance. With that news, Sally promptly sold Giovelli Construction to a corporation based in Houston.

Greg agreed to buy Vince's "straw man" equity from the casinos. Sally did not wish to squabble over numbers, and the amount Greg paid Sally in cash was more than fair. Greg would handle the sale of the extensive real estate holdings Vince had acquired nationwide. Sally, her three children, and youngest niece, Tina, moved from the area. Trisha Giovelli attended college and had been dating Mark Crow. Sally and the children did not have ties to the area any longer. Sally needed to relocate to a locale where her last name did not spawn fear or contempt. Only Sally changed her last name.

Brian Nivaro desperately tried to work out the details to purchase Giovelli Construction. It was too much money and too complicated of a business for him to start in right away. His mentors, Gerald and Greg, assured him that he was better off learning from them and purchasing a company later. He was still too young. Instead, Brian would apprentice the president of the newly formed construction department at Crow Brothers Real Estate Company. He would work closely with architects and contractors. He was granted a handsome salary, a luxury company car, a clothing allowance, and a generous expense account and tuition reimbursement. A master's degree in engineering would be necessary for the president position of the construction department Brian would eventually claim. Brian signed a tuition reimbursement contract similar to the one he had signed to receive his bachelor's in structural engineering. Only Gerald and Greg could arrange for the payments to be paid off the books.

Lawsuits were filed daily. Everyone remotely associated with the hotel was sued. Frivolous lawsuits soon outnumbered the legitimate suits. Hundreds of so-called plaintiffs eventually sued Gerald Crow. When Gerald sold the hotel and office park, the company purchasing the development assumed all risk. All lawsuits filed against him were redirected to the new owners or others involved.

Two of the less profitable casinos were sold to Greg to fund Gerald's expensive legal fees. Publicity surrounded the dismissals to prevent further lawsuits. It would take Gerald two and a half years and an unknown amount of silent cash to have the lawsuits dropped, dismissed, or redirected. Over $2 million in reportable legal fees was spent.

Greg was now receiving the majority of the Las Vegas skim to reflect the majority ownership he had acquired.

The man believed by Greg to be extorting and receiving the skim, Nicholas Cibella, died in a prison hospital of throat cancer in July of 1983. If there were a boss of local La Cosa Nostra at the time, it would have been Greg's father-in-law.

Even if Willie wished to receive the share of the skim he was entitled to as boss, he would have split it with his daughter. Because her husband was the principal owner of the casinos and received the majority of the skim, Willie would not take a penny. It became obvious to Greg that this was the case after Nicholas Cibella died and the cash quickly inflated to an astronomical proportion. Greg knew having tens of millions of dollars in cash was risky, but he remained planted in his belief that having it in a safe took less responsibility than laundering the money to purchase property. Gerald, on the other hand, continued to launder most of the cash into real estate investments.

57

In January of 1984, an investment group based in New Jersey approached Gerald and Gregory and made a generous offer to purchase the Las Vegas casinos.

Greg did not talk it over with his brother as thoroughly as he talked it over with his financial adviser, his wife. Greg soon convinced his brother that the time was right to sell.

Greg believed this was a sign to get out. For almost twelve years, they had gotten away with this highly illegal venture. It did not take much convincing for Gerald to understand they had been extremely lucky financially, and the skimming needed to stop before they were jammed.

Because Gerald and Greg were the owners and the Giovelli clan was gone, the time was right. Within weeks, Crow Brothers and the investors reached a monetary arrangement. However, it would not be time to sell until four huge skims were committed. Following the last hurrah, the documents, offers, contracts, and civil and criminal background consent forms would be submitted to the Nevada Gaming Commission.

Brian Nivaro accompanied Gerald Crow to Las Vegas on a commercial flight. Gerald held a private meeting with James Bucerri, the man who had been handling and organizing the skim operation for Gerald and Greg the entire time of their ownership. James Bucerri was an employee of the Nevada Gaming Commission and had been placed there by La Cosa Nostra bosses back in the '60s.

Gerald needed to multiply the skim by five for two months prior to the actual sale. James Bucerri warned Gerald that this was an easy way to get caught. Any unnatural fluctuations in the accounting were bound to be noticed. Gerald needed the cash. James would normally receive 5 percent. With his percentage, James would cover the fees of the head cashiers and accountants. The receivers paid the couriers. Because of his objection, James would only participate for an additional 10 percent plus a onetime

315

fee of $2 million in cash up front. Gerald had trouble convincing James he did not have $2 million in cash.

After several hours of haggling, agreements were reached. James would receive a down payment of $1 million and an additional 15 percent of the skim. Gerald flew back to Kansas City after giving Brian instructions.

For the last two months of the skim, Brian accompanied James. Once per week, James would audit the books on each of the seven casinos owned by Crow Brothers. Brian had been employed as a cage cashier at all seven casinos for the last two months. Brian never went through the typical background checks conducted by the Nevada Gaming Commission. No pictures, no criminal and civil checks, no fingerprints were ever taken. James Bucerri knew Brian Nivaro was not the typical casino employee.

Before the deposits were made by armored car, the skimmed cash would be divided in a camera and window-proof hidden room attached to the vaults designed by Joseph Giovelli. Each day, James would audit the books on a particular casino, and Brian would work the vault in that particular casino that day. Brian would bring the cash to the special room, while James manned the monitor for the vault.

After the skimming stopped, the applications for the prospective new owners were submitted to the Nevada Gaming Commission. James and several honorable employees of the commission would handle the civil and criminal background check for the new owners.

After the new owners were approved and the transaction completed, James Bucerri was found murdered in a Las Vegas hotel room. The gun used to kill James was found next to his body.

The Federal Bureau of Investigations began thoroughly investigating the murder for obvious reasons. Why did an officer with a law enforcement agency have a safe in his home? The safe had been bolted to a metal stud, which had been cut from the wall. Federal agents had been reviewing the Nevada Gaming Commission for years because of several La Cosa Nostra members nationwide testifying about the skimming. This was going to be a breakthrough.

Several months of record examinations sent up a red flag on the seven casinos sold by Gerald and Gregory Crow. The fluctuation of the profits for two months prior to the sales approval was key.

Then, less than six months after the sale, flight records showed a private plane owned by Crow Brothers flew back to Kansas City only three and a half hours before the body of James Bucerri was discovered. Attorney/pilot Barbara Percival was questioned.

An FBI agent selling information to La Cosa Nostra bosses for the last thirty years immediately notified his loyal friend William Cassivano. William notified his daughter of the current information.

Because Greg was so moral in her eyes, Carol did not want to inform her husband yet. Carol did notify Gerald and Sherry of the impending problem. Carol took all the illegal tender at her home and gave it to her father. She told her father to never let her know the location of the cash.

The cash skimming from the deli chain needed to stop, but Carol knew that stopping the skimming abruptly would send up another red flag, so she had it cease gradually. When Carol moved the cash and informed Greg of the imminent search by the FBI, Greg begged not to know where it was. Carol replaced the cash with rare coins, jewelry, automobile titles, baby books, and a measly $9,000 cash.

Jacob Rosenstingel assured Gerald that he laundered the money adequately and there was no possibility anyone could ever find out.

Sure enough, search warrants were executed for the primary and vacation homes of Gerald and Gregory Crow, the offices of Crow Brothers, and everything else the government could find. Property they owned exclusively as well as all three airplanes and every automobile owned was searched. The searches were conducted over a three-day period. All handguns found were thoroughly checked for ballistics.

The only illegal things discovered in the possession of Greg and Carol were drugs. An ounce of marijuana was found at Greg and Carol's vacation cabin. A quarter ounce of marijuana was found in their primary residence along with three grams of cocaine and a few Cuban cigars. There were a few small remnants of marijuana in the ashtray of his Volkswagen Thing. Greg and Carol were astounded. In the haste of cleansing everything, Carol forgot their recreational drugs. Greg took the blame, and Barbara Percival represented him in order to keep the drug-possession charges out of the media. Greg was sentenced to pay $500 in fines. The illegal items found in Gerald's possession were in Michael's bedroom.

Michael had been attending Park College in Parkville, Missouri. Although the college was close enough to live at home, Michael had an apartment. It was obvious Michael had been running a gambling ring from his mother and father's home. That explained his frequent visits. There were betting slips for college and professional baseball, basketball, and football games. Names, addresses, and telephone numbers of frequent gamblers, including several college athletes and one professional baseball player with the Cincinnati Reds. In addition to the gambling paraphernalia, a half gram of cocaine was found. In addition to the illegal items discovered, the items of concern were cigarettes and cigars.

Michael had nearly died from pneumonia when the medication

destroyed his immune system. Now he was smoking, doing drugs, and probably drinking. Michael had some serious explaining to do.

His baseball playing days came to an end after a permanent shoulder injury cut him from the team during his freshman year of college. He was a golfer now, and a damn good one. He was obviously a big-time bookie now. From the looks of it, he was damn good at that too.

Federal authorities were not interested in a half gram of cocaine with the names and amounts they uncovered on the bookie's betting lists. Gerald was too occupied with his own business to lecture his son. Sherry was too upset and angry with him to speak. Having Uncle Greg lecturing him about drugs and alcohol could be considered a major conflict of interest. Aunt Carol telephoned him at his apartment and let him have it.

She lectured him that federal agents were on to him about the gambling and that he may be arrested. She yelled at him for smoking, drinking, and doing drugs. Michael knew Aunt Carol did her share, but she did not almost die from cancer. It was selfish of him to smoke or drink when he had been given another chance at life. Michael apologized. There were so many people that would be outraged at his drinking and smoking if they knew.

When federal authorities arrested Michael for his illegal bookmaking, he defected and decided to work undercover for them to help arrest and prosecute these major figures. Michael gave the names of several other bookies running larger rings than his.

Nothing criminal could be pinned on Gerald or Greg to warrant an indictment. The Internal Revenue Service appointed an independent accounting firm to audit Crow Brothers Real Estate Company. The government was determined to prove something happened with the downward spiral of profits with the Las Vegas casinos before they were sold. It would take more than a year for the accountants to perform a thorough in-house audit. The audit began in April of 1985.

Gerald and Greg were ordered to set up a private office for the independent accountants. Jacob guaranteed nothing could be detected. Gerald could not mask his frustration and fear. Greg thought not going into the office at all would be sufficient. He lived up to that self-promise.

58

Greg's drinking escalated again to suicidal levels. Greg never went into the office for more than twenty minutes and rarely more than once per week. His son, daughter, and wife were beginning to avoid him. He was out of control again.

One Sunday afternoon in November, while watching a football game on television, Greg noticed his son drinking a beer. It was customary for Danny to have a few sips when he retrieved a beer for Dad. But this time, Danny drank a whole beer by himself. Greg did not want to say a word, knowing he was responsible for this. Mom and Candy were shopping.

After Danny's third full beer, Dad finally asked, "Danny, what in the hell do you think you're doing?" Dad smiled.

"What do you mean?" Danny replied, appearing confused.

"You know what I'm talking about—the beer." Dad pointed. "What do you think you're doing?"

"I'm just having a beer." Danny shrugged his shoulders.

"Listen, young man, you're not allowed to do that!" Dad said sternly as he grabbed the beer can from his son.

"Why? You do it all the time. I'm just having a few." Danny looked confused.

"I'm an adult! You're a kid! That's enough of an excuse. You're not allowed to drink. Period."

"That sucks, man." Danny went into the refrigerator and opened another beer and chugged it in front of his dad.

"Daniel Matthew Crow, you're grounded for one month," Dad shouted! Danny opened another beer and attempted to chug it. Greg never raised a hand to anyone. He seriously contemplated backhanding his smart-ass son. Instead, Greg made a deal with Danny. "OK, I'll make you a deal." Dad took a sip of his own beer. "If you wanna drink beer, then just accept the fact that every beer means another month of being grounded." Dad took

319

another sip and smiled sarcastically. "And I'm talking real grounding." Dad took another sip. "No telephone, no TV, no movies, nothing. Just school." Another sip. "How does that sound, you little smart-ass?"

"Ground me from school too. Then I can just sit around all day and drink beer like you and Mom. Maybe I should start smoking pot too." Dad turned red and noticed he was shaking again. "Then you could bring your friends around and have them see me stumbling around and slurring. That should show me."

"Go to your room, now!" Dad yelled.

Danny had never seen his dad so angry. He needed to push a little further. Danny went to the refrigerator, retrieved two additional beers, and raced to his room.

Dad went into the master bathroom and cried. He looked in the mirror.

That's it. I need to quit drinking now. No more.

In minutes, Dad knocked on Danny's bedroom door. The stereo blared, and the door was locked, so Greg picked the lock with a bobby pin and entered. Danny was sitting on the bed. Dad sat down beside him after he turned off the stereo.

"Point taken. You're not grounded for a month. Only a week for talking to me that way, not for the beer," Dad said as he put his arm around Danny. "I didn't realize I'm such an embarrassment. I can take it. Please, whatever you do, don't ever talk to your mother that way. You're her hero. She couldn't take it if you talked to her like that." Dad needed to fight back the tears.

"I'm sorry, Dad."

Dad took the remaining two beers from Danny's bedroom and poured the open one in the sink and placed the full beer back in the refrigerator.

Candy and Mommy left the shopping center and began to drive home. Mommy lit a cigarette and opened the window a bit as soon as she started the car. Little Candy took one of Mommy's cigarettes and lit it. Candy had practiced in the last week so she would not choke on the smoke. Mommy immediately stopped the car and yanked the cigarette from her daughter.

"What in the hell are you doing, Candy!" Mommy shouted.

"I'm just having a smoke," Candy said in her tiny voice.

"Candy, don't ever let me see that again." Mommy decided to retort with a different message. "Don't ever smoke again."

"Why, you do?" Candy asked innocently.

"I'm an adult! You're a kid!" Mommy yelled.

"At least it's just a cigarette, not pot like you and Daddy smoke outside!" Mommy was stunned that her little girl knew about her and

320

Daddy smoking pot. "You think we don't know, but we do. You and Daddy go outside on the deck or the hot pool every night and smoke pot." Candy smiled sarcastically.

Mommy wanted to smack the grin off her little daughter's face.

"I'm gonna forget you said that, Candy. If you ever smoke again, you'll be grounded."

"From now on, I only smoke when you smoke." Candy pronounced that this was the way it was going to be with a nod of her head.

"Candy, that's not gonna happen." Mommy's blood boiled. "I'm your mother. I'm the boss. Not you." Mommy threw out her own cigarette and began driving home. Fast!

Candy would not look at Mommy. Candy tried to hide her smile. Mommy was as angry now as she had ever been.

After a silent, virtually speechless dinner, Danny and Candy spoke quietly in the upstairs TV room.

"Dad freaked at me. It was scary." Danny laughed.

"Mommy yelled at me and shut up." Candy did not smile at all.

"I'll call Grandpa Willie tomorrow and tell him we finally did it. I don't know if it's gonna work, but I think it might."

"I don't like cigarettes. I don't know why Mommy likes 'em." Candy stuck out her tongue.

"Beer is OK, but I kinda got sick."

"Why do you watch these stupid shows?" Candy went to her room and shut the door.

After the children were asleep, Mom and Dad soaked in the hot tub. Dad lit the customary pipe for the evening.

Carol took one hit and pushed the pipe away. "Greg, I'm not in the mood tonight."

"Me neither." Greg extinguished the pipe.

Carol told Greg what had happened in the car that afternoon with Candy. Greg told Carol about his scene with Danny today. Mom and Dad decided to clean up their act. Mommy quit smoking cigarettes the next day. Dad tried to quit everything at once.

After two days of complete sobriety, Greg decided he could sneak around his kids to drink. He attempted to sneak his boozing for over one month. They knew.

On New Year's Eve, Greg had too much to drink, and a drunken, very embarrassing public scene ensued. He hit on several women that night, so Carol stormed out and drove home from the hotel party. Greg could not get a friend to drive him home, so he checked into the hotel. Carol definitely was never jealous. She knew Greg well enough to know he would not cheat on her without her present, but his behavior that night was unbearable.

Carol broke her promise again and begged her husband to get professional help. On January 3, 1986, Greg voluntarily checked into an alcohol and drug rehabilitation clinic in Center City, Minnesota: The Hazelden Foundation.

Carol met with Greg at the facility twice per week for the duration of his thirty-day hospitalization. Thirty continual days of sobriety had a reverse effect on Greg.

He gradually became resentful and nasty toward everyone with the exception of his wife and kids. He was less inclined to work at the office cluttered with accountants supposed to be independent and instead showed a fiduciary responsibility to the IRS.

Carol had been taking seminar-type classes and notified Greg of the danger of the changing laws in real estate. Because of that, Greg desperately wanted to work with his wife and be done with real estate.

In the middle of March, Greg and Carol met with Gerald and four other officers of the company to negotiate a buyout of his interest.

Greg would ask for a sizable down payment and set up the remainder on an installment plan. No property could be exchanged for payment unless it was easily salable. If this did not work out, Greg announced his intention to sell to an outside interest. This was a threatening proposition.

Greg told his brother that since the casino money was no longer pertinent, the only danger a buyout from an outside interest could present would be control.

Gerald begged Greg to give him time to come up with the investors. He and the other officers of the company would work with extreme diligence.

Greg gave his brother thirty days to come up with the investors or he would sell to an outside interest. Gerald persuaded his brother to give him six months for a counterproposal of this amount, not to mention the nature of it. Greg knew thirty days was impractical and he was afraid his brother would counter him with a one-year proposal to raise the money for his liquid assets. Six months was fine. Greg knew he would be hit with an enormous tax bill if he were to receive that much in huge lump payments. Greg was a master negotiator.

On April 18, 1986, the verdict from the accountants was announced. As a corporation, Crow Brothers owed $14 million in back taxes. No fraud, no commingling of funds. Greg owed over $1 million in back taxes personally. Greg sold enough property to have his business and personal amount of the potential lien satisfied.

I should walk in there with cash just to piss them off.

322

Gerald owed nearly $3 million personally. Gerald had his tax attorney, Barbara Percival, negotiate an installment arrangement with the IRS for his personal and corporate tax debts to resolve the money owed.

Greg began removing personal items from the office to let his brother and the other officers know he was serious. He even burned all of his business cards and other documents in the parking lot. Greg gave his private secretary two notarized notices of his imminent retirement. He recommended she work for his brother. At the same time he did all this, he continued receiving the base salary of $210,000 per month.

Carol did not know what to do. She swore not to say a word to anyone that she knew he was faking this mildly maniacal behavior. She could not be sure he was faking. His behavior at home was also eccentric, but not to the degree of his office life. Sherry begged Greg to see a psychiatrist. Everyone surrounding Greg wished he would start drinking again to end his increasingly bizarre behavior.

When Carol told Greg that people were worried about his sanity, he decided to go one step further. A few times throughout the summer, Greg would make appearances for mandatory meetings wearing shorts and mustard- or motor oil–covered shirts, different color tennis shoes, or boots with his shorts. He was always persuaded to leave. He would show up wearing bow ties and snap-on earrings. Occasionally, he would temporarily dye his hair purple, bright red, or green. He would stay awake the night before a meeting purposely so he could sleep in the conference room.

Gerome was asked to speak with his aging adolescent son. Greg assured his father that he would calm down his behavior at the office. Greg told his father of the success of the deli business and his desire to work with Carol—most of all, his despair over the real estate industry.

After three nights of thinking, Gerome met with his eldest son to arrange the buyout. Greg would be granted a $30 million tax-exempt offshore bank account and a payment equal to $4 million annually for nine years, with the condition that Greg remained a partner on the books, which meant he would be liable for the taxes or losses when applicable. Carol instructed Greg to take the deal with the condition that he could become an active partner again if needed. After the quarterly payments for the duration of the installment, his name would gradually be removed from the agreements. Deal. No counteroffer. Greg received his tax-exempt offshore account by the middle of September.

59

For the last two years, Carol had been attending business, tax, and real estate seminars twice per month in Washington DC. When she became aware of the eventual problems, she encouraged Greg to negotiate a buyout back in March. Now it was imperative. Now it was October 4. The clock was ticking.

When Carol arrived back in Kansas City, she showed genuine anguish and fear in an emergency sense. Greg needed to accept a small payment for the remainder and get off the partnership lists quickly. The general public would know about the changing real estate tax laws soon.

"Honey, we're gonna lose everything you own soon," she said. She explained that the deals Gerald had been making for the last eight years were going to fall through, effective January 1, 1987. "It'll no longer be a benefit to the partners to remain partners after the new tax laws take effect." She sighed because she knew he would not understand anything mathematically complicated. "I'll make this as easy to understand as I can." She did not attempt to hide the fact that she had relapsed on cigarettes. As he drove down the highway toward home, he relapsed also. Afraid of what she told him, he pulled into a liquor store and purchased a twelve-pack. After nine months of absolute sobriety, both felt a relapse was warranted. He parked in a shopping center parking lot and listened. "I know I thought of the original idea, but Gery and the other guys took it way too far. On almost every property you have unlimited partnerships on, the partners are gonna ask for a buyout. Let's say, for example, 50 percent of the partners want a buyout, and that equals $2.7 billion—hypothetically, of course." She smiled because she knew this was a realistic number. "You only have a net worth of almost $70 million, reportable worth anyway, and Gerald has a net worth of almost $300 million. Do the math, Greg. You guys are gonna come up short."

324

"But I don't have anything to do with the company anymore. I'm retired."

"You're still on the ownership deeds of almost everything. I'm telling you, get off the ownership deeds. Give it to Gery if need be. And quick. If not, we're bankrupt!" She enunciated those words and smacked the dashboard with her index finger to illustrate the point.

"If the partners wanna be bought out, why don't they ask for buyouts now?" he asked as he displayed no guilt about the booze relapse. He opened another beer.

"Because most of them probably don't know yet. I bet the ones who do know have been negotiating buyouts for months now. If what you think about Gery is right, he bought the properties out for nothing for the last six or seven years. But appraisals haven't been coming in low for three, almost four years now." She shed a tear and hugged him. "The partnership money you were on is over. You need to find out what is happening with the partnerships, or we're screwed."

For the remainder of the weekend, she explained everything to him on paper. The numbers did not add up. Greg knew his brother had been getting too big the last few years, but he seldom said a word and enjoyed the ride. Now he needed to jump off.

On Monday, Greg walked into the offices as a visitor of the company that bore his name. A private talk with Brian let Greg know that Jacob already knew of the imminent tax law changes. Greg went home, changed into a suit, and set up a meeting with his brother.

"Gery, I want off the partnership deeds as soon as possible. Make me an offer," Greg said as he clapped his hands. Gerald closed his eyes and tapped a Mont Blanc pen on his forehead. "Make an offer, no matter how ridiculous it sounds."

"Gregory, I don't know if we can do that." Gerald leaned forward. Greg noticed he had just been called Gregory again. "Gregory, there's a problem." Gerald continued the business persona. "You and I need to make applications for a few business loans."

"Gery, stop. If what you're asking me to do is apply for fraudulent loans, then you're wasting your time. Carol told me of the difficulty we could have if I don't sell immediately. I wanna be bought out now!"

"Gregory, I'm sorry, we can't do that. We have no money. Partners are already asking to exercise their contractual rights. Originally, we gave them 180-day clauses for us to come up with the money . . ."

"That's not my problem now." Greg chuckled.

"Yes, it is, Gregory. You're still a partner on over $400 million in property." Gerald huffed. "If we can't do this with your help, then . . ."

"What, Gery? We'll be bankrupt. Fuck you! I already know. Carol told me I was on about $300 million. I reserve my right to sell my interests in the partnerships to an outside interest."

"If only you could do that without my signature. I can't sell without your signature on a few things. I'm not bullying you at all. That is the way it is. And we've been getting new apprasails for about ten months. You are on over $400 million in property."

"There are things you own without me, Gery."

"True. But there is very little you own without me." Gerald smiled. "The property you own without me, you can sell anytime. I can't stop you."

"I've been selling it for months. That's over $20 million. I'm talking about the rest of it. I'll accept anything for it."

"Gregory, you can talk to Carol, but I don't see any other way out other than this. Neither does Jacob. He's been a comptroller for over thirty years. Carol has run a deli for fifteen. Which opinion do you trust?"

"Carol! Don't even need to think about it. Do what you think is necessary. One way or another, I'm out."

"Do you really think you're capable of getting out of this without me?" Gerald asked with genuine wonder.

"Absolutely. I know I can. The outside interests are gonna be acknowledged tomorrow or later today."

"Do what you can. Check the contracts again. I have the final say." Gerald smiled deviously.

Greg tipped over his brother's antique desk.

My own brother is screwing me again. This time he has me.

Greg showed several sample contracts to Carol that evening. The legal terminology was way above her head. She recommended a tax and business attorney she knew in Washington DC. She had used him on a few routine deli tax problems over the past two years.

Greg flew to Washington on a commercial flight the next afternoon. The attorney was only thirty-four years of age and a geek to boot. Greg loved him immediately. Attorney Steven Alchwin needed to study the subject contracts in detail, so he recommended Greg use overnight mail and have anyone he could find help make copies of all the contracts. Greg paid Steven a retainer of $50,000. Greg promised another $50,000 if the contracts could be read in a matter of days. Steven let him know that he would have several other real estate lawyers help him study the contracts within a few weeks. Too much time.

Greg suggested giving all the property to charity and writing it off as a tax deduction. That would be immediate fraud. Greg needed an answer

As the Crow Falls

of what to do within twenty-four hours. Not possible. Greg never trusted "house counsel" Barbara Percival, so he agreed.

It is often stated in real estate contracts, "Time is of the essence." It never held weight for Greg until now.

Nothing. Gerald had his brother by the balls legally on all but a few unlimited partnerships. Greg's share in those properties would be sold cheaply and immediately to anyone.

Greg asserted his right of presence and reentered Crow Brothers as a principal partner. Within two weeks, Gerald persuaded his brother to apply for $180 million in fraudulent loans to buy out the unlimited partnerships and keep the company afloat for another two years. In that time, Gerald and Jacob would find investors in order to keep the company themselves. Gerald included a list of what banks or mortgage companies, what cities, and exact orders and times. And, of course, scripts.

Greg was guaranteed he would be bought out. Gerald and Jacob assured Greg that this was a temporary glitch that could be remedied with his help. Gerald borrowed $260 million with the intention of kiting the checks across several state borders for months, if not years.

Unsecured and secured loans were granted. Checks were carefully being kited through express mail addressed to banks and mortgage offices nationwide. Personal couriers unknowingly handled the check kiting in the two-state metropolitan area.

Partners were aware of the looming tax problems and were asking to exercise the buy-out clauses granted them in the original contracts. More partners. More partners. The partners were all granted offers and a few accepted. Some wanted to buy out the remainder of ownership for their own benefit. If not, there would be no benefit. Sold.

This was a major relief, so Greg requested the company sell as many properties as possible to pay the fraudulent loans back quickly.

Gerald hesitated, but Jacob told him this was the easiest and smartest way to resolve this problem quickly. Even if the company needed to take a loss, it was better than getting stuck with loans they may not be able to pay back otherwise. With the process and methods being instigated, this check kiting could continue for years while the numerous subject properties were sold.

By the beginning of December, several smaller properties had been closed. Larger properties were already under contract. In just weeks, Greg had only $60 million in loans remaining under contract. Gerald still had $220 million in loans. The check-kiting scheme worked like a charm. It only worked for six weeks.

60

One of the two personal couriers for the company needed to make a routine deposit and accidentally allowed the pile of envelopes to drop outside his car. Howard Lowell picked up all the envelopes and sat back in his compact car to organize the deposits again. Howard organized the checks that did fall out of the envelopes.

Two deposits were made to banks with similar names on opposite sides of the state line. Southwestern Bank on the Missouri side and Southeastern Bank on the Kansas side. The deposit at Southwestern was for $8 million, and the deposit at Southeastern was for $800,000. Southeastern was usually used for small personal loans. This particular loan from Southeastern was not part of the check-kiting scheme. The $8 million deposit for Southwestern was.

Howard made an honest mistake and placed the wrong checks in the envelopes. He dropped off the deposit envelopes as usual in the loan department of Southwestern. Howard had been told to leave the deposits for Southwestern with Dwight Costello. The deposit receipts from Southwestern were mailed to the accounting office. He dropped it off and drove away without waiting for a receipt, as usual. The deposit for Southwestern contained several checks. The deposit at Southeastern contained only one check.

After an early lunch and the remainder of his route, he made his way back toward the office and stopped to make the deposit for Southeastern at the teller window. The teller immediately noticed the deposit was for too much and paid to the order of Southwestern instead of Southeastern. The teller made a joke about their senility, as she also was in her early seventies. Howard explained his minor setback and drove back to Southwestern to correct the mistake.

Back in the larger bank, he did not see the loan officer he gave the envelope to, so he asked a secretary for assistance. In minutes, the secretary notified him that someone would be with him in a moment. Ten minutes passes. Another ten passes.

Howard is well aware that the deposits he delivers need to be made before two o'clock in the afternoon. The kid working the afternoon shift delivers the late deposits. Howard grows impatient and asks the secretary again for assistance. It is only fifteen minutes till two o'clock. Fifteen minutes pass, and it is now two o'clock. The loan officer Howard gave the deposit to comes in the front door. He opens his desk and retrieves the envelope.

"Hi again, Howard. I knew it was for the wrong bank, so I just left it here, knowing you'd come back. It happens all the time. Southeastern will be part of us anyway soon after the first of the year."

Howard notices out of the corner of his eye the bank tellers are switching over to the next day's business.

"Can you make sure that goes on today's business, Dwight?" Howard asked.

"Sure," Dwight said as he looked at his watch to see it was almost ten minutes after two. "Well, actually, I don't know if I can or not," Dwight replied with a slight grimace. "I'll see if I can."

"Try, or my butt will be in a sling." Howard chuckled.

Dwight made some chitchat with other employees. In ten minutes, Dwight came back with the news that there was no possible way he could direct the deposit to that day's business.

"Oh, well, it's my fault anyway. Let them fire me. Besides, it's too cold outside for an old man like me to do this." Howard walked out, knowing the receipt would be mailed.

Dwight set the deposit on his desk with the intention of making it later. Howard Lowell drove back to Southeastern and made the final deposit. He then went back to the office, clocked out, and drove home.

Dwight prepared to make the deposit and noticed three other loan officers in line. Dwight had a meeting upstairs on the thirtieth floor. After the meeting was finished at five o'clock, Dwight went home for the weekend, knowing if the deposit would be made now, it would automatically be on Monday's business anyway.

61

December 22, 1986

Dwight made the deposit as part of routine. The manager of the commercial department urgently called Dwight into his office. The manager asked what happened to the deposit. Dwight explained the runner made a mistake. That was it. Nothing except a harmless, honest mistake. The manager of the commercial loan department contacted the president and vice president of the bank. The president then contacted Jacob Rosenstingel. There was a huge problem.

An $8 million check deposited by another bank hit Southwestern Bank Friday afternoon and bounced. The exact same amount of the deposit. There was audible panic in Jacob's voice as he attempted to explain. Jacob notified them that the overdraft would be taken care of before two o'clock. The president of the bank had some more bad news. A check this large that bounced had to be reported to the FBI immediately, or the bank itself would be in legal trouble with the Federal Trade Commission as well as the Federal Reserve and countless other government agencies.

Jacob immediately telephoned Gerald in his car to notify him of the imminent disaster. Gerald telephoned Greg at home. Greg went into the office immediately, reeking of booze. Gerald, Greg, and Jacob met privately to discuss what to do. *No fuckin' way.* Gerald's idea was terrible. There was no possibility of Greg walking into a bank with $8 million in cash. Jacob agreed it was a surefire way to get caught in the act of this and more. Immediately, Jacob thought of a plan that may work. Greg knew it would be an illegal plan, so he covered his ears and walked out of the room.

Several accounts in the property management department would be drawn upon that day until enough money was raised to cover the overdraft. In a matter of hours, the already complicated check-kiting scheme would need to be detoured, rerouted, and redesigned. Jacob informed Gerald

330

of the need to borrow a few more million in personal loans to keep the company afloat and cover the already complicated check-kiting operation.

Gerald would apply for $11 million in additional personal loans at small banks around the Midwest over the next two days before Christmas and $14 million the four days after Christmas, while money would be commingled from the property management department to cover the other accounts that were drawn upon and commingled. Several small banks granted unsecured loans within hours of applications because the name Gerald Crow could be put in the bank. Secured loan applications at larger banks in Kansas City, Des Moines, Lincoln, Chicago, St. Louis, Minneapolis, and St. Paul were granted.

Gerald knew he could not borrow this much additional money with his own name. On some of the unsecured loans in other cities, he signed under his brother's name and social security number. Gerald even signed *Gregory* Crow to the documents and applications. Gregory always signed *Greg* Crow. It was risky, but Gerald and Jacob knew it could work.

The Federal Reserve had been investigating Crow Brothers Real Estate Company for the bounced check at Southwestern. The Federal Bureau of Investigations had been investigating them for years after the Las Vegas casino sale.

Between Christmas and New Year's, federal authorities placed a freeze on several accounts of Crow Brothers when the check kiting became obvious. The government could not place a freeze on any personal accounts at that time. Because of the freeze, Gerald, Gregory, and Jacob had to notify banks and mortgage companies that they had minor financial difficulties and could not repay the loans for a brief time. Many banks not notified by the government granted the release of principal payments and only required interest to be paid for one month. The use of the personal loans went into effect. Gerald paid some of the banks with the money he borrowed with the personal loans or money borrowed from other people's accounts in the property management department. For the first time ever, Greg told Carol to somehow get Jacob $10 million in cash to launder.

Over the holidays, partners became aware of the problems when the media printed a small story in reference to a bounced $8 million check. The electronic media then questioned several unnamed sources with the federal government and reported over the airways.

New Year's came, and on January 2, 1987, the telephones at Crow Brothers flooded with partners calling and demanding to know what was going on. Many of the inquiries were notified: "This is all an honest mistake that is being remedied."

Within weeks, Gerald and Greg were being subpoenaed. Specific performance lawsuits from all over the country were served upon them. Suddenly, personal accounts were frozen, but the $30 million offshore account bestowed upon Greg went unnoticed.

It was all over the news, so other rich kids at Danny and Candy's schools harassed them about their dad being poor. Carol could no longer handle the constant finger-pointing and threats.

"Carol, I talked to Gery and Jacob today." He fought back tears. "We more than likely will need to file bankruptcy if we can't work this out."

"Greg, this is gonna eat us alive. We need to divorce so they can't take everything."

He placed his hands over his face and immediately began bawling.

All these years. I have a few financial problems, and she bails.

"I guess I've always been naive. Since the day I met you, I thought you were different. Now I see that you're just the same as all women. It's only ever been the money," he said as he sobbed.

"If you really believe that, then you're sadly mistaken. We'd be together if you never had a dime," she said as she hugged her husband and refused to let go. "I'm thinking of you too. They can take everything from us as a couple if any of it's illegal. We need to get divorced so they can't take the deli money or the deli chain itself." She kissed him on the neck. "Greg, we still have a lot of cash and the offshore account. We can make it if we're smart."

"If you leave me and take the kids, then I have no reason to live." He opened another beer.

"That's so fuckin' selfish of you!" She backed away and slapped him. "You need to find out soon if you need to file bankruptcy and if there's gonna be anything criminal. If you find out something illegal happened, we have no choice but to divorce."

"Find out sooner, so I can give you a reason to leave me sooner." He threw his empty beer against the wall and opened another. "Get out tonight. Leave now! The kids stay with me. Leave." He got right in his wife's face and spoke quietly with his teeth clenched and his evil bloodshot eyes moving rapidly. "Get the fuck out of my company's house now. *Now!*"

She was afraid of her husband physically for the first time ever. She knew he would never hit her, but at that moment, she could not be sure. Instead, he turned his back and chugged his beer. Another beer.

"Greg, please just sit down, calm down, and listen to me. Please." He looked at her as she patted the seat next to her. "For us. Please, calm down."

"There is no *us* if you leave." He slurred. He sat down beside her.

She explained: Since the primary home was under corporate ownership, the liberal homestead laws in the state of Kansas would not protect them

332

As the Crow Falls

under a criminal indictment. She told him her Daddy knew he and his brother were being investigated for bank fraud. The vacation cabin located in Missouri was as good as gone with just the bankruptcy. A divorce was needed in order to survive. Federal investigators and courts could seize everything under a criminal conviction. She said if worse came to worse, he could give up the offshore account. He neared hysterics. He did not know anything, and he knew he understood little.

Gerald was panicky and driven. Gerald and Sherry knew their home was going to be seized in the imminent bankruptcy. They no longer had children at home, so they made the brilliant decision to give enough cash to a friend and launder enough money to purchase a home on the Kansas side, as Missouri had strict homestead laws. They made an offer above the listed price. In addition to the inflated purchase price of $630,000, Gerald and Sherry paid the owners of the home an additional $15,000 in nonreportable cash to move their items into a storage unit. In only two days, they closed.

A huge red flag went up as the sellers hired movers to move their items to a storage unit upon closing. Then two brilliant people, buyers Gerald and Sherry Crow, hired movers to move two miles away to the other side of the state line in the middle of the night.

62

On February 12, 1987, Crow Brothers Real Estate Company filed Chapter 11 bankruptcy as a corporation along with 143 partnership entities. The bankruptcy did stop several lawsuits and foreclosures. Big problem.

Gerald filed a Chapter 7 personal bankruptcy. Personal bankruptcy sent up another red flag after Gerald purchased the new home with no loan and abandoned the castle on the Missouri side of State Line Road in the middle of the night. The FBI had taken surveillance photographs of the move.

On Valentine's evening, Greg was arrested for misdemeanor domestic battery. Carol called emergency, and Greg was arrested with a standard no-contact order. Mug shots. Fingerprints. Full body search. Carol was taken to a local hospital, where photographs were taken showing her bruised cheeks, a bruised neck, and bruised upper body. Police made detailed notes for the record. Carol's father Willie immediately bailed Greg out of jail as *planned!* The children spent the weekend with friends.

When Carol entered her home the following Monday, Greg was naked with another woman, Carol's longtime business partner, Patty. Carol called police again. There was nothing police could do, as Greg did not break any laws. Police again made notes, although there was nothing illegal.

Carol knew Greg was at the US District Court attending his bankruptcy hearing Wednesday and had him served there with a divorce proceeding. Greg collapsed and lost control of his emotions in court. Wednesday evening, when Greg came home with his lawyer and a bodyguard, there was a note.

Greg,

We're going away until you clean up. You have cheated on me for the last time. You're the greatest guy alive, but I can't take any more of the drinking, drugs, and screwing around. I thought it was cute years ago. Now I think you're pathetic. Take everyone else down with you as you ruin the lives of everyone who loves you. Not me. Not our kids. Get help, please. I may or may not call you again. If I do, the kids will talk to you. Not me!

I love you,
Carol

PS Grow up!

Police held Carol's note.

Federal authorities could not waste any more time. The following day, the indictments were announced.

Gerald received fifty-seven counts of bank fraud, thirty-three counts of wire fraud, sixty-four counts of mail fraud, and three counts of forgery. This was the first time Greg became aware his brother had forged his signature.

Greg received thirty-one counts of bank fraud, two counts of wire fraud, and thirty-nine counts of mail fraud. He volunteered to give up his $30 million offshore account.

Jacob received forty-eight counts of conspiracy to commit bank fraud, fifteen counts of conspiracy to commit wire fraud, and forty-five counts of mail fraud.

Mug shots were snapped. Fingerprints were taken. No interviews or interrogations were conducted. Bail was the recognizance of the three.

Greg drove home that night with his lawyer and two off-duty police officers as bodyguards. Greg found some of the furniture missing. All his wife's and kids' possessions were gone.

This was all that was needed to send Greg over the edge he had been teetering on for decades. Steven Alchwin knew Greg was suicidal. Steven was scared for his client and immediately called for mental, if not medical, assistance, as Greg downed eleven beers and a half pint of tequila in minutes. Greg soon found himself surrounded by friends and agreed to enter a hospital voluntarily. After the alcohol was safely out of his system in the hospital, he would be transported to an alcohol and drug rehabilitation program. Because of the court schedule at the time, the rehabilitation would be on an outpatient basis.

Two hours later, Sherry hit her own personal limit and walked out with nothing except her jewelry, clothes, and personal mementos. She knew luxury cars were bound to be noticed. She stopped at a used-car lot and bought a work-van with cash, as she knew her personal checking accounts were worthless. After the automobile purchase, she drove back home for the last time to pick up as much as could be stuffed in the van and have one last word with her husband.

"I don't know what fraud you committed, but if the newspapers are accurate at all, then you should kill yourself now. I've hung on to this marriage for years because I thought you were worth it." Sherry began crying, but not until after Gery did. "I loved you. If you notice I said *loved,* not *love.* Past tense. I fell out of love with you gradually. I should have left you when I found out your secret. I should have blackmailed you. I didn't. I stayed because I thought we could be happy together and because of the kids. They're not kids anymore. It's been one constant embarrassment being with you. Now I can't go anywhere or do anything because of you. I need to leave the city."

"What about the boys?" Gery asked, crying and not looking at his wife.

"They're adults. They're on their own. I called them and told them a few days ago of my departure. I'm sorry that I didn't let you know too." Sherry sobbed as she took one last look at the residence she had recently moved into. "I like this home. Too bad it was purchased with dirty money. I never liked the big house. It's so pretentious. It may be you, but it's not me."

"Sherry, where are you going?"

"Far away from you. You're sick, Gery. You need help." Sherry bowed her head, thinking. "I'm sorry I said that, but it's the absolute truth. You're evil. There are some things I suspect that go with me to my grave. I won't say a word to anyone. I don't love you. Good-bye." Sherry walked out without hearing her husband say a word. She would make one final stop at a storage unit where construction and painting material was used to hide $17 million in cash that Gerald did not know existed. After the $17 million was retrieved, she would go so far away with a changed name that there would be no way anyone could find her, with the exception of her son Mark.

The early evening newscasts were starting. The top stories were the indictments of Gerald and Gregory Crow. Gerome granted an interview as he walked down the courthouse steps earlier that day. Gerald turned up the volume on the television.

"I just know that the tax laws changed and my sons were getting carried away. I'm sure everything will be fine. This is just a temporary setback." Gerome smiled and waved, resembling a politician as the cameras cut away.

Gerald retrieved a handgun and pressed the barrel against his forehead.

He closed his eyes and thought of everyone. Names from throughout his life as he contemplated pulling the trigger. Friends, family, lovers. He released the safety. The mother he could barely remember. Dad. Greg. Sherry. He squinted his eyes, which were already closed. Mark. Michael.

Michael cheated death, and now here Dad was, about to take his own life. Michael was the only reason Dad did not pull the trigger that day. Gerald broke down and decided he should take the medicine he dealt to himself.

Gerome telephoned his eldest son.

"So, Gery, what's going on?" Gerome could hear his son did not sound usual.

"We fucked up, Dad. Nothing else to say." Gerald poured a full glass of vodka.

"Have you heard already that Carol left Greg?" Dead air. "She took the kids. She's gone." Gerome sighed.

"Well then, this isn't going to surprise you. Sherry is gone too." Gerald wailed the tears. "She said we have nothing together anymore. She's gone. Said she doesn't love me anymore. She's gone too."

"Gery, did you know that Greg is going in a nuthouse?"

"You're kidding!"

"Nope. Checked into a hospital a little while ago. After he sobers up, they take him to a nuthouse voluntarily. His lawyer suggested he check in for a few days until he can accept this thing with Carol."

"Where's he at?" Gerald asked.

"I don't know. He wouldn't tell me. It must not be far away, though. Not like when he tried to dry out." Gerome thought for at least a minute before he talked. "I need to make sure you're OK. So Sherry is a money-grubbing bitch. It's not like you haven't always known that."

"Dad, we're finished. Don't add up the debts, it would make you sick." Gerome cleared his throat loudly. "I had my telephones swept for bugs today while I was at court. Don't worry." The phones were tapped. "Dad, there were some loans we took out that we had no business taking. I only did it because I knew we could last for a while and make the money legitimate again if we kept it straight. Then one of our runners made a mistake and deposited a check late. We wouldn't have ever been nailed without that mistake."

"So why do you think it's over? You might just need a little time to get things straightened out," Gerome said, assuring his son. "When I ran it, we faced bankruptcy seven times. We never had to file, but we were usually close."

"Dad, I'm sorry, but you don't know how bad this is. I'm not just bankrupt. I'm going to jail for a long, long time. Greg is too. This is criminal."

"I don't think you'll be going away for that long. But even if you do, Gery, you need to deal with it. Take your medicine and stand up to it. You and Gregy made some mistakes. In a few months, this will all be over. If you do get sent to jail, it won't be for that long anyway," Gerome said as a true optimist.

"Whatever, Dad. I need to go. My lawyer, Barbara, told me not to go in the office anymore. The press would be all over us. I'm not allowed to leave town, so I don't know what to do."

"Just take it easy for a couple of days."

"More like a couple of months, or even years." Gerald cried again as he hung up the telephone.

63

After one week in an inpatient rehabilitation clinic, the remainder of his voluntary thirty days was served as an outpatient. Greg did not want a nasty divorce with everything else going on. He knew he would spend the majority of his time in courtrooms throughout the next year, so his lawyers petitioned the court to resolve the divorce immediately. Greg was not going to dispute anything. Carol was not asking for anything monetary, except for her personal property and one of their four cars. Most of all, she wanted sole custody of the children. Because of the domestic battery Greg pleaded no contest to and the divorce in progress, there was a restraining order against him. Because of the criminal indictments and the trial looming over him, Carol wanted him to receive no contact, and, in turn, Greg was cut off from his children until the criminal trial was complete.

On March 23, 1987, the picture-perfect marriage of Gregory and Carolyn Crow came to an end. It was over. Carol and the children moved from the area.

The sham marriage of Gerald and Sherry Crow came to an end abruptly also. Sherry threatened her husband that if she did not receive everything she asked for, the negatives she possessed would be blown up and distributed everywhere.

64

Greg was in and out of court the remainder of the year. The corporate bankruptcy Greg was involved in stayed unresolved. Much more than being in and out of court, Greg drifted in and out of a drunken stupor. The house was sold to satisfy a few judgments. The once megamillionaire was now virtually penniless. Greg lived and slept in a studio apartment owned by his ex-wife's former business partner.

Greg had always been the neatest person anyone had ever met. Now his place was a pigsty. Patty would often give him maintenance and painting work at the apartment building he lived in to earn a little walking-around money.

Some of the money Patty would pay him had to be coming from Carol. Greg knew this because it was always too much and always cash. Gerome would loan his son enough money to buy a house. Greg was too ashamed to ask.

He rarely went outside the apartment for fear of being killed. When he did leave, he would inevitably return with a female. Even broke, his notoriety remained a powerful aphrodisiac.

Greg was granted a brief visit with his children on Christmas Day of 1987. Carol would not be present, even though the visit was at her father's home.

Grandma Maggie had died after a four-year battle with cancer in October. Willie requested that Greg not attend the funeral because Carol needed to pay respects to her mother and did not want to see him.

Greg asked several questions about his ex-angel. Greg tried to pry several times of his angel and kids' location. Grandpa Willie would come right out and remind Greg he was not allowed to know that by Carol's request.

Greg could not conceal the tears or, more noticeably, his drastic weight loss and constant involuntary shaking. Christmas Day was filled with reminiscing about this or that. The upcoming criminal trial was never mentioned.

Daddy could see Mommy in his daughter. Candy had her Mommy's spectacular eyes. Danny favored Dad. He had the same prominent chin. Although both children had brown hair, there would never be a doubt whom these children were parented by.

At the end of the day, Danny begged his dad to see a doctor about his obvious weight loss and shaking. Hugs and tears all around. As he walked out the door, Willie had a private conversation with his son-in-law on the front porch.

"If you need any money, let me know," Willie said with a smile.

"Thanks, Willie. I'm fine. Thanks for letting me see the kids." Greg hugged his ex-father-in-law. Willie hugged back with his own eyes watering.

"Greg, we need to talk." Willie checked the door to make sure nobody could hear. "I know you don't like hearing things, but you damned well better listen to me now." Willie leaned in toward Greg. "This more than likely involves me too." Greg listened intently. "Jacob is gonna testify against you and Gery."

"How do you know that?" Greg asked.

Willie tilted his head down and smiled.

"Greg, if he testifies about the casino money, you and Gery are screwed. Maybe me too," Willie warned.

How in the world did I fuck up my life this bad?

"Willie, I can't talk to Gery about it. There's a no-contact order. I can't talk to Jacob either. I don't know what to do." Greg sounded as frustrated and shaky as he appeared.

"So you don't know if Gery knew his phones were tapped?" Willie asked.

"He found out about some taps at the office and his home phones, but that was right after the indictments. Gery told me when we could still talk that they only had the taps on for two weeks. If anything was on the tapes, we'd know already," Greg said knowingly.

"Well, the tapes might not say anything about you, but they must say something about Jacob if he's gonna testify."

"I don't know, Willie. I'm scared now, I'm tired, and I'm lost. I'm not thinking about Jacob or Gery now."

"Are you being careful on the phone? You know your phones are tapped."

"Yeah."

"When does the trial begin?" Willie asked.

"January 11 they start selecting a jury. They think it's probably gonna last six, maybe eight months after that." Greg breathed out in frustration. "That's one of the main reasons we couldn't get severance. I'm stuck going on trial with Gery and Jacob. I wanted severance bad, but my lawyers said not yet. They might ask for severance right before the trial. I don't know anymore. As bad as it sounds, I don't think I care anymore." The tears streaming down his face said he did care. "You know, I could probably deal with losing the money, the house, everything. I just can't deal with losing Carol and the kids."

"Greg, everything will be fine. I promise. If you ever wanna talk with the kids, let me know. I'll call them and have them call you."

"What about Carol?" Greg wiped the tears off his face with his coat sleeve. "I'm too old to start over."

"Greg, you know Carol doesn't wanna talk. At least for now. I know she loves you, and so do I. But she said this is too upsetting."

Greg hugged Willie again and walked off. Willie ran the best he could to Greg's Volkswagen Thing.

"Greg, I'll see what I can do. I'll get in touch with Carol." Willie looked at the father of his grandchildren. Willie had seen this look of hopelessness before. His sister, Sandy, looked this way for days before she killed herself. After Greg drove off, Willie immediately telephoned his daughter and notified her of his concern. Carol promised she would call him later. Willie could hear her tears.

Greg went into his studio apartment, opened a beer, and turned on the television. The nightly story on the news about him and his brother came on, so he immediately turned it off. The only thing making a sound was his whimpering as Greg sat on the sofa given to him by his father because all his furniture had been sold to pay debts. The bankruptcy court did not order it. He emotionally could not keep anything he and Carol had purchased together. Emotionally, he could not even keep pictures.

He didn't turn on the stereo. No sound. No light. A big bottle of bourbon to stop the shaking. Chasing it with beer after beer.

Finally, Greg turned on the light over his bed in order to grab his .38 revolver from the nightstand.

He placed the barrel in his mouth. He had to do it. He had no choice. He needed to leave behind the customary suicide note first.

Carol,

I'm sorry about everything. I love you. Never ever forget that. I don't know why I know I have to do this. You were my

342

world. You were my dream. I found a way to screw that up. I love Danny and Candy. I can't take another day without them after seeing them again. I know you think this is selfish. Maybe it is. Maybe I am. I love you.

Greg

Greg placed the barrel in his mouth again. The telephone rang. Only his lead lawyer and his father had the number. It could be a wrong number. He hesitated to remove the gun from his mouth and then thought maybe it was his dad calling to wish him a Merry Christmas.

"Hello," he answered.

"Honey, it's Carol."

The sweetest voice Greg had ever heard. It also angered him to no end that she interrupted his final moment of life before eternal peace was achieved.

"Hi, Carol. Am I the Christmas charity you chose this year?"

Why did I say that? I love her.

"Not at all. I'm worried about you. Daddy, Danny, and Candy told me they were worried about you. They said you're scary skinny and you didn't stop shaking the whole time you were there."

"I needed to lose weight anyway. How're you?" She heard him dragging on a cigarette.

"I'm fine. Honey, I miss you." She broke down and cried. "It's been almost ten months. I love you."

"Actually, it's been nine months twenty-seven days since we spoke. Nine months and one day since the divorce." The exactness of that statement brought a chuckle.

"I need to ask you if you're OK."

"Oh! I've never been better," he said, sarcastically.

"Daddy told me to call you immediately. He said he was worried you might do something stupid," she said, accompanied with a sob.

Her calling me is a sign not to do this.

"No, I'm not gonna hurt myself, if that's what you mean." He realized he still held the gun. He set it down and replaced it with another beer. "Am I ever gonna see you again?"

"Come on, Greg. You know you will. I needed to get the kids away. They were being tormented." She knew she needed to watch her words, as her father made her aware that Greg's phone lines were tapped. "When is this trial gonna be over?" she asked, sobbing and sounding as frustrated as her ex-husband.

"I don't know. Jury selection starts the eleventh. The trial seems like it's probably gonna last for the rest of my life." He slurred.

"When it's over, I'll make sure we see each other. I miss you." She cried.

"Carol, there's a good possibility that I'll be going to jail for a long time."

I shouldn't say that on the phone.

"You probably think that now, but I'm sure everything will work out."

"I don't know anymore. I never knew what was going on, and here I sit, guilty of everything in the public's eyes already."

"Just tell them you didn't know. I'll testify that was the truth. You spent all your time with me." She blubbered.

"It won't do any good if nobody knows where you are. Is there any chance I can find out where you are?"

"No. Absolutely not. You cheated on me. I can forgive you for that. After you hit me, you can't deny anymore that you drink too much. That's not you. You need help. Please get it."

"How do I know you'll still be there if I ever come out of this?"

"You don't. After everything settles down, I might tell you where I am. I know Candy and Danny miss you. I don't wanna deprive them of seeing you, but for now I need to. It's the only way they're safe. Me too."

"What's your name now?"

"Greg, you know I can't tell you that either."

He heard a male voice in the background. "Who's that?"

"It's nobody, Greg. It's the television." She let out a faint laugh.

"I love you. You're my dream. I'm so sorry."

"I love you more. Get yourself straightened out. Clean up, and after the trial, I'll come see you. Maybe during." She wanted desperately to see him and hold him. "Promise me you won't do anything stupid."

"I promise. I love you."

"I love you too. Most of the time." The good-byes were exchanged.

He needed to get rid of the gun for his own safety. He also knew he needed to keep it for his own safety. *I'm so confused.* Back to the nightstand it went.

344

65

On New Year's Day 1988, Edward Rosenstingel, his wife, Meg, and daughter, Brenda, went to his mother and father's home for their traditional New Year's Day festivities. No answer at the door. The family used a pay phone at a nearby convenience store. No answer on the telephone. Eddie knew his mother and father had a secret hiding place for a spare key. The Rosenstingel family entered the home. Eddie and Meg looked in the garage to see if the cars were there. They were. Suddenly, fourteen-year-old Brenda screamed. Eddie and Meg ran upstairs to find their daughter in a frozen stare. Eddie and Meg screamed at the scene that spawned Brenda's screech. Eddie dialed emergency. He and his wife and daughter waited outside for ambulance and police to arrive.

Jacob and Rachel Rosenstingel were dead.

Police took the necessary photographs of the scene before removing the bodies. From the positioning of the bodies, it was determined that Jacob murdered his wife, then took one self-inflicted bullet in his mouth as he held his wife's hand with his free hand. It was indeed ruled a murder/suicide; although the coroner had serious doubts.

A bruise on Jacob's wrists and a contusion on the left side of his face led the coroner to believe there was definitely a struggle. A detective brought in to investigate asked if the bruises might have come from Rachel. Highly unlikely. Her body showed no signs of struggle. She had been shot in the back of the head first and had obviously been turned over. This was staged poorly. In addition to the bruises, blood splatters in the photographs and on the scene led the detective to believe Jacob may have committed suicide *before* he murdered his wife.

For the time being, it would be called a murder/suicide.

According to their religious faith, the Rosenstingels needed to be buried that day. Not possible. A detective would continue investigating the murder scene and autopsy photographs.

Because of the suicide of Jacob Rosenstingel, the criminal trial of Gerald and Gregory Crow needed to be delayed until April 4. The legal team representing Greg and headed by Steven Alchwin filed a motion for severance. Motion denied.

Attorneys for both brothers filed motions for relocation of the trial because of the large amount of publicity. Motion denied. Because this was a white-collar trial, no sequestration of the jury would be necessary.

66

Michael Crow had been walking the course in an amateur golf tournament in Texas and disqualified himself because of a sore back. He knew he hurt his back lifting his golf clubs out of the trunk of his car. Michael regularly visited a chiropractor, but recently the chiropractic treatments did nothing. Michael made an appointment with an internist. After several tests were administered, Michael found out his leukemia was active again. This time, it was caught in time, and his chances of survival were better than before, though still life threatening.

Michael considered that statement a challenge and needed to cheat death once again. He entered the hospital with determination and full knowledge as an adult.

Mark had been attending law school at the University of California, Los Angeles, and immediately flew back home after Greg notified him. Sherry joined a family practice close to her oldest son. Sherry surprised everyone when she arrived with a new smaller nose, a face-lift, and very tan skin.

Michael was happy to see his brother and mother again, but he became extremely angry with everyone making such a big deal about him.

Greg had his ex-father-in-law contact his ex-wife. Greg again spoke with Carol. She could not leave her present location currently, but she assured Greg she would telephone Michael daily. If anything urgent happened, she would take the next plane home. Greg hoped nothing bad happened to Michael. He hated himself for thinking it, but to see and hold Carol again almost outweighed his sympathy for Michael.

No, I'll see her again someday. Mike's health comes first.

Greg and Gerald spoke with one another regularly at the hospital. Under attorney's advice, the brothers agreed to keep the visits and conversation at a minimum and never discuss the looming criminal trial.

Sherry would never see Gerald and made no secret of her hatred for her ex-husband. She stayed at a hotel near the hospital.

One night after only one week back in town, she and Greg had dinner and drinks at a restaurant near his apartment. Something happened, and the ex-brother and sister-in-law ended up sleeping together at his studio apartment that night. Greg was profoundly attracted to her emotionally at the time, and the plastic surgery did wonders for her appearance. Greg said he would get a face-lift if he could afford it. Without Gerald around her, Sherry was mentally looser than Greg had ever seen. After the sex and several more beers, her tongue became way too loose.

"I promised myself I would never tell a soul, but it's been eating at me for years," Sherry said.

She's gonna tell me she knew Gery is gay.

"Are you ready for this?" Sherry asked with a sobbing smile. Greg smiled as he anticipated this. Sherry began crying searching for the correct words. He hugged and kissed her. "I'm almost positive. I think Gery had Charles and Sandy killed."

Nothing short of stunned, Greg jumped.

"That's ridiculous, Sherry." Greg let out a chuckle. "Charles and Gery were best friends. We know Nick Cibella had Ant organize it."

"Greg, hear me out, OK?" Greg looked down at Sherry, and her tears said this was not just anger toward her ex. She explained: Anthony Gilante visited their home frequently for three days prior to the murders. Gerald never met with small-time contractors or painters. "Within weeks of the murders, we were getting all this cash."

"Sherry, we were all getting a lot of cash."

"We were getting twice as much as we did before the murders, and from two different runners." Sherry explained she could hear conversations in Gerald's supposedly soundproof office from an air vent in the utility room. She did not listen intentionally, but one day, while doing laundry, she noticed the sound of her ex-husband's voice in the office through the air vents. She could not hear the whole conversation, but she heard Gerald and Anthony talking two days before the murders and Gerald saying, "'After the baseball game on the twenty-first.' And I heard them bringing up the name Vasallo. I think Gery knew everyone would suspect your father-in-law, so David Vasallo was killed as a diversion." Greg had his eyes closed in deep thought. She explained that the day Kenny Bondano disappeared, Gery had called him that morning. "After that, I never thought he was missing. I think Kenny is dead." Greg held his mouth open and his eyes closed. Sherry told Greg of her opinion on several other murders including Joseph Giovelli, Peter Cassivano, Vito Paglissi, and the Vasallos. "I know

348

As the Crow Falls

Nick has always been suspected of Joseph, but I think Gery did it because he wanted Nick out of the way and he knew Nick's phones were tapped. I think he set it up for Nick to be charged with gambling when he couldn't get him arrested for murder."

"Fuck!"

"I'll tell you something else. Gery wired your office so he could listen to your meetings. I think he recorded most of your conversations, unless he realized it was of no importance. He listened to them in his car and accidentally left one in the tape player of the Rolls I was driving at the time. I found it and listened. It was of you and your father-in-law arguing and yelling about money that Fred Vasallo stole from Anthony." Greg listened to Sherry describe this and instantly remembered the day that argument occurred. "Greg, I made a copy of that tape." Sherry smiled. "To this day, Gery doesn't know the copy exists."

"Where is the tape?" he asked, jittery.

"I have it with me at the hotel." She grinned.

"Let's get dressed and get it." Greg stood up, pulled Sherry to her feet, and they instantly dressed. Several times, they kissed passionately. For some reason, Greg did not consider this a mistake. He knew his attraction for Sherry was intense.

In minutes, they were at the hotel. Sherry popped the tape in the cassette deck of the rental car. Greg listened as they drove back to his apartment. At times, he would fast-forward because he remembered that day and the events surrounding it. He remembered instantly after hearing the tape that his brother had asked for $20,000 cash two days before the meeting of Greg and his father-in-law.

Sherry drove back to the hotel after she insisted on giving Greg $10,000. She joked that it was for gigolo services. She knew his nature and told him he could pay it back to her later. He did not know how long it would be, but he would only accept it if the money was a loan, not a gift. He still had pride.

Greg stayed awake all night, drinking and making a list of the events and Gerald's connections to them. He listed any motive his brother would have had—everything Greg could think of to eliminate his brother. The only motive Greg could see was money. However hard Greg tried, he could not eliminate his brother. Greg knew he could not speak on the telephone, so he drove over to the hotel at six o'clock in the morning to meet with Sherry.

This was the first time Greg had been drinking and driving in months. A towering, mean-looking black police officer pulled him over two blocks from the hotel for speeding. Anyone could easily smell the alcohol. The officer asked Greg where he was going. Greg told the police officer he was going to the hotel and pointed.

The officer made one simple yet threatening statement before driving off. "If I see you driving on the road again before you sober up, I'm arresting you for driving under the influence. I'm following you to the parking lot to see where you park. If I come by there and your car isn't there, Greg, I'm hunting you down and hauling your ass to jail for drunk driving. You got it?"

Greg nodded his head yes. The officer gave Greg the speeding ticket and followed him to the hotel. As Greg walked to the hotel, the officer smiled, waved, then drove off.

He went to Sherry's room and knocked. Sherry looked out the peephole. Because of her paranoia over her ex-husband, she carried an automatic pistol. When she realized it was Greg and not a hit man, she took off her bathrobe and opened the door completely nude. Greg laughed hysterically.

He asked her several questions about events as he wrote down everything. She was never a big drinker, so she remembered everything.

The suspicions of his brother began growing as he and Sherry continued to meet daily, talk, and fool around. He knew he had increasing romantic feelings for his ex-sister-in-law.

Greg pieced all the events together. He knew about Harold and Rebecca Trafficanly. He knew about Victor Spelo. That information came straight from Gery's mouth. Sherry told him of Charles, Sandy, and what she believed happened to Kenny, Joseph, Peter, the Vasallos, and Vito Paglissi.

He listened to the tape and immediately came to the conclusion that Gery was in on the murders of Fred, Wayne, and possibly Peter. He pretty much knew Gery and Vince ordered the murders of Anthony, Sonny, Tommy, and the Lorzanis. He forgot the names of the other people at the scenes. Greg thought he knew about the murder of James Bucerri, but he could not be sure. Greg started to think of how many murders his own flesh and blood was involved with and got violently ill. After a few drinks, he would take a cab to a library to research the other names.

For over a week, Greg made a detailed list of what he now suspected.

Greg wondered if knowing about the three murders all these years and keeping it silent made him guilty also. Greg and Sherry talked constantly.

67

Greg frequently ran into his brother at the hospital cafeteria. Here Greg was, living in a studio apartment, and the extravagant lifestyle of Gerald had barely changed in comparison. Gerald continued to drive a Mercedes. Gerald still had one Rolls-Royce that he put under his father's name. Gerald purchased another large home under his father's name. Greg despised his brother now but never let Gerald know what he now suspected.

One day in the hospital cafeteria, Greg sat down at the table with his brother.

"Michael will get to leave tomorrow. He can't drive, so he's going to stay with me so I can bring him in for his treatments," Gerald said, smiling.

"He's as nice and patient with the doctors and staff as he was as a kid," Greg said with a chuckle.

"I know. I don't know how he does it." Gerald shook his head and grinned. "You know, if something were to happen, Michael's life insurance should pay me quite a bit." Gerald smirked.

Greg stared at his brother and turned bright red.

"That is, without a doubt, the most disgusting, putrid, selfish thing I've ever heard anyone say," Greg snarled with a look of violent insanity on his face. His eyes started darting back and forth. Greg dropped his sandwich and pointed a finger at his brother. "You've said and done some pretty bad fuckin' things before, but that tops everything." Gerald began to interrupt as Greg continued. "That's your son, you fuckin' jerk. What little respect I ever had for you no longer exists, you fuckin' dick. You're scum!"

"Could you please keep your voice down? I shouldn't have said it." Gerald looked around the room to make sure nobody was watching. "I only meant that Sherry, or whatever her name is now isn't on Michael's life insurance. I took that particular policy out on Mark and Michael myself twenty years ago. I've paid a lot into it. Sherry knows nothing about it."

"What does that have to do with anything? You are one sick, sick

351

motherfucker. Michael means more to Sherry than money. He means more to me than any amount. So do my kids and Mark." His eyes darted faster. Greg grabbed the silverware out of Gerald's hands and reached across the table to forcibly raise his brother's head. "If that's the way you think, then Michael won't stay with you. I'll suggest he go out to California with Sherry." Gerald looked down at the table and began to pick up his sandwich. Greg stood up and pushed Gerald's face down in the tray. Gerald began to wipe the cottage cheese off his face, when Greg dumped a bowl of chili on his brother's head, followed by a glass of water and a salad. Everyone in the cafeteria watched as Greg began screaming at his brother. The eyes darted faster. "You may as well murder your son, you fuckin' murdering asshole, faggot, coward!"

Then, with one final flurry, Greg grabbed his brother's Adam's apple hard enough to cause immediate oxygen cutoff and punched him in the mouth with the other fist. Greg just about knocked out his brother and had no regrets.

Gerald cleaned up and drove home with a swollen lower lip and two broken teeth.

Greg immediately walked to Michael's hospital room to see Sherry there. When the opportunity arose, Greg told Sherry what had transpired with his brother. Sherry held her mouth open as Greg told her what Gerald said.

"I just talked to the doctors. Michael is scheduled to go home with Gery tomorrow." Sherry thought aloud, "He can stay in his own apartment if someone stays there with him. If he's released tomorrow, I'll get a bigger apartment and move in with him for a while."

"You have a job in California."

"He's my baby, though. I'll check with the doctors to see if he can stay alone. I know he doesn't want to stay with his dad, or even me. He's getting around fine. They just don't want him to drive. He needs to be here every day for treatment."

"He's an adult now. I can imagine he needs his space." Greg smiled. "I've seen his girlfriend in here. I can certainly understand him wanting to have his own place. She's a knockout."

"You're right. His back may hurt, but that still works," Sherry said, laughing. "I came in yesterday when he was asleep. He didn't know I was in the room. He must have thrown the covers off because I could see it springing every which way." Sherry blushed. "I gently placed the covers back on him and left the room. I was so embarrassed. If he would have woken, he would have been more embarrassed than me." Sherry used her hands to show that Michael had a big one.

As the Crow Falls

"Sherry, I promise, I'd pick him up every day to bring him here."

"I'll just stay here for another week or so. I'll arrange for someone to pick him up when you can't. I'll just talk to the doctors." Sherry did just that.

The doctors let her know that her plan was fine. Because mental health was so important, any unusual circumstances may cause the disease to progress. Living alone may be just what he needs.

When Michael did go back home the next day, his girlfriend, Alicia, announced her intention to move in with him. She worked nights as a waitress; so, for Alicia, bringing Michael to therapy during the day would not be a problem.

68

Mark Crow had been back in town and had rekindled an old romance. Mark and Trisha Giovelli announced their wedding plans. They were almost married years before, but Mark decided to move to California. This time, Trisha was out of school and would move out with him. There was no elaborate wedding, just a simple gathering of immediate family in a courthouse. They needed to have the wedding early the next week. Sally, Amber, Sarah, Tina, and Vincenzo Giovelli Jr. came back to Kansas City for the wedding.

The tension between Gerald and Greg was evident. Neither would look at the other. Everyone present at the wedding noticed.

The criminal trial was only three weeks away.

69

Physicians feared Michael would not achieve remission this time. The chemotherapy and radiation were not working. If nothing changed, Michael would need to enter the hospital again as an inpatient. Something did change.

Mark telephoned everyone, including his brother, two weeks after the wedding. Mark told them that his new wife, Trisha, was already pregnant. Michael acted happy for his brother, as expected. Inside, his stomach turned because Michael knew he could never experience the same joy. Michael was never suicidal, but that night he drank eighteen beers and followed it with several prescribed painkillers and a bottle of peppermint schnapps.

Alicia came home late that evening from her job as a waitress to find Michael suffering from seizures in bed. She had seen him suffer seizures before, though never this bad. These seizures were lasting for four or five minutes each. Between seizures, he could not talk, he could only drool. Alicia tried to help him but started screaming. She called emergency. While she waited for emergency, Alicia noticed a bunch of empty beer bottles in the trash along with a bottle of peppermint schnapps.

Immediately, paramedics entered and strapped Michael to a stretcher. They carried him to the ambulance and tried to revive him because he had stopped breathing. The good sign was that his heart continued to beat. Alicia rode in the ambulance. In less than five minutes, they approached the hospital. Alicia knew.

In less than an hour, Michael Darryl Crow had been pronounced dead. Alicia could not speak on the telephone yet. She loved Michael. She also knew she would be homeless soon without him. Sherry would make sure that would not happen.

Hospital officials telephoned Greg, as his was the only telephone number of a family member Alicia had in her possession. She disliked Michael's father immensely.

In minutes, Uncle Greg arrived at the hospital. Before he tried to phone his brother, he attempted to call Sherry. No answer. He attempted to telephone Mark, but Trisha answered. Greg wondered what her reaction would be if she knew her new husband's father ordered her mom, dad, and both grandfathers murdered. Greg asked for Mark, and Trisha went into a happy ramble about California. Greg gave her the sad news. Trisha gave Greg the pager number where Sherry could be reached. Greg finally reached Sherry.

"Apparently, Michael had several seizures. Alicia called emergency." *I can't tell her about the booze right now.* "I'm sorry to have to tell you like this, but Michael died tonight." As expected, Sherry screamed before she could say a word. "Sherry, he had a good life. Even if it was short."

"Does Gery know yet?"

"No, I called you first. I'll call Dad." Greg tried to forget the fact that Gerald was going to profit from this tragedy. "I'll call Dad and have him call Gery."

"God no! I'll take the next flight," Sherry said, weeping. Greg lost control of his emotions again. "Greg, you're the best friend Michael ever had. I love you. I mean that as a friend. I really love you."

"I love you too. Where are you gonna stay when you get here?"

"I'd love to stay with you tonight. I'll just stay at a hotel. It's already two, your time. I don't know when I'll get there. I'll call you after I check in to a hotel. I need to get packed so I can leave. I need to call my mom and dad. I'll talk to you when I get there." Sherry cried harder. "Are you going to call Carol?"

"I don't know where she is. I'll call her dad in a few hours." Greg tried to stay strong, but to no avail.

"I'll see you when I get there." Sherry hung up.

Thanks for the memories, Mike. I love you. Could my life get any worse?

70

March 29, 1988

When it was time for Michael's wake, the attendance was not as immense as Greg anticipated. The most astonishing treat for everyone was the attendance of several professional baseball and football players who had been corresponding with Michael over the past ten years. At the time, they supposedly knew nothing of his gambling ring.

The greatest treat for Greg was the attendance of Carol. The affection between them had obviously never died, as they hugged and kissed in front of everyone several times at the wake. They had not seen one another in over one year, and the fire between them burned brighter than ever.

After they made love, Greg went home instead of spending the night. Carol was spending the night in the same hotel as Sherry, and the two desperately wanted to talk without Greg present. Sherry did let Greg know she would tell Carol everything they had talked about.

Everyone, especially Greg and Carol, noticed at the wake and funeral that Gerald did everything possible to avoid Greg. Gerald did not cry. Every time Greg looked at Gerald, he was granted an icy-cold stare in return.

At the reception after the funeral, several of the baseball players announced their need to get back to spring training. They had all flown in from Florida or Arizona at their own expense for the sole purpose of attending the funeral of their hero.

Carol whispered a statement to Greg before departure.

"Greg, I love you. I need you and so do the kids. You do whatever it takes to get out of this mess. Do it legally, but get out and call Daddy and you come back to me. I need you." Carol looked at Gerald with vengeance. "I talked to Sherry last night and this morning. I'll keep up on the trial, but I'll get in touch with you soon. I love you. Divorce your brother and come back to me!"

She hated life without him, but she still held to her conviction that the publicity would embarrass and humiliate the children.

Gerald was talking to three officers of the company, including Brian Nivaro. Greg suddenly began thinking of Brian and his tendency toward thrills. Greg remembered giving Brian the money to bail out Anthony. Everything else was the order of Vince Giovelli and his brother. Greg would never be able to prove it. It was just another gut feeling, but a strong one. Greg, of course, never wanted to know anything, yet somehow he knew this. Greg vaguely remembered his conversation with Brian before the murders of John and Janie Lorzani. For a brief time, Greg wondered if he was guilty of that also. Greg knew he was not guilty because he never knew anything.

Greg needed to leave, so he made the rounds. When he approached his brother, everyone stared as Gerald covered his face and smiled a devilish grin—hardly the typical reaction from a father who had buried his youngest son earlier that day. Greg faked an emotional hug toward Gerald. Gerald pushed Greg away. Greg looked his brother straight in the eyes. No words needed to be spoken. The messages in Gerald Crow's eyes were that of hatred.

I know he killed Trafficanly and Spelo, and I suspect him of so many others. Hmm? I never knew anything. They can give me a polygraph, and I'll pass. I'll do it. I'll turn against my brother.

Greg telephoned his attorneys that very afternoon and told them of the need to meet immediately. Greg needed to sing. Not only about the white-collar crimes he had been charged with but also several homicides he knew about.

With Greg's full knowledge, Carol had been paying the airfare and expenses for Steven Alchwin and the legal team to work the case.

Steven could not fathom what he was about to hear. Steven was a top-notch business and tax attorney. When Greg began telling stories of the Las Vegas casino cash, murder, and conspiracy, Steven knew this could only be handled by high-powered criminal attorneys. Steven brought in a lawyer he knew from Detroit. Steven assured his friend over the telephone that the infamous Crow Brothers business fraud trial involved more than just white-collar crimes.

Bradley Gotlieb flew to Kansas City in the early morning hours of Thursday, knowing jury selection was scheduled to begin on Monday. Bradley, Steven, and Greg met in a hotel conference room attached to a suite.

As the Crow Falls

Greg tried to chronologically recall everything that had happened since his induction as principal owner of Crow Brothers. No matter how trivial, Greg gave Bradley and Steven details. Several local attorneys listened with their mouths open as Greg recounted the details of his knowledge of many unsolved crimes and his knowledge of Joseph, Charles, and Vincenzo Giovelli, and their illegal activities, including murder. He never minimized his own involvement in any crimes because he, of course, never knew anything. Bradley had several doubts about Greg being a detective and needed to see the photographs.

Sherry was still in town. Steven telephoned her at her hotel. Sherry was given a thorough interrogation from another attorney in a separate room from Greg.

Steven Alchwin knew how to reach Carol. She arrived in hours. The hotel Carol stayed in was across the street from where the makeshift interrogation room was located. Steven walked back and forth. Carol entered the meeting room with pictures in hand and gave them to Steven. Greg pointed out the items in question in the photographs. Bradley was hesitant to believe Greg until he saw the twenty-four photographs Greg had taken of blood drops in the parking lot of the sports complex. The photographs, along with Greg and Sherry's description of the events surrounding all the murders, had the lawyers convinced.

On Saturday, only two days before opening statements in the white-collar trial, attorneys gave Greg, Carol, and Sherry polygraph tests. Greg passed with flying colors, even when he was questioned in regard to the murders of Harold and Rebecca Trafficanly. Greg replied, "I didn't give the order at all. I just told Joseph that I didn't wanna know." He passed. When he was questioned about Brian Nivaro, he replied, "I met with him and agreed to loan, not pay, his tuition, so, yes, I did give him money occasionally." He passed. "I did give him $21,000 cash to bail out Anthony Gilante—$20,000 of that was Vince's. I told him to bail out Anthony and keep $1,000. Other than that, I don't know." He passed. "I can't prove he had anything to do with the murders of anyone, but I believe Gery and Vince ordered them and Brian carried them out." He passed. When asked about his ex-father-in-law and his involvement in any of the murders and other criminal activities, Greg replied, "I know what I've read, and Carol never told me anything, so I don't know." He passed. When asked about the location of the cash, "I have no idea." He passed. When asked if his ex-wife had the cash, he replied, "I don't think so." He passed.

Carol and Sherry passed their polygraph tests also.

All three interrogations were conducted separately. All the polygraphs matched. In addition to the polygraphs, basic tape recordings were made of all three interrogations.

Normally, attorneys would not play tapes for prosecutors, nor let prosecutors see polygraph results. In this case, they would because of the undeniable matches of the three parties.

"Time is of the essence."

On Sunday morning, the FBI was voluntarily called to interview Greg. Greg went through a more intensive interrogation than the day before. Federal agents especially wanted to see if he would minimize his involvement in the casino skim. He did not. Greg wanted to testify against his brother.

After Greg answered many of the same questions asked by his own attorneys, the FBI knew they had a case. The FBI made Greg aware that attorneys for his brother would shine a light on his drug and alcohol problems. Prosecutors would object. Even if prosecutors were overruled, Greg assured them he could handle it. After agents conducted their own interrogations, listened to portions of the tapes, and reviewed the polygraph tests, Gregory Crow entered the Federal Witness Protection Program.

Greg was denied permission to telephone his father after he entered the program. Greg went into the program knowing he would somehow see his dad again.

Agents notified prosecutors, and the criminal case was continued for sixty days. A new jury would need to be selected.

Federal agents immediately began looking at police investigators' files of the Jacob and Rachel Rosenstingel murder/suicide. A special investigator looked at the photographs and checked the scene again.

Although the physical evidence had been removed, the photographs and other blood evidence led agents to consider this an unsolved double homicide. Federal agents attempted to match some of the fingerprints and could not.

Under a suggestion from Greg, all of the other three living officers of Crow Brothers were arrested on conspiracy to commit bank fraud. All three officers of the company had mug shots and fingerprints taken.

Brian Nivaro matched the fingerprints taken from the home of Jacob and Rachel Rosenstingel. Brian's home and cars were searched. Nothing.

When agents questioned why his prints were in the Rosenstingel home, Brian had a simple answer: "I'm an officer of Crow Brothers. So was Jacob. He and I always talked about the company when he was arrested. I was there all the time. Dust my house and you'll probably find his fingerprints also." Agents did just that. Jacob's prints were in Brian's home.

There was no evidence linking Brian to anything other than fraud. Brian was released on $5,000 bail after his passport was seized.

71

April 5, 1988

Gerald became aware that his brother was going to testify against him. Gerald did not know what had transpired. Greg probably decided to testify against him for the bank fraud and check kiting. All he knew was his brother Gregory was out there. Somewhere.

Gerald's attorney, Barbara, let him know Greg entered the Federal Witness Protection Program.

"Gery, he wouldn't enter the program if this were strictly white-collar." Barbara avoided direct eye contact with her client. "Something else is wrong. Greg is going to testify about your involvement in three murders at minimum. Hundreds of counts of money laundering. Start talking now or find another lawyer!"

Barbara knew some, more than any attorney normally knows. She even participated at times, although she never pulled the trigger. Gerald looked sullen. He closed his eyes to speak.

"Greg never knew anything." Gerald took a deep breath. "I told him I was in on the Trafficanly hit and that I ordered the hit on Victor Spelo." Gerald put his face in his hands and shook his head.

Barbara knew she was breaking the bar code of ethics, yet continued. "Have you ever told Greg of any other crimes?"

"No. He received the cash from the casinos, but he made a special point never to be informed of anything," Gerald said. Gerald went step by step over the three murders, yet he knew there was no way anyone could prove anything other than the white-collar crimes.

Although Barbara knew Gerald Crow and Brian Nivaro were in on other murders, she never could tell anyone because she participated in several herself, including the murder of James Bucerri, which started all of this. Plus the attorney/client privilege. She may be guilty of conspiracy

361

of murder herself if anyone found out Brian killed James for Gerald. After all, she piloted the plane. She knew no other murders could be confirmed.

Barbara needed Gerald to be hit or plead guilty to some bank-fraud charges and serve minimal time. Even so, she may order him to be hit in prison. She recommended she approach prosecutors with a plea bargain for a few bank-fraud charges to test the waters. Gerald agreed to plead guilty to several of the more obvious crimes under the condition that everything else from the original indictment be dismissed. Barbara let Gerald know that nothing else would be offered to prosecutors at this point. Gerald needed to be charged first. She spoke too soon.

A federal prosecutor telephoned her to let her know a warrant for the arrest of Gerald Crow had been issued. The warrant listed the following crimes: first-degree murder against Harold Trafficanly, first-degree murder against Rebecca Trafficanly, first-degree murder against Victor Spelo, and 161 counts of money laundering.

Barbara escorted and surrendered Gerald to the local office of the FBI. Gerald would not say a word, as directed. A bail hearing the next morning would be conducted.

By evening, it was on the news that Gregory Crow had entered the Witness Protection Program in order to testify against his brother.

When Gerome tried to telephone Gregy to ask him why he would do that, the recording let him know: "The number you have called is no longer in service. Please hang up or try your call again. Thank you." Strange. Gerome paid the bill and he never turned off the service. The news said: "Gregory Crow will be protected because of his knowledge of several mob-related crimes stemming from the ownership of several casinos in Las Vegas. The new charges against his brother include money laundering and three counts of first-degree murder. People nationwide are now being investigated." The news made a special point of saying, "Gregory Crow is the son-in-law of reputed Mafia boss William 'Willie the Rat' Cassivano." To say Gerome was flabbergasted would be an understatement.

By early evening, Gerald telephoned his father from jail.

"Dad, everything is fine. This is all a big mistake." Gerome could hear the quivering in his son's voice. "Will you bail me out tomorrow?" Gerald asked. "That is, if they set bail."

"Of course, I'll bail you out." Gerome had a bad feeling. "Gery, can you tell me what's going on?"

"Not now, Dad. I'll tell you tomorrow."

"How much do you think the bail will be?" Gerome asked.

"I don't know. If you come to the hearing tomorrow at nine o'clock, they'll set it. If it's too much, then you can meet a bail bondsman. I'll pay you back."

"I know how it works. I'll be there."

"I need to go. Dad, I'll see you tomorrow."

At the federal courthouse the next morning, Gerome learned the serious nature of the crimes his eldest son was charged with. Gerome wanted desperately to talk with his other son. Not even Gerome could speak with Gregy. Gregy was in the Witness Protection Program already.

Several notable unrelated people were already on the witness list. In addition to Gregy testifying, other relatives, including Sherry and Mark, would testify. Gery had lost one son a week ago, and now the other son would testify against him. Gerome was not sure if he was angry with them for turning against Gery or if Gery had lied to him and was guilty of all he was charged with and more.

Prosecution and defense argued back and forth over bail. Prosecution requested no bail because of the violent nature of the crimes. The defense argued: "Mr. Crow is pleading guilty to three of the bank-fraud charges, but he is pleading not guilty to all other charges. Plus, he has never been convicted and is a prominent businessman locally. Bail should be his own recognizance." Bail was finally set at $1 million.

Gerald instructed his father to pay the $1 million. Gerome needed to go to a bank and have a cashier's check drawn. After four hours, Gerald was finally released. Several armed bodyguards brought him back home. Gerome followed.

"I can't write a check right now, Dad."

"Shut the fuck up, Gery! What's going on?" Gerome demanded with a shout.

"I told you last night. Nothing. It's all a mistake. It's my money anyway, but just to protect you, I'll write you a check later."

"Why is your son going to testify?"

"I don't know yet."

"Why is Gregy going into this witness protection thing?"

"Me . . . Greg is being protected from me." Gerald looked down.

Gerome thought for a long while before he could speak. He stared at his son, who would not look at him.

"Just tell me. Yes or no?" Gerome asked.

"No."

"I can always tell when you're lying. You're lying like a rug!"

Gerome left and drove home.

In his closet was the .45 revolver Joseph Giovelli had given him more than thirty years before. It had never been fired. Gerome loaded one bullet, placed the barrel in his mouth, and ended his life.

In less than two weeks, Gerald had lost a son from an accidental overdose and his father from a suicide.

Greg could not, by design, attend his father's funeral.

The life insurance for Michael needed to be held by a court trustee of the United States Bankruptcy Court. The life insurance for Gerome would not be paid, since he committed suicide. His will had been changed after his sons were charged with fraud. His assets numbering in the $45 million range would be divided between his grandsons, Mark and Daniel, and his granddaughter, Candice.

Because of their ages, Danny and Candy could not receive any money until they graduated from college or turned twenty-three.

72

Depositions were taken from all potential witnesses. Preliminary hearings were conducted. Attorneys on both sides tried to work a plea bargain agreement all through the wait for the beginning of the trial.

Gerald would not turn in Brian Nivaro yet. Gerald knew he was higher profile and, because of the financial aspect, it would do no good. Turning witness against Brian was a last resort. Brian was a small fish.

During the depositions and preliminary hearings, Gerald had been informed that the murder and money-laundering charges looked very shaky. His lawyers assured him the charges might be dropped.

Sherry's testimony in the depositions was worthless to the prosecution and may have been helpful to the defense. Her claim of the abundance of cash in the weeks following the murders of Charles and Sandy Giovelli was worthless because Gerald had not been charged with those murders. The FBI continued investigating those murders. Sherry's testimony about sexual relations with Gerald was pointless. Sherry knew her own sex life could be used to discredit her. Prosecution dropped her from the list.

Mark's testimony proved to be even more worthless. He was taken off the prosecution witness list along with Brian Nivaro.

Brian pleaded guilty to one count of conspiracy to commit bank fraud. Brian was sentenced to one year of probation and a six-month suspended sentence.

Over one hundred potential witnesses were called to give depositions regarding the fraud and forgery charges. Gerald decided that, if need be, he would plead guilty to the three forgery charges for forging his brother's signature.

The most powerful depositions were those given by Gregory Crow. Greg had already been granted complete immunity and had no reason to lie. He never minimized his own involvement in the fraud or the casino skimming. His usual plea of "I only did what my brother told me" worked

365

for the defense. The drug and alcohol past of Greg inevitably would be more of an issue in trial than anyone believed. His testimony about the murders proved to be even weaker as defense attorneys ripped him apart.

The only thing Greg ever said that held weight was "I know what Gery told me. I know where we were standing when he told me. I know he told me the day after someone, probably Gery himself, had Charles and Sandy Giovelli and David Vasallo killed." Occasionally, Greg would throw in something negative about his brother. Greg's opinions of the murders of Charles, Sandy, and David were always objected to and considered irrelevant. Gerald was not charged with those murders. His opinion of the murders of Joseph Giovelli, Peter Cassivano, Vito Paglissi, James Bucerri, and David, Fred, and Wayne Vasallo was considered meaningless. He brought up his opinion of Kenneth Bondano. There was a warrant for his arrest, so that was irrelevant.

Defense attorneys for Gerald accused Greg of recently staging the argument with his father-in-law that was on tape. Making the tape recently constituted another fraud charge that would not be covered under the immunity blanket. Defense argued that even if the tapes were authentic, it was no proof Gerald committed the murders of Fred and Wayne Vasallo.

The prosecution knew the murder and money-laundering portions of the case were getting weaker with every deposition. So did the defense.

No trial. No witnesses. No financial experts. No dramatic testimony.

One week before the trial began, a plea bargain agreement was reached. Gerald Crow plead guilty to twenty-three counts of bank fraud and all three counts of forgery. Gerald was sentenced to twelve concurrent terms of thirteen years at the minimum-security prison in Montgomery, Pennsylvania. He would be eligible for parole in less than four years. He was given thirty days to get his personal affairs in order. He would stay under house arrest until he reported to prison.

This would not stop the civil suits against Gerald that still remained at $142 million.

Greg was angrier at the justice system now than ever before. He never wanted to speak with his brother again. Greg immediately went back to his secret location. Greg nearly paid all of his civil liabilities and only had $10 million in judgments remaining. The remaining property in holding by partnerships not affected by the tax law changes would compensate the judgments.

Because Greg was never convicted of anything, any money remaining would be funneled through the Witness Protection Program. By Greg's estimation, there could be as much as $12 million above the judgments. He would ask for a minimal buyout for the remaining property through the program. Even if there was no money remaining, he would be happy just to have the whole thing over with.

On August 1, 1988, Gerald Crow would report to prison. A nagging cough sent him to several doctors before he reported. All tests administered revealed acquired immune deficiency syndrome. Gerald had full-blown AIDS. Lawyers motioned the court to allow him to stay at home under house arrest for the duration of his life. Because of the progression of the disease, the main treating physician estimated his life expectancy at five years or less. Motion denied. Gerald reported to the prison hospital as required on August 1.

Although Greg stayed mute by his lawyers' request, Greg did write a note that his lawyers' were supposed to read aloud in a press conference, but never did. Here is that note:

> "I know Gery was an animal. If I would have known how bad he was, I would have blown the whistle twenty years ago, and none of this would ever have happened. I think about everything that's happened, and I can't believe what a fool I was. I would like to apologize to everyone for everything. If I could have done anything, I would have. But I never knew anything. I sometimes think my whole life has been a lie. It might anger some people when I say this, but in a weird way drugs and alcohol saved my life. Think about it."

> Greg

AFTER THE FALL

Barbara Percival had her license to practice law suspended for ninety days in January of 1989 after a wiretap caught her in the act of accepting an illegal fee.

On May 13, 1989, Barbara was found murdered in her home. She had been shot five times in the head with a .44 caliber. Ballistics showed it to be one of the same guns used to murder Anthony Gilante twelve years earlier. The investigation to both murders, as well as several other homicides, remains open.

Mark Crow and Trisha Giovelli divorced after less than one year of marriage. Trisha was granted custody of their daughter. Mark changed his name and practices law somewhere in the United States.

When her ex-husband tested positive for AIDS, Sherry Crow underwent several tests. All tests showed she was negative.

In February of 1994, Sherry remarried and resides in the Portland, Oregon, area.

In August of 1990, William Cassivano testified in front of a United States Senate committee regarding the state of organized crime in America. William testified that he never believed Italian La Cosa Nostra existed.

On June 8, 1991, William died at home of complications from heart disease. Over two thousand people attended his funeral, including his daughter, Carol, who arrived swarmed with personal bodyguards. Greg, Danny, and Candy did not want to take the risk of returning to Kansas City.

When his disease entered the final stages, the justice system released Gerald Crow so he could die with dignity at his home. He died from pneumonia on September 18, 1991, only three days after being released from prison. No friends or family visited him in prison. Other than a doctor, he died alone.

Gregory Crow negotiated a buyout from the remaining properties within months, then promptly left the Witness Protection Program and reunited with Carol. Her deli chain was sold to a national conglomerate for over $47 million.

In December of 1991, Greg was arrested for driving under the influence in Eden Prairie, Minnesota. He reentered Hazelden in Center City. He has been sober since.

On Christmas Eve 1992, Greg and Carol remarried twenty years to the day after their first wedding.

In October of 2003, Gregory Crow resurfaced voluntarily and briefly to testify at the assault, extortion and racketeering trial of Brian Nivaro. If there were a boss of Kansas City La Cosa Nostra at the time, it would have been Brian Nivaro. Upon becoming aware of Greg testifying against him, Brian entered a guilty plea to one assault charge, and three counts of extortion. The sentences are being served concurrently at the Western Missouri Correctional Facility in Cameron, Missouri.

Greg could never forgive himself for not attending his father's funeral. During his visit to testify against Brian, he paid his respects at the cemetery. He had a lawyer arrange access for him to see his father's coroner's report. *Cause of death: self-inflicted gunshot wound. Suicide.* Out of curiosity, Greg looked up the coroner's report on the mother he never knew. *Cause of death: massive head injuries from a shovel. Homicide.* The realization slammed Greg, and he vowed never to visit his father's grave again.

The Kansas City faction of La Cosa Nostra, once believed to be the most powerful, tightly controlled and violent organized crime unit in the country, is no longer believed to be a serious threat by the FBI.

If he is not approved for parole before his mandatory release date, Brian Nivaro will be released from prison in January of 2016, when he will only be fifty-seven years old.

As the Crow Falls

Printed in the United States
By Bookmasters